Dedications

Like with every book, my writing group - Linda, Jill, Jim, Randy, Chris, Heather, and Victoria - for helping me see the problems in early drafts.

To anyone who needs healing from trauma. You are stronger than you realize.

"You can't open up the story of my life and just go to page 738 and think you know me.". – **Arin Hanson**

Cover art by Elizabeth Best. See her art on Instagram

@artoferbest

Logo and Chapter Headings by Omni Jacala. See his art on Twitter

@artsyomni

This book was lovingly created by a human, not generated by A.I.

Content Warning. This book contains: Mild sexual situations, physical and mental abuse, dead family, violent deaths, mild swearing, and violent injuries. Please take care of your mental health if you find yourself struggling with the contents of this book.

Discover other titles by R. A. Meenan

Black Bound

Golden Guardian

Shadow Cast

White Assassin

Brothers at Arms

Umber Sky

Gray Matter

Mage

Angel

Facets of Color: Vol 1

The Drover's Tale: Academy

Outlander Sky: Summoner's Fellowship

Angel

Book Four

From the War of Eons Archives

By R. A. Meenan

Starcrest Fox Press

CHAPTER 01

SURPRISE

Trecheon Omnir, car mechanic, reclusive war veteran, apparent mage, and whatever other Draso-damned titles he had earned over the last three and a half wild years, slumped into the battered office chair behind his chipped desk at seven AM on a Tuesday morning in late fall. He dropped a cup of black coffee on the hard surface and ran his prosthetic hand through his red, black streaked quills, wishing for the thousandth time that life could finally feel normal again.

He held up one metal hand and called a marble of fire to his fingertips, bouncing it around like a mini beach ball. Not that life would ever *really* be normal again.

But for the last two and a half years, normal had included friends. Matt, Izzy, Ouranos, Darvin, Roscoe, Sami, and so many others who had filled his life and his heart in ways that he hadn't experienced since before the war were suddenly gone.

The Defenders had headed back to Zyearth after their already long mission to restore Athánatos went longer than expected. According to Matt, they should be arriving on Zyearth at some point today, assuming everything went well on the trip home. The Athánatos went back to their quiet lives on their island. He still had Neil and Ouranos, of course, and all the other friends he had made on Athánatos, but without the Defenders here, visits were less frequent.

Trecheon fiddled with his pendant, making sure it was up and ready to go for Matt's call letting them know they all got to Zyearth safe. He couldn't remember the last time he waited with such anxiety for a simple call. His heart raced just thinking about it. He definitely wouldn't need that coffee today.

God. Why was he freaking out like a schoolgirl with a crush on the quarterback?

He pressed his eyes shut. Because in some sense, that was what was happening. He was, without a doubt, crushing on Matt.

He shook his head. Crush wasn't the right word. That made it feel flimsy. After everything he had gone through with Matt, he needed a better word. More-than-crush. Or something.

At the same time though, he couldn't be certain if what he felt truly crossed into the realm of romance. After all, he hadn't been involved with anything even remotely romantic since the war… and Rebekka.

Rebekka was MIA. Probably dead. And his romantic drive died with her.

Or so he thought.

Maybe.

He pinched the bridge of his snout. He was probably overreacting. Matt's presence had basically given Trecheon permission to be himself again. Escape the PTSD, the memories of war, the life of an assassin, the self-hate… everything. Suddenly he could joke again. Laugh again. Smile. Just make something of himself, build new friendships and cultivate the old ones he had been neglecting with his declining mental health.

His whole life had been a long string of losing control. Theron controlling his family when he was a kid, Granddad controlling his actions as an adult, Ackerson controlling his movements in war, and the war itself controlling his emotions and taking his arms from him, which in turn took control away. Then the problems with his failing business, the terrible world of assassins, the self-hate… his life was broken, and he thought he'd never regain control again.

Trecheon huffed. He flicked a fireball at the wastebasket by the door, setting the paper ablaze. He watched it flare a moment, then he waved a hand and put the flames out.

Didn't help when Matt showed up and he was thrust into a world of mages and mad kings and thrown not only out of control but also out of his element. But Matt had done something no one else had. He had given Trecheon control back. He had actually *asked* if Trecheon wanted to stay involved. And that continued with the rest of his new friends. Suddenly he felt like he had a choice instead of being dragged around against his will.

Life had purpose again.

And that was because of Matt.

For all he knew, he was just misinterpreting his deep friendship with Matt as a crush. More-than-crush. Whatever.

He stared at his black Defender pendant, its dead eyes piercing into his own. Then why did his heart flutter so much when he thought of Matt? His big grin, his handsome face, his casual laugh, the way he patted Trecheon's back, the way he hugged him… Even just picturing him painted goosebumps under his fur. His white and blue fur, his strong green eyes, that golden Defender pendant shining around his neck…

Golden.

Like golden tigers.

Like Sacha.

Trecheon laid his head on the desk. That was the other problem. Sacha Wildpelt, the only Defender who had stayed behind after the rest went home.

That beautiful golden tigress who also had a vice grip on Trecheon's heart.

She was funny, caring, kind, fierce, soft (when she wanted to be) and more than anything, understanding. She never pushed Trecheon to be something he wasn't. Never judged him for his actions. Always empathetic.

Never forcing her control on him.

He painted a star in the air with his fire then waved it away.

Matt was empathetic too, for the most part. Though who knew how long that'd last if he ever found out Trecheon used to be the White Assassin. He still hadn't gathered the courage to tell Matt, even with everyone urging him to. Sacha flat out told Trecheon that if Matt disowned him after learning about his past, she'd disown Matt herself because he clearly wasn't understanding.

But Trecheon wasn't willing to test that. Losing Matt would be like losing a limb. Another limb. He couldn't afford another. And if he lost Matt, would he eventually lose Sacha too? He'd lose both limbs. Be a zombie pulling himself along the ground with his chin, inching toward destruction.

God.

If only he could ignore his feelings for them. But he couldn't. He even caught himself flirting with them. *Flirting.* Natural and suave, which surprised even him since it had been over a decade since flirting ever came to mind. And he couldn't help himself. It came out when he didn't even mean it to. Sometimes he even flirted with both of them at once.

God, they probably thought he was so loose.

His chest ached. Fire lit up his fingertips against his will, but he shook it out.

They probably didn't think that. The Defenders and the Athánatos were the least judgmental people he knew. Never batting an eye at anything – Ouranos' being openly asexual and aromantic, the Athánatos people a society of polygamous relationships, Damianos' attraction to Neil, Neil's relationship with Dami and Natassa… they accepted it all without question or judgement. So different than most Earthlings.

Trecheon breathed deeply. That was what he wanted. A relationship with no judgement or worries. One where he didn't have to pick Matt or Sacha. One where he could have both of them, in perfect balance, like Neil did with Dami and Natassa.

Assuming he could even have *one* of them. Draso's *horns,* why the hell did his heart do this to him? It was losing control all over again. All he wanted was some stability in his life.

It was a good thing that neither of them had the time to really respond too much to Trecheon's uncontrolled flirting anyway. Not with Leah still missing.

That opened a whole new wound. Tongues of fire ran down his quills as he fought the injustice of it all.

He had only known Leah for maybe two hours. Then she vanished while he and Matt were scrubbing spilled soda out of Matt's uniform and they had seen neither fur nor whiskers of her since. Suzy's Café's security cameras were out of commission. No one in the area could get their phones to record video. All they had were some witness statements, but no one was clear on what happened. She had been talking to someone when they were attacked, and a second later, she vanished. Poof. So did her attackers.

All of Trecheon's experiences as an assassin sounded warning bells. Everything felt like a setup – Remove Matt and Trecheon from the picture, kill the security feed, prevent recording, attack and vanish in an instant. But who would set up the kidnapping of some random feline with literally no identity on Earth? It all stank but stalking and kidnapping made zero sense.

They spent every spare moment looking for Leah. Matt and Sacha traded off spending the week at Trecheon's apartment, going out with Trecheon on his days off, or alone when he worked, and leading searches late into the nights.

Sacha and Matt took time to train Trecheon in his magic too, along with Izzy, Sami and Ouranos, which he appreciated. He drew in the air with his fire again, a dragon this time. He wouldn't have this level of confidence without them. And it gave him some much-needed sense of control when he was losing that in the romance department. But it was so hard to focus knowing Leah was out there somewhere.

The Defenders stayed an extra six months to try and find her, a total of two and a half years, but they never did, and supplies had started running low. Staying was no longer an option.

Except for Sacha. Sacha was the head of the Healers, and she wouldn't leave without news about Leah. This week though, she was on Athánatos with Ouranos using her skill to help the still-healing citizens.

Trecheon fiddled with another fireball. Maybe that was for the best. Distract Sacha. Because Draso knew that they may never find anything about Leah.

His pendant beeped.

Trecheon threw himself forward and snatched up the pendant, trying to hold it steady, ready to answer. He took a deep breath. *Calm. It's just Matt. Just talk to him. Make sure he's fine. And for the love of Draso, don't flirt with him. You can control your own feelings for Draso's sake.*

Good luck on that last one. He activated the call and put the pendant down on the desk. A hologram of Matt appeared in the light from the dragon's eyes.

Matt grinned. "Hey Trech."

That damn grin. The familiar nickname. *Draso's wings.* Trecheon smiled, hoping it didn't look forced or uncomfortable. "Hey Matt. Got home safe I guess?" He leaned in and perked his eyebrows seductively. "A month's a long time to leave me hanging."

Matt frowned. "Yeah, well, intergalactic communication is messy."

Trecheon's ears grew hot. "I'm just messing with you, dude. It was supposed to be like us going on a date and you not calling back and like… you know what, it sounds really pathetic when I try to explain it." Damn it, already with the flirting, and he couldn't even get it *right* this time.

Matt laughed. "Don't worry about it. All that matters is we got home safe." He flicked one ear back. "Any more news about Leah?"

"No, or I would have called," Trecheon said. "I hate to say it, but it might be time to give up."

"Tell that to Sacha."

"I've tried, but I think she'd rather chew her own tail off," Trecheon said.

Matt ran a hand through his quills. "She totally would too, if she thought it'd bring Leah back. I wish I never would have brought her along."

"It's not your fault, Matt," Trecheon said. "You couldn't have predicted what happened."

"Still." He leaned in and spoke quietly. "Don't tell Sacha this, but the Master Guardian is talking about just yanking her in the next six Earth months if we still haven't heard anything."

Trecheon snorted. "He'll have to fly down here and pick her up himself. I don't see her leaving any other way."

"Good." Matt winked. "It'd be a good excuse for another visit."

The fluttering in Trecheon's chest returned. "Right."

Matt yawned. "Sorry. For the last two weeks we've been trying to get back on Zyearth's schedule and it's been hell. Didn't help that we dropped here at two in the morning. Jetlag like you wouldn't believe. It'll be nice to sleep in a proper bed for once."

"Well, I offered to let you share *my* bed, but you wouldn't have it," Trecheon said with a smirk. But his smile instantly faded. Damn it!

Matt crossed his arms. "Funny."

"It's not a joke," Trecheon said before he could shut off his brain. "It's an *invitation.*"

Matt eyed him teasingly. "I appreciate it." He raised both eyebrows. "Maybe next time."

Next time? The hell did that mean?

"Sorry," Matt said, chuckling. "I'm too out of it. I'm gonna give Ouranos a call then head to bed. I'll call you both back soon, okay? Let's try to do that when we can. I miss you already."

And Draso's Horns, do I miss you. "Yeah, same."

"We'll plan it then," Matt said. "After I sleep a bit and reset my brain." He saluted. "See ya, Trech."

"Yeah, see ya."

Matt ended the call.

Trecheon planted his face on the desk. "Great job, Omnir, you couldn't resist flirting even when he's a thousand lightyears away."

But he flirted back.

Good. *God.* Matt flirted back. What the hell. He had no right to start that now. Not when he's so far.

And he was so, so far… on a different planet with a job and obligations and a life… And Sacha would join him soon too. Right now she was a hop, skip, and a jump away, but soon she'd be just as unattainable as Matt.

Trecheon formed fists and fought the burning in his chest. Better to let them both go. No romance. He'd lived this long without it. He didn't need it. Just friendship. Their friendship was too valuable to ruin with romance anyway.

He needed control.

He sat up and leaned back in his chair. Better to just enjoy the friendship he had and stop looking to make it deeper. He reached for his coffee.

The door to his office burst open, slamming against the wall. *"Trecheon!"*

Trecheon fell backwards out of his chair and threw his coffee mug into the air with a yip, dumping it all over the floor and shattering the cup. He snarled and pulled himself to his feet.

Then gasped.

There, wearing dirty and bloody American style BDUs and with a literal *Athánatos quilar* at her side, stood their missing healer -- Leah.

CHAPTER 02

LEAH

"Leah?" Trecheon could barely get the word out. "What-- how--"

"Trecheon, we need your help *right now,*" Leah shouted, her voice hoarse. She scratched her matted gray and white fur and adjusted her bent glasses. "Jaden and the others are in trouble and I don't know how to find them, and I hope to Draso Matt is still here because we need a Defender A.I. and he'll be *really interested* in all that went down and--"

"Whoa, slow down!" Trecheon said holding up his hands. "Where the hell have you been? Who's Jaden?" He pointed. "And who the hell is *that?*"

The Athánatos quilar, tall, black, with white tipped quills and a burnt-orange muzzle stared at Trecheon with strangely familiar green eyes behind a cracked set of glasses. "Holy hell. Leah wasn't kidding about your hands." His eyes grew wide. "Oh my god, I am so sorry, that was really rude of me, I don't know what the hell I was thinking--"

Trecheon flicked his ears back and massaged his brow. "Just… *shit*." He waved to Leah. "Who the hell is this? Is this the guy who kidnapped you?"

"What? No!" Leah gasped. "I-Is that what you think happened?"

"You vanished without a trace and no one could find you for two and a half *years,* " Trecheon said, crossing his arms. "Sorry, Leah, but it's a little suspect that you show up randomly with some unknown Athánatos. On the mainland, even."

Leah stood in front of the quilar, her arms out, glaring. "He's not some unknown Athánatos, Trecheon. This is Zeke Brightclaw. He's Alexina's son."

Trecheon's bones buzzed and his eyes widened. "Wait. As in Princess Alexina?"

Leah nodded.

"She's *alive?* "

"I mean, I hope so, but I don't honestly know now…" her voice trailed and she hiccupped.

Trecheon glanced over Zeke again. "You're an Athánatos *prince?* "

Zeke shrugged. "Apparently? I only figured this out myself a few months ago." He rubbed his arm.

Trecheon narrowed his gaze. "Prove it."

Leah glared. "Trecheon--"

"This has scam written all over it, Leah."

"But--"

"No buts," Trecheon snarled. "Prove it, asshole. I've had enough shit in my life to just accept this without question."

Zeke pressed his lips into a thin line. "I can respect that." He lifted his hands and formed magic orbs of every element Trecheon had ever seen. He tried juggling them, but fumbled instead, littering magic all over the floor.

The fireball caught Trecheon's raggedy carpet ablaze, but the snowball and water orb put it out in a hiss of steam, only for the dirt and rock to smash into it, cracking the concrete underneath. The electric marble flew about wildly and singed Trecheon's coffeepot before going out. Zeke scrambled to pull the magic back, but the damage was already done. "Sorry, sorry! I'm still new at this and I'm tired as shit and--"

"It's okay, it's okay," Trecheon said, pulling on some of his own magic to help fight it back. He glanced at the coffeepot. "I think the coffeemaker is toast though."

Zeke pulled back on the power too, extinguishing the last of the magic. "Sorry, I should have just called Archángeli, but they're so worn out after escaping that last battle…"

Trecheon glanced over Zeke. "It's alright, I believe you. Though I assume you're only half Athánatos, with those white quills."

Leah picked at her tail. "Trecheon… Zeke's father is important too. That's Jaden."

Trecheon perked one ear. "Okay, so who the hell is Jaden?"

Leah and Zeke exchanged a look, then Leah turned to Trecheon. "Jaden is Matt's father."

The shocked buzz grew now, blurring Trecheon's vision and forcing him to sit. He steadied himself and looked Leah in the eye. "Leah… Matt's father is dead. He died in the Sol Genocide."

"But he didn't!" Leah said. "Trecheon, we just spent the last several months with him--"

"In bloodied BDUs? Why the hell--"

"Trecheon, we *time traveled,*" Leah said. "And we met Jaden in the past."

"Here," Zeke said. He pulled out a Defender pendant. No… a Guardian pendant. Golden, like Matt's, though battered and worn. He pressed his thumb to the back of it and a hologram appeared from the dragon's eyes.

A white quilar with familiar green eyes and a long ponytail appeared. He spoke about the war and Ackerson and Matt and even Alexina and Embrik, the missing Athánatos. It was like listening to a nightmare, some lying, scheming nightmare, and yet...

And yet...

He even accused Matron Fawn of having a hand in the mobs that called for the blood of Ackerson's detractors. Neil and Trecheon had avoided that with their injuries keeping them from joining the trials, though it would explain how both of their businesses had very difficult starts.

That felt like a strange connection though. Why would the Matron have anything to do with Ackerson? But Leah and Zeke didn't question it, so Trecheon didn't either. Not like it mattered now. Neil had killed her. Maybe he was more justified than he realized.

As he watched, something clicked and his eyes widened. "Holy shit. I've met him before. Jaden. At Atlas."

Leah shifted. "Ronan mentioned he had helped recruit them for Ackerson with you."

"Ronan," Trecheon said. "I remember him too. Black and orange bat, one of Ackerson's--"

"He's a traitor," Zeke snarled with such ferocity that Trecheon jumped. "He killed one of our teammates and controlled the summon that created the Desert Wall."

Trecheon's ears perked. "A *summon* created the Desert Wall?"

"Yeah," Zeke said. "But we took him out. Ronan. I doubt he survived."

Leah's tail twitched. "…He might have since Judgement snatched him out of the air like that."

Trecheon sat back in his chair, as the last of Jaden's message played through. He stared at Leah and Zeke. "Just what the hell happened to you two?"

Leah picked at her tail again. "Zeke and I bound our focus jewels, we time traveled, and we just spent the last few months in the War of Eons in Ackerson's team Mage. We tried to save Zeke's moms at the Battle of DC and we *failed* and I couldn't even save your arms or save Neil from his terrible PTSD and I couldn't save Carter and…" She dissolved into sobs.

Trecheon stood. "You got caught in the War of Eons? With *Ackerson?*" He held a hand to his head. "Good *Draso.*"

Leah focused her gaze on his hand. "Trecheon, I'm so sorry, I couldn't save anyone in Outlander, I just couldn't…"

"Hey, hey, hey, don't start that," Trecheon said, holding out his hands. "I told you on the day we met that everything worked out okay. Don't blame yourself for that."

"But I *knew* and I should have saved you…" Leah sank to the floor.

Zeke kneeled beside her and wrapped her up in a hug. "We just got back to this time after taking down the Desert Wall. Emotions are… high."

"I'd say." Trecheon said, frowning. "You two are clearly out of it. Come on, we'll get you cleaned up and dressed in something decent and get you some Draso-damned rest. You've clearly earned it."

"But Jaden…" Leah muttered.

"He said in his message that we needed a Defender A.I.," Trecheon said. "I'm pretty sure Ouranos has one. So let me get you set up and make some calls. It'll be okay, alright?"

Leah didn't look convinced, but she didn't protest.

Zeke did though. "There's no way you have clothes we can both fit into."

"I don't," Trecheon said. "But both Matt and Sacha left clothes here and they'll do just fine."

Leah perked her ears. "Sacha? As in Captain Wildpelt?"

Trecheon nodded.

Leah's eyes widened. "You had Guardian Azure and Captain Wildpelt in your apartment? What were you doing that meant they left *clothes* behind…?" She clapped her hands over her mouth. "I'm sorry, I shouldn't pry, that's none of my business, I just--"

Trecheon's ears flushed. "It's okay, you're high-strung right now, it's not your fault. Sacha and Matt were helping me look for you and took turns staying with me while they searched. Matt and the others are already back on Zyearth, but Sacha's still here, on Athánatos. Wouldn't leave without you."

Leah hung her head, looking almost shamed. "Call her first, would you?"

Trecheon smiled gently. "Yeah, sure. But time's wasting. Come on, upstairs." He and Zeke helped Leah to her feet. "For what it's worth, I'm really glad you're okay and you're home."

She managed a small smile. "Thanks."

"Of course." He turned to Zeke. "Any chance I can borrow Jaden's pendant? Might need it to convince people he's actually alive and needs help."

Zeke frowned. "It's set to only play that video if it detects DNA close to his own."

Trecheon twitched his snout. "Guess that proves you really are his son then. And Matt's half-brother."

Zeke flicked an ear back, but nodded.

"I can fix it," Leah said. She took the pendant, messed with some settings on the holoboard, then passed it to Trecheon. "S-Should work for anyone now."

Her terrible shaking didn't pass his notice as she handed the pendant to him. "Let's get going then. Get you some rest, for Draso's sake. Matt and Sacha's clothes are probably in my top dresser drawer." He paused. "There might be a pistol too. It's not loaded, but be careful."

Zeke pressed his ears back. "Should I even ask?"

"I'll explain everything later," Trecheon said. "Let's just say it has to do with the war, but It's a very long story and you two aren't fit to hear it right now. Go rest." He herded them upstairs, then flipped the Open sign back to Closed.

This was going to be a wild ride.

CHAPTER 03

MATT AND SACHA

Trecheon made sure Leah and Zeke were set up with blankets and pillows on his spare cots, showed them how to use his shower, and got a frozen pizza in the oven. After each of them drank a full bottle of water, they seemed to calm a bit, though Leah was still antsy about getting to Jaden.

"I should be out looking for him," Leah said, wringing her tail.

"Leah, we don't even know where to start looking," Trecheon said. "And we don't have his pendant to track him. He left information. We'll get to it as soon as we can, okay?"

"You have to take care of yourself first," Zeke added. "Trecheon's right. We're in no shape to go looking for him."

"Okay, okay…" She leaned against Zeke and he wrapped an arm around her.

Trecheon eyed them, but didn't question it. That wasn't his place. "The pizza will be ready in half an hour. Shower, eat, and sleep, okay? I'll be back up once I make my calls."

Leah splayed her ears. "Yeah… thanks."

Trecheon headed back downstairs. Despite his promise to Leah, he reached for Matt first, hoping to catch him before he actually went to sleep. He bounced his foot up and down rapidly waiting for the call to go through. "Come on, Matt…"

Eventually Matt's groggy face appeared in the hologram… shirtless. He wiped sleep out of his eyes. "Hey Trech." He gave him a lazy grin. "Couldn't wait huh? Just can't get enough of me?" He leaned on a pillow.

Trecheon's face flushed. He hoped it wasn't obvious in the hologram. "After all this time, *now* you decide to flirt back?"

"Sorry." Matt chuckled. "Blame the fatigue. What's up?"

Blame the fatigue. Good Draso, did he mean that flirting or not? Geez. "This is serious Matt. We found Leah. Or more accurately, she found me."

Matt frowned and sat up, fully alert now. "Uh oh. Your tone of voice suggests it's not pretty."

"It's hard to say," Trecheon said. "But she's alive, she's fine."

Matt let out a breath. "Thank Draso. What happened?"

Trecheon rubbed his arm. "She burst into my office wearing bloody American BDUs and with, um, an Athánatos quilar."

Matt's eyes widened. "Draso's *mercy*. One of the missing ones? Embrik, or Alexina?"

"Actually… Alexina's son." He explained about Leah and Zeke's jewel bond, the time travel, and their involvement in the War of Eons.

Matt leaned back against his pillows. "Holy *shit.*"

"That's what I said." Trecheon shifted. "But that's not even the wildest part."

Matt blinked. "It isn't?"

Trecheon flattened his ears. "Probably better I show you. Brace yourself, okay?" He pulled up Jaden's Defender pendant.

Matt sat up, eyes wide. His fur puffed up. "Whoa, wait, that's--"

"Just listen, Matt." Trecheon played the recording.

Jaden's worn face appeared in the hologram, and Matt's reaction was instant – eyes wide and glassy, fur and quills standing on end, his jaw loose. *"Greetings,"* the hologram said. *"I've set this pendant to play with either my DNA or any DNA similar to mine. If you're seeing this, then you're family. I don't know if I'm speaking to Matt or Zeke, but whoever it is… you might want to sit down for this."*

"Fire and *ice,"* Matt said. "That's… that's my *dad."*

"I know."

Matt shifted. "Zeke… that's the quilar Leah was with?"

"Yeah," Trecheon said. "He's… your half-brother."

Matt opened his mouth like he wanted to speak, but nothing came out. He kept his eyes glued to the hologram.

"This was recorded on July 22nd, 2038 by the Earth calendar," Jaden continued. *"We had tried so hard to hold out until after Matt and Trecheon first met, but time ran out and we had no choice. I hope Matt doesn't find this too early and mess with the timeline, but this is a risk we have to take."*

"Draso's *mercy,"* Matt said. "That was the extra pendant signal I kept seeing in the pier when I was looking for Izzy right before I met you." His voice came out in squeaks. He listened as Jaden continued about Ackerson and Alexina and their attempts to hide. Matt frowned. "Who's Matron Fawn?"

"Doesn't matter, because she's dead," Trecheon said. "But put simply, she was a mob boss. Not sure what she had to do with Ackerson though. Not a connection I know anything about."

"Dad did, apparently." Matt gripped his head. "Holy Draso… my dad…"

"I hope that this message finds you well," Jaden finished. *"And I hope that you'll find us well too. We'll hold out as long as we can. But… if the worst should happen… know that I'm proud of you. All of you. Leah, Zeke… and Matt. Take care. Find us soon. This military might fear the Angel, but the Angel never met the Defender."* He gave a slight smirk. *"Guardian Azure out."*

The hologram faded.

Matt stared at his comforter, arms limp, hands in his lap. Trecheon's chest ached with an intense desire to reach out and hug him, but of course he was a thousand lightyears away.

"Trecheon," Matt said, his voice shaking. "My father is alive." He shook himself. "How'd he survive? I watched his Gem *explode.* That should have killed him."

Trecheon flattened his ears. Images of Ryota's last moments before his own Gem exploded flashed in his mind.

Matt ran a hand through his quills. "How the hell has he gone this long without us knowing? Why didn't he call us? He clearly had a working pendant. I thought… but Draso, shouldn't he have gotten home by now? Or at least contacted me? Why is he still there? How'd he get involved with Athánatos?" He gripped his head. "Damn it, why *now?"*

"I don't know," Trecheon said. "Something you'll have to ask him when you see him, I guess."

"Assuming he's still alive."

"He is," Trecheon said with more confidence than he felt. "He has to be."

"Maybe."

They sat in silence for several seconds. Matt's breaths came in slow, ragged gasps. He pressed his eyes shut. "…Hell."

Trecheon lowered his gaze. "I uh… I actually met him once before."

Matt shot his head up.

"When Ackerson was recruiting for his teams," Trecheon said. "We went to a draft dodging camp named Atlas that had been attacked and destroyed, trying to find survivors. Jaden was one of them. I just didn't know who he was at the time." He laced his fingers together. "I think Embrik and Alexina were there too. I remember noting that they were very tall and they had strange ear shapes."

Matt pressed his hands together. "My dad married Ouranos' sister. And they had a kit." He shook himself again. "That doesn't even make sense though. How old was the Athánatos Leah had with her?"

Trecheon shrugged. "My age at least I'd say. He had Ei-Ei jewels on though, so who knows." He lowered his gaze. "She mentioned time travel. I suspect that might have something to do with Zeke too. Maybe the Black Cloak's involved."

"Maybe." Matt leaned on his hands. "Draso's mercy… How the hell am I supposed to handle this?"

Trecheon smirked a little, trying to lighten the mood. "I suppose it's a good thing you never developed a crush on Ouranos. He's technically your uncle now."

Matt eyed him, but didn't respond to Trecheon's jab. "This Zeke character. What's he like?"

"Wary," Trecheon said. "Defensive, though also understanding. Hard to tell though, since both of them are so tired and fighting off the effects of the war. He looks remarkably like you, but like he was a negative of you. Black, white-tipped quills, burn orange snout, but also those familiar green eyes. He and Leah are intensely protective of each other." He tensed slightly. "Reminds me of you and Ouranos. Or you and Izzy."

"Comes with the territory of jewel bonding," Matt said. He sighed and managed a small smile. "Though I like to think you and I have the same relationship even without the jewel bonding."

Trecheon's heartbeat quickened and he smiled. "Yeah."

Matt ran a hand down his face and looked off. "My dad… alive. Remarried. Having another family." He shut his eyes a moment. It was hard to tell, but it looked like he was crying.

Trecheon frowned. "Anything I can do?"

"I don't know honestly," Matt said. He faced the camera again. "He's… he's hiding."

"That's what the message says."

Matt pinned his ears back. "I need to get back to Earth. I have to find him." He moved to stand.

Adrenaline spiked through Trecheon's chest, with some intense need that he couldn't name. "I'll find him."

Matt turned. "Trecheon. You'd be going against Angel."

Trecheon waved a hand. "I went after Theron. I can handle Angel."

"Yeah, but you had help."

"I'll have help now too." Trecheon crossed his arms. "Or did you think Ouranos is going to let me hunt down his sister without him? Or Natassa, or Melaina, or hell, even Neil--"

"Alright, alright, I got it," Matt said. He reached out of view then pulled a shirt over his head. "I'm still going to go back. Gotta talk with Izzy and Lance and… and Charlotte." He paused. "Draso, how is Charlotte going to handle this?"

Trecheon pressed his lips tight. "Probably the same as you. Confused, conflicted, worried."

Matt slumped slightly. He was quiet for a long time before he finally spoke. "My father is alive. I should feel happy. Why don't I feel happy?"

"Matt," Trecheon said. Matt met his eyes. "You thought your father was dead. It probably doesn't even feel real. Probably it won't until you actually see him face to face again. I mean, you haven't seen him since you were *six*. That's a whole new worldview to wrap your head around. Give it time, okay? You're fine."

Matt slowly smiled. "Thanks. I needed that." He sighed. "Meeting you has done a whole lot more than I ever expected." He raised one eyebrow. "Next we'll find out that somehow your father isn't dead either."

"It'd be more of an emotional roller coaster if we found Granddad alive," Trecheon said, rolling his eyes. "But Granddad wasn't a mage or a Guardian, so slim chance of that."

"Fair." Matt shook his head. "There's no way I'm sleeping now. I've got too much on my mind. I better get to Izzy and Lance. Figure out what to do next."

"Probably a good plan."

"You said Leah and Zeke were fighting the effects of war," Matt said. "PTSR?"

Trecheon tilted his head. "You mean PTSD?"

Matt flicked his ears back. "I think? We call it post-traumatic stress reaction."

"Ah," Trecheon said. "Same here, except we say 'disorder' instead of 'reaction.'"

Matt winced. "Ugh. Makes it seem like some *disease* instead of a trauma response. Bet you have all kinds of stigma around it."

Trecheon snorted. "You have no idea."

"They'll need help," Matt said. "I'll see if we can get a trauma-response therapist onboard too."

"Good idea."

Matt smiled. "I guess that means I'll be seeing you sooner than I thought, so that's good at least." He pointed at the camera. "Don't get yourself killed going after my dad. It's not worth it."

Trecheon gave a goofy salute. "Aye, aye, cap'n."

Matt laughed now. That felt good to make Matt laugh. He smiled softly. "Alright. I'll update you as soon as I know our plans. See you soon."

"See ya." Trecheon cut the call. He leaned back in his chair. Draso. Matt was taking this hard. He had to find Jaden now.

Time to call Sacha.

Sacha answered almost immediately, grinning at him. "Mornin', Trecheon!" She leaned into the camera seductively, eyes half lidded and her whiskers twitching. "Couldn't stay away, huh?"

Trecheon's ears splayed. "What the hell has gotten into you and Matt that you've both decided now is a good time to flirt back?"

Sacha ran her tongue over her sharp teeth and lifted her eyebrows, leaning forward. "Hun, I've been flirting back with you pretty much since we met. Not my fault you didn't notice. Besides, you started it."

Trecheon's ears flushed. "Yeah, well, I'll have to finish it another time. Sacha… Leah showed up at my shop this morning."

Sacha's face fell and she furrowed her brow, immediately serious. "Is she okay? Was she alone? Did she look properly fed? Was she--"

"Slow down," Trecheon held up his hands. "She's fine, but ah… she showed up with a missing Athánatos prince."

Sacha's golden ears perked. "What?"

Trecheon explained everything as he knew it. "Matt already knows. He's honestly not taking it all that well."

"Can't blame him," Sacha said, wrinkling her snout, her tufted cheeks puffed up. "I'd be freaking out too." She shook her head. "I'm going to pack up and head over there now."

"Wait, please," Trecheon said. "Leah and Zeke were absolutely exhausted, and they need rest. They'll never get it if everyone starts piling up in my apartment. Let me call some other people first. Is Natassa there?"

"She and Damianos are with Neil."

"Good," Trecheon said. "Let me explain it to them first and see how Natassa wants to break this news to Ouranos. In the meantime, let's let the soldiers sleep."

Sacha rubbed the fur of her left arm, a habit Trecheon noticed she did during the few times she was nervous. "I can understand that." She twitched her whiskers. "I hope we can find Jaden."

"Yeah... Me too."

Sacha pointed at him. "Make your calls, but then afterwards, take care of yourself. Find a distraction, get some breakfast out, do sudoku, I don't care what it is. Just don't stop moving until we all get together, okay?"

Trecheon raised an eyebrow. "Why? I'm fine."

"Leah just came back from the war that took everything from you," Sacha said. "You might be fine now, but those memories are gonna come crawling back." She eyed him. "You have a support network now, Trecheon. Make sure you use it. Call me back as soon as we have plans, okay? Don't be alone for long."

Trecheon's short tail drooped. All the memories of his lack of control in his younger years. He hadn't thought of that. And yet, once again, Sacha had. Always concerned for Trecheon's mental health. Always understanding. He nodded to her. "Yeah. Sure. I'll call you as soon as I can."

"Good." She rubbed her arm again. "Take care, hun. Sacha out." She ended the call.

Trecheon sat back. Sacha looked out for him. Matt spoke about how much he missed him. And both of them had flirted back, after all this time.

Yeah, Trecheon's feelings definitely weren't just friendship. If only he could have something more with them. But that probably couldn't happen. Nothing in his life worked that way. He needed to regain control.

Time to call Neil.

NEIL

Neil woke to the sound of his beeping alarm, his mind still foggy. He pulled his pillow over his head, hoping the thing would just stop.

Damianos groaned and shifted next to him.

Neil sighed. Shit. Despite how well Damianos had adapted to much of the mainland, he was still a little put off by the beeps and boops of electronics and Neil had always accommodated him when he spent the weekend over.

But they had been up so late last night playing board games and chowing down on sushi that everything was still a little hazy. They'd been up so late, in fact, that Neil declared he'd take today off. But he forgot the alarm. Curse everything. He sat up, leaned over Damianos, and slid the kill switch on his phone.

Damianos turned over and pulled the covers tight around his yellow, black-streaked shoulders, settling down again.

Neil watched him, a smile creeping across his lips. Who'd have thought that this is what he'd get to wake up to? A handsome quilar sharing his bed every weekend, snoring away in perfect bliss. After the hardships both he and Damianos had had to endure over their lives, this peace was well deserved and definitely needed. He never wanted to let it go.

He turned to his other side. Natassa was already awake and no longer in bed.

Not surprising. She usually woke up far earlier than Neil or Damianos and spent the quiet of the morning reading or painting, and usually making breakfast. Took her a while to get used to the electric stove, but once she got the hang of it, she went all out and they feasted on mornings like this.

It had been a journey to get the three of them comfortable in this relationship, which surprised Neil considering the Athánatos were openly polyamorous.

He had tried everything he could think of to dispel the anxiety and treat them both equally – no favorites. He made a rule about no romantic time during sleeping hours. He tried evenly switching who shared the bed with him – Damianos one night, Natassa the next. For a while he even traded weekends with them, only ever bringing one of them over at a time, so they got equal time with him; no competition.

But it soon became clear that the struggle wasn't because they were worried Neil was favoring one over the other. It was because of the relationship between each other.

Natassa was a Basileia now, taking over after Theron's defeat. Damianos was her subject. And he couldn't seem to get around that dynamic.

Natassa had assured him over and over again that because they were both dating Neil, they should see each other as equals. Call each other by name, avoid the formal titles, treat each other like friends. But old habits die hard and it took nearly a year of Natassa's gentle and patient friendship before Damianos finally started calling her by her first name. By that point, Neil got himself a California king bed and while it was lonely to use during the week, it was plenty big enough for the three of them on weekends.

Eventually Damianos felt comfortable enough for them to share the weekends and the bed, which loosened the odd power dynamic between him and Natassa. The last year and a half had made the two of them very close, to the point where their friendship and comfort with each other often drew stares on Athánatos Island if one of the citizens happened to catch them together.

Ouranos had assured Neil that the citizens would get used to it eventually. Especially if Neil intended to marry Natassa.

Neil rubbed the fur on his bare arm. That one had thrown him off.

Marry Natassa.

Or Damianos. Or both of them.

He hadn't asked yet, but Ouranos had hinted multiple times that marrying Natassa would make Neil a Basileus. A literal king. And he'd share responsibility over the Athánatos. So much of his life had been stuck following. Now it was time to prove he could lead. Take charge. And taking charge over their relationship dynamics was good practice for that. He'd be far better than Theron was.

That would be a little piece of heaven. Married to the zyfaunos he loved, helping to heal the scars Theron left behind, living on Athánatos island, away from the mainland, the worries of work, his past as an assassin… and the pink doe assassins of Triple Fawn. In a place that they could never get to. Safe.

Maybe. After all, the doe had been listening in on those cursed headsets during their entire battle with Theron. He couldn't think they were all that ignorant.

Though they had agreed to let Trecheon and Neil go. And they hadn't bothered them in the years since.

But they also hadn't relinquished their hold on Neil's little brother Philip. He was still trapped in the hell of foster care and Neil couldn't get him out.

Philip would be twelve this year. He had started losing his cub coat last year and was growing into his adult coat. Time was running out.

Poor kid couldn't even have any stability. His social worker was determined to prevent Neil from adopting him and thwarted him at all turns – complaining about Neil's home life, his job, his house, his relationships, limiting visits, trying to set Philip up with other families, who, thankfully, backed off when they learned he had a brother trying to adopt him. Who knew how long that would last though.

The worst was her habit of scheduling court dates and "forgetting" to tell Neil. He had to work damn hard to keep up and make sure he didn't miss anything. There were several notes on the fridge about the one later this week, actually. He had tried complaining about it, because it was an illegal move, but there was only so much their overworked department could do.

Her latest ploy was moving Philip around to other foster families. One such move had happened just two months ago, where he was placed with a brand-new foster parent named Theophania, a blonde-haired, thick-built, ex-military woman apparently trying to "make the world a better place" after her troubles in the war. Philip liked her well enough, but it took all Neil's energy to be cordial to her. After all, this woman had no idea that Philip's social worker had a vendetta. All because she thought Neil had killed Matron Fawn.

Which, admittedly, was true, but she didn't know that.

Thank God Neil had a date scheduled for just the two of them in a couple of days. Some sense of what he hoped would eventually be their normal. Out from under his social worker's hateful eye.

But Ethos, Pathos, and Logos could easily undo all that. This was their doing in the first place. And they hadn't. Who knew what those ridiculous doe thought. He was afraid to ask them directly, unless they tried to ensnare him again.

His piece of heaven wouldn't be complete without Philip. He'd need a way to get him to Athánatos. Then it'd be perfect.

But that was a much bigger fish to fry. For now, it was best to enjoy the comfort and peace of their life.

The gentle smell of pancakes frying rolled into his bedroom, meaning Natassa was making breakfast. Neil yawned. Just a few more minutes of peace before starting the day. He slid back under the covers and wrapped an arm around Damianos. Damianos stirred and leaned into Neil with a contented "Mmm."

Neil gave him a gentle squeeze and closed his eyes.

Then the beeping started again.

Damianos grunted. "Neil…"

"I know, I'm sorry," Neil said, sitting up again. "I must've hit snooze instead of off."

"Neil?" Natassa walked into the room, ears pinned back a bit. "My Heart, your communicator…"

"Yeah, I forgot to turn off the alarm last night," Neil said. He turned toward the phone. But it was dark and silent.

Natassa shifted in the door frame. "It is not your phone," she said. "It is your Defender pendant."

Adrenaline shot through Neil's body, shaking off all sleepiness. Damianos immediately sat up, eyes wide.

Natassa held up the pendant. The dragon's eyes lit up in that eerie blue while it quietly beeped.

Only a few people would be calling him on that pendant now that the Defenders had left Earth. And those few people wouldn't be using the pendant unless there was a massive problem. Neil held out his hands and Natassa tossed him the pendant. Neil activated it and laid it on the bed.

Trecheon showed up in the hologram. He squinted and shielded his eyes like he was being blinded. "Good Draso, Neil. Put on a damn shirt."

"I just woke up, asshole," Neil said with a growl. "Natassa and Dami are over. Took the day off. What's wrong? Why are you calling on the pendant?"

Trecheon's face grew serious. "Are they in the room with you? They should hear this too."

Damianos leaned next to Neil and Natassa sat on Neil's other side. He was significantly shorter than both of them, but both Athánatos leaned down so they could rest on Neil's shoulders. Neil waved a hand. "Well?"

Trecheon rubbed his quills. "There's, ah… gonna be a lot to unpack, so I'll just spit it out and let you ask questions as we go along." He paused, tapping his chin. "Let me start with a question myself actually. That human who's been working with you, who lost his buddy around the same time we lost Leah."

Neil raised an eyebrow. "You mean Andre?"

"Yeah, Andre." Trecheon lowered his gaze. "What's his missing friend's name again?"

"Zeke Brightclaw," Neil said.

"Black quilar, white tipped quills, burnt orange snout?"

Neil flicked his tail. "Yeah. Why?"

"Well, um." Trecheon wrinkled his snout. "We uh… we found Leah."

Neil's bones buzzed. "Oh my god."

"Or more accurate, she found me," Trecheon said. "Burst through my office door this morning. And she had Zeke with her." He pressed his lips together. "Did you know Zeke is an Athánatos quilar?"

Neil's eyes widened. *"What? Athánatos?"*

"But how is that possible?" Natassa asked. "All Athánatos are confined to the island except--"

"Except Embrik and Alexina," Trecheon said. "Apparently Zeke is Alexina's son."

Damianos gasped and Natassa drew her hands to her snout.

Neil wrapped his arms around them both. "This is some space opera bullshit, Trecheon."

"It's more complicated than just that too," Trecheon said. "Because his father is Jaden Azure. Matt's father."

Natassa stiffened next to him, and Damianos shivered.

Neil frowned. "Isn't he dead?"

"Evidently not," Trecheon said. held out the pendant and played part of the recording.

Neil just stared. A scraggly hologram of a pure white quilar who looked far too much like Matt spoke about things only a veteran of the War of Eons would know. God, he even sounded like Matt.

"I guess when Matt and I had left Leah at the café, Zeke showed up and then Angel attacked them," Trecheon said, cutting the recording off and tucking away the pendant. "They fought and accidentally bound their focus jewels the way Matt and Ouranos had. And they time traveled, like the damn Black Cloak. I need to ask them if he was involved, honestly." He shook himself. "But they got caught up in the War of Eons with Mage, along with Jaden, Embrik, and Alexina."

"Holy *shit,*" Neil said. "They were *Ackerson's?*"

"Yeah," Trecheon said. "Though no more willing than we were. But I guess they helped take down the Desert Wall."

"Christ on a bike, Trech." Neil pinched the fur between his eyes. "Slow down. The hell am I supposed to process all this shit?"

Trecheon shrugged. "I said it was a lot."

"Right." Neil sighed. "But they're safe."

"Safe as can be," Trecheon said. "I have them showering and resting now. They were a mess. I also gave Matt a call, and he's on his way back, though it'll likely be a month or more to get here. In the meantime, we have to find Jaden, Embrik, and Alexina."

Neil pressed his eyes shut. Damn it. That was it again. No more safety. No more peace. Back into the fire. He held Damianos and Natassa close.

Time to be the leader.

And they suddenly felt very… fragile. His heart thumped against his chest.

"Neil?"

"I know," Neil said. "Let me give Andre a call. He'll probably want to bring his boyfriend too."

Trecheon lowered his gaze. "Is that safe?"

"Considering his boyfriend is Chadwick Moonbeam, I think so."

Trecheon flicked an ear. "One of Ackerson's."

"Not anymore willingly than us."

"Fair," Trecheon said. "Might as well bring him along."

"I'll set up a meeting tonight with everyone," Neil said. "Probably sometime late tonight on Casino Beach since we're gonna be talking aliens and mages and shit. I'll send you the details once I've talked with Andre."

"Gotcha," Trecheon said. "I'll have Zeke and Leah with me." He turned to Natassa. "Natassa, I've already explained things to Sacha since she'd want to know about Leah, but you should be the one to talk to your family."

"I will give Ouranos a call," Natassa said. "If… Zeke is really family, we will all want to be there."

Trecheon furrowed his brow. "Sorry to dump all of this on you at once. I know it's a lot to take in."

"We will survive," Natassa said. "As much as I am struggling now, the news, overall, is good."

Trecheon smiled. "Good. Take care, all of you. See you tonight." He flipped off the hologram.

Natassa leaned on Neil's shoulder.

Neil pressed a kiss to the top of her head. "You okay?"

"I will be," Natassa said. She wrapped an arm around Neil's stomach. "I had thought my sister dead. I had already mourned. The fact that she survived is hard enough to process. But to learn she has also married Matt's father and had a child?" She shook her head. "Seems… strange. And somehow too good to be true."

It did, honestly, and if it wasn't for that pendant recording, Neil would have thought Leah was full of it.

Natassa smiled. "But… that would mean Matt is actually family. Real and true family, not just in name. There is light in that." She gave Neil one more squeeze and kissed the side of his head. "I will go to the living room to speak with Ouranos and give you and Dami a chance to wake properly and dress."

"I'm pretty freakin' awake after that call, but I hear you," Neil said. "Give my regards to Ouranos. If he or anyone else wants to crash here for a bit before the meeting, they're welcome to."

"Thank you, my Heart." She left the room.

Neil turned to Damianos. He sat on the bed, hands in his lap, staring at the covers. Neil frowned. "Dami?"

"Is this to be our lives?" Damianos said quietly.

Neil frowned. "What?"

"My childhood was full of fear and uncertainty because of the Basileus," Damianos said. "Then I came of age and watched as my family and friends waged war with the mad king, staining the battlefield red with their blood, or black with the ink of the Shadow Cast and leaving me one by one until Theron imprisoned me."

Neil reached over and held Damianos' hand.

Dami squeezed it back. "And then… you. Coming into my life like an emerald prince, pulling me from imprisonment, giving me a chance to find myself, to find purpose again. To find love…" He frowned. "And peace. But only for two years. A snap of the fingers compared to the long decades afraid and alone." He turned and met Neil's eyes, his own glassy. "Is this our fate? To face turmoil, uncertainty, fear, only for a snap of peace before being thrust into the flames once more?"

Neil bit his lip. He pulled Damianos close. Damianos laid his head on Neil's chest and gripped him tightly.

God, he felt so damn fragile. Like if Neil let go, he'd vanish into the wind, never to be seen again. Neil shook off the feeling and took a deep breath, drawing on every ounce of strength he had.

"I don't know what's going to happen with this," Neil said. "And I don't want to lie and say it'll be fine, because I don't know if it will be. But I promise this. We will have peace again. And if I have anything to say about it, it'll be a long peace next time."

"Will it?"

Neil's mind wandered to his imagined perfect future – married and happy to Dami and Natassa, living on Athánatos and doing something good for the people there, with Philip at his side, safe and happy and free. He'd never get his "magic hit" as an assassin – saving lives by taking out the right dictator or mafia boss. Those days were behind him. But he could damn well do good in other ways. Make up for all the bad he'd done in his life.

He pulled Damianos up, cupped his hands around his face, then drew him in for a long, deep kiss. Damianos physically relaxed, his shoulders slumping gently. He gripped Neil's hand on his cheek and leaned into the kiss, causing Neil to smile. He loved that he had that effect on Dami. He pulled back after a moment and locked eyes with Damianos again.

"When I say I promise, I mean it," Neil said. "I'm going to get us through this. You just have to trust me."

Damianos gently gripped Neil's wrist. "I trust you."

"Good," Neil said. "Now let's get dressed and go meet this missing Athánatos prince, huh?"

CHAPTER 05

GUILT

Leah woke up from another fitful bout of sleep, breathing heavily, sweat soaking her fur. Every time she closed her eyes, another nightmare ate at her. Sometimes it was actual memories from the war. Sometimes it was something seemingly mundane. Walking the Defender campus, having lunch at the café with Trecheon and Matt… then suddenly some unknown monster appears and destroys everything in sight.

Sometimes she watched Ari die over and over and over in increasingly destructive ways, and she could do nothing about it.

All the other nightmares ended with Zeke's death. Or Jaden's. Or even Matt's.

Leah laid her arm over her face. Was this going to be every night from now on?

"Hey," Zeke said. "Can't sleep?"

Leah sighed and sat up. Zeke sat at Trecheon's rickety table, a soda in one hand and a piece of pizza in the other. He wore a green shirt and a pair of black pants, similar to the street clothes Matt had been wearing when they had first landed on Casino Beach all that time ago. His glasses had tape around one of the temples. A gentle smell of baking banana nut bread filled her nose, mixing with the smell of melted cheese and processed meat. Contemplation.

It was so strange seeing him in a normal environment. Like they hadn't just fought a massive summon and ended a world war. They were just… having a pizza party.

Maybe that was how life would be from now on. Never really normal again.

Leah flattened her ears and looked down. "No. Kept having nightmares."

"Thought as much," Zeke said. "I could feel them."

Leah wrinkled her snout. "Sorry…"

"Not your fault," Zeke said. He passed her a plate with pizza and a soda. "Trauma will do that to you."

Leah took the meal, her brain swirling around the word "trauma." She frowned. "Does Earth really think of post-traumatic stress as a disorder?"

Zeke shrugged. "I suppose so." He sat back in the chair. "I wish I could give you advice on working through it, but this is the first time I've experienced it so acutely myself. I don't have anything to give unfortunately."

"It's okay. I'll figure it out." She forced a smile. "We'll do it together, right?"

Zeke smiled and nodded. "Yeah."

She glanced around the room. A pair of cheap prosthetic arms and a repair kit sat on the coffee table in Trecheon's living room. Leah winced.

Zeke flattened one ear. The burning smell of a hot pan hit Leah's nose. Worry. "Don't blame yourself for that, Leah. Trecheon told you not to, and you were going after my moms with me."

"And I failed to save them too," Leah said bitterly.

"You gave me another moment with them," Zeke said. "I got to talk to them again, hug them again. That's invaluable."

Not as valuable as having them alive. Leah said. But she kept it to herself, hoping Zeke didn't hear. She knew she shouldn't feel sorry for herself. Zeke and Trecheon were the ones facing loss. She was making this about her. That was selfish.

But if you can't save others, what kind of Defender are you? the Thought Factory echoed in her head.

Leah snarled. *I'm Guardian material. Jaden said so himself.*

Yeah, before you lost Zeke's parents and all of Outlander.

Leah formed fists. *That wasn't my fault!*

"Leah…" Zeke said softly. "I keep smelling something burning."

Leah shook herself. "S-sorry, just… caught up in my thoughts." She stared out the window. "What time is it anyway? It's dark out."

"It's about 11 PM." Trecheon walked into the room. Leah turned. The red and black quilar crossed his biomechanical arms and frowned. "How you holding up? Get any rest?"

Leah stared at his arms, a double sense of guilt washing over her. She squeezed her eyes shut a moment. *Don't make this about you!* She turned and bit into her pizza. "…A little."

"Good," Trecheon said. "Because we're gonna be headed out to Casino Beach in few minutes here."

Zeke perked an ear. "Why? We were just there. It's a ghost town."

"We're meeting some people there," Trecheon said. He nodded to Zeke. "Your family, mostly."

Zeke shuddered.

Trecheon flicked his ears back. "All of us wanna help Jaden. We'll figure out what to do from there."

"Why are we meeting them so late?" Zeke asked. "And why on that old dilapidated beach?"

Trecheon crossed his arms. "Mainly because of the Athánatos. You'll see when we get there."

Leah turned to him. "Trust me, Zeke. There's a reason." Zeke shrugged, but nodded. She met Trecheon's eyes. "Are you doing okay?"

Trecheon froze for a quick moment, but then shrugged nonchalantly. "Fine. Closed up the shop to give you guys some quiet, then did some sudoku. That shit's riveting when there's nothing else to do." He waved a hand. "Come on. They're waiting."

Leah stared a little longer at his metal hand, then shook herself and stood. Captain Wildpelt's clothes were a little big on her – she had to roll up the legs of the black pants and the blue shirt hung kind of loose around her shoulders, but it was better than bloody BDUs.

Zeke walked up to her and wrapped an arm across her shoulders. She leaned into his hug.

Trecheon eyed them again.

Leah twitched her tail. "I'm sure you're wondering, but there's nothing romantic between us."

"That's fair," Trecheon said. "I didn't want to assume, but cultural habits die hard."

Trecheon led them to his garage and his same old truck still stood there. The group piled in. Leah sat in the back, but Zeke sat up front to accommodate his long legs. Leah watched as he adjusted the seat.

Again, a totally normal, everyday action. And yet it felt so alien. There had been no seat adjusting while they were in the field. You just made it work and hoped you were okay. She pressed her eyes shut and huddled on the bench.

"Seatbelts on," Trecheon said. "Don't wanna get pulled over this late at night."

Seatbelts. Did the Humvee even have seatbelts? She couldn't recall. The habit had been lost though, so probably not. Another mundane task erased by war. She pulled her seatbelt taut.

"I don't want to push you two for info about what happened," Trecheon said, starting the engine. "But if you want to talk about it, I'm here to listen. I lived it too."

Leah shifted in her seat. The seatbelt chaffed her neck fur. "I... have a confession, Trecheon."

Zeke frowned. "Leah."

Trecheon's quills bristled. "If this is about not saving my arms, Leah-_"

"I let Carter go."

Trecheon turned, one eyebrow raised. "Wait, *what?*"

"I saw him at the field hospital after the Battle of DC," Leah said. "H-He went into Neil's tent when he was having a PTSD episode. I should have spoken to him. Said *something*. But he walked out and I just... let him go."

Trecheon stared wide eyed. "But you saw him. He was alive."

"Y-yeah." Leah folded her hands in her lap. "I can understand why you say Matt looks like him. They're very similar."

"Did you see where he went?" Trecheon asked.

"N-No," Leah said. "Commander Reddy came and talked to us afterwards and I didn't see Carter again."

Trecheon's jaw dropped now. "Commander Reddy? They were in DC?"

"The Commander is the one who led us to the Desert Wall assault," Zeke said.

Leah flicked her ears down. "I don't suppose you knew what happened to them?"

Trecheon shook his head. "No. Anyone connected to black ops and Ackerson essentially vanished after Ackerson's trial. For all I know, they're dead."

Zeke folded his arms and looked away.

Trecheon turned back around and drove the car out of the garage. They rode in silence for several minutes. Streetlights blazed in the windows, burning Leah's eyes. She took off her glasses and huddled in the seat, pulling her knees up to her face.

Zeke glanced back, ears pinned. He reached over and grabbed her hand. She squeezed it, forced a smile, then turned back to the window.

They drove for what was probably an hour, with only the occasional hiccup from Trecheon's old truck to keep them company. The Thought Factory swirled, but couldn't land on one particular topic, making Leah's head feel like alphabet soup. She had to focus.

"How did you and Neil avoid it?" Leah asked.

Trecheon stopped at a red light and looked back. "Avoid what?"

"The problems with Ackerson's supporters."

The light turned green. Trecheon continued on. "Good question, honestly." He waved a hand. "We were so messed up after the war that we didn't have the strength or energy to speak out against Ackerson. I don't think any of the news sources picked up that we were connected to Ackerson. The only reason they picked up on anyone was because they chose to come forward against him in the first place."

"You dodged a bullet then," Zeke said. "I suppose Leah and I have too, technically."

"Considering you two were so secret that no one seems to remember you, yeah," Trecheon said. He glanced at Zeke. "You know a human named Andre?"

A strong smell of spice stung Leah's nose. Shock. Zeke stared at Trecheon. "Andre! Is he okay? How do you know him?"

"He knows Neil," Trecheon said. "He's been looking for you as long as we've been looking for Leah." He shrugged. "I can't be certain, but he might be there tonight."

Zeke held his head in his hands. "God, I hope so…"

Another hour passed and they parked at the old, battered Casino parking lot. Trecheon led them down the beach toward the Pyramid casino. Leah clutched Zeke's hand. He shook during their entire walk.

Trecheon led them to the pyramid. They entered and walked toward the conference rooms.

Zeke tensed, gripping Leah's hand tighter. His anxiety rippled through her almost like a disease, setting off her healing magic. She pressed cooling healing energy through his body, though it did little to calm him.

Trecheon opened the door to Conference Room B.

And they met the gentle, yet shocked brown eyes of a tall, dark-skinned human.

FAMILY

Zeke stared, adrenaline rushing through him, mixing with some strange, deep-seated worry and an unrecognizable scent from Leah.

Andre.

His best friend, his flying partner, his reason for living, standing there wearing simple jeans and a white shirt, almost identical to what he wore the day Zeke had vanished. Like nothing had changed, and yet, *everything* had.

Andre stared back at him like he saw a ghost – motionless, his face frozen in some shocked, wide-eyed look. In a subtle movement, he pressed his lips together, uncertain, shaking.

Zeke couldn't stand it anymore. He reached over and pulled Andre into a deep hug. He couldn't manage words, only soft squeaks and sobs. His eyes burned.

Andre reacted immediately, gripping Zeke so tight it hurt. He buried his face in Zeke's shoulder. "…Thank god." His voice trembled, and he barely spoke above a whisper. "Oh, thank god…"

Zeke took off his glasses and pressed his forehead into Andre's shoulder. "Andre, I am so *sorry.*"

"Don't say that," Andre said. "You're here now, ain'tcha? You're safe, you're okay." He sniffled and squeezed Zeke even tighter. "God, you're okay… I thought I'd never see you again." He held him for a moment longer then pulled back. He stared at Zeke, eyes glassy, a big grin covering his entire face. "Hell, you look like shit."

Zeke put his glasses back on and smiled back. "Thanks, asshole."

"Love you anyway," Andre said. A warmth built in Zeke's chest and ran through his entire body. Andre tilted his head slightly and lifted a hand. "Are these the jewels from your good luck charm?"

Zeke nodded. "Yeah."

Andre reached a hand toward them, but then pulled back, frowning.

"It's okay," Zeke said. A soft smell of hot chocolate entered his nose. Leah smiled up at him.

Andre ran a finger down the Ei-Ei jewels. "How the hell do they stick to you?"

"Your guess is as good as mine," Zeke said. "The story of how I got them is a freakin' epic novel. I'll have to tell you sometime."

Andre furrowed his brow. "They'll never let you fly again with these."

"Don't think I want to anyway," Zeke said. He shook himself. "Draso's wings. That's a life change I wasn't expecting, but I think it's true."

"…Sisters save us."

Zeke turned. Three Athánatos who looked strongly like Alexina stood there, staring at Zeke with the same shocked expression Andre had. He recognized one immediately from Leah's mental image. "Ouranos!"

Ouranos stood straight up, his pupilless, teal-green eyes widening. He opened his mouth like he wanted to say something, but nothing came out.

Leah stepped in front of Zeke, her ears back, uncertain. "Ouranos, Natassa, Melaina… This is Zeke. He's Alexina's son." She shifted. "And Jaden's son too. Matt's father."

The Athánatos with a cream-colored snout stared a moment, then smiled hesitantly, her purple eyes lit up. The other, with light blue eyes, cream-colored dots across one brow, and orange ear tips, also tried smiling, though she shrunk back slightly.

Family. A new family.

A new life.

Images of Zeke's moms just before they died shot through his mind. Their final hugs wrapped around him, their gentle "I love yous," echoed in his head. Something bit at him, but he couldn't tell what.

Ouranos smiled warmly, which set Zeke's teeth on edge. He pushed back the feeling. Ouranos perked his ears. "The resemblance is uncanny," he said. "To both Alexina and Matthew. But also wonderful. So very wonderful." He reached a hand out to Zeke. "May I be the first to welcome you?"

Zeke flicked his ears back, but he reached forward and took Ouranos' hand. His uncle's hand.

His *uncle.*

Ouranos gripped Zeke's hand in both of his and shook it enthusiastically. "Welcome home, nephew. We are delighted to meet you."

Zeke tried to smile, but failed. *There's nothing wrong. It's just your uncle. Alexina would want this. Your moms would want this. You've earned this new life.*

A pain struck his heart as images of his moms' deaths blasted his mind. He could almost feel them surrounding him, wrapping their arms around his shoulders, protecting him. He leaned back into their hug.

Leah glanced up at him, ears flat. She slipped her hand into his free one and cooling healing energy radiated through his body, bringing him back to reality. He shook his head free of the images and forced himself to relax. Ouranos was family.

He should smile at him. He managed a ghost of one. Hopefully that'd be enough. "Thanks."

Ouranos grinned with an uncontained joy.

Family. Support. Love. Ouranos had only known him for thirty seconds, and he was ready to treat Zeke like they had known each other their whole lives.

So why did it feel so wrong?

The cream snouted Athánatos offered her hand. "I am Natassa. This is Melaina." Melaina smiled sheepishly. Zeke took Natassa's hand, trying to hold in the shivers. Natassa smiled. "Welcome." She flicked her ears back. "I know we are urgently looking for Jaden, but when time permits, if you have any news at all about Alexina, we would be glad to hear it."

"Yeah, sure, of course," Zeke said.

The door behind them opened. Zeke turned. A golden tiger wearing a black shirt and uniform pants similar to the ones Leah had been wearing when they first met walked in, looking slightly harried. She had a Defender pendant around her neck. "Back from patrol, but I haven't seen--" She paused the moment she saw Leah.

Leah turned. She stared a moment, then saluted with a sweep of her fist over her chest. "Captain Wildpelt, I--"

"You're *home,*" the tiger said. She took three big steps and drew Leah into a hug. Zeke expected Leah to recoil considering the hug without question, but instead his senses washed over with warm cookies baking. "Thank Draso. I thought we had lost you." She stepped back and looked

Leah over quickly. "Any wounds? Pain? Did Trecheon let you get enough sleep? Have you had anything to eat?"

Leah held her hands up. "I'm fine, Captain. Really."

She eyed Leah, then turned to Zeke. "Is she?"

Zeke blinked. "Why are you asking me?"

"Trecheon said you have a social bond with her," the tiger said. "I know what that looks like. I saw the effects in Matt and Ouranos for over two years. So what do you think?"

Zeke frowned. He glanced at Leah, ears back.

Leah stared up at him, brow furrowed, a singe of a hot pan hitting his nose, drowning out the baking cookie smell. Edging on panic. *I'm fine for now. Please tell her that, or she won't let me go looking for Jaden.*

Zeke flicked his tail, flattening one ear. *Leah, you need time to process everything. Staying behind might not be a bad thing.*

Zeke, please... Leah said. *I have to save him. We'll need everyone helping. I can't sit this out. Please...*

The stink of rotting food filled his nostrils, making him feel sick.

The tiger poked her head between them and eyed Zeke. "Well?"

"Give 'em time, Sacha, geez," Trecheon said. "They've been through hell and back."

"Exactly why I need to know if Leah's okay," Sacha said.

Zeke pressed his mouth into a thin line. Leah's pleading bombarded his mind. "She's fine," he said, against his better judgement.

Sacha narrowed her gaze. "Really?"

"Really," Zeke said. He turned to Leah. *But both of us are getting help as soon as we can after this. Okay?*

Leah chewed her lip and picked at the tip of her tail, but she nodded.

Sacha watched Zeke another moment, then sighed and shook her head. "Fine. I'll believe you. For now." She turned to Leah and gently gripped her shoulders. "If you need to stop or take a break or get help for anything, you let me know, okay?"

Leah nodded. "Of course, Captain."

Sacha's shoulders relaxed. "Good." She smiled. "And while we're on the mainland, it's Sacha, okay? No military titles. Draws too much attention."

Leah flicked an ear back, but nodded.

"Well then," a deep voice said. "This has been quite the reunion." Zeke turned. Chadwick, one of their partners facing the Desert Wall, stepped forward from a corner of the room, a smile on his dark furred face. He twitched his tail, the faded jaguar spots barely showing up in the dim light. "Good to see you Zeke, Leah."

Leah grinned and moved to hug him, though she paused. Chadwick crossed the gap and hugged her anyway, though Zeke noticed he was careful not to let bare fur touch. Protect her from her healing powers. She squeezed him back, her thoughts running through Zeke's mind.

It's good to feel wanted.

"Good to see you too!" Leah said. She stepped back. "But what are you even doing here? Did Jordan make it? What happened after we vanished?"

Chadwick held out his hands. "One step at a time, please."

"Wait," Andre said. "You two know Chadwick?"

Chadwick nudged him. "I told you so." Andre eyed him.

Zeke turned to Andre, one eyebrow raised. "I'm more curious about how *you* know him."

Andre smirked. He wrapped his arms around Chadwick's neck. "He's my boyfriend."

Zeke blinked a moment, then laughed. "This is the exotic car repairman you wanted me to meet?"

"Absolutely," Andre said. "But somehow you've met already." He paused and rubbed his chin. "How the hell'd that happen?"

Zeke flicked his ears back, and all the waves and waves of information about mages and Zyearth and time travel and Defenders and summons came rushing into his mind at once, melting into a sticky, gooey mess and Zeke had no idea how to untangle it in a way Andre would understand. He glanced at Leah, his mind blank. "Suddenly I realize why you struggled to lay everything out to me the day we met."

"If it helps," Andre said. "Chadwick's shown me some… things." He glanced around. "Not sure how much I can share here though."

A new Athánatos, with deep yellow fur and black streaks, stepped forward. "We are all mages here," he said. He glanced over at one corner.

A puma in a green bomber jacket carrying a sword stared at him with a smirk and one eyebrow raised.

A sharp smell of spice hit his nose and he could practically feel Leah's fur stand on end. A name ran through his mind. *Neil.*

So that was Neil.

"Well, most of us," the Athánatos continued. He gripped Neil's hand, then turned to the group. "Those who are not are at least aware of magic."

Neil nodded to Andre and smiled. "Neil Black. Sorry all our interactions up to this point have had be through the phone. Though I suppose that's what happens when we're both frantically looking for people. I'm guessing you and I are the only not-mages around here. Might as well get to know each other." He nodded to Chadwick. "Maybe swap dating stories sometime. Dating mages is not something I get to share with many people." Neil held a hand out to Andre.

Andre took Neil's hand with a grin. "We'll start a fan club."

Ouranos cleared his throat. "If I may." He turned to Leah. "Trecheon said you have a pendant from Jaden, one that will hopefully lead us to him. Perhaps we should see what we can do with it."

Leah frowned. "But what about Jordan?"

All mirth left Chadwick's face. "Jordan's... dead."

Leah held her hands to her snout.

"I'll explain in greater detail later," Chadwick said. "But right now we have to get to Jaden before he becomes Ackerson's next victim. Let's see this message."

Zeke swished his tail side to side, feeling anxious, but nodded. He pulled out Jaden's pendant, activated the message, and set it down for everyone to listen.

CHAPTER 07

CAREFUL PLANS

Leah sat in a dented plastic chair as Jaden's message played, her hands folded neatly in her lap. She resisted the urge to pull at the fur on her tail. Captain Wildpelt… Sacha… she knew Leah's nervous tell and Leah couldn't let her see.

She couldn't give any excuse for them to pull her out of the mission to find Jaden. Nothing was more important.

The hologram held the rapt attention of everyone in the room. It was almost two minutes before anyone spoke.

Andre leaned back against a wall, bracing himself with his foot. Despite his height and his obvious strength, he had an air of calm and warmth around him that immediately put Leah at ease. No wonder Zeke liked him so much. Andre shook his head. "Maybe I'm wrong," he said carefully. "But this makes it look like you fought in the War of Eons."

Zeke shifted next to Leah. "We ah, we did."

59

Andre lifted a brow. "What crazy magic is that? Time travel?"

"Basically, yeah," Zeke said.

Andre snorted. "Shit, dude. Magic I can understand, sort of, but time travel? How?"

"It's complicated," Leah said. "But it's a reaction from my magic and Zeke's magic clashing."

"I can confirm it happens," Ouranos said. "Matthew and I experienced the same sensation when we accidentally formed our own social bond. Though we only lost a day." He turned to Leah. "It seems you lost far more."

"We got dumped a few months away from the Battle of DC," Zeke said. "Something like eight or nine years in the past."

"Then you lost years coming back," Trecheon said. "No wonder you're both so out of it. Time travel jetlag."

"Jaden mentioned Alexina was pregnant," Natassa said. She flicked her tail and sat in another plastic chair. "Does this mean we should expect to find them with a child?"

"Draso's mercy, I hope not," Zeke said. "Because she was probably pregnant with *me.*"

The room grew silent as everyone stared at Zeke. Leah reached over and gripped his hand.

"Zeke, I love you man, but you must've hit your damn head," Andre said. "This message is three years old. If that was you, you would have been in the *womb* when I first met you as an *adult.*"

Zeke shrugged. "Jaden said that too when we first met." He flicked his ears back. "He accused the Black Cloak of abducting me and moving me out of my own time."

"So the Black Cloak was involved then," Trecheon said, his voice bitter.

"He was one of our teammates," Leah said. "He followed us for a majority of our time together. I don't know how we would have gotten through it without him."

Trecheon crossed his arms. "He did similar things for us, but that doesn't mean I trust him."

"He saved Leah's life," Zeke said, giving Trecheon a pointed glare. "Healed her after she got shot point blank with a rifle. That's gotta count for something."

The yellow Athánatos, Damianos, tilted his head confused. "Healed? But the Cloak has cloaking powers."

"That was how he helped us create Cast charms," Ouranos said, nodding his head. "Unless he has two powers."

"Unlikely," Sacha said. "That's really rare."

"But not unheard of," Trecheon said, juggling tiny fireballs. "If I have it, it can't be that rare."

"Hun, I don't think you realize how rare you are," Sacha said. "The last recorded Gem user to have two powers was Vyse Gildspine – Izzy's grandfather. And he died something like a hundred and fifty years ago."

Trecheon wrinkled his snout. "Okay... rule that out then. Geez." He straddled a chair and leaned against the back of it. "So do you think it's possible he actually abducted you?"

Zeke gave a slight shrug. "He never denied it. But if he did... I assume he did it for a reason."

"But why take you to some place outside of your own time?" Melaina asked. "Why not bring you to Athánatos?"

Chadwick frowned. "The Desert Wall."

Trecheon snorted. He tapped the back of his chair. "I could see that. It'd mean Zeke had the age and training to help take it down."

Leah twitched her whiskers and hunkered down in her chair. She didn't like the idea of the Cloak shuffling Zeke around in time just for convenience like that, but at the same time… it made sense. She gave in and pulled her tail into her lap anyway, picking at the hairs.

Melaina folded her hands together. "The Black Cloak is a product of Athánatos," she said. "The role was created as a way to connect to mainlanders should we need their help fighting Judgement."

"The summon that we fought at the Wall," Zeke said.

Melaina nodded. "The Cloak's mission, above all else, is to stop Judgement from rising again. If that mission meant he had to move Zeke to another time, he would do it, consequences be damned. But… he is also an ally. I do not believe he would take Zeke by force. If he moved you, then there was a reason."

Silence enveloped them again. Leah dropped her tail and sat on her hands to keep herself from picking at it again.

Ouranos breathed deeply and voiced what they were all thinking. "If this is truly how the Cloak operates, then that means something happens to Jaden and Alexina." He turned to Zeke. "How old were you when you were adopted?"

"I was only a baby," Zeke said.

"Hmm," Ouranos said. "Then something has already happened to them."

Sacha tapped the floor with her long tail, her ears back. "Makes me wonder if we should even bother looking then. We might be too late."

"We *can't be*," Leah said. "We have to try. It isn't an option." She glanced at Chadwick. "Do you have any idea where Jaden might be?"

Chadwick shifted, his tail swishing side to side. "No, and you can blame Ackerson for that. Any of us who spoke out against him were blacklisted. Made it unsafe to go outside. We had to fade back into the shadows and hope no one remembered us. Which worked for a while. But very recently, Ackerson started going after us again." He bristled his fur. "From what I understand, the military reopened the investigations, particularly in connection to the various political assassinations lately. They wonder if he's connected to the White Assassin."

Trecheon froze in place, then turned to the wall.

Chadwick's ears twitched. "Jordan's family had a big business with the casinos, so he used his influence and money to get us all to safety. New locations, new names, new businesses. I don't know where Jaden went — that was a necessity to keep us all safe. Jordan initially gave us regular checks to help us survive, but about a month ago, it just stopped coming. Tried contacting Jordan, tried his family. Nothing. Everyone is gone." He sighed and leaned back. "His family's Gems are missing too."

Andre rubbed Chadwick's shoulder. Chadwick smiled sadly and patted Andre's hand.

"Why did Jaden mention Matron Fawn?" Neil said suddenly, startling everyone. His voice was so strained and tense, it shook Leah's bones. Neil stood straight up, ears pinned down, fangs bared slightly, tail twitching wildly. His fur stood on end and his brow furrowed deeply.

Trecheon tensed up next to Leah, holding himself rigid on his chair.

"She works with Ackerson," Zeke said. Leah's fur puffed up, but the soft smell of brewing tea kept her calm. Zeke's anger was directed at an enemy long dead. Zeke continued. "Or worked with, I suppose, since she apparently got herself killed."

"She did," Chadwick said. "The papers claim the White Assassin got her."

Andre shivered next to him. Trecheon's ears flattened and he slumped into the chair.

"Considering the hell she put us through, she deserved it," Zeke said bitterly. "She killed one of her sisters."

"One of the triplets?" Neil asked.

"Quadruplets," Zeke said. "The Fawns... once had a had a fourth sister."

Leah stared at her hands. Ari's smile, her gentle touch, her fierce anger, her comfort and laugh coursed through her like an electric shock.

All of that. Gone.

"How do you even know this?" Neil asked.

"They worked with us on a hit," Zeke said.

"What?" Trecheon said. "In the war?"

Zeke nodded. "They worked for Ackerson in Hunt. Ackerson had us chasing down people in the Matron's smuggling ring." He rubbed his arm and leaned against the wall. "It was a trap though. Both the Matron and our target worked with Ackerson."

Leah pulled her knees up to her chin and hugged herself. The chair squeaked loudly in her ear.

"Smuggling ring?" Trecheon asked.

"For focus jewels," Leah said quietly. "It's a long story, but Ethos told us that they were originally trying to fight the smugglers. Then the Matron decided it would be more profitable to work with them instead."

"They also helped us take down the Desert Wall," Chadwick said. He frowned. "I didn't know there had been a fourth."

Leah buried her face in her knees. *A fourth.* Like Ari was just a number instead of a living, sentient creature. A statistic instead of a lost friend. Her hands shook.

"Why the hell would the Matron kill off one of her own assassins?" Trecheon asked.

"They didn't *want* to be assassins," Leah said, lifting her head. "But the Matron killed their mother, took over the Family, and forced them to train as assassins since they were eight years old. All they wanted was--"

"Did they feed you this pathetic sob story?" Neil asked bitterly.

Leah paused, staring. Her heart pounded. "They… I mean… that's what they told us."

"And you *believed them?*" Neil snapped. "They're *assassins. Mafia.* Those disgusting, black-hearted--"

"They were our *allies!*" Leah snapped, louder than she intended. Neil stepped back, surprised. She formed fists. "They were our *friends.* We traveled and worked with them for *months.* Ari helped Zeke contact his parents. They helped us fight Sharp and they took down the Desert Wall with us. All they wanted was their freedom, and I couldn't give that to them, I couldn't save Ari and she *died in my care with a knife in her throat--*"

"They *killed my parents* and took my baby brother *hostage!*" Neil roared. Leah sat straight up, ears flat. Damianos and Natassa turned to Neil, eyes wide. Neil snarled. "I don't want to hear about benevolence and freedom and whatever other goddamned lies they fed to you when they took *everything from me!*"

Leah stared. Her vision blurred with unexpected tears. "…B-But why would they do that?"

Neil turned his head, but didn't speak.

Sacha gently placed her hands on Leah's shoulders. There was no unfamiliar disease or injury in her touch, but there was… tension. She looked Neil straight in the eye. "Neil. You need to tell everyone here what happened with you and the Fawns." She turned to Trecheon. "Both of you do."

Neil stared at the floor. Both Damianos and Natassa came and wrapped their arms around him. He leaned into their hugs, then gave a shuddering breath. "I'm the White Assassin."

Leah's whole body buzzed and she felt slightly numb. Andre gasped and Chadwick grunted.

"We both are," Trecheon said, ears drooping. "Don't take all the blame."

Zeke tensed now and moved closer to Leah and Andre. "That explains the gun in your drawer then."

"You two are assassins…?" Leah asked quietly.

"Were assassins," Trecheon said, leaning on the back of the chair. He stared at the floor. "We dropped it just after we met Matt and the others."

"We weren't assassins by *choice,"* Neil said. "Not at that point anyway. I killed Matron Fawn because I thought I could use the skills I learned in war to do the world some good. She was ruthless. Killed hundreds, possibly thousands, and would continue to kill more. And rumors in the assassins circles said that the Triple Danger wanted out. I thought I'd give them that out by killing their Matron."

Leah frowned. "I thought… I mean… that'd be doing them a favor. It's what they wanted to do themselves. They weren't assassins by choice either."

He crossed his arms and looked away. "So they say. But they retaliated. Killed my folks. Used their influence to make sure I couldn't adopt Philip, then told me that I had to give them a million dollars to get him back. I work in HVAC. I can't make that kind of money. So back to assassinations I went, because that was the only way to get the money we needed. They took evidence from every kill, so if I went after them or went into hiding, they'd take it right to the authorities and I'd face life imprisonment or death and Philip would be stuck in foster. I was at their mercy." He pressed his eyes tightly shut. "And I dragged Trecheon into it with me."

"I volunteered," Trecheon said. "You needed the help to make up all that money."

"Wouldn't have needed to if I didn't do that stupid shit in the first place," Neil said. "I know what happened. I used you."

"Neil," Trecheon said. "This isn't all on you. I was involved too. I just happened to not have anyone they thought was worth retaliating with. Her blood's also on my hands."

Neil glanced at him, ears down, but he nodded. Natassa held him tight and Damianos pressed his forehead to Neil's shoulder.

Leah frowned. "Do the Defenders know?"

Trecheon waved a hand. "All of the ones who were on Earth do, and possibly your Master Guardian." He crossed his arms. "Everyone except Matt." He pointed a finger. "And no one better tell him. That's my job."

"One you should have finished ages ago," Sacha said, eyeing him.

"*I know,*" Trecheon said. "I know." He slumped over the chair.

Zeke rubbed his chin. "Something isn't right here."

"You're damn right it's not," Neil snarled.

"No, I mean, I can't see the doe doing that to someone," Zeke said. "They didn't want to be assassins. And yet here they are pulling the same thing on someone else?"

Neil crossed his arms. "You think I don't know who killed my own family?"

"I didn't say that," Zeke said, holding his hands up. "I think their behavior is strange. Someone's pulling their strings."

Leah flattened her ears. "Ackerson."

"No doubt," Zeke said.

Neil raised an eyebrow. "So what?"

Zeke shook himself. "If the Fawns are being coerced by Ackerson, then they might also know something about Jaden," he said. "So I'm going to find out for sure if they are." He held out a hand to Leah. "With me?"

She stared at his hand then took it.

Trecheon stood. "Absolutely not. I'm putting my foot down here."

Zeke flicked his ears back. "But--"

"No buts." Trecheon glared. "They may have been your allies in war, and yeah, maybe they hated the what the Matron did to them, but that doesn't change the fact that they have maimed and killed and ruined lives. It doesn't change how they've kept Neil and I as their personal mafia puppeteers while holding Philip hostage. They are *not* allies. No one is going after them."

Zeke furrowed his brow and narrowed his gaze. A strong smell of burning entered Leah's nose.

But Trecheon lifted his chin and set his quills ablaze. "No. Arguments."

Zeke snorted, but backed down. Physically anyway. The burning smell only got stronger.

Ouranos stepped forward "Perhaps we can pick this up again when we know more." He picked up Jaden's pendant off the table. "In the meantime, I have an A.I. on Athánatos who can tackle this puzzle Jaden has left for us. Pilot was recently repaired and should be in the right shape to handle it. I can start tonight. After all the information we have, I dare say sleep will evade most of us for the rest of the night."

"Once we have information about Jaden's whereabouts, we'll meet back here," Chadwick said. "Make plans, figure out what to do next."

"It may be safer to meet on Athánatos," Melaina said. "Away from prying eyes."

Zeke swallowed hard. A smell of hot peppers hit Leah's nose. Almost… like fear.

Chadwick frowned. "You're okay with Andre and me being there?"

"Of course," Ouranos said. "You are welcome to our home."

Chadwick smiled.

Neil glanced off.

Trecheon met Zeke's gaze, his face softening slightly. Zeke pressed his lips together and looked away. Trecheon sighed. "It's a plan then, I suppose."

Zeke cleared his throat. "Before we go." He turned to Andre. A strong smell of coffee brewing, something contemplative, hesitant even, entered Leah's nose. Zeke's nervousness ran through her like a cold chill. He took a deep breath and gripped Andre's shoulder. "I need to speak with you."

CHAPTER 08

HEART TO HEART

Zeke walked out onto the beach with Andre beside him, his heart pounding. This shouldn't be this difficult. He just wanted to talk to Andre about fixing the relationship they had lost. Yet he was sweating and nervous like he was about to lose him.

They neared the water's edge before Zeke finally convinced himself to stop. But speaking was a different beast.

Andre gripped Zeke's shoulder. "Hey, everything okay?"

Draso's wings, how could he put all he had faced into anything coherent? Where the hell would he even start? The pain and loss of war, so immediate, so fresh, drowning out the longer, drawn-out pain of watching his relationship with Andre slowly deteriorate because Zeke wouldn't speak up about his own feelings on it. Because Zeke had been so busy just *existing* that he hadn't taken the time to really *live* and enjoy what he had. He took a deep breath.

Just start the conversation. Talk about what you miss. Ask if we can start over.

But that's not what came out.

"I saw my moms again," Zeke said. "At the battle of DC. Alive." His voice barely rose above a whisper. "I… watched them die."

Andre's eyes widened. He gripped Zeke's shoulders and met his gaze. "Oh god, Zeke, are you okay?"

"I…" Zeke's chest ached and his vision blurred. He had told Leah it was okay. And it was, he knew it. He couldn't have them and the life he had now. He accepted that. But at the same time… They were gone. Again. He stared at Andre, emotions bubbling, trying to find the words.

But Andre reacted first. He gently removed Zeke's glasses and pulled him into a deep hug. "Just let it all out, man. I'm right here."

Zeke tried to say he was okay and ask why Andre had removed his glasses. But all the emotions of the war, of the loss of his parents, of Andre's firm, familiar hug that had been absent for so long stole the words from him.

He pressed his face into Andre's shoulder and sobbed instead.

His whole body shook as his mind whisked him away from the beach and dropped him back into the Battle of DC, trading the cool, calming ocean for a warzone. His body grew hot, jittery, his mind, absolutely terrified. One thought crystalized.

Save his moms.

And he had failed.

He had *failed.* He had known exactly how they were going to die and he hadn't stopped it.

They're dead. They're gone.

You failed.

In some vague hallucination, he fought through waves of heat and rubble and enemies, trying to reach his parents. They lay on the ruins in the distance, blood soaking their outfits, limbs twisted, while they sobbed quietly, staring blankly into the broken air, tears running through their soiled fur. Too far, too far, *too far*. Gone. *Gone*. He had lost them.

YOU FAILED.

He couldn't escape DC. The burning city dragged him deeper and deeper into its homegrown hell.

Then Andre's gentle hand on his back, patting him. His voice, echoing, distant. *You're here. You're safe. You're present.*

He reached for Andre… and failed. DC's fires and rubble and war wrapped around him, holding him fast. His parents called to him in broken voices. *Zeke! Zeke!*

Listen to the waves, Andre said, his voice distant. *Feel the spray on your quills. Taste the salty air. Smell the brine of the ocean.*

Zeke pushed back at the debris, the fires, the smoke. He had to escape.

Stay. Find your moms. Don't lose another chance to save them.

But it was all in his head and he knew it. He needed to be back. Get Jaden.

Jaden.

His eyes flashed open. The dead casinos were barely visible in the light of the broken streetlamps, blurry without his glasses. But Andre's hug felt closer and more real than ever before. He clung to that, forcing his eyes to stay open, focused. The tears ran down his snout. He slowed his breathing, concentrating on the sounds and smells of the sea.

Andre wouldn't let go.

Zeke pressed his forehead to Andre's shoulder and centered on his hug, his soft breathing, the fabric of his shirt, his heartbeat pressed against Zeke's chest. *Calm. Calm...* He took one more deep breath then pulled back from his hug with Andre.

Andre held on to Zeke's shoulders, steadying him. He furrowed his brow, his mouth twitching like he was trying to speak but couldn't find the right words.

Zeke forced his body to relax. "I... I think I just had my first PTSD panic attack."

Andre smiled sadly. He handed Zeke his glasses. "Hopefully your last, but considering the hell you went through, I ain't betting on that. You holding together?"

"Yeah..." Zeke put his glasses back on. "For now anyway."

"You wanna talk about it?"

Zeke rubbed his arm. "Yeah, honestly." The two of them sat in the sand and he gushed – about his moms, Ackerson, the battles, the magic, the Fawns, the hits he took out, Ronan's betrayal, the Desert Wall. And of course Jaden, Alexina, and Embrik and... and Leah. Leah especially. It came out faster than he could process it himself, but when he finished, an hour had passed. Andre listened patiently.

"Sounds like you had quite a ride," Andre said. He shifted on the sand. "Leah... She seems good for you."

"She's amazing," Zeke said. "She's patient, understanding, and fierce when she needs to be. Having this social bond with her is extra special too. We're like two halves a whole. We can read each other before we even speak. I wouldn't trade it for anything." He shook his head. "Not... not even if it meant I still had my moms." He held his head in his hands. That was true, wasn't it. His eyes burned. "Draso's breath, that's really true... Does that make me a bad son?"

"'Course not," Andre said. "Sometimes good things come from tragedy, and it's okay to admit that. Healthy probably. S'what my therapist would say anyway."

Zeke looked up. "Your therapist?"

Andre rubbed his arm. "Yeah, been seeing a therapist for a couple years now." He frowned. "I took it real hard when you vanished. Picked up a pretty bad bout of depression." He tried smirking but it didn't quite look right. "Hadn't had a chance to say it yet, but it's probably okay you ain't gonna be flying anymore, because I ain't either."

Zeke stared, eyes wide. "What? Why?"

Andre laced his fingers together. "When you vanished, I put all my spare time into looking for you. But it wasn't enough time. So I asked the Major if he could sign off to get me discharged for mental illness. Just fake it, you know? That way I could spend *all* my time looking for you."

Zeke frowned. "There's no way the Major would do that."

"He did," Andre said. "But not because he thought I was faking it. He had me diagnosed before he signed me off. That's when I had to face the reality of it head on. Definitely had depression. I'm glad the Major forced the issue. Got help through VA services. Wouldn't have been able to afford it otherwise."

"Andre, I am so sorry…"

"I don't wanna hear it," Andre said, holding up his hands. "Not like you had a choice."

"Is that where you learned those grounding techniques?" Zeke asked.

"Yeah," Andre said. "I always thought PTSD only came from like, abuse, car accidents, war, whatever. Something big and damaging. But turns out losin' your best friend without warning can have the same effect." He smiled. "But you're here now. I couldn't be happier and I mean that.

And I'm glad you had Leah to pull you through the war." He eyed Zeke with a smirk. "Hope she's not gonna replace me."

Zeke shot his gaze up, frowning, his ears flat.

Andre frowned. "Sorry, that was supposed to be a joke. Didn't come out right."

"No, it's…" Zeke formed fists, trying to stop the shaking. He reached out and took Andre's hands and held them tight. "I honestly wanted to talk to you about that."

Andre tilted his head.

Zeke breathed deeply. "Andre… we… we used to have something really special with our relationship. Like I have with Leah now. Openness, understanding, love. And we still have most of that, but when I came out to you as ace/aro, we lost something important."

Andre smiled and gripped Zeke's hands. "The hugging, touching, that stuff."

Zeke flattened an ear. "…Yeah. I really miss that. I know why you backed off. You were giving me space, trying to work through your own feelings, but we never repaired that part. And I didn't realize how much I missed it until I had it again with Leah. And it's great to have it with her but…" He squeezed Andre's hands, his heart pounding. "I want that with you again. With us."

Andre smiled. "Well. 'Bout time you brought that up." He pulled Zeke into a bear hug. "I'd want nothing more."

Zeke sighed. His body relaxed and he hugged Andre back tightly. Thank Draso.

Andre broke the hug after a moment. "Now, before we all pass out after this late night, introduce me to Leah properly, yeah? I wanna know this woman I'm sharin' you with."

"Yeah, sure," Zeke said. Relief washed over him. He got to his feet and helped Andre up. "She's a mage too, with healing powers. Just a heads up, she can see your ailments just by touching you."

"Damn, really?" Andre said, brushing sand off his pants. He paused. "Does that work with mental illness?"

Zeke rubbed his chin. "You know, I don't know. I'll have to ask her."

"Still. Hell of a power," Andre said. "That must mess with her head a lot."

"I think it's better for her with me now, but yeah," Zeke said. "Her planet kind of sees it like a disease, like it's some big personal invasion. People avoid her."

Andre wrinkled his nose. "God knows I've been there. It sucks when people reject you for a part of yourself that you can't help. I'll won't make a big deal about it." He paused. "Wait. You said 'her planet.' Does that mean she's an alien?"

"Yeah, from a placed called Zyearth."

Andre blinked, then chuckled. "Guess Chadwick really wasn't pulling my tail with that extraterrestrial talk. I thought he was full of it. That's a hell of a worldview to reimagine."

"You're telling me," Zeke said. He wrung his hands together. "I haven't brought it up yet, but eventually Leah's gonna want to go back home. I'm... gonna have to decide if I want to go with her."

Andre frowned. "Wow. Yeah just... geez." He rubbed the back of his head. "That'll be more than just a worldview change if you do."

"It's a ways off," Zeke said. "This is more immediate. I'm... trying not to think about it."

"I get it." Andre pointed at Zeke's Ei-Ei jewels. "So, ah... speaking of sensitive topics right now, but... do those things give you long life like Chadwick's does?"

Zeke flicked an ear back. Shit. He hadn't thought about that. Leah had long life. Not immortality like him, but at least a long enough life that he'd never have to think about it. But Andre… "Yeah, actually. It, ah, makes me immortal. Not invincible, but… from what Alexina told me, I get to choose my death. I won't ever die of old age."

Andre paused, silent for several seconds. "Yeah. Thought as much." He shook his head. "Magic I can handle. It's weird, but not totally unbelievable. But the fact that you'll both outlive me… The fact that you might move to a whole 'nother planet. That's gonna take some time."

Zeke's body buzzed. Of all the consequences he thought of with getting these jewels and accepting his bond with Leah, this wasn't one he considered. Shit.

Andre shook his head, then wrapped an arm across Zeke's shoulders. "Let's have those hard conversations later. Gotta survive this hell hole first. And we need to get Chadwick and Leah involved anyway."

"Yeah." Zeke leaned into him.

Andre grinned. "Yeah, I've definitely missed this. C'mon, let's get back to the others. I wanna meet Leah. Especially since we're all gonna be workin' together on finding your dad." He chuckled. "As weird as that is to say."

Zeke flattened his ears. "You're planning to help?"

Andre smirked. "My guy, I spent the last three years looking for you. I ain't gonna abandon you now. Y'all need all the help you can get."

And there was that strike to the bones again. "Andre… If Angel really is the group that chased Jaden into hiding then we're going against some powerful mages."

Andre's smile faded. He folded his arms and lowered his gaze. "And?"

"And you're not a mage."

"I'm a solider."

"It's not the same thing."

Andre sighed. "Look. I'll stay off the front lines if you want, but I ain't abandoning this all together. You ain't. Chadwick ain't. You two are my life. I'm not gonna sit on my ass and do jack shit."

Zeke's bones buzzed now. "Andre…"

"Don't try to talk me out of it," Andre said. "Not happening. Alright?" He gripped Zeke's shoulder. "Might as well get used to it. Let's go."

They headed back, but the buzzing in Zeke's bones wouldn't stop.

By the time they entered the room, only Leah, Trecheon, and Sacha were still there. Trecheon leaned against the wall, his eyes droopy. Sasha sat on a sofa in one corner, with Leah sleeping on the cushion next to her, her head on Sacha's lap. Sacha rested a hand on Leah's shoulder.

Zeke frowned. "Everyone left?"

Trecheon yawned. "Ouranos was antsy to get started on decoding Jaden's message. Chadwick and Neil are driving them to the Athánatos portal." He nodded to Andre. "Chad said he'd be back for you when he's done."

Zeke raised an eyebrow. "Athánatos portal? The hell does that mean?"

Trecheon grinned. "You thought time travel was strange, just wait til you see how we get to the Vanishing Island. That's where Athánatos is."

Zeke held his head. "No more worldview shifts, please. I've had enough lately." He turned to Leah. "She fell asleep, huh?"

Sacha rubbed Leah's shoulder. "Reluctantly. But yeah."

Zeke's tail twitched. "You're from Zyearth right? I thought they had a problem touching a healer-S."

Sacha lifted her chin. "I'm head of the Healer's department. It wouldn't do to have me reject Leah based on a power she can't control. I've been trying to squash that stigma for decades." She gently patted Leah's shoulder. "Leah knows she can trust me."

Zeke tilted his head. "I was under the impression Leah didn't have any friends."

Sacha flicked her tail. "Hard to be friends with your superior officer."

"I heard that," Andre said.

"Yeah, same," Zeke said. He folded his arms. "She hardly got any sleep earlier. Too many nightmares. If she's sleeping now, I'd rather not wake her. Think I could carry her to the truck?"

Sacha smiled. "How chivalrous of you."

Zeke narrowed his gaze. "Only if chivalry applies to friendship. We're not romantically involved."

"Sorry, wasn't trying to imply you were," Sacha said. She leaned back and grinned now. "But for what it's worth, chivalry does apply to friendship too."

"Aww, how sweet," Andre said. He slapped Zeke's shoulder. "I'll remember that the next time you carry me to bed."

Zeke rolled his eyes. "Let's just get her to the apartment while she's still peaceful." He gathered her up in his arms. Carefully, he poked at her brain, looking for stress without waking her.

A soft, warming smell of hot cocoa wafted past his nose, and she cuddled close to him, but she seemed agitated. He held her close and surrounded their bond with relaxing, calming images, creating a safe atmosphere. Him by her side, a warm blanket around her, gentle rain against a window. She relaxed in his arms.

Now if only Zeke could relax his buzzing bones.

Andre smiled. "You really love her."

Zeke nodded. "I do."

"Make sure you tell her that," Andre said. "We could all benefit from hearing it more."

The door opened and Chadwick walked in. "Hey hun. You ready to go?"

"Definitely," Andre said. He gave Zeke a half hug, careful not to disturb Leah. "Take care, Zeke. I better see you tomorrow. You still ain't introduced me to Leah proper."

"We'll be there."

Trecheon nodded toward the door. "Come on, Prínkipas, let's get you and Leah home before we wake her running our mouths." He led the way to the truck.

Zeke followed behind, holding Leah close, praying to Draso that whatever A.I. Ouranos had could break Jaden's code quickly.

Draso, let Jaden and the others be safe…

CHAPTER 09

SHADOWS

"That's quite a bike collection you've got there," Zeke said.

Trecheon glanced up from the back of the truck. Zeke and Leah had slept into late afternoon and Trecheon let them. Ouranos' A.I. Pilot hadn't had any luck with Jaden's pendant overnight, so they might as well rest up.

Trecheon had been up since the ungodly hour of 6AM, wasting time with sudoku and a phone game of Tetris, unable to sleep. Sacha had been right. Memories flooded his head of the war. Weirdly, Tetris had been a better distraction but only because those invasive ads on the app gave him something to grumble about.

He kept a close eye on Zeke and Leah. Neither of them seemed to sleep well either, but they had each other at least. Draso, Trecheon missed Matt and Sacha's company. He probably should have called Sacha, actually. She'd chew him out for it later.

Andre had showed up on a motorbike around 3PM saying he'd like to take Zeke to the apartment to get his stuff. Since Zeke had no family, Andre got his affects after he vanished.

"I also want my computer," Andre said. "That weird A.I. has been working on this thing all day and hasn't got a freakin' clue. Maybe I can help."

Trecheon doubted it, but if it kept them distracted, what did it matter?

So here they were, gathered in Trecheon's garage, tired and antsy as hell.

At least the bike collection seemed to awaken something in Zeke. He nodded to the back of the garage, all lined with Trecheon's motorcycles.

Trecheon stood in the truck's bed. "Thanks. It's grown in the last couple of years, I'll admit. Call it a favor from the Black Cloak."

Leah eyed him. She finally seemed a little more herself today, Zeke had said, now that she had a proper night's rest. While they both insisted they weren't romantically involved, they certainly were physical with each other. They had pushed their cots close together and Zeke had slept all night with an arm over her.

She crossed her arms, frowning, her brow furrowed in confusion. "What does the Black Cloak have to do with your bike collection?"

Trecheon leaned against the cab of his truck. "It's kind of a long story, but let's say his time traveling antics cost me an arm, an expensive security system, and several days' worth of lost work. He paid me back after we took down Theron, and then some. I've been collecting and restoring trashed bikes in my spare time." He flicked his ears back. "Honestly, most of that spare money went to our savings for Philip's ransom, but I had to do something else for my own mental health."

Zeke picked up a black and silver helmet from the display shelf. "Where do you get your helmets? I have a hell of a time finding ones that fit."

"All the ones you see there were custom fit," Trecheon said. "Laughing Jackal Customs owed me a favor." He grinned. "Several favors." He nodded to Zeke. "You ride?"

"I do," Zeke said. "After the War of Eons Air Corps propaganda, it's practically a requirement for pilots."

"Not that I'm complaining," Andre said grinning.

"I thought I heard Andre mention flying," Trecheon said. "I'm Marines myself."

Zeke smirked. "Something, something, military branch rivalries, right?"

Trecheon chuckled. "Yeah, well, none of us fit there anymore anyway. Screw made-up rivalries."

Zeke turned the helmet over, one ear flattening. "My moms had bikes. I probably should have kept them, but it hurt to look at them, so I sold them after their deaths. Haven't owned a bike since, though on rare occasions I'll rent one and just shoot the breeze."

Trecheon pressed his lips together. "My Granddad got me into bikes. He vanished when I was 18, right before the war." He shook his head. "I still have his somewhere, but I won't ride it. It sucks, but I get it."

Zeke rubbed his arm. "Yeah."

Andre snaked an arm around Zeke and gave him a squeeze. "When this is all over, we need to go riding."

Zeke frowned. "If I can find a helmet, sure."

Trecheon pointed to the helmet. "Try that on. If it fits, you can have it and we'll work on a bike together."

Zeke raised an eyebrow. "Really?"

"Sure, what the hell."

Zeke grinned. "Thanks." He slipped off his glasses and pulled the helmet over his head. "Cozy." He tried putting his glasses back on through the open visor, but they didn't quite fit. "Needs some adjusting though."

Leah picked at the tip of her tail. "I hate to spoil the mood, but we should really get going. I want to get to the Athánatos portal before dark."

"Take the helmet with you and adjust it on the way," Trecheon said. "There's a portable toolkit on that last shelf you can use."

Zeke smiled. "Thanks." He snatched the kit off the shelf.

The group piled in the truck and Andre straddled his bike. Trecheon buckled up, careful of the shoulder holster and his pistol. With all the bullshit around Ackerson being active again, he didn't want to be without it. Leah huddled up in her seat in the back of the cab. Once again, Trecheon had to remind her about seatbelts.

Zeke held the helmet in his lap and tinkered with it. "So if you lost your granddad at 18, that makes you…"

"31," Trecheon said. "Almost 32. I suspect you're around the same age."

"28," Zeke said. He paused. "…I think. Do I count the years I was missing? God." He shook his head. "Maybe I should, since it's what my ID will show. It'd mean crossing the 30 threshold without fanfare though." He tapped his Ei-Ei jewels. "Not that age matters much anymore."

"Yeah, I'm still getting used to that myself," Trecheon said. He flashed a grin. "Just wait til you hear what it does to your reproductive system."

Zeke rolled his eyes. "Not planning on a romantic partner ever in life, and if I want kids, I'll adopt. Means nothing to me."

"Probably a good thing," Trecheon said with a laugh.

They continued on until they hit Andre's neighborhood, a swanky collection of apartment buildings in a massive gated community. Trecheon parked in the visitors parking, a multi-story garage, and took a spot on the fifth floor. The place was packed. Leah stuck close to Zeke's side.

Andre pulled into a motorcycle spot near the stairs. He took off his helmet. "It's a bit of walk. Sorry 'bout that." He waved them down the stairs. "Don't touch the elevators. They don't work half the time." He pointed to Zeke. "Take the helmet and hide the tool kit under the seat. They'll be targets for thieves around here." Zeke nodded and grabbed it.

Trecheon raised an eyebrow. "I thought this was the nice part of town."

"Since when does this shithole have a nice part?" Andre said.

"Got me there."

Andre led the way out of the garage toward a far-off apartment building. They walked in silence for several minutes, on a thankfully empty sidewalk.

"Trecheon," Leah said quietly. "Why White Assassin?"

Trecheon perked both ears. "Pardon?" Andre and Zeke both glanced at him.

"Neither you nor Neil have white fur," Leah said. "So… why White Assassin?"

Trecheon flicked an ear and his quills bristled. "I only killed corruption. People who used their power to hurt others. It was a poor attempt to convince myself that what I did was okay. All it did was make me hate myself more." He rubbed his arm. "Matt had to pull me out of that."

Leah looked up. "That's why you care about him so much."

Trecheon's ears flushed. "One of the reasons."

"Captain Wildpelt… er, Sacha seemed like she was doing that for you too."

"Yeah," Trecheon agreed. "She's been a real solid rock for me. Even more so with Matt not here."

Leah smiled. "They're good zyfaunos."

While they walked, Trecheon stared at the concrete. They were good zyfaunos, both of them. He had been in a depressive slump and they pulled him out. Matt's unconditional love, his care, his smile, his laugh, his touch. Sacha's understanding, her concern, her pushing him to do the right thing. His chest swelled again and he pressed his eyes shut. *Damn it.*

Andre let them into the apartment. "Sorry it's a mess."

It was anything but. Clean, old fashioned furniture, marble counter tops, plants everywhere, classy paintings. Basically the opposite of Trecheon's messy living space.

Zeke snorted. "This is messy?"

"Chad would say it is," Andre said. "Haven't vacuumed yet today. Fur everywhere." He vanished down the hall and returned with a couple of backpacks and a messenger bag. "These are yours, Zeke." He passed the backpacks to him. Zeke and Leah each shouldered one. "Give me a mo' to water the plants or Chad'll kill me." He filled a watering can. "Make yourselves at home."

Trecheon turned toward the living room when someone knocked on the door.

Everyone froze. Andre narrowed his gaze. He pulled a pistol out of his messenger bag and loaded it.

Trecheon already had the Lowry out, his heart racing. Carefully he peeked through the peephole.

Something covered it.

"Get behind me." He activated a shield. Leah did the same, pulling Zeke behind her. Andre aimed his pistol at the door and moved next to Zeke.

Trecheon smashed the door open, pistol at the ready. But no one was there. He turned. A folded piece of paper had been taped to the door.

His heart felt to his stomach, a familiar adrenaline rush invading his spine. He snatched the paper off the door and opened it up.

Blank.

Zeke peered over Trecheon's shoulder. "Blank?"

"No." He ran back inside and held the picture up to the window. A faint icon of a three-quarter moon appeared.

Trecheon stared wide eyed. Oh *shit*. Why *now?*

Zeke frowned. "What's with the picture?"

"A message to me," Trecheon said. "One of the things the Fawns used in our assassin days."

Andre's eyes widened. "The *Fawns?"*

Trecheon nodded. "Three-quarter moon means serious danger, and we have a shadow." He shoved the paper in his pocket. "Back to the truck. Go!" He stowed the pistol, then dashed out of the apartment and toward the parking garage at a brisk pace. Leah and Zeke followed behind, gripping each other's hands. Andre wouldn't let go of his gun, but he did stuff his hand into his messenger bag, glancing around anxiously.

Trecheon fought the itch to grab his gun again. He drew on his magic instead, letting little embers build on his metal fingertips.

It took half the time to get to the truck as it had to get out of the garage. Trecheon glanced around the whole walk back, but didn't see anything. Bad sign. *Very* bad sign.

By the time they got to their floor, most of the other cars in the lot were gone, which was extra strange considering how packed it had been. Only Trecheon's truck and Andre's bike remained. *Oh god, oh god.*

Trecheon held his hands out, stopping the others. He bathed them in a shield. Leah did the same. "Wait--"

The truck exploded, shooting waves of heat and fire across the garage, slamming into the group. Trecheon flew back and smashed into the wall. Zeke tumbled back and caught himself on a bollard, and Andre tumbled over him.

Leah flew the farthest and went over the edge of the concrete railing, screaming. She barely grabbed the edge, scratching deep grooves into it with her claws.

Zeke scrambled to his feet. *"Leah!"*

Trecheon leapt up and the two of them ran for the wall. Leah's fingers were just visible over the top of the concrete. Zeke leapt to grab her when her hands slipped out of view.

"Leah!" Trecheon leaned over the edge, but neither he nor Zeke could reach her. She fell, screaming.

"Archángeli!" Zeke shouted. The summon appeared, but was too far off. Trecheon's heart dropped to his stomach. Zeke's magic went haywire, spewing plasma and dust and wind, mimicking his panic.

Something black and green flew through the air and crashed into Leah, leather wings flailing, catching her and vanishing into another floor of the parking garage in a loud crash.

Zeke ran for the stairs and Trecheon followed. They found Leah two floors down.

And a black, green streaked bat sat next to her.

CHAPTER 10

FLYING BLIND

Zeke gasped. "Angus!"

"Zeke?" Angus said. The black and green bat glanced around, but didn't seem to focus on anyone. "Thank the Great Zephyr. Come check on Leah, hurry!" Zeke dashed over and dropped by Leah's side. She wrapped her arms around his neck, breathing in ragged gasps.

Trecheon pushed back his building magic, but remained wary. "Zeke, who the hell is this? Is that Ronan's brother?"

Angus blinked rapidly and turned his head this way and that. *"Shit*, do I hear Trecheon?"

"Yeah, he's right there," Zeke said. He leaned in closer to Angus' face, but Angus didn't react. Zeke's eyes grew wide. "Holy hell, are you *blind?*"

"Squalls and gales," Angus said. He scrambled to his feet. "Trecheon being here throws the whole prediction off." He dug into the pocket of his

black slacks and pulled out two keys. "Plan B. Which of you has the bike helmet?"

"I do," Zeke said. He pressed his lips together.

"Shit, shit, *shit,* " Angus said. "Okay, forget Plan B, this is like… Plan L." He held the keys out to Zeke. "Zeke take the blue key, Trecheon, the silver one." But then he paused and pulled his hands back. "Wait, is your friend Andre here?"

A motorcycle rev echoed through the garage and Andre rode up to them. "Holy shit, is Leah okay?"

Angus spat off a string of some language Trecheon didn't recognize. *"Crosswinds."* He held out his hand. "Take those keys!"

Zeke flicked his ears back, but didn't protest. He tossed Trecheon the silver key. "Got 'em. But what--"

"No questions!" Angus pulled out three earpieces. His gaze focused on the ground, but he tossed them to Zeke, Andre, and Trecheon without a problem. "Put these in. Zeke on the bike in space E34 and Trecheon and Leah in the car in E37. Andre, stay close to Zeke. And I mean *close.*" He pointed toward the parking spaces. "That way. Hurry!" Then he pulled a tiny mirror out of his pocket, mumbling.

Trecheon flicked his ears back. "What the hell is--"

"We don't have time," Angus said. "I managed to get you away from the car bomb, but Trecheon threw a monkey wrench into my map and I have to compensate or we're all *dead.* I'll direct you through the earpieces."

A piercing screech of tires echoed through the garage.

Angus snarled. "You've got one minute to get going. I'll explain when I can. Go!" He turned and headed for a wall, chittering quietly. He pressed his hand against the wall and it opened up, revealing a tiny room, then he vanished into it. *"One minute!"* The wall swung shut.

Another tire squeal.

Trecheon pushed Leah and Zeke. "Go, *go!*"

They ran for their respective spaces. Zeke put the earpiece in and pulled his helmet over his head and fit on his glasses before sliding down the visor. Andre slid up next to him. "For the record, this is a *terrible* idea."

"I don't even know what the hell we're *doing,*" Andre said.

"Bags!" Trecheon shouted.

Andre and Zeke toss their bags to him. "Careful with that messenger bag!" Andre called.

Trecheon opened the door to the car, a fancy silver sports car unlike anything he had ever seen. He threw the bags behind the seats and sat down while Leah took the passenger seat. The thing looked like a spaceship, with unrecognizable dials, a very empty dashboard, and no display screen.

And crucially, no starter. Or steering wheel. "What the hell? What *is* this thing?"

Leah gripped the seat. "It's a *Pendragon.*"

Trecheon eyed her. "What?"

Leah smashed a button on the center console and a strange, cone-shaped hole appeared in the middle.

About the size of Trecheon's Gem. Trecheon stared.

"This is a *Zyearth* car," Leah said. "Put your Gem in there."

"What the hell is a *Zyearth* car doing here?" Trecheon exclaimed. "I can't drive this thing!"

"Well, I can't drive at *all*, so you've got to figure it out!" She put her seatbelt on and huddled on the seat.

Trecheon snarled. He slammed the Gem in the center console and the car lit up with hologram read-outs. A steering wheel popped up in front of him. He pressed the familiar earpiece to his ear.

And a massive white SUV with police-issued bull bars came barreling down the ramp from the floor above them.

"Go *now!*" Leah shouted.

Zeke peeled out of his space and zipped away, ripping around the pillar and heading down the ramp with Andre at his heels. Trecheon jammed the accelerator to the floor and tore off after them. "Hold on!"

"You all have a flair for dramatic escapes," Angus said over the earpiece. *"Two more seconds and you would have been shark food."*

Trecheon growled. "Look, I don't know who the hell you are, but you'd better get talking. What are you doing here? How'd you know about the car bomb?"

"Ask Leah," Angus said. *"And yes, for the record, I'm blind. Blame Angel. Hell of a price to pay for fixing my scrying problem, but if it saves your asses, maybe it'll be worth it."*

"Leah, the hell is scrying?" Trecheon asked.

"He can see into the future," Leah said, pulling her ears down over her head. "But scrying is really difficult to get right."

"Which is why I'm struggling now," Angus said. *"Trecheon was an unknown, and no offense dude, but having you there absolutely screwed my prediction map. I don't know how the hell I'm gonna get you all out of there now."*

The SUV barreled behind them. Zeke nearly scraped his knee on the concrete pavement banking around a corner and went down another ramp. Trecheon followed him, making as tight a turn as he could. The SUV had to slam on the brakes to follow them or risk falling over.

"Running out of time here, Angus," Zeke said over the comms. *"If you've got any idea, now's the time to share it."*

"Okay, okay," Angus said. *"Start with the garage. What floor are you on?"*

Trecheon pressed the earpiece. "Second."

"Got it. Give me a moment." He went silent.

The seconds expanded into years, pounding into Trecheon's head as the tires squealed and strained with his wild driving. The SUV screeched down a ramp to an adjacent parking row and accelerated, putting it parallel to them with only support pillars and cable barriers separating them. He growled and slammed the accelerator. "Screw this--"

"Brakes now!" Angus shouted. Trecheon's foot slipped, but he pressed hard against the brakes, shooting tire smoke into the air, blinding them both. Zeke and Andre stopped next to them, lifting their back wheels as the bikes came to a halt.

Someone in the SUV rolled down a window and a rifle muzzle poked out, spraying the air with a short burst of bullets, albeit poorly aimed. Leah shrieked.

"Go, go, go!" Angus shouted. *"Leah, shield everyone, now!"*

"Leah, shield us all!" Trecheon cried. Leah held her Gem in her lap and a shield burst forth around them, flickering green, then purple, then vanishing, but leaving behind an iridescent sheen.

"Leah, don't overwork yourself!" Zeke shouted, though she couldn't hear him through the earpiece.

Leah shivered in the seat next to Trecheon, breathing heavily, eyes squeezed shut.

"Drive!" Angus shouted. *"Follow my directions!"*

Trecheon squealed out of there. "I don't even know you!"

"Either do what I say or get everyone killed," Angus said. *"Which do you want?"*

"I want to know who the hell you are!"

"If I tell you, then you really won't listen."

"Trecheon, just listen to him!" Zeke shouted. *"We don't have time!"*

"But where are we *going?*"

"I don't know yet!" Angus said. *"Give me time and do what I say!"*

Trecheon snarled. He whipped about a pillar and sped toward the exit. He tried calling fire to his hands. One well-placed fireball and that car was toast.

But he couldn't even manage a spark. The car drained all his energy.

"No! Not that exit!" Angus shouted. *"Go to the one exiting on Main!"*

"How the hell do you even know where I *am?*"

"Fewer questions, more driving!"

"Damn it, Angus!" Zeke shouted. He turned the bike sideways, slid to a halt, and tore off toward the other exit. Andre cursed loudly and followed suit.

Trecheon cursed. "Where's the e-brake on this?"

"The Gem!" Leah shouted.

"Of course." Trecheon gripped the wheel tight. "I need both hands, hit the brake!"

Leah slammed her fist against the Gem and Trecheon spun the wheel, kicking up tire smoke and drowning them in echoing shrieks as the Pendragon rotated. He dashed for the Main Street exit.

The SUV headed right for them.

Trecheon swerved and missed the car by millimeters, taking off their door mirror with a loud *clonk.* He checked the rearview. The SUV shrieked to a halt and the hatch opened. A red wolf hung out the hatch, half a dozen tiny drones floating around his head.

Leah stared wide eyed at the side-view mirror. *"Caster?"*

Trecheon turned. "What?"

"It can't be Caster!" Zeke shouted into the earpiece. *"Jaden ran a sword through his gut!"*

Trecheon's stomach coiled in on itself.

"Watch yourself!" Andre called.

Several drones zoomed forward and exploded against the asphalt, sending debris into the air. Trecheon swerved to avoid it. "Shit!"

Zeke skidded about the rubble. *"No freakin' way! How'd he survive?"* Andre nearly crashed into a pillar, but he managed to avoid it.

Leah huddled on the seat and shut her eyes tight, forming fists. Her shimmering shield expanded, reflecting light in all directions, blinding Trecheon. He squinted. "I can't see!"

"Just keep going straight!" Angus shouted.

Gunfire echoed through the air now, but nothing pierced the car, thank Draso. Though how Leah's shield held, he had no idea.

"Hard left when you leave!" Angus called. *"Zeke, Andre, you need to be on the inside line."*

"What does that even mean?" Zeke said.

"On our left, Zeke, on our left!" Leah shouted.

"You can hear me?!"

"Yes!" Leah yelled. "Everything you're hearing and all your thoughts are bleeding into my mind, just *get on the left of the car!*"

Zeke shook his head and maneuvered on Trecheon's left, Andre close by. They hit the exit and tandem-turned hard left, barely squeezing all three vehicles through the exit.

A gun-metal gray sports car zoomed next to them from the right, running alongside them, matching their speed and nearly smashing into the door.

"Shit!" Trecheon said. "Angus!"

"Sharp right!" Angus called.

"There's a *car* on my right!"

"Just do it!" Angus called.

Trecheon glanced at the car. One window rolled down, and a stag appeared, holding a rifle. Trecheon cursed and yanked the wheel hard to the right, smashing into the other vehicle. Leah's powerful shield dented the front quarter panel and sent the car into an uncontrolled spin. Gunfire sprayed everywhere as it tried to rebalance and the stag gripped the side of the car trying to avoid sailing out the window. Bullets pierced Leah's shield until it shattered, penetrating their own car.

Trecheon winced as bits of metal and seat stuffing flew everywhere, his heart pounding in his chest, and every quill standing on end, just waiting for that well-known pain of a bullet wound. But thankfully nothing happened.

Then Leah drew in a sharp breath and groaned.

Trecheon turned. She gripped her arm, blood soaking her outfit and fur. Trecheon's eyes grew wide. "Oh, *shit.*"

"I-I'm fine," Leah said, breathing sharply through her teeth, strangely calm. "Bullet grazed me. Superficial. Just *go.*"

"Leah, you better hang on!" Zeke shouted. *"And Trecheon I swear to Draso, if you don't get her to safety--"*

Trecheon pressed his foot to the pedal and tore down the road, guilt and anger washing over him. His shoulders tingled near the arm mounts, magic building, desperate to escape and heal Leah. "You'll have every right to beat the living shit out of me."

"Believe me now, asshole?" Angus snarled.

"Yes." Trecheon gripped the steering wheel tightly. "Just help me get Leah to safety."

"Safety is a long way off," Angus said. *"We're headed to the shipping docks."*

A burst of lightning shot up Trecheon's spine. "Son of a bitch."

The SUV and two more sports cars burst from the parking garage and gave chase. Trecheon cursed.

"Left here," Angus said. *"And no more questions."*

CHAPTER 11

FAWNS

The shipping docks. It *had* to be the shipping docks.

"Right hand here," Angus said. *"Then quick left. This is a backway onto the docks, been unused for decades, so it's perfect for--"*

"Less talk, more directions, Angus!" Zeke shouted, his voice strained.

Trecheon followed the directions carefully, methodically, focusing tightly on that and nothing else. It was all he could focus on. Someone else controlling him. Not the five cars chasing them down, peppering the air with gunfire when the slightest opening appeared. Not Zeke and Andre following alongside, helpless, unprotected. Not Leah, bleeding, silent, in the passenger seat.

Not Ryota's blood soaked into the shipping dock concrete, calling out to him.

"Through that barrier!" Angus called.

Trecheon shook himself and blasted through the wooden beams. Zeke and Andre followed, their bikes wailing in his ears.

Focus on the driving.

Zeke had tried burning the cars with magic, but couldn't manage more than a few marbles of plasma, which bounced harmlessly off their hoods. He manifested one good fireball, but it flew between the vehicles, missing everything. They were just moving too fast.

Trecheon still couldn't manage anything at all, what with every atom of power going into driving this ridiculous thing. He longed for his pistol, but with Leah out of commission and with his frantic driving through metal containers, he couldn't afford to have a hand off the wheel. Neither of them were in a position to shoot, assuming either of them could even get in a shot at this speed. And somehow, despite the speeding and shooting and incredibly loud noises, not one sign of law enforcement. Not that that would work in Trecheon's favor, considering the prejudice against zyfaunos.

What he wouldn't give to have Matt and Sacha at his side right now.

Or Ryota.

They drove between the shipping containers, weaving around workers and cranes, those gray and white cars following close behind.

Focus on the driving.

Then the smell of the sea penetrated the car, calling out to him, coaxing memories of that battle to his mind. Ryota, fighting beside him, blasting the air with fire and electricity, melting Cast left and right, while more took their place. The Black Bound elixir, running up Ryota's fingers, his wrists, his shoulders, his neck, his snout--

"Angus, where to next?" Zeke's voice drew Trecheon out of his stupor and he blinked, trying to refocus.

Angus hadn't given any directions in the last several minutes.

Zeke spoke again, more frantic this time. *"Angus? Directions?"*

Trecheon strained his ears.

Nothing.

Leah moaned in the seat next to him. Their pursuers hunted them down with relentless speed.

Trecheon's heart leapt to his throat. "Angus? Don't drop us now. Where to?"

Still nothing.

"Shit." He turned away from the open platforms and toward the forest of shipping containers. "Zeke, Andre, lose yourselves in the containers. We've lost our contact."

Andre growled. *"But--"*

"Just go or you'll get yourself killed!" Trecheon weaved around the containers, his heart thumping. Too fast, too unpredictable. If the cars didn't catch them, they were bound to smash into a container.

The moment he entered the container canyons, the pack of five pursuer vehicles broke up and spread out, vanishing among the metal boxes. Trecheon's body buzzed. Not good. "Leah, as much as you can, keep track of Zeke, okay? Andre, stay close to Zeke so we know where you are. We're on our own."

"Already on it," Leah said.

Trecheon glanced at her. She seemed far more focused, determined. Ready. He didn't know where that came from, but he was grateful for it.

One of the cars appeared on Trecheon's right. Leah shouted, forming a massive glowing shield. "Hit it!"

Trecheon veered right and smashed the rival car. It spun and embedded itself in a shipping container. Out for the count.

Leah groaned. Blood soaked her uniform and hand, staining the white and gray fur red.

They needed out of here *now*. Trecheon zoomed forward.

Zeke whipped past him and vanished into the stacks of containers. One of the sports cars chased him. Trecheon snarled and turned hard left to follow.

A thick built, brown-haired human with sunglasses, leaned out the passenger window. He stared at Trecheon a moment, brow furrowed in anger, then turned and aimed a rifle at Zeke.

Leah leaned forward and let out a short scream. *"Trecheon!"*

"Give me a shield on the left quarter panel!" he shouted. He pulled alongside the enemy vehicle and performed a PIT maneuver, pressing his nose to the side of the car's trunk and forcing it into a spin.

Then he ducked.

The enemy car spun hard right, tires squealing as the driver tried to get it back under control. The gunner sprayed bullets everywhere, smashing into containers and breaking windows in their car, raining glass around them, though thankfully the bullets burned up in Leah's overpowered shield around the two of them.

He could only hope Zeke and Andre got out.

"Holy shit!" Zeke shouted over the earpiece. *"What the hell did you do to him?"*

"Are you two okay?" Trecheon said.

"Yeah, we're--"

"Trecheon, Zeke, Andre, go!" Angus shouted, cutting them off. *"Make two quick lefts and you'll find an open shipping container, get in, NOW. Go!"*

Shit. Trecheon zoomed off after the bikes, scrapping the paint on the corner of one container as he made his first left, then the second.

Leah huddled even closer in on herself, eyes wide, her breaths shallow and forced. Shock taking hold.

Trecheon gritted his teeth. *If Angus is wrong about this, I'll kill him myself!*

But, sure enough, there was an open container in front of them, dark as hell. Zeke and Andre vanished into the container, enveloped in black.

"You better not hit them, Trecheon!" Leah snapped. Trecheon followed, slamming the brakes. The smell of burned rubber filled his nose, but thankfully the car stopped without hitting anything.

Then the doors slid shut. The only light came from his and Leah's glowing Gems, which barely lit up anything.

Someone opened the passenger door.

Trecheon whipped his Lowry out of the holster and aimed it in the dark. "Don't move, asshole!"

"Drop the gun, Trecheon," a smooth female voice said, setting Trecheon's quills and fur on edge. "I'd hate to have to turn your priceless piece into a water pistol."

Trecheon's heart stopped. No. *No.* It couldn't be. Not--

"Pathos!" Leah said.

Trecheon blinked, letting his eyes adjust. Sure enough, one of the pink doe had poked her head into the car, the red from Trecheon's Gem making her pink fur look like blood. Adrenaline shot through his spine and all his training, his fear, his desperate need to obey and his equally desperate need to escape bombarded his mind all at once, threatening to break him.

The doe smiled at Leah. "Long time no see, pussycat. Glad to see you're alive and kicking."

"Leah!" Zeke slid next to Pathos in the dark, with Andre barely visible behind him. The doe pulled herself out of the car and Zeke took her place, kneeling besides Leah. He reached forward like he wanted to hug her, but seemed to think better of it, seeing the blood. "Holy *shit.* You need a healer--"

"Zeke," Leah said, breathing frantically. "That human shooting at us a second ago. I swear to Draso it was Sharp."

Zeke's ears perked and his quills and fur puffed up. "No way. How could he do that *blind?* Hell, how did he even survive?"

"I don't know," Leah said. "But it was him, I swear it was."

Pathos leaned in now, holding an electric lantern. "Worry about him later. Are you okay?"

Leah stared at her a moment and her breath cooled slightly. "Yeah." She rubbed her arm near the injury. "Strangely, when I got hit, it kind of focused me, like I was back in battle and suddenly I could think clearly again." She stared at the floor, her eyes wide. "Oh Draso, that's *terrifying.* Is that--"

"Don't think about it," Trecheon said. He yanked the Gem from the car and reached for Leah's wound. "Sit still. I'm not as good at healing as I am with fire." The Gem glowed again as he worked on her.

She sighed relief, though she still shook so hard that Trecheon could feel it buzz through his metal prosthetics. "...Why did it take being wounded to ground me? What is wrong with me?"

Trecheon chewed his lip, working around her wound. "I did that too, Leah."

She glanced up.

Trecheon breathed deeply. "Instead of feeling safe when I was out of war, I felt unfocused, wild, even a little insane. It was one of the reasons why I got stuck in assassin circles. Holding a gun and living on adrenaline was the only way I could cope."

Leah frowned. "Just... one of the reasons?"

Trecheon glared at Pathos through the car window. Ethos and Logos appeared next to her. Andre stared a moment, then backed away into the darkness, hands up. Ethos crossed her arms, but Logos wouldn't meet Trecheon's eyes. He snorted.

"Yeah. Just one."

"You can hate us all you want later," Ethos said, her cold, no-nonsense voice grating on his ear. "Right now we have to survive."

"Any time now, girls," Angus said over the comm.

Trecheon pinned his ears back. "Is Angus working with *you?"*

"Yes," Ethos said. "A choice he made after his brother killed our other sister, Ari."

"Who the hell *don't* you have working for you?" Trecheon snapped.

"Trecheon, another time!" Angus said. *"I promise you we'll explain everything, but you're teetering on the edge of death here, so enough windblown questions!"*

Ethos turned. "Sisters?" The other doe nodded. Ethos eyed Leah and Trecheon. "Might wanna get out. Grab your bags."

Trecheon didn't have to be told twice. He scrambled out of the car, snatching up the bags. Leah stumbled out into Zeke's arms, and Andre pulled them both close to the wall.

Every atom in Trecheon's body demanded he burn them to hell. Except one. The tiny, quiet memory of Leah painting them in an entirely different light in the war. He fought every instinct and held back.

Logos held out a fist-sized figure of a doe's head, in pink crystal. She tossed it to Ethos. "You be the Bleeder for Pathos, then I'll be your Bleeder."

Trecheon frowned. "Bleeder?"

"Fire and ice," Leah said quietly, pointing to the crystal doe figure. "You have a *Blood Crystal.*"

Ethos nodded. "Trecheon, I'd appreciate a shield if you wouldn't mind."

Trecheon narrowed his eyes.

Ethos lifted her chin. "I'm not *ordering* you, I'm *asking* you. If you couldn't tell, I'm trying to repair what I broke."

"Whatever the hell good that does," Trecheon said, though his heart raced at the defiance.

Ethos' only response was to turn her head, frowning. It was strange, seeing her so meek. He shook himself and waved everyone against the wall to shield them.

Ethos moved close to Leah and gripped her hand. "Catch me if I fall." Leah wrapped an arm across her shoulders and nodded.

Zeke twitched his tail. "Leah, is that wise? Your magic."

"I don't know," Leah said. "So you better prop me up just in case."

"You do your magic shit," Andre said. He braced against the wall and held them both. "I gotchu."

Zeke pressed his lips into a thin line and reached mentally for her.

Trecheon's stomach roiled. The casual, trusting way Leah and Zeke interacted with the doe grated on his psyche.

Pathos laced her fingers together and stretched her arms out. "When I do this, it's going to make a lot of noise. We'll have a very limited window before our enemies find us. I'll do my thing, take the Crystal, then let Ethos do hers and we'll need to get out immediately. Do you understand?"

"I don't even know what the hell you're doing at all," Trecheon snarled.

"It'll become clear once they start," Angus said. *"Ladies, our window is shrinking."*

Ethos leaned closer to Leah. "Do it."

Pathos pressed her hands to the sports car and pushed.

The pink doe crystal glowed brightly, blinding Trecheon for half a second. Then the top of the car violently ripped off and went flying into the opposite wall in a crash of metal and glass and the doe crystal's light faded.

Ethos gasped and collapsed. Leah managed to catch her, grunting. Zeke leaned into them both, stabilizing them, but he struggled.

Against his better judgement, Trecheon braced himself against Zeke, holding the whole group up.

Once the car's roof settled on the bottom of the dirty shipping container, Ethos wearily passed the doe crystal to Pathos and stepped toward the car. Leah helped her walk.

Trecheon stood, torn between helping and recoiling. Zeke covered him though, and moved to Ethos' other side. She pressed her hands to the car, leaning heavily against it. Trecheon ground his teeth. "I still have no idea what's going on. Why the hell are you taking the top off? You're removing one of the few flimsy protections we have."

Ethos ignored him. "Leah, catch Pathos." She flexed her fingers and the pink crystal burst into radiant color again, as did the car.

Pathos instantly passed out. Leah caught her. "Oh my *gosh,* she's--"

"Is she breathing?" Ethos asked.

Leah wrinkled her snout and lay her hand near Pathos' nose. "Yeah, but--"

"Then she'll live." Ethos stepped back and the car's glow faded.

Trecheon gasped.

While there was still no roof, the car was now fully fixed, but instead of two seats, it sported nine, complete with seatbelts. The silver paint had been fully repaired and it shone like it was freshly washed.

Trecheon stared. "The *hell?"*

"Get in, now!" Angus said. *"You've got about a minute, hurry! And don't question anything, Trecheon! Lysander's almost there to open the door."*

Trecheon snarled, more confused than ever. He pushed aside his questions, leapt into the driver's seat, and slammed his Gem into the console. It lit up and beeped at him. Andre and Zeke helped Pathos get in, with Leah following behind. The doe had regained consciousness, but still seemed quite dazed.

Ethos got into the passenger seat, spiking Trecheon's adrenaline even higher. She fastened her seatbelt. "Head for the water."

Trecheon raised an eyebrow, incredulous. "Are you joking? We're on a platform. The water's a hundred feet down!"

"Less talk, more driving," Ethos said. "Trust us and live or ignore me and don't."

The doors opened wide. A strange half-lion, half-zebra centaur creature with violet eyes stood on the outside. Trecheon's fur stood on end. "What--"

"Go!" Angus shouted.

"Trecheon, just listen to Angus, we don't have time!" Leah called.

Trecheon growled and slammed the pedal down. The car flew out of the shipping container in a cloud of tire smoke.

"Left!"

Trecheon hung a sharp left.

The white SUV followed close behind. The centaur aimed a pair of colorful orbs of energy at the vehicle, but the car smashed through the creature, breaking it apart in a thousand light motes. Trecheon gagged.

"Summon," Ethos said. "He'll be fine. Turn right here. Drive to the water's edge."

"What the hell do you expect us to do when we get there?" Trecheon said.

"Leap into the sea."

Trecheon stared.

"Just *trust me,*" Ethos said. "Go!"

This is suicide. He should head back out. Go for the Athánatos portal. Head for the police. *Anything* but leap into the sea.

But Trecheon gritted his teeth and drove through the shipping containers towards the dock's edge. He caught quick flashes and deafening sounds from the remaining cars chasing them. Without a roof, they were far easier targets. He pulled on his power for a shield.

Surprisingly, one popped up, though it left a purple tint behind. Weaker.

He glanced behind him. The same brown-haired man leaned out of one of the windows of the SUV with a rifle again, his eyes hidden behind a pair of dark sunglasses.

Zeke gripped the seat. "Holy *shit,* that *is* Sharp!"

Ethos turned. "Logos, take the blood crystal. Leah, support her. This is gonna be tough on her. Zeke."

Zeke stood straight up.

"Do you trust me?"

Trecheon's belly churned, threatening to expel his breakfast.

"I trust you," Zeke said, which only made Trecheon queasier.

"Then when we go over the edge, I need you to pull the ocean up to meet us," Ethos said.

Andre gasped. "When we do *what?*"

Ethos pressed on. "Tell me you can do that."

There was a long pause. The SUV appeared on Trecheon's left.

"Tell me you can, Zeke."

"I can try," Zeke said.

"No. You can't," Ethos said. "Either you do it and we live, or you don't and we die. *Tell me you can.*"

Elemental marbles floated around the car and Zeke's Ei-Ei jewels glowed, catching in Trecheon's rear-view mirror. "Fine. I can do it."

"Good."

"There's the edge!" Andre shouted.

A gap in the shipping containers led to the entrance to the docks, a flat, dirty platform made of nothing but bare concrete.

And yet it was so familiar to him. Because this was the dock where Ryota died saving Trecheon's life. And here he was gambling away that gift following the Fawn's orders *again*. His chest ached with the loss and mixed with his fear, making his whole body feel ill.

Trecheon flattened his ears and ground his teeth. He slammed the pedal harder, pushing the car to its limit. If he didn't take this at full speed, he'd never convince himself to do it. "Hold on!" His fingers locked around the steering wheel.

Ethos gripped the dashboard, her hands glowing.

And the car sailed off the concrete into the air.

SUMMONS

Trecheon could only stare wide-eyed as they careened over the edge, his brain fighting for survival, trying to grasp on to some semblance of control.

The nose of the car plummeted toward the sea.

"Zeke!" Ethos shouted.

Zeke shouted something unintelligible. The harbor water bulged up to meet them.

But not fast enough.

Ethos gripped the dashboard. "Zeke, more power!"

"I'm doing the best I can!" Zeke cried out. Half a dozen other elements flew about his person, nearly hitting Trecheon.

"Your best needs to be better!" Ethos called.

All Zeke could do was shout. Leah and Andre gripped his arms. The water bulge grew but only slightly.

The light from Ethos' hands made Trecheon's whole world go white.

The vehicle crashed into the ocean bulge, spraying water everywhere, coating his face before engulfing him completely. He struggled for fresh air as the impact shot sharp pains up his legs.

But then the car broke the surface of the water. And kept going.

A roaring engine sound pounded Trecheon's ears and water sloshed on either side of him as the vehicle glided smoothly along the surface. The light faded.

They were no longer in a car, but a long, thin speedboat.

Ethos slammed the dash. "Hit the gas!"

Trecheon slammed it, more pain shooting up his leg, and the boat slicked along the surface, headed for the harbor's exit. He turned back to the platform.

The remaining cars chasing them had managed to stop by the edge and several people climbed out of them. They were already far enough away that Trecheon couldn't make out faces, though he caught at least one dark haired human among them. Probably that Sharp character.

Zeke stared forward, hand out, jaw slack, like he couldn't believe what had just happened. "I'm sorry, I couldn't--"

"Zeke, brace yourself!" Leah said. "Logos is struggling, and I need the power to heal her!" Trecheon glanced at her. The pink doe stared up blankly, her jaw loose, eyes wide. Leah pressed her hands onto her body. Zeke winced, gritting his teeth.

A loud roar echoed over the harbor. Trecheon looked up.

A blue and lavender bird… no a gryfon, stood on the edge of the harbor, its massive, blue lined wings spread impossibly large.

And next to it… a dragon.

A Draso-damned *dragon.*

It spread large black and blue feather wings and roared, shaking the very air around it.

Trecheon flattened his ears, eyes wide. "Oh *shit.*"

Leah shrank back. "A wyvern!"

The human figure lifted a hand. Both creatures leapt up into the air and swooped over the water at breakneck speed.

Trecheon peeled off toward the harbor exit.

Zeke snarled. "We are not doing this. *Archángeli!*"

In a whoosh of wind and a violent bird shriek, Zeke's summon appeared overhead and dove after the rival summons. Trecheon looked back briefly.

Archángeli paused in the air, spun in a circle, and wind whipped up around them, catching sea water and shooting wild waterspouts into the air. The waterspouts danced along the ocean surface and chased the wyvern and gryfon.

Trecheon made it out of the harbor and into the open sea. "How long do you think Archángeli can hold them off?"

"I have no idea," Zeke said. "They--"

The gryfon reared its head, roared loudly, and in a flap of wings, shot lightning through the air, crashing into Archángeli. The electricity coursed through the hawk, and they vanished in a puff of multicolored light motes, sending the leftover lightning into the sea.

Zeke flicked his ears, jaw slack. "How…?"

The wyvern and the gryfon turned their sights on the group. Electricity spread out from the gryfon's wings and water spun around the wyvern in whirlpools.

Trecheon pushed forward. They were *dead.*

Zeke tried shooting magic at it – fire, electricity, even big boulders – but nothing hit. The thing was too agile and Zeke's magic too weak. Trecheon dodged the waterspouts left and right, spraying water everywhere, but the dodging severely slowed them down.

Then Zeke collapsed in his seat. "I can't…" He turned to Leah.

"I don't have any power to give," Leah said. Logos was awake now, but just barely. Her eyes were half-lidded and she panted while leaning against Leah.

The wyvern shot overhead, its long taloned feet reaching forward and scraping against Trecheon's shield, cracking it.

The shield shattered. Trecheon ducked.

But a massive black-winged creature smashed into the wyvern with a loud whinny. Trecheon looked up.

An alicorn had pierced its long, crooked horn straight through the wyvern's chest and dragged it away through the wind.

Leah gasped. "Magna!"

The wyvern roared and bit down hard on the alicorn's neck. The alicorn snorted angrily, seemingly unaffected by the bite, but then the wyvern lifted a taloned foot to the alicorn's head, dug its claws into the alicorn's eyes and raked them down its face. The alicorn screamed something otherworldly and a dozen sharp stones appeared from its wings and pierced through the wyvern's skin and feathers. The pair of them hit the drink and vanished in a spray of colorful motes.

Trecheon stared, slackjawed.

"Don't relax yet," Angus said. Trecheon glanced in the back. Angus sat between the doe and Leah.

Trecheon gawked. "How the hell?"

"I rode on Magna," Angus said. "And you have to admit, she was a bit distracting." He pointed, though his gaze didn't follow his finger. "Don't go to Sol. You'll attract our enemies to the way onto Athánatos and blow all of this for us."

The shrieking *caw-caw-caw* sound of a sea eagle hit Trecheon's ears. The gryfon was still right behind them.

"Fine," Trecheon said. "Omnir island it is." And Ryota's final resting place. Good god, he didn't need this shit. "Why the hell did you stop giving us directions? Maybe we could have avoided all this."

"Someone's messing with time," Angus said as he crawled into the passenger bench between Ethos and Trecheon. "Not that you did a good job listening anyway. But it ruined my scrying map. I lost contact with the timeline."

Trecheon turned to him. "The Black Cloak."

Angus chewed his lip and folded his leather wings into his lap, rigid and tense. "Can't think of anyone else."

"I don't know who the hell this Black Cloak character is, but I don't like him," Andre said.

"Watch out!" Ethos called. The purple gryfon bore down on them.

A white, blue-tipped gryfon who looked strongly like Matt smashed into the purple one and dragged it into the sea with a loud squawk. Trecheon's heart leapt into his throat and he glanced around, but could only see splashes and bubbles.

The white, blue-tipped gryfon leapt out of the water. Droplets gracefully flicked off its feathers.

"Rashard," Ethos said.

Leah stared. "That means--"

"Trecheon!" a voice called. A damned familiar voice. Trecheon turned.

The Black Cloak. Riding alongside them on the back of a red, black-streaked gryfon that looked uncomfortably like himself. The Black Cloak stared at Trecheon with cold blue eyes.

Trecheon glared back.

The Black Cloak pointed. "See that ship? Go around it. Pretend you're headed back to shore. Now, goddamnit!"

Trecheon looked where the Cloak pointed. A massive cargo ship headed there way, leaving big waves in its wake. Trecheon's heart grew cold. "Are you serious? If we get hit by that thing--"

"You won't," The Cloak said. "Just trust me."

"Why the hell should I *ever--*"

"Trecheon, just do it!" Leah shouted.

Trecheon snarled and pressed harder on the pedal, even though they were already going at full speed. That damn Cloak.

A splash echoed in his ears and he turned. The purple gryfon had escaped the ocean and tackled the white and blue gryfon. The pair battled it out, talons flying, sending fistfuls of feathers and fur into the air while lighting and ice clashed through the sky, bathing the sea in diamond dust.

Then they suddenly vanished.

Cloaking.

"How the hell can you do that?" Zeke said. "You're a healer!"

But the Cloak didn't answer… because he had vanished too.

"Damn it!" Trecheon weaved around the ship. "Zeke, can you push back the wake from the ship?"

Zeke flattened his ears. "I don't… I don't know."

"Try," Trecheon said. "The thing's too close!"

Zeke chewed his lip. He held out a hand and "pushed" as Trecheon ran alongside the ship's wake. The water flattened, but only slightly. Fireballs and ice marbles floated around Zeke's head. He batted at them like flies. The boat rocked madly in the wake of the ship.

"Just keep heading for Omnir Island!" The Cloak's disembodied voice barely registered over the roar of the engine and the splash of the waves. "And don't slow down!"

Trecheon snarled. He aimed the boat toward the island's shore, fighting to keep his anger under control. What did he mean don't slow down?

Ethos reached over and laid a hand on Trecheon's Gem.

Trecheon roared at her. *"Don't touch that."*

"I'm going to enhance it," Ethos said, glaring back. "If you're really going to go into that island at full speed, we need a shield, and you won't make it strong enough without my help. "

Trecheon bared his teeth. "If you hurt that Gem--"

"Then I'm sure your friends will happily end my life," Ethos said. "I dare say your Guardian would hunt me down himself."

Trecheon's face flushed. She meant Matt. "He's not my Guardian."

"Tell him that."

He snarled. "Just do what you're going to do."

"Leah, see if you can do individual shields on all of us," Ethos said. "I'm not sure how well a blanket shield will help."

"I'll n-need to borrow some power, Zeke," Leah said, her voice trembling.

Zeke gripped her hand. "Take all you need." Andre pressed his forehead to Zeke's shoulder.

The shore came up far too quickly. Trecheon gripped the wheel and called his strongest shield. The air shimmered with their shields, blinding everyone.

Then they vanished too.

"Everyone hold on!" Trecheon shouted.

The boat hit the shore.

It slid through the trees, crashing through bushes and brambles, crunching everything it touched, knocking Trecheon around. Eventually he let the steering wheel go and huddled in on himself, shutting his eyes, hoping the impact wouldn't be too bad. Branches blasted by them, scraping against the shield, grating on his ears.

One cracked through his shield and pierced his shoulder. He held in a scream – the branch had only caught his biomech – then rebuilt the shield as best he could.

The boat caught on a particularly large object and threw itself forward, smashing into their shield, before finally coming to a stop. Trecheon waited several seconds before he opened his eyes.

Everything was visible again, including a large scar in the landscape from their vicious run through the foliage. A massive divot in the ground, broken trees and bushes, leaves and grass everywhere. No one could possibly miss that.

Though as he stared, the bushes, dirt, and trees started pulling themselves back together. One of the Phonar phoenixes, the earth one Pax, flew gently through the woods, using his magic to heal the scar. It looked completely untouched when he was done. He landed on a branch near them and waved a wing. The branch piercing Trecheon's shoulder pulled out and his arm fell limp at his side.

It was one of the few times he felt grateful for the biomech. Everything ached, but he pushed through it and said the first thing that came to mind. "Soldiers, sound off."

"Praeses Nealia alive and accounted for," Leah said. She winced. "Ow."

"Lieutenant Brightclaw okay," Zeke muttered. "Good god, I'm gonna be sore for days."

"Andre sounding off, and I ain't using my old rank." He groaned. "Holy *fu--*"

"I'm fine," Angus said, shaking his leather wings and brushing dust out of his poof of hair. "Girls?"

"We're okay," all three doe echoed at once. Trecheon shivered.

The boat's hull was nothing but splinters, but the cabin was relatively intact. Trecheon peeled himself out and landed on the soft dirt. He shook his good arm and smoothed out his quills. *Ow.* Gonna have to get Leah or Sacha to fix this soon as. And who knew when he'd be able to fix the biomech. He longed for his spares.

There was a loud whooshing sound and the two gryfons the Cloak had been with earlier landed gently in the circle of trees. The Cloak slid off the back of the red and black one. "Good work. Pax has covered up the scar so no one should--"

Trecheon whipped his pistol out of his holster and aimed it directly between the Black Cloak's eyes.

THE CLOAK

The Cloak immediately threw his hands up in the air. Both gryfons flared their wings and hissed at Trecheon, but he didn't flinch.

Trecheon clicked off the safety, his hand shaking. He wished for the millionth time that he could feel the pistol in his palm again to prevent accidental firings, though somewhere in the back of his mind, he didn't actually care if he fired by accident. "Stay right where you are, asshole."

Leah zipped in front of the Cloak and held out her hands. "Trecheon, *stop.*"

"*Get out of the way, Leah,*" Trecheon said. "I'm sick and tired of this bastard running our lives. I'm done with it, do you hear me?"

The Cloak narrowed his piercing blue gaze. "I don't run your lives. I just guide you."

"*Bullshit,*" Trecheon said. "Taking Zeke away from his parents and dropping him outside of his own time isn't guiding. Jumping in the past and stealing my arm isn't *guiding.* Sending Leah and Zeke ten years in the past to fight a war they should never have been involved in *isn't freakin' guiding!* "

"Their jewel bond sent them into the past, not me," the Cloak said.

"Don't pull that crap with me," Trecheon snarled. "I'm an assassin, dickbag. I know how to make someone disappear. You didn't 'guide' Leah and Zeke. You *kidnapped them.*"

Zeke stepped forward now, but wouldn't get too close. "I think that's a bit extreme."

"It absolutely is *not,*" Trecheon said. "It's got all the signs. Security cameras not working, phones can't capture anything, conveniently drenching Matt in soda to get us out of the picture just before you two disappear. I don't give a flying *shit* about your claim that their jewel bond sent them that far back. Ouranos and Matt are far more powerful and they only lost days. Leah and Zeke lost a *decade.*" He snorted. "No trails, no evidence, no leads. The perfect disappearance. You did this." He flicked his ears back. *"Tell me I'm wrong."*

Both Leah and Zeke glanced at the Cloak.

The Cloak took a deep breath. He waved his hand and the two gryfons vanished. "I only do what I have to."

Zeke gawked. "Are you *serious?*"

"After I defended you!" Leah said. "Why would you do that?"

"You saw how the dominos fell," the Cloak said. "You two found each other and healed broken parts of yourselves. You took down the Desert Wall and ended the war. You found the missing Guardian--"

"The Guardian who's still missing because you pulled us back!" Leah said. "That didn't fix anything!"

The Cloak stepped back. "Your actions saved countless lives, Leah--"

"We also lost lives," Ethos snarled. "Ari is dead. And Jordan and his family, and possibly even Jaden and the others."

"I did what I had to," the Cloak snapped, which made Trecheon jump. "You think I want to do this? Do you think this brings any kind of pleasure? None of you know the real me, but I know all of you. *Intimately.* I know who lives, who dies, who's permanently injured physically and mentally, and *I can't do anything about it.* Do you understand that?"

Trecheon stepped back.

The Cloak shook himself. "You're right. I do have to control some aspects of the past because otherwise all of you will *die*. This whole *planet* will, and more besides. But that means I have to watch people I care about lose life and limb and *I can't stop it."* He gripped his head.

Zeke lowered his gaze. "You said the world destroying summon was an exaggeration."

"I lied," the Cloak said.

"So how do we know you're telling the truth now?" Zeke snarled.

The Cloak shut his eyes. "…You don't. Unfortunately."

Trecheon pressed his lips together, torn. On the one hand, the Cloak had a point. But on the other… "If you knew everyone's suffering ahead of time, you'd do everything you could to stop it."

The Cloak furrowed his brow. "I have done all I can with whatever power I have, Trech," he said. "You have to understand that."

Trecheon ground his teeth. "Don't call me that. That's for friends."

Then Trecheon's pendant beeped.

Still snarling, he holstered the pistol and pulled up his pendant. Matt was on the other line. Trecheon's ears flushed. He turned his gaze at the Cloak, speaking through gritted teeth. "If you really had done all you could, I would still have my natural arms." Before the Cloak could respond, he answered Matt's call, anger and shame warring in his belly like fire and ice. "Hey, Matt."

Matt's ears immediately perked up and his eyes widened. "Holy hell, Trech, what in Draso's name happened to you?"

Uh oh. "Does it look that bad?"

"Your quills are a *mess,*" Matt said, ears flicking back. "And your *arm.* Is that hydraulic fluid? Are you okay?"

"Let's just say we had quite a race right now," Trecheon said, rubbing his quills and trying to flatten them. He shot a quick glare at the doe, then turned back. "But we're fine, we're okay."

Matt eyed him. "You're sure? I don't want to hear you put your life on the line trying to find my dad."

"We haven't even started looking yet honestly," Trecheon said. "Haven't broken his encryption yet. This was… something else. But I promise you, we're okay." He brushed a hand casually through his quills, trying to change the subject. "You heading over here now?"

"We're leaving in an hour," Matt said. "I'm taking the whole gang with me. Charlotte too. She's determined to see Dad."

Trecheon flicked his ears back. Matt's sister. "She's not gonna press a sword to my throat like you did is she?"

Matt smirked. "I doubt it, but if she does, she'll be thrusting it while striking a pose. She's a champion fencer."

"Thanks for the uncomfortable image of a sword through my gullet."

Matt grinned now. "Hey, you're the one who keeps bringing up *swords.*"

Trecheon chuckled, but his throat burned. Was he flirting or what? Good Draso.

"That's not all though," Matt said, seriousness returning to his face. "Some of Dad's old friends are coming along. Larissa, our Domini Defender, her wife Viri, and the Master Guardian, Lance."

Yikes. "No pressure or anything."

"They want to put in every effort they can to find Jaden," Matt said. "Assuming he's…" He pressed his lips together. "So you haven't broken the encryption?"

"Not that I've heard. We're waiting to see what Ouranos and Sacha have been able to find out from his pendant," Trecheon said. "We're, ah…" He glanced at the doe. Shit, should he go to Athánatos at this point? Reveal it to the Fawns? Shit, shit, *shit,* this got a hell of a lot more complicated.

Logos poked her head around Trecheon's shoulder, shooting chills through his body. She smiled, almost slyly. "You really are the spitting image of Jaden, minus the blue in your quills."

Pathos edged in now. "And like a negative of Zeke. You were right, Trecheon." Zeke shifted uncomfortably.

Ethos leaned over and grinned. "I hope Jaden can play piano half as well as you do."

Matt's eyes widened. Shock rushed Trecheon's body, flushing his face.

Ethos chuckled. "Yes, we're aware you're our casino's famous piano player."

Trecheon gritted his teeth.

Matt narrowed his gaze. "So you're the Fawns."

"We're allies," Logos said. "We worked with Jaden in the war. He's a dear friend. We've got a lot of resources to work with. If Jaden's alive, we'll find him. Don't you worry."

Matt lifted his chin. "You're mafia."

"Not by choice," Ethos said. "But I promise you will use our ill-gotten gains to find your father. We owe him."

Matt kept his face neutral, but he nodded. "Thank you. I mean that."

Trecheon bared a fang and glanced off, his blood boiling.

Leah pressed herself into the picture, looking sheepish. "Hi, Guardian Azure."

Matt's shoulders relaxed and he breathed a sigh of relief. "Leah, thank Draso… we were so worried. Trecheon let me know what happened. You doing okay?"

"I could be better," Leah said. "But… at least I'm here."

"I'm so glad. I've let your uncle Garnet know you're okay." Matt smiled, but the smile didn't extend to his eyes, and he flattened his ears. "And… you met my dad."

Leah smiled now. "Yeah."

Matt shifted. "I… um…" He checked himself and perked his ears again, though stiffly. "What… what's he like?"

That hit Trecheon like a kick to the gut.

Leah flicked an ear. She pulled her tail up and picked at the hairs. "He's… fierce. A warrior. A bit standoffish, but I think that's expected when he's faced as much loss as he has."

"He's learning," Zeke said, pushing his way next to Leah. "And I respect him for it. I don't know what you remember of him when you were a kid, but he's trying to be better. I hope he'll be better still once we find him again." He took a deep breath. "He's a good man. I mean that. I'm… I'm proud to call him my father. Even if the relationship is strange at this point."

Matt perked his ears. "Oh. You're Zeke."

Zeke's ear twitched and he nodded.

Matt rubbed his arm. "Thank you. That means a lot coming from… family." He looked off. "Draso's mercy, that's strange to say."

"Strange for me too," Zeke said. "My family… they…" He shook himself. "Never mind. We'll talk when we see each other in person."

"Yeah," Matt said. "I'll see you soon then." He turned to Trecheon. Trecheon's ears flushed again. "Trech, I'm counting on you to take care of them. But also take care of yourself, okay? You're too important to me. Same goes for Ouranos." He rubbed his head. "I mean, same goes for everyone, really but…"

"I get it," Trecheon said. He smiled. "They're in good hands. See you soon."

"I'll try contacting you again in a week or two," Matt said. "Hopefully you'll have some news huh?"

"Yeah."

"Take care." The hologram cut out. Trecheon stared at the dead pendant, emotions swirling through his mind.

He had to get to Jaden. He just had to.

Ethos lifted her eyebrows and smiled. "Well. You really do have quite the crush on him."

Trecheon dropped his pendant and clenched his fist, setting the air ablaze.

Everyone leapt back.

He turned to Ethos. "The hell is your problem? You have no right. *No goddamned right* to make comments about my life and my relationships." He waved a hand. "What the hell was that anyway? Why are you *here?* You told me you were dropping your hold on Neil and me, and yet here you are, running my life *again.* You claim you're *allies,* but what the hell allies are you? Here you are running for your lives like the damn FBI raided you!" He gritted his teeth. "But it wasn't the FBI was it? It was freakin' *Angel.* Chasing you away from the resources you just told Matt you have. You aren't allies at all, you're *burdens* coming to us like we flippin' owe you something. Well, we *don't.* We almost *died* for your worthless tails!"

"Trecheon." Leah's sharp voice shook Trecheon's core and he faced her.

She had her staff out, clenching it tightly, brow furrowed, fangs bared. His fire didn't even phase her. "We saved four lives today. Eight, if you count our own. This was not *worthless*. Life is never worthless."

Trecheon stared at her, his heart pounding in his ears.

"We haven't lost access to all our resources," Ethos said. "We have lost some, admittedly, but we're still valuable to this. We made sure of it. For Jaden."

"For yourselves," Trecheon said bitterly.

"Trecheon, *stop it.*" Leah took a step forward, fur bristled up. "I know they hurt you and you have every right to be angry, but for the love of Draso, this is *not* the time to go after them." She waved vaguely to the dense forest. "Jaden and Alexina and Embrik are out there, waiting for us. We've lost enough life to the War of Eons and Ackerson's hand. But we saved four more. Focus on that, not on the past."

Somewhere in his head, he knew she was right. Life was precious. He knew that intimately as an assassin. It was why he wanted to turn himself in every time he made a kill, even when the scum deserved it.

But righteous anger burned in his chest anyway, fanning the flames surrounding him. "Fine. I concede." He turned to Ethos. "But know this. You made my life a living hell for *years*, controlling literally everything. I was ready to *end it all* because I felt so incredibly worthless, so broken, so trapped that I didn't see a way out. Then Matt showed up and gave me a reason to keep going. Matt, Sacha, Izzy, Ouranos, Darvin, Roscoe, Sami, *everyone*. I have a family." He pointed a blazing finger at her. "Don't you get near it." He turned to the Cloak. "You either." He flagged down Pax. "We're going to Athánatos now, and I swear to Draso, any one of you steps a hoof out of line, you're bar-b-que. I finally have a home to fight for, and I'm not taking any chances."

Ethos flicked her ears back. "Fine. Understood."

Zeke leaned forward. "You said you saved resources for Jaden. Does that mean you planned this?"

"In a manner of speaking," Ethos said.

"Good *Draso,* could this get any worse?" Trecheon said.

"I know you have no reason to," Ethos said. "But trust us."

"I'll trust you when you prove yourself trustworthy," Trecheon snarled. "Until then, you're the enemy. So tread lightly." He marched off toward the Athánatos portal.

Angus rubbed his arms and shook his leather wings. "Well then. This is going to be quite a roller coaster.

Assassin

Neil leaned against a wall in one of the inner sanctums buried in the Athánatos Palace, his tail swishing side to side anxiously. His body itched with anticipation, waiting for info about the pendant's encryption. A fierce weariness dug into his bones, but he pushed it aside. He had been here all night, trying to hold the group steady, keep up morale, but they were all so exhausted that nothing he did worked well.

The sooner they got Jaden, the sooner he could try and find that happy stability again.

And the sooner Dami and Natassa could rely on him again. God, he felt so powerless.

Ouranos had Jaden's pendant plugged into a reader with his A.I. crystal power unit connected to it. By this point, everyone had gathered in the royal family's personal chambers - Chadwick, Sacha, Ouranos, as well as Melaina, though Natassa was working on some important administration thing with Damianos.

Sacha leaned over the pendant working on the hologram interface, her expression contorted with intense concentration. Everyone else sat on little wicker chairs and chaise lounges, sipping water or sneaking evening snacks from the tiny buffet along the back wall.

It almost hurt to watch them. Because of his connection to Natassa and Dami, Neil had had the privilege of weekend evenings with the royal family. It was a symbol of comfort, of hard-won peace, and of the likely future where he'd be married to Natassa, helping to lead Athánatos. But now, with everyone here, with the anxiety in the air, it no longer meant peace. It no longer meant a bright future. It meant apprehension, fear, uncertainty. Neil's happy little ritual turned on its ass.

He shook his head. He shouldn't think that way.

Pilot's miniscule figure appeared in the holobulbs, flickering in and out of sight, his blue-green fairy wings flapping calmy. Sacha had said that the colonization-era A.I. had been carefully repaired and restored during Ouranos' time on Zyearth, but he still struggled to keep up with the power demands of modern Zyearth technology.

Ouranos folded his arms, his brow furrowed, frowning. "Any luck, my friend?"

"A little," Pilot said, snorting rainbow fire out of his nostrils. It dissipated in the shape of tiny stars. Pilot lashed his tail. "I think. His encryption codes are old. It's probably a good thing you had -*bzzt*- me on board for this or you might be out of luck. A modern A.I. may not have these codes." He lifted his head in a tiny display of pride.

Sacha smirked. "Caesum could probably do it, considering he was a Golden Guardian A.I. for Jaden."

Pilot rolled his eyes. "That -*bzzt*- dragon would just fanboy out over Jaden and never get anything done. He'd probably overheat trying to force the decryption."

Ouranos smiled patiently. "Still bitter over your encounter with him?"

Pilot huffed, throwing his head back. "Absolutely not. That ridiculous sycophant can *-bzzt-* suck my tail."

Sacha chuckled.

Neil picked up a delicate cheese pastry from the table and nibbled it, trying to distract from the anxiety.

Natassa walked in. Neil's shoulders relaxed and he jogged over to her. She hugged him and melted into his arms. He held her close, drawing in the warmth, trying to reassure her. She sighed and her body relaxed. "Any word about the pendant?"

"Not yet," Neil said. "Where's Dami?"

"He is pacing outside." She flattened her ears and leaned against Neil. "He is nervous."

He rubbed her arm. "Understandable. Let me go talk to him, okay?"

"Of course, my Heart." She kissed the top of his head. He smiled, grabbed another pastry, and walked out, looking for Dami.

The yellow, black streaked Athánatos wandered back and forth, wearing a path in the dirt under the crystal trees just outside the Palace. The setting sun painted everything in a blood red, which stung Neil's heart.

Neil flicked his ears back, then walked up to him. "Hey. Pastry?"

Damianos waved a hand. "No, thank you."

"Dami," Neil said. "You gotta eat. For me at least. Okay? You haven't eaten all day. Don't think I haven't noticed." He passed him the pastry.

Damianos glanced at the cheese pastry and took it, but didn't eat it.

Neil frowned. He wrapped his arms around Damianos, stopping the pacing. "It'll be okay. Alright? I promise. Everything will work out. I've got you."

Damianos held him tight, but didn't respond. He laid his head on Neil's, shuddering.

Neil buried his face in Dami's neck, running hands down his bare back and letting his breath warm Dami's fur. "Remember our first kiss?"

Dami paused and chuckled. "An interesting time to bring this up."

"Better that no time at all." Neil pulled back and held Dami's head in his hands, meeting his gaze. "I fought hard for that memory."

"Harder than you needed to," Dami said, smiling. "All you had to do was confess your feelings to me. Instead you put on a show."

"I *courted* you," Neil said, smirking. "Like an Athánatos should."

Dami laughed now. He looked deep into Neil's gaze. "From the moment we had peace, you have done everything you can to fit in here. To keep Natassa and myself comfortable instead of insisting we conform to your ways." He pressed his forehead to Neil's and closed his eyes. "It is a trait I admire in you. My emerald prince."

"Someday I'm gonna figure out what that means," Neil said.

"I am sure you will," Dami said. "With your own research because you insist." He pressed a long, loving kiss to Neil's forehead. "I hope it will bring you great joy when you learn. It is a title well earned." He pulled Neil close, sliding his hands into Neil's jacket and under his shirt, stroking the fur.

Neil buried his face in Dami's chest, little shivers running up his spine. "My point, Dami, is that I fought hard for that kiss. I fought hard for this relationship, this peace. I'm going to continue fighting for it. Trust me, okay?" He reached up and kissed him, wrapping arms around his neck. He pulled back and stared into Dami's violet eyes. "We'll get Jaden. Escape Ackerson. And we'll have our peace back again."

"Neil…?"

Natassa. Neil frowned, but pulled away from Dami.

She stood in the entrance way to the palace, her eyes wide and her ears flat against her quills.

Neil's adrenaline immediately shot up. "What? What happened?"

"Trecheon and the others have returned," Natassa said. "And they have some… unpleasant company with them."

Neil's heart dropped. He ran up the steps with Dami and Natassa at his heels.

He saw the flashes of pink before anything else. He stopped in his tracks, his heart seizing, as a thousand bad memories ran through his mind, all congregating on one word.

Assassin.

Neil's fur stood on end and he held his arms out in front of Damianos and Natassa. Not them. Not *here. Not his home, damnit!*

The three doe, Ethos, Pathos, and Logos, stood at the entrance to the room with a green and black bat at their side. Leah, Zeke, Andre, and Trecheon walked in behind them… with the Black Cloak. Trecheon looked about ready to kill someone.

Ethos pressed her finger to her snout and smiled slyly. "I hear we've got information on a missing Guardian. Let's get him."

TIME BOMB

Trecheon's body buzzed as he followed the deer into the palace. The three pink doe who had ruined his life walked in like they owned the place, like they *always* freakin' did. Angus followed behind, his wings slightly unfurled, tilting his head this way and that while his ears twitched. Leah, Andre, and Zeke followed Trecheon and the Black Cloak slunk in behind them.

The Cloak steadied himself against a wall, glancing around warily. His presence didn't seem to bother any of the Athánatos, but Andre refused to look away, eyes wide. Chadwick narrowed his gaze, but gave him a friendly nod, which the Black Cloak returned.

Neil bared his teeth at the doe and unsheathed claws, ready to pounce. *"What the hell are you doing here?"* He turned to Trecheon. "What the hell were you *thinking?"*

"You wanna tell them *no?"* Trecheon snapped.

Ethos was unfazed. She crossed her arms and raised an eyebrow. "I thought you wanted to get Jaden. Time's wasting. So where are we going?"

"No one's going *anywhere,"* Trecheon said. He pointed at the Fawns with his good arm. Little tongues of fire clung to his quills, mimicking the flames of anger in his gut. "The hell happened just now? What was that crystal you used? How in Draso's name do you have a *Zyearth sports car?* What is going *on?"*

Sacha moved to Trecheon's side, which cooled him, but only slightly. She itched her left arm. "Draso's mercy, Trecheon, your arm!"

"Later."

Ethos stood straight and still, expressionless. "The stone is a Blood Crystal. We use it to steal energy from each other and enhance our Wishing Dust."

"That's what you were doing," Leah said. "I've never heard of a Blood Crystal being used that way. Normally it's used for big destructive spells."

Ethos shrugged. "That was the original intent, but the Wishing Dust canceled it for some reason, so we had to find another use. A bit unconventional but--"

"That is *not* the most important part of this story and you know it," Trecheon snapped. "Why are you here? And why is Angel going after you? You're a powerful mob with the resources to fight back. What the hell is going on?"

The three doe exchanged looks. Ethos sighed and sat on one of the chaise lounges, her sisters following her. They almost blended into one being sitting like that. Ethos licked her lips and tapped her fingerhooves. "Alright then." She turned to Trecheon. "You won't believe me, but we are as much victims of Ackerson's control as you are. Today was us finally breaking free of that control, at great cost."

"So you were *lying* when you said you still had your resources," Trecheon said.

Ethos lifted her chin. "We have enough resources to help."

"We were hoping to wait until you found Jaden before pulling the trigger," Pathos said. "But Ackerson moved first. We didn't have time or we'd lose our window."

Logos nodded. "Or worse, Ackerson would use us and our resources to kill Jaden and use you, as he has so many times before."

"What other times?" Neil asked.

"That's the long version," Ethos said. "Which we don't have time for. But let's just say Ackerson is a... shrewd negotiator."

"That doesn't answer the question of *why the hell you're even here,*" Neil snarled. "You said you released us. You were *out of our lives.* You claim to be Ackerson's victims, but you haven't even explained *how.* So what the hell is going on!"

Ethos exchanged a glance with her sisters. She turned to Leah and Zeke. "Ronan survived the battle of the Desert Wall."

Zeke's eyes widened and Leah drew her hands to her snout. Angus snorted and crossed his arms, his ears twitching.

"He's been under Ackerson's employ since the war ended," Ethos continued. "But hiding in the shadows. From what we know through our contacts, Ronan managed to heal himself, but at a massive cost."

Trecheon raised a brow. "He healed *himself?*"

"Ronan and I have Continuum Stones," Angus said, bitterness dripping through every word. "He can heal himself by reversing time on his body. But big wounds cause time glitches. His body will jolt and glitch while it tries to resync with current time." He frowned, looking off. "Healing wounds like that would mean *years* of time glitching. Every second alive would be agony. He'd struggle to sleep, struggle to eat, struggle to *function*. Most don't survive it." He shook himself. "Unfortunately, he has. So far at least."

"And apparently he's well enough to work again," Ethos said. "Because two days ago, Ackerson sent him out on some kind of mission. We think he's going after Jaden, Alexina, and Embrik."

Neil cursed. Trecheon threw a punch in the air and turned away, gripping his head.

Ouranos stepped forward. "Where?"

"We don't know," Pathos said. "But I don't think that's Ackerson trying to hide it. I think he sincerely doesn't know. But somehow he thinks Ronan and Judgement will be able to find him."

Natassa flicked her tail. "Which means we are running out of time."

Neil snarled. "But what do *you* want with Jaden?"

"Jaden is a friend," Logos said. "But more than that, this is an opportunity to get out from under Ackerson's foot and finally remove Angel."

"If you're willing to help us," Ethos added.

"Our time is limited," Pathos said. "For us three, and for anyone else under his employ." She pointed to Neil and Trecheon. "That includes you two. We all have an expiration date and we edged very close to it. We just struck first."

Everyone grew quiet. Trecheon's insides twisted in knots when he failed to put his feelings into words, making him feel queasy. "Well," he said quietly. "Seems like we really don't have a choice."

Neil let out a low, feral growl, his fur on end. He bared his teeth at the Fawns, though he didn't move.

Ethos lifted her head. "I know it means next to nothing," she said. "But I am sorry that this had to happen this way. We didn't want any of it." She turned to Neil, her ears pinned back and a rare look of empathy on her face. "None of it."

Neil only looked away, his eyes glassy, growling under his breath.

Trecheon huffed. "I'd welcome you to the team, but you're really not welcome at all." Leah cleared her through. He ignored her. "Regardless, we can't do anything until we get Jaden's location." He sighed. "While we wait, I need to get back to the garage. Gotta get my spare arm or I'm useless."

Ethos shifted. "I'm sorry but… you can't go home."

Trecheon's bones buzzed. "What?"

Ethos exchanged glances with the other doe. "You and Neil are part of the cost of breaking ties," she said. "Ackerson used us to keep you under his thumb. Once we pulled the trigger to get out, we… forfeited that. You have no home to go to now. Ackerson knows where you live." She rubbed her arm. "Go home and you're dead."

Trecheon's jaw dropped and his ears rang.

"It may not mean much," Ethos said, her voice piercing Trecheon's eardrums. "But while you were away from your homes, our agents retrieved the most sensitive items. Phones, computers, IDs, etc. I don't know if Ackerson's agents will actually strip your places. Frankly I think he'd see it as a waste of resources, though Angel might not feel the same. But if he does, we've saved at least some of it. We'll get it when it's safe."

Trecheon stared at the ground, ice and fire swirling in his belly while he tried processing their words. His vision blurred.

His home… gone. His motorbike collection. Everything connected to his Granddad. His tiny war memorial. Carter's dog tags. The piano Matt bought a few years ago for Christmas so he could play for Trecheon. The scarf Sacha knitted for him for his birthday. His clothes, spare arms, custom helmets, game systems… His safety.

All gone.

He sat on one of the wicker chairs.

Neil let out a long breath. "…Poor comfort," he muttered. Natassa wrapped her arms around him.

Chadwick stood. "We need to take charge of this problem, *now.*" He turned to the doe. "If what you say is true, we're all targets after that attack, more so than ever before. As much as Ackerson might want Jaden and his team, he's missing. That makes him small potatoes compared to the rest of us still living out in the open. He won't wait for us to find Jaden first."

Ouranos twitched his tail and lowered his gaze. "He has some knowledge of Athánatos. I have no doubt he will attempt to find us here."

"Likely," Chadwick said.

"Then we need to prepare," Ouranos said. He waved his hand and Pax and Jústi appeared. Natassa and Melaina exchanged glances and summoned their phoenixes too. Excelsis and Deo, the black raven and white egret fire phoenixes, and Lumen and Sémini, the stone kori bustard and water falcon phoenixes. Their elements flew about the room, making the whole area sparkle. Competing scents stung Trecheon's nose.

Andre stared, wide eyed.

Zeke flicked his ears back. He breathed deeply then held out his hand.

Archángeli appeared, slowly, from thin air. They wobbled a bit, likely still out of it from the battle on the water, then landed on the couch behind Zeke, fluffing their eagle feathers and gently squawking.

Ouranos perked his ears. But he smiled. "Archángeli… it is nice to see you again, my friend."

Archángeli perked up, then gently mantled their wings, sending a gentle breeze through the room. *The pleasure is mine, Prínkipas.*

Zeke furrowed his brow and looked away.

Ouranos waved the summons to him. "Muster the Archons," he said. "Athánatos is in danger." The Phonar nodded as one and took off through the open ceiling, vanishing into the sky.

Natassa watched them fly off. "I will say it again. You should have been Basileus in my place, brother."

"If I have my way, I will never carry that title," Ouranos said. "Our family failed in this responsibility. It is time we have someone with better perspective." He glanced over at Neil.

Neil perked both ears and his eyes grew wide. He stood tall and lifted his chin. "If that's what Athánatos needs." Natassa slipped her hand in his.

Ouranos smiled softly. "We shall discuss it when things are not so dire. But I believe it is."

Chadwick cleared his throat. "If I may redirect us. While it's great to have Athánatos as a safehouse, it's not a solution. We can't stay here permanently, especially if we go after Jaden."

Neil crossed his arms. "We need to know who we're up against." He turned to the Fawns. "Supposedly you know what that is. I loathe to ask, but what can you tell us?"

Ethos lowered her gaze and frowned. "Not much, unfortunately. Just like in the war, the members of Angel are a deep secret. But we've confirmed a few, and suspect others. Angus?" Angus walked to Ethos and held out a black messenger bag. She took it. "This has all the information we currently know. It'd be best if we had a blank wall somewhere to lay it all out."

"I will have one readied tonight," Melaina said. "We can begin tomorrow. In the meantime, the palace staff will find beds for everyone. I dare say none of us are leaving the island today."

Andre folded his arms. "Glad I watered the plants then…" Chadwick smiled, in spite of everything.

Sacha wrapped an arm around Trecheon. "Come on, hun. Let's see if we can get your arm repaired. Pilot can run double duty and Leah and I are trained in biomech repair." Leah stood.

"Tomorrow," Trecheon said, not taking his eyes off the doe. He closed his eyes and mentally reached for his emergency passphrase. *Emergency release: IAmTheWhiteAssassin.* The broken arm collapsed to the floor and he picked it up, gripping it like a club and glaring. "I'll sleep on this tonight so you can set me up wherever the Fawns are setting up their suspects wall."

Ethos flicked her ears back.

Sacha frowned. "Trecheon--"

"Don't," Trecheon said. He glared at Ethos. "I go where you go. No questions. This is my *family.* My *home.* And I don't trust you to be alone. You eat and sleep and piss where I can see you. You're here because you and Ackerson gave us no choice, but you aren't *welcome.*" He narrowed his eyes. "Do I make myself clear?"

Ethos narrowed her gaze, but she nodded. "Crystal."

REPAIRING

Trecheon sat on a hard wooden chair with his broken arm laying on a battered table next to him, trying to fight back the aches and pains in his shoulder and phantom arm.

He had spent the whole night half-awake, watching the doe from his makeshift bed, daring them to make a move.

And he wasn't alone. Even though Neil usually slept with Dami or Natassa in a comfortable room, he had opted to sleep in the big community room Melaina had set up with beds, also keeping one eye open and on the Fawns.

Everyone else slept soundly, which annoyed the hell out of Trecheon. More so when Leah and Zeke chose to sleep next to them and slept far more soundly than they had in Trecheon's apartment.

He shook himself. He shouldn't be angry about that. It was a product of their time in the war, nothing more.

But still.

Melaina had led them into this dark, sunken room early the next morning so the Fawns could set up operations. "It will give us privacy from the rest of Athánatos," she had said. She left after that saying she couldn't stand staring at the murderers. She had had enough of that in her life.

No one could tell if she meant the pictures of Angel or the Fawns themselves. Not that the distinction mattered much.

It was well past lunch at this point, and Trecheon's stomach shouted at him. But he brushed it aside. Fixing his arm was more important and they were almost done.

Still no word on decrypting Jaden's pendant.

Ethos, Logos, and Pathos stood in front of the wall now, carefully pinning up pictures, clippings, and string, connecting all the members of Angel as they knew it. Ouranos leaned against the adjacent wall, arms crossed, staring at the floor, and Zeke sat at a table with Chadwick, helping to sort pictures. Andre stood next to the doe, studying the pictures. Though he also kept one eye on the Fawns. That didn't escape Trecheon's notice.

At least he had one ally.

Leah had a tool kit out, and Sacha's portable fabricator was hard at work printing several parts from Trecheon's biomech. Pilot used a floating tool to repair parts of the arm. An easy enough task while also working on the decryption upstairs, but it also showed his age. The drone frequently paused in its work, dropped out of the air, and generally took a long time on simple tasks. Trecheon didn't know if it was his computing power or the distance between the drone and his core, but something kept him from working 100%.

Thankfully Leah worked on his shoulder without Pilot's help, despite the pain. He winced every time she came near with a screwdriver. "I hate this."

Leah paused. "S-sorry, am I hitting a nerve?" She shook herself. "Sorry, I mean a literal nerve, not like..."

"I got it, it's fine," Trecheon said. He winced again. "The phantom pain is just really bad after a hit like that."

Leah frowned. "W-want me to try healing it?"

Trecheon lifted his head. "Think that'd work?"

"I don't know, honestly," Leah said. "But I could try."

"Sure, give it a shot."

She pressed her hand to his busted shoulder and cooling healing energy flowed through his skin. He sighed. "Thanks. That's much better."

Leah smiled, then went back to repairing his shoulder mount.

It was short lived though. Every twist of the screwdriver shot pain through the phantom limb, bringing tears to his eyes. Leah paused every now and then to heal again, but it did very little.

"Explain more about these Angels," Ouranos said.

Trecheon narrowed his gaze at him. He'd known Ouranos for a good three years now and considered him as close a friend as Neil. Usually he was cheery, helpful, and kind, which helped keep the mood light despite their desperate search for Leah at the time.

But now… now he was angry. Dangerous even. And Trecheon had to remind himself that he had once been Matt's enemy, with the power to match. Good thing *he* wasn't Ouranos' target.

Ethos finished a pin and turned to Ouranos. "Which one? They all have fairly elaborate stories."

"What about this group here?" Ouranos said, pointing to a bunch of photos lined in a circle.

Trecheon hadn't been paying too much attention to the Fawn's wall until that point, but the moment he saw the pictures, his blood ran cold.

Ethos crossed her arms. "They call themselves the Patriots. Subset of Angel who've made themselves believe they were sent to save their respective countries. Some of the few Angels we know a lot about, mainly because they're incredibly tight knit, fiercely dangerous, and strangely loyal to Ackerson. Also loud. They don't believe in hiding in the shadows. They nearly assassinated--"

"--President Floretta," Trecheon said, his voice quiet.

Ethos flicked her tail and raised an eyebrow. "You know?"

Trecheon stared at the floor. Part of him wanted to keep it to himself. That war was private. However... "My brother Ryota helped them." He leaned on his good arm. "We've met before, in the war. Found them while we were trying to get into Canada."

Zeke's tail lashed at the mention of Canada.

Trecheon breathed deeply. "Later Outlander was called to hunt them down when they attempted to assassinate President Floretta since Ryota worked with them."

Chadwick glanced through a bunch of photos. He pulled one out - Ryota's old military photo. "Ryota Omnir." He turned to Trecheon. "He's your brother."

Trecheon flicked his ears back. "Yes."

"Do you know where he is now?"

Trecheon stared at the floor. "...Dead. He gave his life to save mine while we fought Theron off."

Chadwick frowned. "I'm sorry to hear. For what it's worth, he died a hero."

Trecheon shrugged, fighting the ache in his heart. "At least you don't have to pin him up on the wall."

"This is true," Chadwick said. He tucked Ryota's picture in a folder.

Logos walked up to the table. "Well, that eliminates one of the traitors from Outlander. Now we just have Rebekka."

Pain shot through Trecheon's heart like someone had pierced him with an ice spear. He narrowed his gaze. "She's dead."

"She's MIA," Logos said, lifting her picture off the table. "We've never been able to confirm that she was dead, but she was incredibly close to Ackerson in the war. So until we know more," she plastered the silver fox on the wall near the other defectors. "She goes up."

Trecheon's chest ached. Just what he needed – Rebekka's gaze bearing down on him. Her memory came with a slew of other anguish that Trecheon didn't have the energy to explore. "Until we confirm she's alive," he said. "Can we pretend she's dead?"

Chadwick turned to him. "Why?"

"Please don't ask me to explain why," Trecheon said.

Logos flicked her ear. "Ah. Yeah. Sorry about that." She moved her picture to a dark spot on the wall, then stepped back. "There. That's all we know, laid out as neatly as we can."

Neat was the wrong word to describe it. The wall was plastered haphazardly with images, string, writing, maps, you name it. Each member of Ackerson's old teams lined the wall, grouped with their old names - Outlander, Hunt, Guardian, Chaos, and Mage - each picture complete with a profile stating whether they were dead or alive, what magic they had, whether they had been seen with Ackerson since the war, and every detail the Fawns knew about them.

It looked like a Draso-damned hitlist.

"Quite a list," Ouranos said. He flicked his tail. "I will go and see if the Phonar have returned with the Archons. We should all familiarize ourselves with these people if we expect to face them while searching for Jaden." He bowed to the group and left.

Andre stood and looked over the wall. "Looks like a madman's ramblin'. If I hadn't seen magic firsthand, I'd call you all nuts. No offense, hun."

"None taken, only because it's from you," Chadwick said. He headbutted Andre's shoulder and Andre gently scratched Chad's head.

One of Pilot's drones floated down the stairs and projected a hologram of the fae dragon. "Andre? I could use assistance with the decryption and you're the only one with a laptop. Leave it to a Golden Guardian to mix Zyearth tech with this primitive Earth stuff."

Andre chuckled. "Sure, be right up."

"I'll come with you," Chadwick said.

Ethos stepped forward. "Here. Take my laptop. Got some intergalactic codes on it. Might be useful."

Andre nodded. He gave Zeke a hug and they followed the drone upstairs.

A big list on the side named all the currently known Angels. Zeke stood and looked it over. "Hey. Got a pen?"

Ethos frowned. "Did we miss one?"

"Caster."

Ethos crossed her arms. "Jaden ran a sword through his gut."

"I know," Zeke said. "And yet we saw him chasing us with exploding drones while fetching the Fawns. Don't ask me how, but he survived."

Pathos flattened her ears and passed Zeke a pen. "That's not good. I thought we had a good understanding of everyone Ackerson used openly. If Caster is alive and openly fighting..." She trailed off.

Trecheon flicked an ear. "Can you pause a moment, Leah?" Leah put her tools down. Trecheon stood and glanced over the list of Angels. Far more than he expected if he was honest. All laid out like a damn to-do list.

Like back to being an assassin. He hated this.

He frowned. Rebekka's name still stood there, in bright red. He took the pen from Zeke and crossed it out.

Ethos frowned.

Trecheon put the pen down. "She's dead, Ethos, until we see otherwise. If you really expect me to help with this, you'll let me keep that can of worms tightly shut."

Ethos sighed, but didn't protest.

Trecheon tilted his head. "Tell me more about this Caster guy." The red wolf grinned wildly in his picture. "Is he a mage?"

"I don't think so," Zeke said. "But he's got those custom Paper Wasp Nanos with really powerful explosives in them. I don't know how they work, but they're formidable."

"Yeah, I saw them when they were chasing us," Trecheon said, pinching the bridge of his snout. "We're lucky we survived." He sighed. "And you say Jaden stuck a sword through his stomach."

"That's right," Leah said. "I don't know how he survived." She stared at the slim piece of paper with names scribbled all over it, narrowing her gaze. "Hey, Pilot?"

Pilot flittered close to her in a trail of colorful motes. "What can I do for you?"

"Are you connected to Galactic InterPol's databases here?" Leah asked. "Sharp's got a pair of summons and I want to see their history."

Pilot faded in favor of floating 1's and 0's for a moment, then nodded. "Certainly. What can you tell me about the summons?"

"Odd pair," Leah said. "A lavender gryfon with electric magic and a black and blue wyvern with water magic. That should be specific enough. Odd pairs are rare. Summons tend to bond with members of their own species."

"Sorry, nothing's -*bzzt*- coming up."

Leah froze. She turned. "What?"

"I said -*bzzt*- nothing came up," Pilot said. His wings shuddered. "No such pair exists."

Leah blinked. "Blanket search gryfon and wyvern pairs then."

"Already did," Pilot said. "Nothing. I have a dragon with a hippogryff, but the dragon is gray and green and the hippogryff is bright red. But that's the closest I've got for you."

Leah's fur stood on end. "Try searching another odd pair. A lion/zebra centaur with a black alicorn."

A second later Pilot popped up with Angus' summons. "Here you go. Lysander and Magna, joined Angus Lightwind in UX 5807, registered that same year." He flashed their record, which showed their magic specialties, their living origins, and their last eleven summon masters.

Leah stared.

Trecheon narrowed his gaze. "So if you can't find Sharp's summons, what does that mean?"

Leah twitched her whiskers and furrowed her brow. "It means he has an unregistered summon pair. Which makes me wonder who else might."

Trecheon threw up his hand. "Great. More to worry about."

The paper on the wall listing the Angels caught fire suddenly and burned to cinders. Logos and Pathos yelped and leapt back.

"Sorry, sorry!" Zeke said. Dozens of elemental marbles hovered around Zeke's head and shoulders. He stood and moved away from the table, taking the magic marbles with him. "Sorry, it's just… all these mages, all this *magic*, and… Andre has no protection."

Trecheon narrowed his gaze. "Zeke."

Zeke looked up.

"When we find Jaden's location, you need to stay here."

Zeke's eyes widened. "What?"

"This has been happening since we met," he said. "Magic marbles all over my office, unable to hit anything while we were chased, fighting to get the magic to work on the water. You're so stressed, you can't control it. The last thing we need is your wild elements giving Angel a trail to follow."

"It won't!" Zeke said throwing his hands up. "I can *handle it.*"

Trecheon crossed his arms. "Then shut your magic down."

Zeke pressed his eyes closed and formed fists. But rather than shoving the magic away, the fireball doubled in size, flew around the room, and smashed into the picture of Rebekka, setting it ablaze. Zeke yelped and tried to put it out with water, but the water ball flew around and struck Trecheon in the face instead. Trecheon spat and wiped his fur.

Leah ran over, ripped the picture off the wall, and stamped out the flames. She frowned. "Maybe he's right, Zeke. Your mental state--"

"Oh *my* mental state," Zeke snarled, making Leah jump. "What about yours? Don't think I can't smell it. There's been this steady burning ever since our first meeting with Chadwick." He waved a hand. "I never should have told Sacha you were fine. You're *not.* You need to be *resting.*"

"*I need to be out looking for Jaden!*" Leah shouted. "He's being *hunted* and we're hiding here like *trapped rats.*"

"We *are* trapped rats," Trecheon said. "It's not safe--"

"We're *Defenders,*" Leah snapped. "We're soldiers and mages and *dangerous.* Jaden and Embrik and Alexina are out there alone, and if they aren't dead now, they sure as heck will be soon now that Angel is on the alert and looking for them!"

Everyone in the room grew silent.

Leah seethed, breathing fast, her fur puffing up. "You're not saying anything, because you know I'm *right.*"

Zeke stood slowly, holding his hands up. "Can you sit, please?"

"*Why?*"

Trecheon held his hand up too. "You're glowing."

Leah paused. She looked at her hands. A faint, green glow covered her fur follicles, wafting off her body in waving tendrils.

"I… can smell the magic," Zeke said. "It's like… like burning plastic."

"I smell it too…" Trecheon said.

Zeke frowned. "Leah. You're out of control."

Leah glared at him. "You're one to talk."

"Both of you are," Trecheon said. "Look at you two. Neither of you are in control." He shook his head. "I'm sorry, but I'm going to recommend to the group that the two of you stay here for the rest of this mission."

Zeke furrowed his brow.

Leah flicked her ears. "Trecheon--"

He held up his hand. "You can't go after Jaden. It's too dangerous. Not when you can't control yourselves." He frowned, his quills drooping. "I know that's not what you wanna hear, but you literally just got back from war. Trust me, I know what that feels like, and I know how hard it is to admit it. But you need R&R and I can't think of a better place for that right now then Athánatos."

Leah flattened her ears, staring at the floor. "But Jaden…"

Ethos stood and gently gripped Leah's shoulder. "You need a break, hun. Let's go see if we can find Sacha to finish Trecheon's arm. Maybe see what we can do to help Andre."

Trecheon bared his teeth. "Ethos--"

"I won't hurt her," Ethos said, glaring at Trecheon. *"You* have every right not to trust me. But that doesn't apply to Leah. She can make her own choices. And she needs a break. If it makes you feel better, I won't leave her side."

Trecheon snarled. "It *doesn't.* "

"Trecheon."

Trecheon turned to Leah.

She stared at him with hard, yet distant eyes. "I promise she'll stay by me. But… I need a break."

Trecheon frowned. He shook his head. "…Fine. Against my better judgement."

Leah nodded to him. She and Ethos left the room.

Logos and Pathos stood.

Trecheon growled. "Don't you *dare.*"

"We haven't eaten yet," Logos said, glaring Trecheon down. "Come with us if you want, but you can't deny us food."

"I'll go with you," Zeke said. Little gusty twisters gathered around his feet, but he pushed them aside and turned to Trecheon. "This conversation isn't over yet." He walked up the stairs with Logos and Pathos following.

Trecheon watched them go up, then turned back to the wall, seething. Where did Zeke get off like that? He didn't know the Fawn's like he did. He had no right.

The wall stared back at him. A dozen faces, all enemies, pinning Trecheon down.

He scanned the powers they had. Mostly unfamiliar focus jewels. Continuum Stones, Wishing Dust, Blood Crystals… so many names, and so much unpredictable power. Wishing Dust especially. Their specialties didn't even make sense to him. Body morpher? Item tracker? Fear monger? There was only so much he could infer.

His damaged shoulder ached terribly. He rotated it, wishing for the hundredth time that he could just pick up his spare parts from his apartment. But that ship had sailed. Everything precious and important still on the mainland, aside from their own families.

Shock blasted his spine and all his fur and quills stood on end. Not all from their families. They missed one.

Philip was still on the mainland.

He dashed out of the room.

THE VEIL

Neil stood on Natassa's left, arms crossed, as all the Archons assembled in the audience chamber of the royal family.

Well, almost all the Archons. The House of Embrik's seat stood empty. Normally Melaina would represent Embrik, but Natassa had her busy around the palace searching for rips in the Veil. Ouranos and Natassa had both decided that one of the best things they could do to protect Athánatos was to seal it fully away.

Neil shook himself, old memories of first meeting the Shadow Cast while chasing Ryota invading his mind. He had been dragged through one of those broken portals in the Veil during the ensuing scuffle, wrapped in the body of a Shadow Cast, barely able to breathe or think.

He pushed it aside, glancing away. Didn't need that trauma clouding his brain right now.

Neil didn't understand it full himself, but apparently only royal family members and the Archons could magically repair the invisible rips. And rips could be *anywhere* on the island. Ouranos had said many simply lead to other broken places on the island, but any of them could lead to the mainland. Or lead a mainlander here.

Natassa grew quiet after that, but Neil didn't press her on it.

But this would be a massive undertaking. One that needed all hands on deck and a lot of time. Things they didn't quite have. A shame they didn't have Embrik or Alexina there to help out. Hopefully they'd find the two of them alive and well with Jaden.

Hopefully.

Natassa sat at the head of a round table in the large, well-lit room. Neil had been here a couple of times. Normally there'd be food, drinks, small talk. The Athánatos liked good company. But now, nothing. Utter silence. Empty table. Just the Basilea and her Archons.

Natassa had encouraged Neil to sit, but he couldn't. This kind of thing needed standing. He needed to prove he could help lead. He needed the illusion of strength, to fool himself even if it didn't fool the others.

Ouranos stood on Natassa's right, chin high, face blank, clearly trying to keep the Archons calm. Most seemed to be, though several eyed Neil with a dark gaze. Neil racked his brain, trying to connect their colors with their titles. The green, black streaked Archon, Windrik. The blue, black streaked Archon, Mistik. The brown, black streaked Archon, Dustrik. All staring at him.

He breathed deep, trying to keep his face neutral. Electrik, Damianos' father, smiled at him and nodded encouragingly. At least one of the Archons was fully on his side.

He sighed and turned to the large, ornate perch on the side wall, highly polished and decorated with colored jewels. Seven of the eight Phonar perched there.

Including the new one, Archángeli. Zeke's summon. Alexina's son.

That still freaked Neil out a little.

As the last Archon, Dustrik, sat, Natassa stood. "Greetings, my Archons. *Erini mazi sas.*"

"May the Sister shine on us," the Archons replied as one. *"Erini mazi sas."*

"Erini mazi sas," Neil and Ouranos said quietly.

"We have gathered here for some interesting news," Natassa said. "This will be shocking and you will all have questions, but I ask that you ask them in an orderly manner. Then we need to get to work."

Archon Electrik raised a hand. "If I may pose one question, My Lady? Before we get started?"

Natassa nodded to him.

Electrik stood, his yellow and black quills rustling. He pointed to the Phonar's perch. "I see we have Archángeli here, but not Kyrie." His expression grew dark. "The Phonar redistribute to the royalty when they die or when they have children. If Alexina had died, we would see both Phonar. Since we do not… is it safe to assume she has had a child? And that that child is among us?"

Natassa nodded, a small smile on her face. "Excellent analysis, Electrik. That lays out the situation well." She addressed all the Archons. "Electrik's deduction is the reason for this meeting. First off, we have found the missing Defender healer Leah. She appeared at Trecheon's place of work two days ago with an Athánatos Prince in her company."

The Archons stood as one, eyes wide, tails lashing. Magic clung to their fur.

"Sit please, my friends," Natassa said. The Archons glanced at each other and slowly sat back down. "This prince is indeed Alexina's son, which she had with another missing Defender, Jaden Azure. Matthew's father. She and Embrik found him not long after leaving the island during the war and she and Jaden married on the mainland."

Frostrik stood, silver and black quills bouncing.

"Frostrik?"

"Since we do not have Kyrie here," he said. "Does that mean Alexina is still on the mainland?"

Natassa nodded. "We believe so, yes. She, Embrik, and Jaden are being hunted by an Earth enemy and his team of assassins called Angel. We are working to locate Alexina and the others before Angel does, though our time and resources are limited."

"However, our enemy is not so limited," Ouranos said. "He has resources and power that we do not fully comprehend. We do believe though, that he is well aware of Athánatos since Embrik and Alexina was in his employ during a world war on the mainland."

Windrik narrowed their gaze. "They worked *with* this madman? Whatever for?"

"Unknown," Natassa said. "Though it should be noted that Trecheon, Neil, Leah, and our new prince Zeke all worked for him as well, but none were willing. Likely Embrik and Alexina felt the same."

Windrik lifted their chin then turned to Neil, glaring slightly. Neil fought hard not to sneer back.

Natassa didn't notice though. "Because Angel is aware of our island, we are going to start a coordinated effort to seal all the rips in the Veil and block any passage he might take."

Dustrik stood now, brown quills shaking. "We have not done a full sweep of the Veil since before the war," she said. "Is it possible to eliminate all of the rips?"

"It will be quite a chore," Ouranos admitted. "So we intend to act logically on this. We will start with the palace - Lady Melaina has already begun - and I will ask that the Archons and any of your family willing and able work on rips near your own villages. If we have time, we will move out from there. But protecting the population centers are our priority."

Mistik stood now, smoothing down blue and black fur. "And if our home is breeched in the meantime? We need a way to keep our people safe and communicate if there is trouble."

"We have always used the Phonar for communication in times of trouble," Frostrik said.

"We have always had *eight* Phonar," Mistik countered. "And if we are truly to face mainlanders again, with their destructive weapons and instant communication, we will be at a desperate disadvantage. The Phonar are not fast enough."

The room grew silent.

Neil lifted his chin and perked his ears. "Ouranos. The pendants."

Ouranos turned to him.

"Before Matt and the others left, they fabricated pendants for everyone," Neil said. "I bet Pilot could fabricate something similar. Instant communication."

Ouranos smiled. "A good solution. We should speak with him about it as soon as we can."

"That does not fix the problem of invasion," Windrik said, shaking their green quills.

"I've been thinking about that too," Neil said. "The rips in the Veil often lead to other places on the island, right? But you can make them on purpose. *Direct* where the rips go. That's how you got it to Sol and how we got the rescued Athánatos off the mainland on the docks." He turned to Natassa and Ouranos. "Can you use the rips to create portals to other parts of the island?"

Ouranos' eyes widened. "I... have not considered that."

Bouldrik stood now, gray quills trembling, her eyes wide with excitement. "Try it, my Prince! It need not go far. Perhaps to the library? As a test?"

Ouranos nodded. He stood back from the table and held out a hand, tugging at strange invisible strings, using a method for quick creation like Ryota had showed them on the shipping docks years ago.

A twinge of pain ripped through Neil's heart.

The portal slowly opened and the shimmers in the air transformed. A clear image focused from the sparks. Floor-to-ceiling bookshelves covered in old bound books, scrolls, and artwork. The Athánatos Library.

A few Archons clapped and Bouldrik let out a little cheer.

"Excellent!" Natassa said.

Windrik leaned back in their chair. "I do not like it. Creating more rips on purpose weakens the Veil. We need it as strong as possible."

"I concur," Mistik said.

"As do I," Dustrik said. "But only on the condition that it causes actual harm."

"Unfortunately, we don't have time for tests," Neil said. "Not if we want to protect Athánatos."

Windrik lifted their chin, glaring down at Neil. "I realize you have been courting the princess and Electrik's son. But that does not give you the right to tell us how we should protect our people. We have been doing it before you were *born.*"

Neil glanced at Natassa to see if he was expected to defend himself. She nodded to him. He took a deep breath and puffed out his chest, hoping his voice wouldn't squeak. "With all due respect, Archon, your mad king, almost entirely by himself, turned your entire island into mindless Shadow Cast, despite your flashy magic and powerful bird summons. He was one of your *own* and you still failed to stop him. You had to get outside help."

Windrik huffed, crossing their arms.

Neil lowered his gaze. "There's nothing wrong with getting help, and you have it readily available." He waved a hand. "I worked for this asshole going after us. I know how he operates, how he thinks. And I'm familiar with the kind of tech he'll bring here. I'm the expert. So, *with your help,* let me use that knowledge to protect Athánatos with you. We'll all be stronger for it."

The room grew quiet again. Neil's heart pounded in his ears.

Frostrik stood. "I stand with Lady Natassa and her courter."

"As do I," Boulder said.

Electrik stood. "I also stand with him." He turned to Windrik. "My friend, I know you have reservations, and I dare say we all do. But these are desperate times. Our people should come before our reservations. If this is a way to protect them, let us use it."

Windrik lowered their gaze. "Fine. But I demand further testing be done before we make this a permanent solution."

"I concur," Natassa said. "I appreciate your concerns but also your desires to put your people first. Both have been noted. Before you leave to begin your searches to find Veil rips, Ouranos will train you in creating rips to the palace. This is a safe haven. Should any of your homes be breached, you can evacuate here."

"I'll go get Pilot working on those comms," Neil said. "We'll get this under control."

The Archons all bowed. Electrik met Natassa's eyes. "May we hear good news about your sister soon, my Lady. We are all waiting and ready to help."

"And please keep sir puma at your side," Bouldrik said with a wink. "He is a fantastic problem solver."

"All of Athánatos benefits from Lord Neil's presence," Electrik said, smiling at them both.

Neil's ears grew hot and he turned away. *Did he really say lord…?*

Windrik rolled their eyes and walked out.

Frostrik stood now. "I will speak with my family about our plan and I eagerly await the communicators and training." He smiled and bowed. "With your leave, my Lady."

Natassa nodded. "We will send the Phonar when we are ready to gather again."

The Archons left one after the other. Neil dropped the façade, heaving a breath. *God* that was nerve-wrecking.

Ouranos gripped Neil's shoulder with a grin. "Excellent thinking, brother. You make a fine partner for my sister. I am honored." He turned to Natassa. "I will go speak with Pilot myself and work on ways to train the Archons. Windrik and their allies will come around. Rest a moment and join us when you are ready." He bowed and left.

Neil watched him walk off. Natassa walked up behind him and wrapped her arms around him, resting her chin on the top of his head. He relaxed in her arms, letting the tension vanish. "Natassa? Did Electrik really call me Lord or am I dreaming?"

She giggled. "This is no dream." She sighed and snuggled into his fur. "Though I wish some parts of this was."

He sighed and gently gripped her arms. "You and me both."

She gently kissed his head. "Regardless of the situation though, I agree with Ouranos. You fit the role well. Even when arguing with stubborn Archons. An important skill to develop." She gently squeezed him. "I look forward to making our partnership more permanent."

A shiver ran up Neil's spine. He looked forward to it as well, but a tiny twinge of fear still clung to him. Sure, he made some good suggestions, but what did that really mean? Skills with suggestions doesn't make someone ready to lead. And yeah, he had allies, but at least three of the Archons dismissed him.

He still had a lot more to prove.

And protect.

"We should see how Trecheon is faring with the Fawns," Natassa said, releasing her hug.

Electricity ran up Neil's spine. The damn Fawns. A fire lit in his belly as they walked out. Those Fawns took everything from him. He wouldn't let them take anymore. Not here. Here he was in control.

But then ice ripped through his veins and he froze in place. Here he was in control. But not on the mainland.

Not where his other heart was.

"Oh God… *Philip.*"

Natassa's eyes widened. "Oh, *Sisters.*"

"I have to find Trecheon. *Now.*" He ran.

CHAPTER 18

HEALER

Leah walked into the palace, staring at the ground, mentally playing her fight with Trecheon and Zeke over and over in her head. The emotions, the smells, the fear…

The glow on her fur.

She paused, trying to rebalance.

Healers didn't do that. Healing was an invisible power. And yet, here she was, growing green tendrils on her fur.

She really was out of control.

Bile built in her mouth as a thousand thoughts flooded her mind, competing for attention, digging into her anxiety, pulling her apart, atom by atom.

Zeke likes Andre more.

Trecheon doesn't trust you.

You're not helpful.

You can't protect either of them.

Andre has been Zeke's best friend for years – you barely know him.

He doesn't actually want you.

He lied.

You failed him.

You failed his parents.

You failed Trecheon and Neil and Carter.

You failed Jaden.

"Stop!" Leah shouted.

A hand gripped her shoulder. "Leah?"

Leah whipped her head about. Ethos.

The pink doe frowned. "You okay?"

Leah blinked at her a moment, then pulled her uniform jacket tighter around her and walked off, her heart racing.

She had trusted Ethos in the war. But here… now… after all they had done to Neil's family. After their dubious connection to Ackerson.

Who knew.

Someone cursed.

Leah paused and looked down a hallway. That was Andre. Though she couldn't make out the words, she heard Chadwick talking as well. He must be having trouble.

She violently shook her head and clutched her jacket. The Thought Factory kept spitting at her. She pushed it back, though it echoed in her head, then headed down the hall, not caring if Ethos followed or not.

The hall led into a small audience chamber. The room was only about twice the size of Leah's own tiny office back at home, though it was airy and bright and homey. There was a long wicker couch along the far wall and a small wooden desk, but that was about it. Bright light shone through the ceiling holes, painting pictures in the dust and on the walls.

Sacha sat on the couch, her brow furrowed. She nodded to Leah when she walked in, but didn't say anything.

Ethos crossed the room and sat next to her. Sacha narrowed her gaze, but still kept silent. Not that Ethos would have noticed. The pink deer stared at Leah blankly, her face devoid of emotion, but one ear lay flat against her head, giving her feelings away. She was worried.

Andre sat at a makeshift desk with three laptops surrounding him, typing away at one of them. The blue of the screens mixed with the light from the ceiling holes and left strange highlights on his dark skin. Chadwick stood next to him, a deep frown on his face, his ears pasted back. A handful of pastries sat on Andre's left, surrounded by cloth napkins. He stared unblinking at the screen, his lips moving slightly as he typed. His brow furrowed and he gritted his teeth. *"Shit."* He slammed his fist to the desk, shaking the laptops and making Ethos jump.

Chadwick growled quietly, though Leah took it more to mean worry than anger. "Problem, hun?"

"This hellish encryption," Andre said. "I don't know why the hell Pilot thought I'd be helpful here. Only half of this code is familiar. The other…" He tapped away at one laptop. "Doesn't help that I'm not at my normal battle station. Working on three separate laptops sucks enough as it is, but it's extra bad when two of them ain't even mine."

"You're welcome to give mine back," Ethos said, arms crossed.

"Can't," Andre said, clearly missing her sarcasm. "That's where I'm analyzing the foreign code."

"Sorry, Andre," Sacha said. "We work with what we've got. Pilot's an old A.I. and has limited functions."

Andre eyed her. "How old?"

"Quite literally thousands of years," Sacha said. "I could check his properties, but he might consider that rude.

Andre blinked at her, then shook his head and shrugged. "At least I grabbed the powerbank, or we'd be hurtin'. Though not sure how long they'll hold." He sat back. "Don't suppose you electric mages can charge a battery?"

Leah shifted. "You could ask Ouranos. He's got to power Pilot somehow." She frowned. "I-I'm not super technologically savvy. How do you break an encryption?"

Andre leaned on his hand, shaking his head. "Code analysis or brute force. Pilot's force-feeding the pendant a thousand passcode combinations a second, hoping to find a match since he goes *way* faster than my grubby paws can. Meanwhile, I'm trying to analyze the program's coding and find patterns so I can reverse engineer the passcode. Didn't think of the whole 'from a different planet' bullshit though." He leaned back on the wicker chair. "I'm kicking myself for that now." He shook his hand and sucked in a breath. "Damnit, I caught the edge of the table." A trickle of blood ran down his pinky.

"Oh, I can take care of that," Leah said. She paused. "I-I mean, if you want me to. I uh… I can see your ailments and medical history if I touch you. It's part of my magic."

Andre smiled. "Yeah, Zeke mentioned. It's cool though." He held out his hand. "I hope I don't overwhelm you. Bein' a fighter pilot leaves lotsa scars."

Leah perked both ears in surprise. No one had ever warned her about their own history. No one had ever *cared* to.

Andre frowned and looked at the small wound. He pulled his hand back. "Actually, can you see mental health?"

Leah flattened one ear, prepping for a familiar argument. "To a degree. Not enough to be able to identify it by name, but I can see feelings and sometimes I'll get flashbacks associated with injuries. The worse the trauma, and the more recent the trauma, the more likely I'll see it. If you don't want me to see it, there's no shame in that…"

Andre furrowed his brow. "But does it screw with *your* head?"

Leah rubbed her arm. "I-I'd be lying if I said it didn't. Though I'm a lot better about that than I used to be." She flicked her tail. "I can handle it most times, but I'll admit, some trauma affects me more than others. Trecheon losing his arms, for example. That… really knocked me down."

Andre glanced down at his pinky. He shook his head and picked up a discarded napkin. "I'm not putting you through that shit for something tiny like this." He wiped the blood clean.

Leah frowned. That definitely wasn't expected. "Andre, I can handle it."

"It ain't about you bein' able to handle it," Andre said. "It's about me not wantin' to overwhelm you."

Leah lowered her head. "But…"

"Leah," Andre said. "You just got back from a bloody *war*. I'm a soldier. I know what special hell that is. You don't need my trauma on top of your own. Work through that first, 'k? If I really need you, I'll call on ya, but no sense in dumpin' more on you when you're still recovering."

Leah's heart warmed. "I… Thank you. No one has ever taken their own trauma into consideration for me before."

Andre lifted a brow. "Really? Never?"

Leah wrinkled her snout, twitching her whiskers. "Zyearthlings… they don't really know what to do with my magic. Healing is stigmatized enough, but healing when I can see and feel your whole medical history? I might as well see right into your soul for how invasive it is. No one can fathom it, and they're too concerned with what I might see… they don't care about what I might *feel.*"

Both Andre and Chadwick stared at her with wide eyes. Leah shrunk down, a blush blooming in her ears, making her feel hot. "Sorry, I didn't mean to dump all that…"

"Did you say healing was stigmatized?" Chadwick said.

Leah blinked. "Y-Yeah."

"What the hell for?" Andre said. "I'd kill for magic healing powers." He paused and leaned on his good hand. "Bad choice of words." Chadwick chuckled.

Leah shifted. "I-I suppose I should clarify that it's only stigmatized in the Defenders… When you've got a support power in a military full of powerful elemental users, healing is seen as weak."

"Bullshit." Andre leaned back in his chair and crossed his arms. "Even more of a reason not to push you for this stupid cut. Someone oughta think about your wellbeing before foisting themselves on you."

Sacha smiled. "Good man. I knew I liked you." She waved him over. "Lemmie take care of that. I don't have Leah's specific healing power. It won't hurt me."

"Sure," Andre said. "Thanks."

Sacha healed the cut. "No, thank *you* for actually thinking about your healer. It's a nice change of pace."

"Should be all around, but I hear ya." He turned to Leah. 'Sides, we need your head intact to get Jaden and fight these damn mages. And more than that, Zeke needs you, and he sure as hell don't need me accidentally screwing with his life partner."

Leah pulled her tail into her hand and picked at the guard hairs. It was strangely refreshing to hear an outsider's perspective on her magic. But… "Are you okay with that?"

Andre tilted his head. "With you bein' Zeke's new winglady?" He turned and faced Leah, though he gazed at the ground. "I'ma be honest. It's a new worldview. I thought I'd lost him. Then he just shows up outta the blue with a new best friend and magic and shit, having survived the war that took his folks. And both of us ain't pilots anymore. Trying to cope with all that, plus the fact that he's gonna outlive me by hundreds of years…" He wrung his hands together. "…And Chadwick is too."

Chadwick wrapped his arms around Andre's shoulders.

Leah perked her ears. Finally, she could be useful. "You can Gem share with Chadwick," she said. "It won't grant you magic, but you can live as long as Chadwick does. If you wanted to of course."

Andre perked up. "Really? I thought humans couldn't use Gems."

Leah rubbed her chin. "Base humans can't normally, because you don't have innate magic. Most Earthlings are base humans."

"Plenty of other extraterrestrial humans have innate magic and use focus jewels," Sacha said. "I don't know how true it is, but there was rumors during Jaden Azure's time as Golden Guardian that he and his partner Dyne bound a base human to a Gem. It'd hurt like hell, but it's proof of concept. If it's real."

Andre leaned back. "Good God. Magic, time travel, space travel, and now humans on other planets. The hell did I get dropped into."

Sacha grinned. "Better dropped in than dragged in."

Andre laughed. "Aight, I'll give you that."

Leah shifted, swishing her tail. "Even without innate magic, you two should still be able to Gem share, I think. We can ask the focus jewel specialist Jaymes Fogg on Zyearth once this all calms down. Jaden… Jaden might know too." She slumped down. "…We really needed to get to Jaden."

"You will," Andre said.

"But not *fast enough.*" Leah slumped onto the wicker couch next to Ethos. "Every second we waste trying to get this dang decryption puts him and the others in further danger."

"Then we need this thing unlocked yesterday," Andre said. "I'll keep at it. We'll get it. K?"

Leah sighed. "Yeah."

"Leah," Chadwick said. "Maybe your time would be best spent looking over the information the Fawn's brought us working on a plan to fight them with Trecheon and Zeke."

"It'd be better spent looking for Jaden."

"Then this is the first step," Chadwick said. "And it'll keep your mind occupied."

She threw her head back. "Okay, you're right." She turned to Ethos. "If you have any other resources that can help…"

"Then I'll be there in a heartbeat," Ethos said.

"We got this," Andre said. "Go see your partner."

Partner. She rubbed her arms. At least Andre was understanding. She stood.

"Hey Leah?" Andre said.

Leah turned to him.

He smiled. "I'm really glad Zeke had you when he was trudging through hell. Thanks for taking care of him."

She blinked, but nodded. "We really took care of each other, but you're welcome." She blinked and looked away. "I wish I could have saved his moms though."

"Don't do that," Andre said. "No one heals thinkin' of what ifs. You deserve better."

Leah shrugged. "Sure."

"I ah… don't wanna hug you just yet while you're still recovering," Andre said. Leah flicked her ears back. "I know that sucks ass, but I just want you at the top of your game first, k?"

"I understand," Leah said. "Thanks for caring. I mean that."

Andre nodded. "So until hugs are on the table, how about finger guns?"

Leah smiled. "Sure, if you show me what those are."

He lifted both hands, index finger and thumb extended, and pointed at her over and over with a goofy grin. "Finger guns. *Wapow!*"

Leah giggled now. "I like that." She pointed right back at him.

"Hey, you got it." His grin faded into a softer smile. "Friends?"

Leah nodded. "Friends."

"Fantastic." Andre gave her a goofy salute. "Go tell Zeke he better treat you right or I'll kick his ass." He turned back to the computer.

"I'll be staying here for a bit to help with the decryption," Ethos said.

Leah frowned. "I promised Trecheon--"

"And I'm more useful here," Ethos said. "Chadwick will watch me." She smiled at him. "Won't you?"

Chadwick flashed a thumbs up.

"I will too," Sacha said. "If Trecheon gives you hell about it, I'll kick his tail."

"So go," Ethos said. "Spend some time with Zeke. Calm your mind if you can. You need it."

Leah let her shoulders relax. She nodded and left the room, headed back for the basement. Trecheon would be mad, but she trusted Chadwick. It'd… it'd be fine.

At least that interaction with Andre was exactly what she needed. She hadn't even heard the Thought Factory spewing lies. She'd finally won.

But Jaden is still missing, it said, oh so quietly. *And you're not doing anything about it.*

She stopped.

That one wasn't a lie.

You're a disgrace, the Thought Factory spat. *Jaden was wrong about you.*

Leah shut her eyes tight and flattened her ears. *Jaden told me I was Guardian material. I value life!*

Then why aren't you saving Jaden's life?

Her heart ached. The Thought Factory collapsed into flames in her head.

A Thought Monster rose from the ashes, tearing into her mind with vicious claws, teeth, and horns. She flinched, a raging headache ripping across her forehead.

You are nothing more than a scared, pathetic kitten.

Leah gripped her head. "No… No, I'm not…"

Can't save anyone. Not Jaden. Not Zeke's moms. Not Outlander. You're no Defender.

"No!"

"Leah!"

Leah shot her head up, her vision blurry from unshed tears.

Trecheon ran at her, full speed, his expression frantic.

PHILIP

Trecheon ran up to Leah, his heart pounding. "Leah, tell me you've seen Neil."

Leah flattened her ears, her eyes glassy. "N-No… What's wrong?"

Trecheon frowned. "Leah, did something--"

"Trecheon!"

Trecheon turned.

Neil ran up to him, Natassa at his heels, panting. He stopped in front of them and leaned on his knees. "We gotta get to the mainland," he said, huffing. "We left *Philip.*"

"I know," Trecheon said. "I thought of that too. We need to get him here before Ackerson goes after him and uses him as some kind of leverage." *Or worse, just flat out kills him.*

"Let me go with you," Leah said. "You need a fighter and a healer and--"

"No," Trecheon said. "Absolutely not. This is too sensitive to bring anyone along."

"But--"

"What's going on?" Sacha walked into the room with Ethos beside her. "I heard yelling."

Neil turned to the doe, snarling. "Give me back Philip. *Now.*"

Ethos perked her ears, then glanced at the ground, frowning. "We've been trying, actually," she said. "Ever since we released you after the Athánatos and Basileus problem was resolved."

"It's been almost *three years* since the incident with Theron," Trecheon said, crossing his arms, tongues of fire in the air. "You're telling us you can't fix a problem *you created* in that time?"

"No," Ethos said. "Because we didn't create the problem. Ackerson did, through us."

"Do you think that *matters?*" Neil bared his teeth. "My little brother is out there where Ackerson could get him! Get him back!"

Ethos flattened her ears and lowered her gaze. "We have no control over Philip," she said.

"Then who *does?*" Neil said.

"The state," Ethos said. "Though Ackerson has friends in high places. We think he's been using that knowledge to move Philip around and hold him hostage." She rubbed her arm. "Believe me, we have done everything we can to try and get him back under our control and pass him over to you, but our attempts only caused..." her voice broke. "...hardship."

Leah frowned. "W-what kind of hardships?"

"That's personal," Ethos said.

"I don't care," Neil said. "What are you going to do to help me get him back before Ackerson takes him?"

Ethos bit her lip, bending one ear back. "I can't do anything. My hooves are tied."

Neil growled, throwing a fist through the air.

"Noted," Trecheon said, catching his fist on fire. He turned to Neil. "We'll take care of this ourselves. Let's go." Neil nodded and they marched toward the portal to the mainland.

Sacha slid in front of them, hand out. "Slow down, hotheads. Your arm is being repaired. You're not going anywhere, especially alone."

"It's what we've always done," Trecheon said. He moved around her.

Sacha cut him off. "When you had no one else. But you have a support network now, Trecheon."

"Don't try to stop this, Sacha," Neil snapped. He tried skirting around her again.

"I'm not trying to *stop* you," Sacha said, blocking them. "I'm trying to talk some sense into you. You shouldn't do this *alone.*"

Trecheon bared teeth. "I need to take charge!"

"You need to let others support you!" Sacha said, pointing at him.

Natassa formed fists, little elemental marbles floating above her head. "You are not leaving without us."

Neil frowned. "Natassa, we--"

"*You are not,*" Natassa said. "It is not up for discussion. You would not let me face my father alone. You cannot expect me to let you face Ackerson's demons alone."

"Nor me," Damianos said, walking into the room. "As long as we are connected to you, Philip is family. We go after him together."

Trecheon furrowed his brow. He turned to Neil.

Neil glanced at them both, his shoulders slumped. "...Fine. You're right, much as I hate it."

Sacha crossed her arms. "Trecheon, your arm is broken. Stay here and get that taken care of."

"But Philip--"

"I'll go with Neil to get him," Sacha said.

Trecheon's stomach churned at the thought of her going after Angel. "Sacha, you're--"

"If you even think to pull the 'you're only a healer' shit on me, I swear to Draso I'll break your other arm," Sacha snarled, her rounded ears flattening against her head. "I'm a Draso-damned *Defender--*"

Trecheon stepped back. "I'd never say that, I'm--"

"You're staying here," Sacha snapped. "And I'm going with Neil. End of story. Don't argue."

Trecheon stared deep into Sacha's eyes. This wonderful woman who had been so comforting, so supportive, so caring, so wonderful... that he had fallen in love with her.

But... once again someone was running his life. Telling him what he could and couldn't do. Didn't matter that she had a point. He was so sick of not having control.

He was done with it. He shut his eyes tight and rotated his shoulder.

Sacha took a step back.

Trecheon lifted his head. "I'm not staying here."

Sacha flattened her ears, her tail drooping. "Trecheon."

"Don't," Trecheon said. Sharp pain ran through his chest as if an icicle shot through his heart, but he kept his expression under control. "This is my family at stake. And I'm not standing idle." He turned to Neil. "Take who you want, but we need to *leave.*" He whipped about.

This time, the Black Cloak stood in his way.

Trecheon glared. "Don't you start."

"You want me to use my knowledge to protect you," the Cloak said, his voice deep and dangerous. "Fine. That's what I'm doing." He lifted his chin. "If you leave this room right now, Philip will die."

Neil let out a terrifying choked sound.

Trecheon faltered, taking a step back. He narrowed his gaze. "How do I know you're not lying?"

"You want to take that risk?" the Cloak said. "Go for it. I can't stop you. But the moment you step out of this room, there is no turning back. Period."

Trecheon growled. Damnit. Damn him. Damn everything!

Neil moved in front of the Cloak and sized him up, despite being shorter than him. "If you're really going to start using your knowledge to help us, then tell me right now. How do I save Philip?"

The Cloak lifted his chin. "Stay here."

"Give me another option, asshole," Neil said. "Because I'm *not* staying here."

"There *is* no other option."

Trecheon scoffed, shaking his head. "You haven't changed anything."

"Every word out of my mouth changes everything," the Cloak said. "Whether you believe me or not."

Neil violently flicked his tail. "Thanks for nothing. I… I choose not to believe you. We're done." He turned to the others. "Come on, let's go."

"Wait."

Neil stopped.

The Cloak hesitated, then shook himself. "Look. I can tell you two things. One, don't go tonight. You'll kill him if you do. Go tomorrow. You have a normal visit. Go to the house then." He paused. "Two, take Angus with you."

Neil lifted a brow. "Angus?"

"Yes." But the Cloak didn't elaborate.

Neil stared at him a moment then snorted. "Fine. Tomorrow." He stomped off. Natassa and Dami followed behind, wrapping arms around him.

God, what Trecheon wouldn't give to have someone wrap him up like that. He sighed. "Leah, let's finish getting me fixed up. I'm going with him."

Sacha frowned. "Trecheon, I--"

"It's my family, Sacha," Trecheon said, turning to her. *Mine.* What very little I have left. And I need to take charge. Get him myself. We need to control this. Even if you don't understand it."

Sacha flattened an ear. She took a deep breath, nodded, and walked off. "Just don't die," she muttered.

Trecheon furrowed his brow. That wasn't ominous at all.

"Trecheon."

Trecheon glared at the Cloak.

The Cloak's eyes softened and he lowered his voice. "I'm dead serious when I say you can't go tonight. That will guarantee you won't get Philip. I know you don't trust me, but believe this. Okay?" He walked off.

Trecheon watched him, his heart ripping apart.

CHAPTER 20

CONFINEMENT

Neil lay on Natassa's large bed, but his mind couldn't focus on anything. He needed sleep. He needed to be *resting,* damn it.

He needed to be on the mainland getting Philip. And he couldn't. Curse the Black Cloak. Curse Ackerson.

He stared up. Maybe this is what he deserved.

Natassa walked in the room, wrapped in one of the extra-soft Athánatos towels, having just taken a bath. Steam followed her, clinging to her tail. "Greetings, love. I have a bath warmed for you if you want it. Some peace before you go to get Philip tomorrow."

Neil turned, looking her over. God, she was so beautiful… so perfect.

And she was stuck with him. An assassin, still picking up the pieces of a wasted life. Someone who forgot his own brother in the middle of what essentially equated to a gang war.

No wonder half the Archons didn't trust him.

He lay back on the bed and covered his face with his arm. "I don't deserve peace."

He expected Natassa to tell him different. Or lie to him. Or maybe even confirm it. It was true after all.

But instead, she said nothing. That hurt worse than anything she could have said. Maybe he finally blew it.

After several seconds of silence, he moved his arm and looked around. Empty.

But not for long. Natassa walked in, dried and dressed, and took his hand. She pulled him off the bed and toward the bathing room, one of the few fully private chambers, with a stone bath large enough for three people at least. He followed her dully, his mind a fog.

She gently stripped off his clothes and helped him into the large bathtub, rewarming the water with her own fire magic. Then she took a soap sponge, lathered it up, and rubbed it over his chest and shoulders.

He frowned. "Natassa--"

"Hush," she said. "I will not have you beat yourself up so." She looked him in the eye with her gorgeous violet ones. "You need peace. You *deserve* peace, my heart. You have support. A family." He opened his mouth, but she pressed a finger to it, shutting him up. "You have survived too much to give up now."

"I am here, Natassa."

Neil turned. Damianos walked in, his face awash with worry. He strode quickly to the bathtub.

Neil frowned. "Dami."

"Natassa called me," Damianos said. He kneeled beside her and grabbed another sponge.

Neil shifted uncomfortably. "You don't have to--"

"We are going after your brother tomorrow," Damianos said. "Together. I cannot predict what will happen, but the Black Cloak's words do not fill me with hope. I hope we will come out of this safely. But in case we do not, we should relish the peace we have now." He rubbed soap in his hands and began massaging Neil's scalp. "You promised me peace and I accepted that promise. But I should have promised you peace as well. We are partners and our peace is something we work on together."

Neil let Dami lather him up. He shut his eyes. This… he still didn't deserve it. But maybe he could work until he did. He turned to them both. "Join me?"

Natassa chuckled. "I have already bathed, but I will leave you two to enjoy each other. The bed is open to all of us though." She gave Neil a long kiss, then hugged Dami gently. "Take care." She walked out.

Neil met Damianos' eyes. "Dami?"

He smiled, then stood, slipped his pants off, and slid into the water. Neil rinsed the soap off his body, then pulled Dami close to him, tangling their limbs together. Dami stroked his back, pulling him into a deep kiss, pressing himself against Neil.

Neil lay in the middle of Natassa's bed that night, Dami on his left, Natassa on his right. His two lovers snuggled close to him, sleeping quietly. Peace. Safety. Comfort.

He stared at the ceiling.

They deserved that peace. That safety. He'd have to make sure that he'd make that permanent. For them, for Athánatos, and… for Philip.

Hold on, kiddo. I'm coming.

CHAPTER 21

EMPTY

Neil clung to his battered old chopper as he had a thousand times before, forcing himself with all his might to stay under the speed limit. He couldn't afford to get pulled over. His fingers hurt from his vice grip on the handles.

One phrase ran through his mind.

Get Philip.

But some quiet, nagging voice kept whispering back. *You're too late. He's gone. Ackerson already got him. You should have been here yesterday. You failed.*

He couldn't have. He *couldn't have*. He had lost everything already. He couldn't lose Philip too. There was no happy ending without him. No peace without him.

But Philip could already be dead.

He shook himself, nearly falling off the bike. "Focus. He's not dead. He's fine. Screw that anxiety and just get to him. This is… a normal visit."

The plan was for Neil to get close, call his foster parent Theophania, get Philip, and get out. If she didn't answer, he'd go up to the door. And if he still got no answer… well, that's why Trecheon, Natassa, and Damianos were following in a van the Fawns had lent them.

And Angus, as the Black Cloak suggested. Neil didn't see the point with the Cloak's nonsense, but at the same time, it couldn't hurt bringing him along. The black and green bat, though clearly wary of the Cloak, didn't seem to mind going anyway, and he had piled in with the rest of them, taking a mirror with him. Trecheon mentioned he could see into the future. Neil didn't know how the hell he did that, but why question anything anymore? Magic got more and more wild every time he learned something new about it.

Neil bit his tongue until he tasted copper. Against Sacha's advice, he brought an Athánatos hunting knife. It wasn't a sword or gun, but it was better than nothing. He hid it in the bike, but that also meant it was out of reach. He just had to hope nothing would happen.

Focus. Get in. Get Philip. Get out.

Bursting through the door was a last resort though, no matter how anxious he was. Because if he did, it put everyone, particularly Philip, in danger. And even if they escaped, Neil would become a wanted man. With all the shit going on around him, that was the last thing he needed. They'd have to hide away forever.

Though they'd likely have to hide away forever anyway. Picking Philip up and not returning him would be seen as kidnapping.

Ouranos had promised him that he and Philip would have a home on Athánatos. Which was great but… not the way Neil wanted. That was exile, not freedom.

Curse everything.

Neil turned down Philip's street and caught a glimpse of the house at the end of the block. Typical suburbia, with cookie cutter homes, solar panel roofs, painted shutters that didn't actually work, neatly trimmed lawns, a few baby trees, and clean sidewalks. The neighborhood usually had lots of cars in the driveways, but on a random weekday in the middle of day, most everyone was gone for work.

It made everything feel empty and alone.

Neil pulled over near one corner and pulled off his helmet. Trecheon drove their van on by, parking several houses down from Philip's door, waiting for Neil to make a move. Neil breathed deep. Calm. Collected. Take charge. Can't have her noticing anything's off or… He pressed his eyes shut. He pulled out his phone and put in the call.

The rings blasted out his ear drums, but the rest of the world went totally silent. He forced his breathing to calm and he counted the rings. 1… 2… 3… 4… 5…

Then silence.

Neil's fur bristled. It didn't go through? He was about to try again when a robotic voice spoke dully over the phone.

"We're sorry, but the number you're trying to reach has been disconnected."

Adrenaline ran all the way to the tip of his tail. That couldn't be right. He tried again.

1… 2… 3…

"We're sorry, but the number you're trying to reach has been disconnected."

"No, no, no…" Neil tried again. Same five rings. Same dull message. He double checked the number. Same one he had always used.

You're too late.

Without even bothering to put his helmet back on, he started up the bike and dashed for the house, sliding sideways into the empty driveway. He dropped his helmet in the side car and ran up the patio steps.

Trecheon, Dami, Natassa, and Angus had already piled out of the van and ran for the house.

He couldn't hide his fear anymore. He panic-pressed the doorbell and smashed his fist against the door. "Theophania! It's Philip's brother! Open up!"

He waited.

Nothing.

Trecheon walked up behind him, his ear twitching. "Neil?"

"There's no answer!" Neil said. His tail puffed up wildly and he paced on the patio. "Phone line's disconnected." He turned and banged on the door again.

Damianos exchanged a glance with Natassa. She flicked her ears back, hopped off the patio, and pressed her face against the darkened window, trying to look in.

Neil ground his teeth. He dashed to his bike and retrieved the hunting knife. All caution to the wind. Philip was in danger.

"The house is empty!" Natassa exclaimed by the window.

That did it. Neil raced back up the patio steps and pounded his foot against the door. It flew open in two kicks and he dashed inside.

Natassa was right. The whole house was empty. No furniture, no drapes, no appliances. Every surface had a thin layer of dust, like it hadn't been used in years.

Neil gripped his head. "No, no, no no no no." He paced. "Where are they? What the hell do I do?"

Trecheon gripped Neil's shoulders. "Stay calm. We'll find him." He turned to Angus. "If ever there was a time for your scrying to work, it's now."

Angus rubbed his temple, his wings shaking slightly. "Give me a second." He sat cross-legged on the filthy floor, staring blankly forward, a small mirror in his lap, perfectly still.

"Jesus, Mary, and Joseph…" Neil said. He flexed his fingers, trying to expel the nervous energy. Damianos tried reaching for him, but he shoved his hands in his pockets and stared at the floor. There was no comfort for this.

Angus shook violently, blinking rapidly. He ran his hands down his face.

Neil tapped his foot. "Well?"

Angus furrowed his brow. "Patience."

Trecheon flattened his ears. "We don't have *time.*"

"*I know.*" Angus flicked his wings and resettled, keeping his unblinking gaze forward. "But scrying isn't just making predictions like a fortune teller. Time is an everchanging phenomenon, dictated by choice and happenstance. I don't see time as linear. I see hundreds of possibilities. When I found Leah and Zeke were found, I spent hours scrying and planning out every possible outcome for that chase. I wasn't calling in real time. I was reacting based on a map I had already built. And right now, for Philip, I'm building a map."

Neil furrowed his brow. "In the mirror."

"That's how scrying works."

"Then how does the Cloak do this so quickly?" Damianos asked.

"The Cloak isn't a scryer," Angus said. "He's not giving you information based on a prediction map. He's telling you what *will* happen because he *lived* it."

Trecheon frowned. "That implies the Cloak is one of us."

Angus nodded. "Yes, it does."

Trecheon shuddered.

Neil growled under his breath. "Well, I'm not waiting until you're finished. I'm calling his social worker." He pulled up his phone again. Took a while to get a direct line to Philip's social worker Miss Piper, but eventually he got through. He put it on speaker.

"Record this," Angus said suddenly, still not blinking. He held out a phone.

Trecheon raised an eyebrow, but he took the phone, held it near to Neil's, and hit record.

The smug housecat spoke. "Piper here."

"Where the hell is Philip?" Neil demanded. "His foster home is *empty*. It looks like it hasn't been lived in in *months*. I visited Philip less than two weeks ago. Where is he?"

The line went quiet for far too long.

"Well?"

"You're not privy to that information," Piper said, her voice cold.

"What?" Neil snapped. "That's my brother! Of course I am! Where do you get off?"

"You missed his last hearing."

Ice seized Neil's heart. "I… what? His next hearing is Thursday."

"His last hearing was last Friday," Piper said. "Ten a.m. You failed to show."

"But it's *not.*" Neil formed fists. "My fridge is plastered with the right date!"

"A slot opened up," Piper said. "The hearing got moved up."

The ice in his heart spread through his whole body. "I wasn't informed."

"I have it in my notes of five attempts to contact you--"

"I don't give a shit about your notes!" Neil said. "You changed the date without telling me *again* in an attempt to keep me from him. You've been doing that for almost a year! That is *illegal.*"

"Well then," Piper said. "You'll just have to take it up with your lawyer. Good luck finding one who will take you with your reputation. And our department is absolutely swamped too. It'll be years before legal will catch up." A smug pause. "I'm sure Philip will find a home by then, now that you're no longer interfering."

That nasty, disgusting, sneaky-ass *bitch.* Did she even know what she had done? "You--"

Angus stood quickly and held a hand up, his wing shaking. "Mr. Black, as your lawyer, I advise you refrain from finishing that sentence."

Neil faltered. "What--"

But Piper faltered too. "Hold on, what lawyer?"

"I'm sure you'll be hearing soon, Miss Piper," Angus said. "Good day." He pressed the button to end the call, still staring off, then turned to Trecheon and stopped the recording.

Neil gawked. "The hell was that?"

"Evidence," Angus said. "In case we end up in court." He grinned. "And before you ask, yes, I am a lawyer. The Fawns put me through law school after the war. In return, I keep their business out of legal trouble." He turned to Trecheon and passed him a business card. "Send that recording to the email listed here, then turn off the wi-fi on the phone. We need to protect that."

Trecheon took the card and raised an eyebrow. "Is this even legal?"

"This state is a one-party consent state," Angus said. "Only one party needs to consent to being recorded." He pointed vaguely to Neil. "That's you."

Neil flattened an ear. "Okay… good I suppose, but that doesn't help--
"

Trecheon growled and spread out his hands, shielding all of them, glancing around the room. His ears twitched. "Stop talking. We're not alone."

Shit, shit, *shit*. He unsheathed the hunting knife and stood in front of Damianos and Natassa. He might have lost Philip. He wasn't going to lose anyone else.

Then the silent air ripped in half as Philip's violent scream tore through the house.

OLD ALLIES TO ENEMIES

Neil's ears rang and he glanced frantically around the room. "Philip! Philip, I'm here!"

Another scream ripped between his ears.

He dashed for the back of the house. "Philip! I'm coming, hold on!" But the back of the house was just as empty as the rest of it.

Damianos appeared behind him. "Neil?"

"Out of the way!" Neil rushed past him.

"Stop, please!" Philip again.

Upstairs. He ran for the staircase.

Trecheon zipped in front of him and held his shoulders. "Neil, what the hell is going on?"

"That's *Philip,*" Neil said. He struggled in Trecheon's grip. "Let me go!"

Trecheon frowned. "What's Philip?"

Neil snarled. "Didn't you hear him *scream?*"

Damianos came up behind Trecheon. "There was no scream, Neil."

But another scream echoed on the second floor.

Neil wrenched himself free of Trecheon and double-timed it up the stairs into the darkness, panic gripping his heart. "Philip, hold on!"

Something shot out of the dark from the second floor and wrapped around Neil's body in a thick coil. Neil yelped and dropped his knife, struggling.

The strange coil tightened its grip on Neil.

He roared, kicking and wiggling, trying to fight back the increasing pressure. "Let me go!"

Then he saw a human hand attached to the end of the coil. *Holy shit, the coil was an* arm.

He yipped and struggled harder, full panic setting in now, trying to unsheathe hand claws, though the tight grip held him fast.

The hand flew by his face. In an act of desperation, he sunk his fangs into it.

Something in the darkness shouted and the hand/arm/coil thing unwrapped quickly, the hand flailing about, shooting blood from its wound in all directions, staining the white walls. The sudden release made Neil lose his balance and he tumbled down the stairs, crashing into Trecheon and Damianos. They landed in a pile at the bottom.

Trecheon recovered quickly though, and bathed them all in a shield. Waves of electricity and ice shot down the stairs, colliding into them. The shield held, but the force of the magic pushed them all back and scattered them around the room.

Neil got to his feet, adrenaline pumping hard through him. *Shit, shit, shit!* Protect Natassa, protect Dami…

Too much to protect and not enough power to do it. And Philip--

A massive brown bear crashed down the stairs on all fours, mouth open wide, roaring, while half a dozen elements rippled through his fur. Neil's thoughts vanished and he scrambled away. The bear turned on Dami, flashing his teeth at him, saliva flying everywhere. He leapt.

But then he stopped midair. He blinked, confused, but then went flying into the opposite wall.

Angus moved in front of Neil, arm out, a snarl on his face. His fur puffed up and he flicked his ears back, flaring his wings slightly. *"Otoydi, Jaska."*

Neil stared, his jaw slack. *"Jaska?"*

Trecheon stared at the great bear. "Draso's *breath.*"

The bear stood up straight, shaking himself and adjusting his wide black pants. He growled.

Three colored jewels on either side of his eyes glowed brightly.

Natassa gasped. "Sisters help us. He has Ei-Ei jewels."

Jaska snorted. He spoke with a thick Russian accent. "You should have died in the war, *Outlanders.*" He held his hands out and electricity rained down on them.

Damianos gathered all of it, letting it run through his fur and build at his fingertips. He glared at the bear, lightning running through his fur. "Wrong element choice." He shot the magic right back.

A sharp metal rod shot down the stairs between Jaska and the lightning and pierced the wooden floor. The electric magic gathered around it.

"Heads down!" Trecheon shouted and formed shields in front of everyone. In a powerful boom, the lightning dispersed around the room, crashing through the house, ripping through the walls and smashing through windows, leaving everything cracked and scorched.

Neil crossed his arms in front of his face. Natassa dashed next to him and used her own magic to fight off the flailing electricity until it vanished.

The rod retracted back up the stairs and a thin human with thick white hair and a well-trimmed beard walked down, glaring. He held up his arm as the rod retreated into his own body and reformed into a hand. "Well then. I wasn't sure I believed Ackerson when he said some of you actually survived."

Neil's tail puffed up and he flattened his ears. "Vincent." First Jaska, now Vincent. Two members of the strange team Outlander had found running along the Canadian border while trying to get into the country illegally during the War of Eons. These people were creepy at best and downright dangerous at worst. Carter had warned against working with them, but since the strange team had promised Outlander a way into Canada, they did anyway.

One of Neil's biggest regrets. Because this was also the team Ryota defected to after he betrayed them all.

"So how is your brother, Trecheon?" Vincent said. "Still living under your shadow?"

Trecheon bared his teeth in a feral snarl and Neil roared. Natassa answered with a blast of fire.

Vincent held up his arms. They flashed and morphed into metal before spreading to cover him from the torso up. Natassa's fire hit the shield. It glowed red, but didn't penetrate.

But while his arms had transformed into something useful, his legs had ballooned into massive, grotesque blobs and melted along the floor. Vincent grunted as his body slid along the bare wood like butter on a saucepan, but he kept his arms held up.

Angus turned his head. "Natassa, to your right! Ice, now!"

Natassa whipped to the right as a wave of fire bore down on them. She bombarded it with iceballs, exploding the magic into hot steam, cutting visibility.

Neil waved his hands, trying to dispel the steam. "Natassa! Dami! Trecheon!"

But Angus found him instead, gripping his shoulder. "Take off your shoes and go get your knife. It's on the third step up."

Neil frowned. "Take off my *shoes--?*"

"No questions!" Angus said. "That's what almost killed Trecheon!" He vanished into the steam.

Neil snarled. He kicked off his boots and dashed for the stairs. Sure enough, his hunting knife lay on the third step. He picked it up.

A heavy furred hand gripped his shoulder and lifted him up. Jaska. Neil whipped his hand around and stabbed Jaska in the wrist. The great bear roared and dropped Neil. Neil stumbled back.

Someone wrapped their arm around Neil's neck and yanked him down, gripping the hand that held his knife. "That wasn't very nice."

Neil snarled. "Luana." Another human from Jaska's strange team.

"You have a remarkable memory," she said, her accent biting at his ear.

"And better aim." He pulled his hand free and stabbed at her side. But she let him go and rolled, escaping.

Jaska stumbled to her. "Heal!"

She frowned, but nodded and pressed her brown hand to his injury. The wound closed, but as it did, a slash formed under Luana's cheek. Blood flowed down her skin, catching in her black hair.

Bile filled Neil's mouth and he retched.

Jaska charged.

Neil dove left, tucking into a roll, holding his tail close to his body. Holy *shit*. How the hell were they supposed to fight this?

"Stay away from him!" Damianos shouted. "Natassa!"

Natassa threw several electric marbles at Damianos, then turned back to her enemy, a brown-dark haired, heavy-built woman with elemental magic, another from Vincent and Jaska's team. Dami caught the electric marbles and blasted magic at Jaska and Luana.

But Vincent appeared with another lightning rod hand and dispelled the magic. "Didn't learn the first time, I see."

Trecheon leapt up at Vincent, hands blazing with flames, but he smacked him away with his lightning rod arm. He shook it and the tip sharpened, while half his face expanded several times its normal size. He flung the arm forward and pierced Trecheon's shoulder. He roared and the arm snapped off its mount and fell uselessly to the floor.

Vincent flared his nostrils and shot at him again, though he missed. "Stand *still*." His swollen face distorted his voice.

Neil flattened his ears and charged Vincent. He whipped behind him and stabbed the knife into Vincent's shoulder. Vincent gasped and pulled his hand back. Trecheon scrambled out of the way, dragging his broken arm with him. His Gem whined with power and the electric *pop pop pop* of a shield snapped against Neil's ears.

Neil snarled at Vincent, shaking him. "What the hell did you do with Philip?"

But Vincent could only stare as his eyes rolled into the back of his head, his mouth open in a silent scream. Without warning, a dozen sharp blades shot out of Vincent's back.

Neil yelped and dodged, pulling his knife back, as the blades ripped through his bomber jacket, nicking his flesh. Vincent turned on him, eyes wide as his face drooped down his skull like melted modeling clay. He held his hands to his skin, trying to push it back up, panicking.

Trecheon lifted his broken arm like a club, staring wide-eyed.

Vincent shot another sharpened lightning rod at him, cleanly missing. But that only hastened his melting face. His scream finally found a voice as all the skin, flesh, and blood sloughed off his skull and he collapsed to the floor. His brains exploded through his eye sockets, and the blades on his back shrank, forming ribs pierced through organs, though the lightning rod remained.

Neil did throw up that time. Trecheon leaned over, gagging.

Luana backed along the wall. "He… Vincent…"

The other human Natassa had been fighting stopped as well. She threw up too, then shook herself and dashed out the backdoor. Luana followed her, her hands over her mouth.

Jaska wasn't so easily deterred. "You will die for this!" He charged Trecheon.

Neil pushed aside the nausea and leapt on Jaska's back.

Jaska roared and reached back, but he only scraped a shield. Trecheon still had the sense to protect them. Neil muttered a silent thanks, then dug his feet, claws out, into Jaska's back, and wrenched his arm under Jaska's thick chin. "Where's Philip, Jaska? Answer me!"

Jaska snorted, though the snort turned into a choked sound. "As long as I draw breath, *zlodey*, you will never see him again." He reached behind him, pounded at the shield until it shattered, then grabbed Neil's jacket, and pitched forward, throwing Neil across the room. Neil managed to catch himself and roll, but every smack against the bare wood floor beat another bruise into his body.

Damianos turned the last of his electricity on the bear. But Vincent's strange lightning rod arm still held its shape and drew all the electricity to it, sapping the remaining magic from Dami. The lightning tore through Vincent's remains, shooting flesh and blood into the white walls.

Jaska charged him, teeth and claws out. Damianos' eyes widened and he leapt to the left, but Jaska caught him in the chest with his massive claws. Damianos screamed and blood flew everywhere.

Neil bellowed. Filled to the brim with adrenaline, he lifted his knife, and leapt on Jaska's back again, digging the blade into the nape of Jaska's neck. The great bear hollered, flipping his head back, stumbling. Neil ripped the blade out, curled his hand around Jaska's neck and stabbed it into his throat, spilling blood everywhere. Jaska gurgled a moment, then crashed to the ground, unmoving.

Neil left the knife and ran to Damianos. Dami lay on the ground, heaving breaths, staring blankly, hands covering the massive, jagged wounds in his chest. Neil ripped off his jacket and pressed it to the wound. *"Trecheon!"*

Trecheon stumbled over, dropping his damaged arm to the floor. "Move the jacket." Neil did and he pressed his good hand to the wound. Damianos cried out.

Tears blinded Neil, and his heart pounded. He gripped Dami's hand, but the Athánatos' grip was weak, so very weak... *Not Dami, not Dami, for Draso's sake, please not Dami!* "Trecheon--"

"I'm struggling," Trecheon said, his voice shaking. The wound slowly started healing, but blood still spilled everywhere, staining Dami's yellow fur. "With all the fighting and my weak healing and the constant shielding, I'm pretty drained. The last thing I want to do is push too hard and get the acid going."

The seconds ticked away like hours. Neil pressed his forehead against Dami's shoulder, gripping his hand tight. Damianos laid his head on Neil's, shaking, his breath coming in tiny gasps. Natassa sat next to them and supported them both. She sniffled quietly, muttering something in her native language.

Trecheon stopped with a hiss and shook his hand. "Kai's bloody *wings.*"

Neil glanced down. The wound still looked angry and red, with little pools of blood in the wide gashes. His heart fell. "You didn't finish!"

"I'm totally spent," Trecheon said. "I need a moment to recharge--"

Neil pounded a fist into the wall. "Damnit!"

"Here." Angus kneeled by them now, a first aid kit in his hands. "Found this in the van. Sorry I vanished for a bit, but this was one of the stronger possibilities and I had to do something. Wrap him up. He'll be fine until Trecheon is better."

Neil snarled. "Trecheon said you have *summons.* Why the hell didn't you use them?"

"Because Sharp literally ran a car through Lysander," Angus said. "And apparently Sharp's wyvern has a venomous bite. It'll be a while before Lysander or Magna are ready to fight again." He turned to Neil. "I've got your jacket. Don't leave your knife behind."

Natassa began the long process of wrapping Damianos' massive wounds with Trecheon doing what he could to help with one arm. Neil couldn't quite make it out, but he thought he heard him muttering about the Cloak being right. Shit hit the fan.

He tried not to think about it.

Neil retrieved the knife from Jaska's throat, shaking and helpless. Blood was everywhere – the floor, the stairs, even the ceiling from Vincent and Jaska's violent deaths.

And all over Neil's fur. How much of that was Jaska's… and how much was Dami's?

And worse still… if Philip wasn't here, where was he?

CHAPTER 23

FAMILY

Zeke wandered through the palace, trying and failing to keep his magic under control. Draso's *claws*. This shouldn't be that hard. But he had woken up with magic floating about his head and hadn't been able to get rid of them all day. People *stared*.

What was all that training with Embrik for anyway? They had spent *weeks*. And control just slipped through his fingers.

Channel your emotions into your magic, Embrik had said. *Don't fight them. Use them.* And he was *trying.* All the pain, the worry, the anxiety coursed through him. He balled it up and held it close to his heart, trying to pull his magic to it. But the magic refused to cooperate and flew about his head in shining marbles, like a miniature solar system.

Why did Leah have so much control over her own magic? Even when she had been glowing, she wasn't endangering anyone. She still controlled it. And she had just as much trauma around all this as he did. Wasn't fair.

Didn't help that Pilot still hadn't broken Jaden's encryption. Andre had been up all night with him, trying to crack it. No dice. Andre looked so exhausted that Zeke insisted he stop and go sleep. He did, reluctantly, promising to return that afternoon.

A fire marble smacked into the wall, spilling ash everywhere.

Zeke cursed. This was dangerous. He left the palace and made his way to a large clearing in the middle of the garden. The well-kept trees and bushes lined a big scraggly clover lawn covered in wildflowers. It'd be beautiful if Zeke wasn't so dang upset.

Ouranos was there, with six Athánatos of various colors, talking about something Zeke couldn't quite make out. Each one wore a simple diamond pendant and several drew strange red lines in the air. Zeke chewed his lip watching them. Why did he seem so bothered by Ouranos? Or any of his Athánatos family? Something in his chest ached every time he saw them, but he didn't understand why.

Once again, he could feel his moms gripping his shoulders, whispering in his ear, holding him tight. The ache of their loss churned through him. The elemental marbles whipped about his head even faster, swirling and spinning, shooting water, ice, and pebbles into his quills.

It hurt. Why did it hurt?

He gritted his teeth. *Channel the emotions. Use them. Just like Embrik said.* If he could just control the magic, it wouldn't be so bad, even if he couldn't make it go away completely. He pulled the emotions toward his heart again, but it spread through his whole body instead, forcing more marbles of magic out from him. He tried pulling on the marbles in an effort to direct them, but they stubbornly refused to follow directions. Exhausted, Zeke sat defeated on a bench on the edge of the lawn and crossed his arms, focusing on Ouranos and the Archons talking about sealing rips in this thing called a Veil.

He sighed, then leaned on his hands. This was his heritage. Technically his home. His uncle, his aunts, where his mother came from. He had a whole family he had never been aware of, creeping in and trying to push their way into his heart. Trying to replace the family he had lost.

His mothers' phantom hands massaged his shoulders, whispering in his ear, begging him to stay. He growled.

"Zeke?"

Zeke looked up. Ouranos smiled at him, chasing away his moms' ghosts. His eyes, though pupilless, looked at him with such kindness, but Zeke couldn't convince himself to smile back. "Oh. Hi."

"Mind if I sit here a moment?" Ouranos asked.

A marble of fire whizzed through Zeke's field of vision. He flattened his ears. "Do you really want to?"

Ouranos waved a hand and gathered his elemental marbles into a ball. Then he flashed his hands forward and the magic vanished.

Zeke flicked both ears back.

Ouranos took a seat and folded his hands into his lap. "You are worried, nephew."

Zeke winced. "Don't… don't call me that. Not yet."

Ouranos paused a moment, then nodded. "I understand. My apologies." He leaned back. "Does your worry stem from your struggle to control your magic?"

Zeke wrung his hands together. Magic built under his collar and rippled through his fur, but he pushed it back as best he could. "Yeah. Partially."

"You also worry for Jaden, Embrik, and Alexina."

"I mean, yeah," Zeke said. "But it still feels kind of… abstract. I don't even know if they're alive."

"Andre and Leah then," Ouranos said. "They are more concrete."

Zeke looked away, his tail lashing. "Leah… she's facing that bad trauma and I'm worried she's going to hurt herself. But she's such a strong-willed person, even if she doesn't believe it. She gets tunnel vision and it's hard to change her mind on something. I know she's going to keep going anyway, but I feel like it's my job as her partner to keep her from pulling some stunt. And she has a better case too. She can't hurt with her magic and she has perfect control."

"Perhaps," Ouranos said.

Zeke formed fists, tightening them until it hurt. "And Andre… He shouldn't be involved with this at all. He should be hiding away here and staying safe." He leaned forward. "But with my magic doing this, I can't protect either of them." He gritted his teeth. It wasn't right to blame his magic. This was on him. *Good god, I'm a mess. Lashing out, letting my magic control me. I should be* better *than this…*

"I also struggled with my magic when I was first bound."

Zeke turned to Ouranos.

Ouranos offered him a sad smile. "I am unsure how much you know about how magic is distributed amongst our people, but most of us are only granted immortality. It is only the royalty who have any magical ability. As a long-lived people with few historical examples and massive gaps in our history, this means we have very little in the way of help if someone struggles to control that magic."

"So what do you do then?" Zeke asked.

"Fight with it, mostly," Ouranos said. "Which goes against the nature of Athánatos. Culturally we are pastoral and peaceful. Some of us even question the point of the jewels granting us magic, when the Veil protects us from the outside world and we are not prone to fighting with ourselves. Though that belief was questioned when Theron began his mad attack on us all."

Zeke closed his eyes a moment, huddling in on himself, ears flat. "My grandfather."

"No," Ouranos said, his voice dark. "He was an enemy, nothing more. He lost his right to any family or royal titles." He released a breath. "Regardless. We are not typically a people of war. Elemental magic, however, is mostly regarded as a tool of war. So we believe that if one struggles with it, the only way to learn control is to learn war."

"But I did that," Zeke said. He stared at his hands, as little tongues of fire and drops of water danced on his palms. "Embrik worked with me for weeks during the war. And in battle, it was generally fine, but then we got back and couldn't find Jaden all this stuff with Andre and Leah came up and…"

Ouranos turned to him. "I had done this too. I spent decades learning war. And while those were valuable lessons when war came to my door, they did nothing to help me control my magic. It only fed my anxiety and fear, and made me associate the elements with stress and battle. So when stress overtook me, my control waned."

Zeke's tail swished slowly. "Like me."

"Indeed," Ouranos said.

"But you have control," Zeke said.

Ouranos held up a hand. "I do now. War was not a good teacher. I needed a different one."

Zeke tilted his head. "Who?"

"My mother," Ouranos said. "She taught me peace. Meditation. Music. And those, in turn, taught me control."

Zeke lifted one brow and grimaced. "Meditation."

"It is a slower process," Ouranos said. "Because one of meditation's teachers is patience and patience requires time."

"We don't *have* time."

"We have some time," Ouranos said. "If only we look for it." He stood. "Zeke, would you accompany me while I repair rips in the Veil? I can teach you what I know and start you on this journey, if you so choose."

Zeke flicked his ears. "What good am I to rips in the Veil? I don't even know what that is."

"The rips can only be repaired by members of the royal family," Ouranos said. "You are royalty. It would be a good lesson in patience, and I could teach you a little of our history while we travel."

Zeke wrinkled his snout. "Can I think about it a moment?"

"Certainly," Ouranos said. "We will be splitting into search parties in about five minutes though."

Yikes. "Yeah… Thanks."

Ouranos bowed, then walked back to the Archons.

Zeke picked at a loose thread on his pants. Why was he hesitant to go? Not like he could do anything else. Trecheon set down the rule that he couldn't go on assassination hunts.

Deep down, he knew Trecheon was right.

But why did it feel wrong to go with Ouranos?

His moms clung to his shirt, their claws digging in.

Screw that. Screw everything. He needed to be useful. This was being useful.

Hey Leah, I'm gonna go with Ouranos and fix rips in this veil thing. Okay?

No answer.

Uh oh. Was Leah still mad at him about yesterday? She hadn't seemed that way last night. *Leah?*

Yeah. Her voice sounded hesitant. That burning hot pan smell returned. *Be careful.*

Zeke pushed his glasses higher on his snout. *You okay?*

Yeah, Leah said, the smell returning two-fold. *Fine.*

Zeke breathed deeply. *I'm... I'm sorry for what I said yesterday. It wasn't right.*

It's fine. But the smell of angry hot peppers burned his nose.

Leah...

It's fine, Leah said. *Be careful.*

Zeke exhaled. It definitely wasn't fine. But he knew better than to push her. *Yeah. Sure.*

Leah didn't respond.

Zeke snorted. *Screw this whole day.* He stood and walked to Ouranos. "Hey. I'm ready. When do we start?"

Ouranos smiled. "Now, if you like. Follow me. Have you ever ridden before?"

Zeke's ears went cold. "...Ride? Like horses?"

Ouranos chuckled. "Not exactly. Let me take you to the stables."

CHAPTER 24

MISSING

Leah sat on the wicker couch in Andre's makeshift office, with Sacha on her left and Ethos on her right. She leaned back, chewing her lip.

Trecheon and Neil should have called by now.

The Black Cloak's message yesterday hung about her like chains. She didn't want to say anything, but she noticed the Cloak never said they'd get Philip if they left today instead of last night. Just that Philip would die if they left sooner.

So yeah, maybe they avoided disaster last night. But that didn't mean there wouldn't be problems today.

"I know I'm asking this in vain," Sacha said, leaning on the couch arm and glancing at Andre. "But I'm bored. Found anything yet?"

Andre sat back cursing. He wiped his eyes and yawned loudly. "No."

Ethos flicked her ears back. "You should have slept more."

"Can't."

"Zeke will murder us all if you kill yourself from lack of sleep," Ethos said. "I'd rather not be burned alive."

"I'm fine." Andre shook himself and slapped his face. "Just need coffee." He paused. "Do you Athánatos have coffee?"

"Here." Melaina walked in with a tray of ornate mugs and passed them around. "It is not easy to get, but those of us confined to the mainland during the war developed a taste for it." One of the palace staff walked in with a tray carrying a small pitcher and a bowl of something brown and grainy. Melaina thanked the staff member and took the tray. "Milk and *záchari*. A sweetener made from the *zácharienno* plant. It is akin to the 'raw sugar' you get on the mainland."

Andre picked up the mug and took a sip. He smiled, melting into the chair. "Just what I needed." He glanced at the pitcher of milk. "Cow's milk?"

"Ah, no," Melaina said. "We raise llamas and *gída-nadé*, a cousin of the goat. That is essentially goatmilk."

Andre raised an eyebrow, but poured a little in his mug, with a spoonful of the *záchari* and stirred it up. He sipped it, then raised both eyebrow. "Wow, good stuff." He grinned. "Thanks."

Melaina bowed, smiling, then passed the pitcher and bowl around for everyone else.

Leah prepared a cup of coffee and sipped it cautiously.

You're sitting here in perfect comfort, drinking coffee without a care and Trecheon and Neil are out risking their lives for their loved ones, the Thought Monster spat into her mind. *That should be you. You should be with them. You should be looking for Jaden. He's counting on you. The supposed Guardian material.*

Leah held her breath. *I am Guardian material. Jaden said so himself.*

He'd take it back seeing you now. Failing at your one task. What is wrong with you?

She scrunched her face up.

Sacha's pendant beeped. Leah lifted her head. Sacha frowned and put her coffee down. "Neil?"

"Philip is *gone!*" Neil shouted over the comm. His ears lay flat against his skull.

Leah's whole body buzzed.

Sacha sat up now. "What?"

"The house is empty!" Neil said. "Right down to the carpets! And Dami…"

Sacha held out a hand. "Neil, slowly. What happened?"

Neil took several slow breaths. He recounted everything that happened. Leah's stomach roiled as she listened. She picked at the guard hairs on her tail. Neil growled as he finished the story. "I have no idea where Theophania took him…"

Leah perked her ears. "Theophania?"

"His foster parent."

Oh Draso.

Ethos stuck her head in now. "Built woman, ex military?"

Neil narrowed his gaze at her, but nodded.

Leah shook herself. "And you said you heard Philip screaming?"

"Yeah, but we couldn't *find him* anywhere--"

"You wouldn't," Ethos said.

"Neil…" Leah said quietly. "I know that Theophania. She was one of Ackerson's in Team Chaos. A Wish Duster. She's an illusionist. She makes people see or hear their worst nightmares."

Neil's ears paled. "Oh *Christ.*"

Ethos glanced at her. "What did she do to you?"

Leah picked at her tail. "She made me think my team had abandoned me. And made Zeke think Jaden shot his parents in front of him."

Everyone grew silent for a moment.

Leah pulled at her tail hairs. "You can fight back though, if you just refuse to believe it. It doesn't affect you. Didn't for me anyway, when her partner Vera did the same thing. I think they have the same magic…"

"Well," Sacha finally said. "Good news is that means Philip is probably alive. Bad news, it means she's been in on this from the beginning."

Neil cursed loudly.

Sacha let him shout himself out before speaking. "How's Dami now?"

Trecheon pressed his face into the hologram. "Not great, but alive. My magic gave out though. Gotta wait until it comes back."

Sacha's face went blank. "Let me see him."

Trecheon raised an eyebrow, but he maneuvered the pendant so Dami was in full view. The yellow and black streaked Athánatos lay on the ground, resting fitfully, gripping Neil and Natassa's hands. The bloodied bandages didn't look good.

Leah's face grew fully neutral now, out of habit. A healer's mask. Don't let the injured know how bad it is. Don't let them despair or they'd sabotage their own healing.

Don't let their loved ones freak out and stress the patient.

Trecheon narrowed his gaze, clearly trying to read Sacha's expression. Some healers had tells, though usually things only other experienced healers could really recognize. Izzy, for example, had a subtle twitch in the ear, and one of Leah's mentors let his voice get so neutral he almost sounded bored.

Sacha though, was much harder to read. Her face was so steady, so calm. Which could almost be a sign in itself. One whisker on her left side twitched slightly. One of her more subtle tells. Not good, but Leah kept it to herself.

Sacha eyed Trecheon. "And how are *you?*"

"Fine," Trecheon said. "Just the biomech. The other arm, of course, so now I've got two busted arms."

Leah flicked her ears back. "We still have Pilot's scans. M-Maybe Pilot can get started on fabrication."

Trecheon shrugged. "It'd be easier to go to my apartment."

"No," Ethos and Sacha said together.

He glanced off.

Ethos narrowed her gaze. "Trecheon, I cannot emphasize enough how bad an idea going to the apartment would be. You'd be signing your death warrant. Don't. Go."

Trecheon glared at her, teeth bared. "You don't control me anymore."

"This isn't about *control.*"

"So do *you* have anything that can help me?" he demanded. "Parts, fabricators, spare arms? Because these Zyearth parts don't fit well and I have limited mobility when I need it the *most.*"

Ethos flicked her ears back. "Sorry. No."

"Of course not," Trecheon said. He rotated his bad shoulder and turned to Sacha. "Just get me the parts. Better than nothing. But only slightly."

Ethos pressed next to Leah, chewing her lip. "So Luana and Florina escaped, but Jaska's dead now?"

"And Vincent," Neil said. He rubbed one arm. "He... Christ, how do I even describe that?" He ran his hand down his face. "I stabbed his shoulder and a bunch of knives exploded out his back and... and turned into ribs and organs and shit when he died." He gagged. "Christ *almighty,* I'm gonna have nightmares about that for years."

Andre shuddered. "Holy mother of *Christ.*"

"Body morpher," Leah said. "More Wishing Dust. Ari… she and I saw it with Sharp."

"Hopefully not like this," Neil said. "His face melted off his skull when he died."

Trecheon gagged and turned away.

"He overloaded," Pathos said, walking into the room. Logos stood next to her, frowning. "When a morpher uses too much power at once, they can't compensate and end up exploding parts of their own bodies." She lowered her gaze. "This is the first I've heard of a body morpher transforming themselves into metal though. I suspect this is new. And greatly untested." Her face softened.

"You have to bring Philip back." Neil said, ears flat. "You told us you still had some of your resources. Use that."

Ethos folded her hands together. "I'm sorry Neil… But if I try to get into the systems to get information on Philip's whereabouts using our credentials, Ackerson will pick it up immediately. He'll move Philip. Or worse, kill him." She paused, silent, though Leah picked up the subtle hint.

Philip might already be dead.

Ethos looked away. "I wish I had more for you, and I understand what you're going through. I'm sorry."

Neil stared a moment, then gritted his teeth. "Don't. Give. Me. *Sorry.*" He stood. "I took out El Dorado's most notorious mob boss, and a goddamned magic smuggler, and you *set me up* to kill her because you wanted her dead too, and what do I get? *My whole family is dead.* I'll never see Philip again. And you give me *sorry?* You claim you *understand?* How the hell can you pretend you understand loss like I do?"

Ethos flicked an ear back. "Ackerson--"

"Don't give me excuses," Neil said. "I don't give a shit if Ackerson was the one pulling the strings. *You* were the ones pulling the trigger. And now I've lost Philip too! *Are you freakin' happy now?"*

Pathos stepped forward. "Neil, you have to understand--"

"No I don't," Neil said. "All I understand is Philip is gone and you can't do a goddamned thing about it, and you can't even use your supposed power to find him!"

Andre pushed between Ethos and Leah and met Neil's gaze. "I'll find him."

SONG

Zeke looked up at the giant mule stag towering over him in the massive stable box. "You have *got* to be kidding me."

The stag stood at least two meters tall at the shoulder, sporting a dark gray coat with white spots, white fur fluffed up on his chest, a white snout… and two massive tusks protruding out of the top of his mouth, which dropped below his chin. He snorted hot breath at Zeke, fogging his glasses, glaring at him with fierce brown eyes. His polished silver antlers gleamed in the beams of sun poking through the stable ceiling, and he wore a dark green bridle with no bit.

Ouranos grinned, standing next to a different stall. "They are majestic creatures, are they not?"

"They freakin' *terrifying,*" Zeke said.

The stag narrowed his eyes, and Zeke could swear he smirked before lifting his head high, almost proud.

Ouranos chuckled. "I am sure he takes that as a compliment."

"Sure."

"They *can* understand us," Ouranos said. "To a degree. Like us, they are long lived, though they need no jewels to be so. Caj there is older than Matthew. He leads the pack and has been with us for long enough that he has picked up quite the vocabulary."

"Pack," Zeke echoed. "Don't deer run in herds?"

"Herbivore deer, perhaps." Ouranos walked to Caj and stroked his chest. The stag pressed his head against Ouranos, closing his eyes. "But the mule deer on Athánatos are omnivores, leaning mostly on the carnivorous side. So we call their groups packs."

"Holy *hell,* " Zeke said. "What do they eat?"

"Fish, mostly," Ouranos said. "Sometimes birds if they can catch them. On rare occasions a wolf pup or a fawn from the herbivore deer on the island."

"Jesus," Zeke said. "And you expect me to *ride* that?"

"You will ride Caj's youngest daughter, Kia," Ouranos said. He nodded to the stall behind Zeke. Zeke turned and found a much more reasonably sized deer, standing about a meter and a half at the shoulder. Just tall enough to look Zeke in the eye.

But her antlers branched chaotically, and added at least another half meter to her height. "Didn't you say daughter?"

Ouranos carefully pulled Caj out of his stall. "Yes. The doe have antlers too, and unlike the males, they do not shed. They just continue to grow. Helps them defend fawns. Males can get quite aggressive around them." He nodded. "Open the stall, take her bridle, and follow me. She's very mellow and will follow Caj." He headed out of the stable.

Zeke eyed Kia. She looked up at him with, ironically, doe eyes, and almost seemed to smile. He sighed, picked up her bridle, and opened the stall. Like Ouranos said, she fell into line behind her father. Zeke frowned following next to her. What had he gotten himself into?

It only got worse when Ouranos told them they rode deer bareback. It took far too long to get Zeke comfortably on Kia's back. It had been easier riding Rashard through a blizzard. Thankfully Kia was very patient with him.

Once he finally got settled, Ouranos spoke gently to Caj and they traveled into the woods near the villages. Bird songs filled the air, mixing with the gentle rustling of leaves swaying in the breeze and everything smelled strongly of pine and mahogany.

"It is good to have the mule deer back again," Ouranos said. "When the Basileus started losing his mind, I released all our animals for their own safety. Thankfully Caj and his pack returned to us the moment they knew it was safe."

Zeke clutched to the reins, trying to stay balanced. "Do you use them often?"

"Depends," Ouranos said. "Athánatos is quite a lot larger than it appears to be from the mainland. It takes about a day to travel its length by deer-drawn carriage." He frowned. "Neil suggested we use the Veil to create portals between each realm, though some are wary that this will cause more unintended rips, and rightly so. We will only use them in emergencies. The Veil protects us, so this is why we must periodically hunt for rips and repair them."

"What is the Veil?"

"It is a magical shield to protect us from outsiders," Ouranos said. "It is why the mainlanders call this The Vanishing Island. They can see it from the outside, but the Veil prevents them from entering the island. It 'vanishes' if they get too close. Only rips in the Veil can allow for anyone to go on or off."

Zeke pushed his glasses up on his nose and carefully rebalanced. "So that portal we took on Sol…"

"The only planned portal on or off the island, for now," Ouranos said. "And I plan to seal it as soon as I am able. I do not believe it safe."

Kia carefully ducked under a low hanging tree branch. Zeke followed her example. "And we're out here looking for rips. How will I know when I see one?"

Ouranos clicked at Caj and they turned left. "There are several possible signs. A floating portal. A shimmer in the air. Matthew called some of the rips 'glitches,' saying they were reminiscent of the electronic problems Pilot faces. But for a royal, the biggest sign is *feel.*" He turned to Zeke. "Your first lesson, Zeke. Feel for the rip. It will feel uncomfortable, unfamiliar, sometimes even dreadful. Nothing like your normal state."

Zeke flicked his ears back. "My normal state is already in turmoil."

"Which is why this is a good exercise," Ouranos said. "Because in order to recognize the turmoil around you, you need to calm the turmoil in yourself. Kia can lead the way. Hold the reins loosely. Take deep breaths. Reach for your senses and let them guide you. If you find yourself focusing too much on what you see, close your eyes and let your other senses take over." He smiled. "And know that this will take several tries to get right. You will need time."

Zeke slashed his tail. *We don't have time!* But he bit his tongue. He closed his eyes and focused his other senses, trying to remember grounding exercises. Hearing first. *I hear… birds. Leaves rustling. Wind blowing by quills. The clip-clop of our steeds.*

Andre screaming for help.

His eyes flashed open and he glanced around frantically for his friend. But they were deep in the woods now, far from the village and palace. His fur puffed up slightly. That wasn't real. Andre was fine. He was safe.

Try again.

Feeling next. *I feel… the soft, rough leather of the reins. A breeze against my skin. The coarse hair of the doe under me.*

Mom and Mama gripping my coat, digging their claws into my flesh.

He jolted again, opening his eyes, and nearly falling off Kia. She shifted her weight to catch him, snorting loudly, but thankfully stopping his fall. He let go of the reins and hugged himself, checking for scratches.

Nothing. Nothing but shaking.

"Deep breaths," Ouranos said again.

Zeke breathed deeply, letting the shakes run through him. He held Kia's reins again and she practically purred at him. *Deep breaths…* Perhaps… smell next. *I smell… pine. The sea salt, floating through the air. The musk of stag.*

The stink of Leah's blood from the rifle wound.

He gritted his teeth. *No!*

But then… Ouranos started singing.

Sisters brave,

Sisters free,

Meeting under mahogany tree,

Facing their mother,

Wild and wrong,

Fighting back Shadows,

With a new song.

Zeke opened his eyes and stared at Ouranos. He spoke in the Athánatos language, but the words translated in Zeke's head, courtesy of Archángeli. The translation was slightly out of sync, but somehow the juxtaposition made the melody that much more beautiful. Ouranos continued.

Sisters afraid,
Sisters four,
Sealing their fate,
Closing the door.

Zeke closed his eyes, focusing on the scents again, letting Ouranos' song keep him grounded. *I smell wildflowers. Fresh, clean water. A faint smell of a fire, cooking.* He breathed deeply, slowly, deliberately.

The First is the Purge
Erasing our minds,
The Second, the Seal,
Hiding our shame,
The Third is the Veil,
Protect us from hurt,
And the Fourth is the Cloak,
Our ally, alert.

Oh, Four Sisters,
Statues in slate,
Holding us close,
Lying in wait.

Ouranos started the song over, though quieter this time, forcing Zeke to focus his hearing to understand it. And as he focused, his other senses focused too, chasing away his lingering fears. Peace he hadn't known in years washed over him as his surroundings grounded him. A taste of salty ocean air, a particularly complicated bird song, the feel of Kia's fur as he lay his hands on her neck…

Then a spike of something sharp rushed through his mind, breaking his peace and turning his attention left. He opened his eyes and stared into the woods.

And he saw it. A tiny shimmer in the air. "Glitchy" as Ouranos had said.

A rip in the Veil.

"There." He pointed.

Ouranos clapped his hands. "Fantastic, nephew!" He frowned. "My apologies. Zeke." But he smiled. "An excellent first attempt. And you seemed to find yourself again, if only for a little while."

"Yeah," Zeke said. He smiled back. "Thanks."

"Of course." Ouranos slid off Caj and walked to the rip. "I will seal this one and teach you how to seal them with the next one."

"I assume that since you have portals open on purpose, you can also create them."

"I can," Ouranos said. He ran his hands over the shimmering air, muttering quietly. The shimmer slowly faded. "I can teach you that too, if you like."

"I would, actually. Eventually."

"Very well." Ouranos hopped back up on Caj. "I will find the next one. Practice your meditations."

Zeke nodded. "That song… Was that about Judgement? Alexina and Embrik gave us a little info about her."

Ouranos breathed deeply. He whistled at Kia and she walked up beside Caj. "Yes. A song of our history," he said. "The story of Judgement, her creation, and her defeat, temporary as it was. The song is… incomplete. Likely because of the Purge." He flicked an ear and his tail twitched.

"Judgement was a Basilea of Athánatos. And it was she who created Shadow Cast."

Zeke frowned. "I remember Alexina telling us that. So those four titles…"

"The Four Sisters magic fighting Judgement back," Ouranos said. "Judgement's daughters. The Seal sealed away Judgement, making it impossible to summon her again. The Purge erased the memories of the Shadow Cast, Judgement, and all surrounding events from our minds and histories. The Veil created the Veil we see today, cutting us off from the outside world. This is as much to protect us as it is to protect the world *from* us. And finally, the Cloak, an outside ally, passed down through generations should they ever be needed."

Zeke frowned. "Hold on. You said the Seal prevented Judgement from being summoned."

"It did, once," Ouranos said. "But much of the Four Sister's magic is failing. You can see it in the statues outside the palace. I will show you sometime, when the situation is not so dire." He looked off. "It is only a matter of time before all the magic fails."

Zeke's bones buzzed. "What then?"

Ouranos tensed, his quills on end. "I do not know."

Zeke and Ouranos spent the next three hours finding and sealing the rips. Zeke got better and better at finding the rips just by feel and watched with fascination while Ouranos sealed each one.

But when it came time for him to try it himself, it ended in disaster. Zeke sat hard on the forest floor, defeated. "I can't do it."

"It takes patience, Zeke," Ouranos said. "Let us try once more. Pick a familiar element."

Zeke sighed. He lit his hand ablaze.

"Weave the magic through either side of the rip," Ouranos said. "Think of it like sewing fabric together."

"I don't know how to sew."

Ouranos chuckled. "Another activity we can try sometime then, perhaps. I find sewing very grounding. It might be beneficial to you."

Zeke's tail twitched. "That's not helpful *now.*"

"Try to picture what you know of sewing," Ouranos said. "Weave the magic."

Zeke tried on and off for nearly twenty-five minutes, but couldn't get a single weave to work. He growled. "Ugh… I give up."

Ouranos gripped his shoulder firmly. "There is a skill to it. We will try again after you are more comfortable with your magic. I will take over from here."

By the time they finished their sector, Zeke was worn out and famished, though despite his failure with the seal, more content then he had been since… well, since he met Leah, really. Maybe even before that. And Ouranos… Maybe Zeke did have room in his heart for Ouranos as family.

A spike of pain shot through his chest. He frowned. Maybe not. Not yet.

After a quick trot back to the palace, they put Caj and Kia in their respective stalls and Ouranos made sure they had plenty of food and water. As a pair of stable hands walked in to help out, he slipped a handful of pecans and blackberries to Zeke. "It is her favorite treat," he said.

Zeke held them out to Kia, which she ate quickly before rubbing her nose against his head, making him chuckle.

Ouranos smiled. "Next time, I will teach you how to brush them, but for now, let us eat." They entered the palace.

"I should call Leah for food," Zeke said. He reached into his mind. *Hey Leah, we're back. I'm starved and Ouranos is getting lunch. Wanna join us?*

We've ah, got a situation here actually…

Zeke's fur stood on end. *Uh oh. What's going on?*

Philip is missing, Leah said, and she gave a breakdown of everything that happened. The shock running through Zeke's fur grew as she spoke.

Ouranos perked an ear. "Is everything okay?"

"Give me a moment," Zeke said. He reached out for Leah again. *So what's the plan? What are we gonna do?*

We wait, Leah said. *It's not great, but we don't have a choice until we find Philip.*

But who's looking for him if we're all waiting?

A smell of hot peppers and chilled alcohol ripped through Zeke's senses. *Andre is.*

CHAPTER 26

PARTING

Zeke stood in the palace's royal chambers his body buzzing with worry.

Andre had all his equipment packed up and on his back and shoulders, staring at the portal to get back to the mainland.

And leave Zeke behind. In a home that was both his and not his.

Taking away his best friend. Again.

His mind replayed his conversation with Andre on repeat, trying to figure out where he went wrong. Where he had lost him.

Zeke had run into Andre's makeshift office, his ears ringing, just as Andre finished packing the last of his stuff. "You're *leaving?*"

Andre had paused, staring a moment at Zeke. He chewed his lip, then flung his bags on his shoulders. "I got to."

"But *why?*"

"Wi-fi's no good here," Andre said. "Something about the Veil getting in the way. And I gotta get this kid, Zeke."

Zeke searched for any excuse to keep him here. "Andre, you aren't trained in this…"

"I found and decrypted your moms' files," Andre said. "Deep in restricted vaults, connected directly to Ackerson. I still got my in." He turned to the doe. "They'll give me what they have, and I'll find him."

Zeke twitched an ear. "That'll put you on Ackerson's radar."

"So what?" Andre said. "I already am being with Chad and being friends with you. Might as well go full tilt."

"Andre, that's *dangerous,"* Zeke said.

"So's Philip being with a nightmare-producing monster."

"But…" Zeke chewed his lip, then took Andre's hand. "This is putting you right in the path of Ackerson's Angels. Didn't we say no trails when you decrypted my moms files?"

"This is different," Andre said. "This is a living person in danger. Ain't the same."

Zeke winced. That stung, even though he knew Andre was right. Both Zeke's ears flattened now. "How the hell are you gonna fight back if Angel comes after you? You don't have magic."

"Don't matter," Andre said. "A kid's in danger and I ain't gonna stand by if I can do something."

"But--"

"There is no 'but', Zeke," Andre said. "I have to do this."

And he had let go of Zeke's hand.

Zeke flexed his fingers now, feeling cold and empty. He couldn't stop Andre from leaving.

And he couldn't leave with him. His magic kept him bolted to this spot, to protect his friends and allies as much as himself.

Andre, Chad, Pathos, Logos, and Sacha were all going. The Fawns claimed they had a safehouse where Andre could work in peace and where everyone on the mainland could sleep on decent beds.

Never mind that all their resources were compromised and Ackerson likely knew everything about them, but whatever.

Chadwick wouldn't leave Andre's side.

Sacha confided in Leah that she didn't trust the Fawns. Understandable. Despite everything they had been through, Zeke wasn't sure he trusted them either. Though she hid her true motives saying she needed to go take care of Damianos' injuries before they got worse.

But that left Zeke and Leah alone on this island, paralyzed to do anything.

The magic marbles around his head doubled now, both in size and number, flying about in panicked solar system of elements. No ancestral song would fix it. His heart ached.

Leah walked up to him and slipped her hand in his. He clung to her, though a twinge in his mind wedged itself between them, reminding him that Leah had perfect control and wasn't a liability with her magic the way he was. He was the one holding them back.

Andre turned and met Zeke's eyes. "It's gonna be alright, brother."

Zeke pressed his lips together. He turned to Pathos and Logos. "It better be."

"Trust them, Zeke," Ethos said, walking next to him. She had offered to stay behind for when Pilot broke Jaden's encryption. She met his eyes. "Like you trusted us in the war."

Zeke flattened his ears.

Andre frowned deeply. He passed his bags to Chadwick then drew Zeke into a bear hug.

Zeke buried his face in Andre's neck, gripping his shirt and holding him tight. His brain recorded everything - his scent, the feel of his hands, his breathing, his heartbeat, everything. It could be the last time.

It could be the last time.

Andre snuggled into Zeke's fur. "I just got you back," he said. "I ain't losing you again. I'll be back. I'll be fine."

Zeke squeezed him again, but couldn't speak.

Slowly Andre pulled back. He offered a sad smile, then turned to Leah. "Take care of him, okay?" He flashed finger guns at her.

She smiled softly and flashed fingers guns back at him.

Then Andre got his bags back from Chad and they all walked through the portal. Ouranos, true to his word, sealed it up.

And they were gone.

Leah gripped Zeke around the middle and buried her face in his chest. He held her tight, unable to look away.

He didn't know how long he stood there staring.

CHAPTER 27

SAFEHOUSE

Trecheon's body buzzed with worry sitting in the back of the disguised van that came to pick his team up from Philip's old house.

About an hour after the call to Sacha, two vans showed up with some bullshit carpet cleaning and instillation business plastered on it, and several zyfaunos and people in dirty jumpsuits hopped out. Trecheon had been ready to shoot them on sight, but Angus waved him back. "They're with the Fawns," he said.

That did little to change Trecheon's desire to shoot them.

They came in, carefully rolled Damianos in a fake carpet roll, then got him into the van. They passed out uniformed coveralls to everyone else and began cleaning. Packing up bodies, bleaching out blood, replacing destroyed flooring, even panting. Like it never happened.

Efficient.

One of the workers, a familiar gray cat, took the driver's seat of one of the vans. Trecheon unzipped his jumpsuit and gripped his gun with his one good hand. One suspicious move and she was done.

"You can let the gun go, Trecheon," the cat said. She turned to him, her green eye sparkling with orange dust. "One of my Wishes prevents guns from firing around me. The other protects me from mage magic."

Trecheon cursed.

The drive through town in a dark, windowless van unnerved him, but he managed to keep it together and work on healing Dami. He certainly wasn't perfect, but he was a hell of a lot better by the time they got to wherever they were going. Eventually the van stopped and the back doors opened.

And they had their safehouse. A broken down, cavernous warehouse, long abandoned, in some Draso-forsaken suburb, with tinted windows, almost no light, and no electricity. Just blankets for warmth, batter-powered fans for cooling, and a lifetime supply of flashlights. The air stank, and the walls, strangely, absorbed every sound, deadening everything to the point where it almost felt like a coffin.

At least the cots were new and relatively comfortable. A shame there was no privacy.

The gray cat did have something for Neil and Trecheon though. All their effects from their apartments, or at least the stuff the Fawns deemed "important." Computers, phones, etc, plus a few clothes, an old hoodie, and, oddly enough, camouflage makeup and balaclavas from his assassin days. He didn't even know he had that anymore.

Though all of the electronics had had their histories wiped and internet connections permanently disabled. At least Trecheon could still play Snake and Tetris.

The black cat passed out water, canned food, and army rations, with no utensils or napkins. Trecheon triple checked the seals on everything before he'd let anyone eat it.

Sacha and the others showed up soon after and she immediately went to work on Damianos, her healer's mask on fully. Damianos had long passed out and didn't even react to her poking and prodding the wounds.

Neil wouldn't leave his side. The pain in his face physically hurt to look at.

While Sacha worked, the cat led Andre and his equipment downstairs. Chadwick went with him, but so did Trecheon. Don't trust anyone. Thankfully though, it was just a simple room, the only room with electricity, and the only place Andre could work.

And work he did. All day. Hardly ate or drank, just pressed his nose to the computer, searching databases for any sign of Philip, sweat beading down his face from the computer's heat dump.

But night came, and he had nothing. Chadwick had to wrestle him into bed. With nothing else to do, the rest of the gang picked cots and drifted into uneasy sleep. Only Sacha and Trecheon stayed up, working their magic on Dami while they could.

"Healing therapy," Sacha called it. "Normally we'd have equipment and round the clock healing to help with it, but we'll have to make do." She gently rubbed Dami's shoulder before pulling a blanket over him. She leaned over, totally spent. "We have to."

Trecheon lifted his now-repaired arm, listening to it squeak and stall. The part Sacha's fabricator made didn't quite work, and it made movement from the shoulder almost impossible. Draso, what he wouldn't give for one of his spare arms…

"Sorry," Sacha said. "My fabricator is really meant for Zyearth parts. Trying to get an Earth part with just scanning and no plans was probably bound to fail. But at least the arm is in the socket again."

Trecheon sighed. "Sure."

Sacha watched him a moment, then stood up. "I'm gonna hit the sack. Get me if he gets worse, though I don't expect he will. He could probably heal just fine on his own now, if we weren't in such a dire situation ourselves." She sighed. "If nothing changes, wake me in four hours. I should be good to hit him again."

"Sure," Trecheon said again, flexing his fingers. They stalled too. "I should be good… soon. Then I'll see what I can do."

Sacha nodded and made her way to an empty cot.

Trecheon turned the sound off on his phone and pulled up Tetris again. Might as well do something to pass the time. But after the fifth failure based solely on glitchy fingers, he had had enough. God, he needed his spare.

He bit his lip. What would it take to get it?

The Fawns had permanently disabled his internet. But Andre had to get internet from *somewhere.*

He glanced at the cots. No one moved. Even Sacha had already passed out. He did what he could do for Damianos' healing, then headed down to Andre's little box. No one guarded it.

Then he pulled up his phone. They might have removed his Wi-Fi capabilities, but they never said anything about hardwire. Fifteen minutes of fiddling later and he got his phone on Andre's secure connection.

He went straight to his home and office security system.

This was one of the most idiotic things he had ever done.

But the security footage was clean. The last time anyone was in that apartment or office was right after Trecheon left with Leah, Zeke, and Andre - the Fawns' agents picking up his important things. A shame they didn't think to grab his spare arms.

But his connection was secure - no one would trace him checking it. The house was just as they had left it, spare arms on the table and all. All his checks were in place - no one had messed with the cameras. The van was right there for the taking.

And he was so tired of people controlling his decisions.

After a good hour drive through the city, he pulled up to his district and parked his van in one of the alleyways several rows down from his shop. He got out, heart racing, while Ethos' words echoed in his brain. *If you go to your home, you're dead.*

This really was idiotic. Suicidal even. He paused in the alleyway, gripping his gun in his glitchy hand and trying to calm his breathing. Draso's horns, what he wouldn't give for Darvin's cloaking power right now. Or even his whole team.

Or maybe he should just go home.

He growled. *No.* He wasn't going to let the Fawns control him anymore. He turned off his cameras, flipped on his own looped footage just in case Ackerson was watching, then pulled his balaclava and hoodie out of the back of the van.

He muttered the security key for Laughing Jackal, grateful for the favors they owed him, then made his way to their shop. He'd take the back way, using the communal hallway that held customer bathrooms. In and out and back by dawn.

"Trecheon."

Adrenaline hit him like a lightning bolt and he whipped about, ripping the pistol from his belt, aiming it at a dark figure behind him. But the figure gripped his hand and pulled, catching Trecheon off balance and throwing them both to the ground, pinning Trecheon on his attacker's weight. He struggled, snarling. "Let go of me!"

"Absolutely not," a feminine voice said. "I should smash your arms to *bits* for this stunt. What the hell were you thinking?"

Trecheon blinked. Wait. "Sacha?"

"Yes, Sacha!" Sacha said. "Be grateful I found you instead of Angel."

Trecheon's eyes grew wide. "What-- how-- did you follow me?"

"In a sense," Sacha said. "I woke up, found you and the van missing, and made the logical conclusion." She shook him. "This is unbelievable. After everything the Fawns said? With all this danger? What were you thinking?"

Trecheon struggled under her. "I was thinking that I'm *useless* with the parts I have and we need all the help we can get once we can go after Philip. As I am now, I'm a liability. I need my arms."

"And this idiotic plan *isn't* a liability?" Sacha snapped.

Trecheon narrowed his gaze but didn't deny it. "Could you let me up?"

"Why should I?" Sacha said. "I'm gonna rip those arms off and drag your sorry tail home." She ran fingers over his shoulders. "Where's the release on this?"

"Sacha, just *listen,*" Trecheon said, wiggling his shoulders away from her. "No one's been here. I scanned my entire camera footage since I've been gone. The system didn't alert about anything and everything's exactly where I left it."

"As far as you know."

He twitched an ear. "Unless someone has Wishing Dust that turns them into an undetectable ghost, I'm going to assume it's fine."

"What if they're cloaked?"

Trecheon paused, but he snorted. "Cloaking would still leave traces. Doors opening. Items moving on their own. Dents in the couch cushions. Scuffs on the carpet. I know how it works. Any open doors and I would have had an alert on the system."

"Then what if it's looped footage?"

"It's not," Trecheon said. "I leave multiple clocks with the date and time all over the cameras in inconspicuous places just for this reason. Besides, any looped footage would still have my coffee pot. Zeke accidentally destroyed it when he showed me his magic to prove he's an Athánatos prince." He frowned. "He also cracked the concrete floor in my office. Damn him."

"What if they're just watching the place then?" Sacha said. "Just waiting to snipe you the moment you enter the front door."

"We're not going through the front door," Trecheon said. "All the shops here are connected by a back hallway to get to customer bathrooms. We're gonna cut through Laughing Jackal customs. I know their code."

Sacha raised an eyebrow. "We?"

"This'll go a lot faster if you come with me."

"I'm dragging your ass *home.*"

"Sach, we're already here," Trecheon said. "And you know how useless I am with those parts. We need to get these or we'll be short on people to go after Philip."

Sacha fell silent. After a moment, her weight lifted off Trecheon's back. He got up slowly, rubbing his head. "Ow."

Sacha sighed. "I'm going to regret this."

"I already do," Trecheon said. "Follow me."

Cutting through Laughing Jackal and sneaking into Trecheon's office was a breeze. Almost too easy, but Trecheon didn't question it. And just like he saw on the cameras, everything was completely untouched.

"Okay," he said. "We have limited time." He passed her a list and a shoulder bag. "This is what I want. Find what you can and let's get out of here."

"Thought you were just getting you arms."

"I am," Trecheon said. "But I need proper repair tools. And a few keepsakes."

She glanced over his list and her ears drooped. "Matt's music sheet from Christmas, the scarf I made you last year, the family ornaments, teammate's dog tags… Shouldn't you be focusing on what you *need?*"

He turned to his war memorial in silence and carefully picked off every dog tag, picture, and Carter's last message, dropping them into a pocket in his bag.

Sacha flicked her ears back. "I can make you a new scarf, hun."

Trecheon stared at her a moment, his mind wandering back to that first Christmas together. *"I only picked up knitting last year,"* Sacha had said. *"You're the first one to get a gift out of it."*

He shook his head. "Trust me. I need everything on that list."

They worked in silence in the office for several minutes, picking at Trecheon's war memorial, snatching important tools from the garage for his biomech, and securing recorded camera footage. Then they headed upstairs to his apartment.

The moment they entered the living room, an eerie anxiety grabbed Trecheon's heart. He tried to push it aside, but then Sacha spoke.

"Hey… Trecheon? I have a confession to make."

He turned to her, eyes narrowed. She looked… meek. Perhaps even annoyed? What was with that expression? It filled him with dread. "What?"

She chewed her lip, her face moving quickly from one expression to the next. "I… told Matt you were the White Assassin."

CHAPTER 28

SILENCE IN THE LIVING ROOM

Trecheon met her gaze, eyes wide, his heart racing. "You… what?"

"I told Matt," Sacha said. "I… I didn't mean to, but he called right before we left Athánatos and he was asking questions about the Fawns and how they knew you and it just slipped out and--"

"You *told Matt*?" Trecheon demanded. "What did he say? How did he react? The hell were you *thinking?"*

Sacha shifted from foot to foot, her ears pasted back. "I uh… Well, remember I promised that I'd disown him if he left you?"

Trecheon's heart sank and his head buzzed with worry and stress, making him feel sick. His whole world crashed around him. "Don't tell me he--"

"I lied."

His broken heart shattered into dust now. "…You… lied…"

She rubbed her left arm. "I am so sorry, Trecheon, but the more I think about it, the more I can't do this. I can't be friends with an assassin. I won't turn you in, but when Matt and the others get here, I'm going home, and you're on your own."

Her voice faded while he stared at the ground, frozen in time, pain running like sharp needles through his veins, cementing him to the spot.

This couldn't be happening. This couldn't be *real.* Sacha... Matt... gone... Sacha betraying him... Matt leaving him... He gripped his head. No. No, no, no, *NO--*

Something thudded to the floor, and he whipped around, drawing his pistol, ready to destroy anything in his path after all he had lost.

But all he saw was a body.

A human woman with short red hair, light skin, and thick arms lay on the ground halfway behind his couch, facing away from him.

He stared, dumbfounded.

Someone crashed into him, holding him tight. He fought until he realized it was Sacha.

"Oh, thank *Draso,"* she said. "Trecheon, I couldn't see you, I could only hear you arguing, I promise, I didn't tell Matt about you being an assassin, I would never do that..."

Trecheon blinked, trying to refocus his world, focus on the body in his living room, anything but focus on Sacha telling Matt he was an assassin.

But she hadn't. It wasn't real.

Right? He didn't know what to believe.

Then his mind flashed to Neil freaking out in the house looking for Philip. And he wasn't there.

The body in the living room suddenly lost all color and collapsed to black dust on the carpet. Trecheon leapt back, and Sacha shielded them both. He lifted his pistol again, his quills catching fire.

"Trecheon."

Both he and Sacha turned. Trecheon's set his hands ablaze, his heart still racing.

A blue otter walked into the living room from his office. She frowned, her tiny ears pinned back.

Trecheon snarled, holding his hands out. "You did this."

The otter held up her palms. "Hear me out."

Trecheon bared his teeth and his quills caught fire. *"Hear you out? Hell no. Stay back--"*

"Just *listen,*" she said. "I'm one of Ackerson's--"

"I know that."

"--And I want out."

Trecheon narrowed his gaze, keeping his pistol up. The fire faded, but just slightly. "Explain."

"Ackerson is dangerous," the otter said. "We all know that. And he's trying to cover his tracks. He's using us to do so, sure, but what happens when everyone else is gone? We're next. We all know it. Everyone has an exit plan." She narrowed her gaze. "You're my exit plan."

"And we're supposed to just trust you," Sacha said, lashing her tail about.

"Of course not," the otter said. "But I have information you want. You get me out, I give you said information."

"What could you possibly--" Trecheon said.

"I know where Philip is."

Trecheon shot forward and flattened the otter against the wall, pressing the gun to her head. *"Where is he?"*

But she didn't even flinch. "Get me out and I'll tell you."

Trecheon shoved the gun harder into her skull. "Tell me or *die.*"

"I'm not afraid to die," the otter said, her expression unchanging. "Only the manner of death. A gun doesn't scare me." She pressed her eyes shut a moment, then pierced Trecheon with her gaze. "Ackerson does."

He gritted his teeth. After all the years he worked with Ackerson, he knew that intimately. He stepped back. "Fine. We--"

The door to the office opened downstairs, ringing the customer bell. "Kitta, I know you're here."

The otter's eyes grew wide. "Ronan."

Sacha's fur puffed up. "The summoner."

Trecheon formed a fist with his glitching hand. "The traitor."

"Hide," Kitta whispered harshly. "If he sees you, we're *all* dead. Go!"

Ronan's footsteps echoed up the stairs.

Trecheon cursed. He pulled Sacha into the bathroom. She furrowed her brow. "Trecheon, this is a terrible hiding spot."

"Trust me." He quietly pulled back the curtain to his shower, pulled them both in the tub, and shut the curtain again. Then he pressed a tile on the wall and a hidden door opened up, revealing a tiny room with thickly padded walls and benches.

Sacha shot him a look, which he ignored. He pulled them both inside and carefully shut the wall, dropping them in total darkness. Trecheon slid back a tiny door on the wall, and a sliver of light poked through a slitted peephole just under the windowsill. Thank god he had found that shower curtain with a transparent top half so he could survey the room.

"It's mostly sound deadened," Trecheon said quietly. "Also, before you ask, no, I've never sat in here while you took a shower."

"I respect you better than that than to ask," Sacha said. She smirked, barely visible in the dark. "Besides, if you wanted to see me naked, all you had to do was ask."

His cheeks flushed and his pants grew uncomfortably tight, but he waved her off, gazing through his peephole.

Sure enough, Ronan walked into view. He was a bit blurry through the curtain, but recognizable. Something was definitely off though. His body glitched and jolted and flashed like a broken video game character. He stared Kitta down, though he struggled to keep his head facing one direction. Next to him stood what looked like an Athánatos quilar… sort of. It wore no clothing and dripped like it was covered in thick, black mud.

And it had wings. *Wings.* Big, drippy wings. It lifted its finger and spun the black mud around the air, filling the whole apartment with a terrible, awful stench.

Judgement, Trecheon thought. *The bastard actually has Judgement.*

Kitta stood her ground against Ronan. "And what the hell are you doing here?"

"The cameras glitched out," Ronan said, his head glitching left and right. "Boss wanted me make sure everything was okay." He glanced down at the pile of black dust. "Guess it's not."

Kitta frowned and kicked at the dust. "She only had a year. Didn't expect she'd go out this soon though."

"She should have had another month," Ronan said. "Theophania stole too much."

"Tell her that."

"I just might," Ronan said. He turned to Judgement, his wings glitching now. "Can you clean that up?" The slimy summon crossed its arms, flicking mud over Kitta and Ronan. Ronan rolled his eyes. "I didn't say you were my servant. But that has lingering power in it. Might be useful to fight this ridiculous glitching."

The creature shook its head, then extended a long inky arm and wiped up all the dirt.

"Thank you." Ronan turned to Kitta. "Time to go."

Kitta flicked her fat tail. She crossed her arms. "Fine."

Ronan turned toward the exit. Kitta flashed a glance back toward the bathroom.

"Trecheon's war mementos are missing."

Kitta turned to Ronan, her fur standing on end. "What?"

"The mementos," Ronan said. "Did you take them?"

Kitta scrunched her face up. "Why would I take them?"

"Why would anybody?" Ronan said. "Except for the person who owns them." He turned to the bathroom.

Trecheon shut the peep hole immediately, cutting off all light, and shielded them both. Shit, shit, *shit.*

Quiet footsteps. The dramatic curtain pull back. Trecheon shut his eyes and grabbed Sacha's hand.

But… nothing. After a moment, the footsteps walked off, though Trecheon didn't dare open the peephole again.

"One of Ackerson's idiotic goons must have stolen it all," Kitta called, her voice muffled. "Little money grubbers probably thought they could sell it or something. Maybe you should stop looking for imaginary burglars in the shower and go find Jaden already. I got this."

A rush of wind and a smack of something heavy hitting the ground echoed against the shower walls. A second passed before Ronan spoke.

"Don't speak to me like I'm a *child,*" he said. "Lest you forget who has the universe's most powerful summon."

Kitta gagged, but then let out a choked laugh. "A loser who can't even complete the one job he's given?" More pounded body sounds, with Kitta grunting. But she laughed again. "Go ahead and kill me. Be faster than what Ackerson wants."

No! She knows where Philip is! He set his fist ablaze.

But Sacha grabbed his arm. He turned to her and she shook her head, mouthing *summon*.

He cursed quietly.

"I won't kill you," Ronan said. "Ackerson can still use you." Another body thud and Kitta cried out. "But he can use you roughed up."

There was a scuffle and Kitta screamed. "Let go of my fur! Let go!"

"Stop squirming or I'll have Judgement encase you in a Cast," Ronan said. "You'd be surprised how hard they can squeeze without actually killing you."

The scuffling stopped.

"That's what I thought." A pause. "Grab the Blood Crystal." A moment passed, then Kitta cried out again and a series of *thud, thud, thud* sounds crashed down the stairs into Trecheon's office. He listened for the front bell, his heart racing.

It rang.

Trecheon waited a good five minutes, listening for any movement, any sign they were still there. But… nothing. Carefully he slid open the wall and they climbed out into the tub.

"Get the stuff," Trecheon said. "And get out *now.* " He moved quickly, adrenaline pumping through his system faster than it had since the war.

Briefly, he glanced over where Vera's body had fallen. No leftover dust. Judgement had picked it clean.

He went to work without another word, pushing the uncomfortable image into the recesses of his mind. Add that to the list of nightmare fuel he had gathered so far with this outrageous life.

Bags full, they left, not even bothering to put Trecheon's spare arms on.

CHAPTER 29

CONSEQUENCES

"You did *what?*" Neil shouted.

Trecheon winced, his heart racing as the full weight of his idiocy hit his chest. "I know, it was stupid."

"It was more than *stupid,*" Neil said. "You put everyone here in danger. You compromised *everything.* Why would you do that?" He paused, rubbing the fur on his snout and sighing. "No, don't answer that. I know why. But goddamn it, Trecheon…"

Trecheon and Sacha had gotten back to the safehouse just as the sun peeked out over the ocean. The rosy-fingered dawn that Ouranos had so often associated with Matt. Over the years Trecheon had started associating it with Matt too, as the Guardian got up for his morning run and came back just as the sunlight hit Trecheon's apartment window.

But now it was just a symbol of how much he had screwed up. How much time he had wasted and ruined with this ridiculous stunt. He should have let Sacha drag him back.

Trecheon sat hard on a cot. "I know. Trust me, I know. The whole thing was a shit show. But it happened. Can't change it."

"At least he has his arms now," Sacha said, leaning over Damianos. He still hadn't woken up, though the wound looked better.

Though it would have been much better if Sacha had pulled Trecheon back and they had spent the night healing him. Draso's mercy, he had done so much damage.

Pathos stood tall, narrowing her gaze at Trecheon. "Trecheon--"

"Don't start," Trecheon snarled, desperate to throw the guilt and anger anywhere else. "This is your fault in the first place."

"It's our fault we're stuck in hiding," Logos said, crossing her arms. "It's not our fault that you can't follow directions."

Trecheon flattened his ears. "You said I'd die if I went home. I got out. So maybe your directions were pointless." The words felt hollow even as they left his mouth.

"Are you serious right now?"

Trecheon turned. Andre stood to his full height, glaring daggers at Trecheon.

Trecheon narrowed his gaze. "Stay out of it, Andre."

Andre flexed a hand. "You don't get it, do you? You *compromised everything.* Openly used our van, told the enemy we're looking for Philip, even gave away your one hiding spot in your apartment. And for what?"

Trecheon gritted his teeth. "These arms were useless."

"They were *damaged,*" Andre said. "Not useless. When you're on the field, you work with what you have and only pull this dangerous shit when you have no other choice." He crossed his arms. "But that wasn't the point anyway. That was the excuse. This was about fighting for agency."

Trecheon stood and stared him down. "Until you've lost *yours--*"

"*I have,*" Andre said. "We all have. The war, the military, Ackerson, the Fawns, and hell, all this friggin' trauma stole it from us. And we're all fightin' for it back. But you made a *choice* and that choice took away what little agency we *all* had. Now they know we're alive, we're angry, we're desperate for Philip." He glared. "Losing control sucks ass, but you don't win it back by taking away *everyone's* control. And that's what you did."

Trecheon hunched down, ears flat.

Andre glanced off, his face softening slightly. "But what's done is done. Can't change it. All we can do is roll with the punches." He turned to Angus. "Don't suppose you can use your timeline shit to find Philip."

Angus shrugged. "I can try." He turned to Neil, his dark eyes not quite meeting Neil's. "When and where did you see him last?"

Neil rubbed his arm. "At that house about a week ago."

Angus flicked his ears back. "Hmm. Got a lot to sift through, but it's a start. Don't expect an answer for at least a day though." He pulled out his mirror, sat comfortably on one of the cots, and began his weird meditation.

"That's a start," Andre said. "But now we're extra short on time. The enemy knows we're lookin' for him. He's a liability and not worth hangin' on to if they can't use him."

Neil cursed, burying his face in his hands.

"We need to up the efforts," Pathos said.

"We need help that I can't give," Andre said. "I ain't gonna get this done fast enough, and I doubt Angus will either. I need Pilot."

Natassa frowned. "He is attempting to break Jaden's encryption."

"And he ain't done it yet," Andre said. "It's been nearly a week, and now we have a new priority. Like it or not, this is more important." He turned back to Trecheon. "I know you mages sometimes think with your magic instead of your brains, thinkin' you're all invincible. But you ain't. And you're putting all of us in danger. Think about that next time you take away others' choice like that." He eyed Sacha and even the Fawns. "All of you."

Trecheon closed his eyes, his face twisted in agony. God… He walked off toward the far end of the warehouse.

Sacha watched him a moment, then shook her head. "I'll call Leah."

Trecheon sat hard on a rusted old bucket, letting the shame wash over him. It swirled in his mind like alphabet soup, making his head spin.

He never should have gone.

"Hey."

He turned. Pathos stood there, ears flat against her head. "Can we talk?"

He glared at her, all the shame morphing to anger. Yeah, Andre was right. Trecheon had made a shit show of this whole thing with his selfishness. But the Fawns had started the whole thing. "Here to throw my mistake in my face?"

"Here to apologize," Pathos said. "For what it's worth."

"Not much."

Pathos sighed. "I know." She turned away, hugging herself. "Our lives have been used to hurt others from the moment we could walk. We've been desperate to escape since we could form words. We had to take our one shot." She flicked her ears back. "But Andre's words hit hard. We escaped, yeah, but our choice took away any choice the rest of you had. We should have thought of that and we didn't." She stared at the ground. "I'm not making excuses. Just… looking for understanding."

Trecheon turned to her.

She met his gaze. "We're beyond hope, Trecheon. We've caused too much hurt. But you have a chance to redeem yourself. Don't let it go to waste." She walked off.

Trecheon watched her, flattening one ear.

Redeem himself. He shook his head.

Back to giving up control. Because that was apparently the only way to fix this. He stood and slowly walked back to the group like a robot, leaving a part of himself still sitting on that bucket.

CHAPTER 30

Narrow Thinking

Zeke paced back and forth in the room with all the Angels' information, listening to Pilot quietly hum while his processes worked through Jaden's encryption. His head swam.

The night had bombarded him with terrible nightmares, vicious anxiety, and the smells of trauma, though he couldn't tell if that was from Leah or his own brain. Previously the only smells he had gotten from their bond had been food related but last night he smelled the stench of blood, ash, smoke, and gunpowder, locking him in the battlefield at the War of Eons.

It never looked quite right in his mind though. Smells didn't match up with the battle he had lived through. Too often it looked like Athánatos. A peaceful village, a welcoming palace with bright gardens and colorful birds. But the scents lingered. They built in his nose, filling his head, and destroying any peace he might have found.

And all the while his parents called to him in some far-off distance. He chased them through the island, but they only grew farther away the more he ran toward them.

At least twice he woke up in a cold sweat. Leah always woke with him and got him back to sleep with her arm across his chest.

Then the nightmare started again.

"Did you get any sleep last night?" Ethos asked, breaking Zeke from his thoughts.

He paused, blinking at her, trying to focus his vision. He pressed his lips together. "No."

She raised an eyebrow. "Then sit down."

He shook his head. "No."

"Zeke." Leah met his gaze. "You need to rest." She had her tail in her lap again, pulling at the guard hairs, leaving a tiny bald patch.

Zeke flattened his ears. "But--"

"Nephew," Ouranos said. Zeke turned to him, his quills and fur puffed up. Ouranos twitched an ear and frowned. "Zeke. Please. Sit down, for your partner's sake if not for your own."

He bit his lip then reluctantly sat. She leaned against him and he wrapped her in his arms.

And immediately thought of Andre. Damn it, he never should have let Andre go to the mainland alone. He gave Leah a squeeze, his heart ripped in two.

Leah's pendant beeped.

She sat up straight and fumbled with the pendant, pulling up the hologram. "Captain?"

"Hi Leah," Sacha said. "Any news from Pilot?"

"No, unfortunately," Leah said. "Anything with Philip?"

Sacha flicked her ear back. "Nothing good." She explained what had happened last night. Trecheon had gone to his apartment and met a pair of Angels, essentially giving them away. Adrenaline rushed Zeke's spine and the solar system of magic marbles appeared above his head, swirling around his ears and quills. "Now we need Pilot here," Sacha continued. "Philip has to take priority and that means we need more computing power to find him."

Neil stuck his face into the hologram. "Sorry Leah… I know that's not what you want to hear, but you have to understand."

Leah picked at her tail again. The hot pan smell hit Zeke's nose. Frustration. Hesitancy. But she nodded. "Yeah… I get it."

Pilot's colorful hologram flittered in front of them, his faerie wings leaving behind tiny sparkles of light. "I don't have to stop this process to -*bzzt*- do that one," Pilot said, his voice just a little too cheery considering the subject matter. "I can make him a smart copy of myself."

"Absolutely not," Sacha said. "There's a reason we removed copy programming from A.I.s."

Pilot huffed, throwing his head back, sending sparkling motes into the air. "Just because so-called *modern* A.I.s can't -*bzzt*- handle it."

"It's not about handling it, Pilot," Sacha said. "Smart copies take several hours to create, are prone to terrible errors, and are a security risk. Hell, it's known to change entire A.I. personalities. No guarantee that you'd even be the same. And frankly I'd rather not have a smart copy running around in Earth's technology."

Pilot flicked his tail like an angry cat. "As if Earth technology could harm me."

"But they sure as hell could detect you and blow our cover."

Zeke pressed his lips tightly together, fighting back fear. What if Ackerson *did* detect him? It was one thing for Trecheon to be seen, but what about their digital footprint? Ackerson was aware of Zyearth and Defender technology after all and Trecheon had already compromised them. He--

"They haven't detected me yet," Pilot spat. "And I -*bzzt*- lived here for literally *millennia.* "

"No good," Sacha said. "That doesn't mean they won't find you *now.* No smart copies."

Zeke sighed relief.

"H-how about a narrow copy?" Leah asked.

Zeke whipped his head to her. A smell of lemon hit his nose but Leah didn't look at him.

Sacha perked an ear. "A narrow copy."

Leah nodded. "We still use them in the library for various search engines. Pilot could make a narrow copy with his infiltration software. Less of a chance of errors, not as much a security risk, and you can fit a narrow copy with a kill switch that he can activate if he's caught, no harm done. It'd only take a few minutes."

Sacha sighed. "Even with a kill switch, he can still be caught."

"But he can't be interrogated."

Zeke flicked his tail. "Leah, even getting *caught--*"

"A-At this point, does it matter?" Leah shrugged. "They're already aware of what's going on... Might as well throw everything we can at them."

Neil whipped his gaze to Sacha. Zeke wrung his hands together.

"P-Plus we could still work on this encryption," Leah said. She wrung her tail between her fingers, picking at the fur. "We can do both and the risk stays the same..."

"I know, I know," Sacha said. "Fine. Against my better judgement, Pilot, you can make Andre a narrow copy of your infiltration software. But *only* your infiltration software, do you understand?"

Pilot flicked a clawed hand up to his head, scattering rainbow sparkles everywhere. "Yes Ma'am!"

"Good."

"This shouldn't take long." Pilot's hologram froze in place as code washed over his form.

"I'll take the narrow copy to the mainland," Zeke blurted out.

Sacha eyed him. "Zeke, that's not safe. Look at you, your magic is all over the place."

"Then I will go with him," Ouranos said. "I have a feeling we are coming to a head with this battle for Philip and you may need the power to hold Angel back while we retrieve him."

Leah stood. "Then let me go too."

"No," Zeke said, the adrenaline doubling.

Leah turned to him. "Why not?"

Zeke's mind raced. *Because you're safe here. Because I already have one piece of my heart in danger on the mainland and I can't stand the thought of both of you there. Because this is the only way I can make sure you're both protected.* He pressed his lips tight. *Because I need a reason to come back here. I need another reason to keep living.*

But he buried those thoughts deep in his mind. "Because... we have the bond. If the pendants don't work or if we can't use them while getting Philip, we can still communicate. Keep us up to date."

Ouranos nodded. "That is a good plan, honestly. If you do not object, Leah."

Leah flattened both ears. "Sure."

"Done!" Pilot called. "Narrow copy finished." A small device popped out of Pilot's hub. "I applied it to this *-bzzt-* memory drive. It's defunct technology, but it should be compatible with anything Andre's using."

Pathos stuck her head in the hologram. "I'll be on Casino Beach with our van. Get there as soon as you can."

"We'll be there," Zeke said. Leah slowly dropped the hologram.

Ouranos stood. "I will make preparations. Be ready, Zeke." He left.

Zeke turned to leave as well.

"Are you sure about this?" Leah said quietly. A smell of burning chocolate accompanied her question.

Zeke frowned and turned back to her. "What do you mean?"

Leah met his gaze. "Zeke, you can't control your magic."

Zeke narrowed his eyes. "I have Ouranos. He can help."

"You can't rely on Ouranos forever," Leah said. "Especially when Philip is in danger…"

"I won't put Philip in danger--"

"Not *intentionally*--"

"*Stop,*" Zeke said. "Just because you have perfect control over your perfect magic doesn't give you the right to comment on mine."

Leah's eyes widened and a panicked smell of burning peppers stung Zeke's nose. "I-I wasn't… I didn't…"

He paused. Too far. But he pushed aside the discomfort and crossed his arms. "Look. If it makes you feel better I'll stay behind when they go for Philip, but damn it, I can't just sit here when Andre is on the mainland without me. He's not a mage and he's putting himself out there without any real protection. I can protect him. You understand that, right?"

Leah gripped her tail and didn't speak. She only nodded.

The smells suddenly vanished, sending a cold chill down his spine.

Ouranos stuck his head into the room. "Zeke? Is there anything you need to pack?"

Zeke's ears twitched. "Yeah… Coming." He frowned, glancing at Leah. "I have to do this. But I'll be back. Okay?" He held out a hand to her.

But she didn't take it. She nodded again, then stood and walked to the wall of assassins, pretending to be interested in it in a way that fooled no one.

Zeke watched her a moment. He took it too far. But at the same time… He shook his head, snatched up Pilot's memory stick, and walked out.

Andre needed him.

DECRYPTED

"You really sure about this, Zeke?" Ethos asked.

Leah stood next to her in the royal chambers next to the only exit off Athánatos. Just as she had done a couple of days ago when Sacha and the others had left. She had felt so alone then, but at least she had had Zeke.

Now she had only Ethos. And she wasn't entirely sure she could trust her.

Though something in her mind also questioned whether she could trust Zeke. A mini monster, feeding off the anxiety and fears from the Thought Monster filling her head with thoughts. One thought path in particular rose above the others.

He used your magic against you.

Your control.

Your weakness.

He disregarded your struggles.

He's just like everyone else. He doesn't understand the pain that comes with being a healer-S.

You're alone again.

Her chest physically ached as her mind zipped through that thought chain over and over and over again, zapping it through every neuron, every mental process, every inch of her skull until it melted together like glue and shut down all other functions. No amount of telling herself that those were just intrusive thoughts made them go away.

She was alone again.

Zeke hoisted his backpack higher up on his back. He glanced at Leah, chewing on his lip. She could sense him poking at her mind, asking to come in, but the thoughts pushed him away to the point where she didn't even get smells anymore.

And he stopped pushing.

He turned to Ethos. "I'm sure. We've got this. Just let us know when Pilot finds Jaden's location."

Ethos flicked her ear, but she nodded. "I will. Be safe, okay?"

Zeke nodded. He looked at Leah again. He took a step forward. Just one step. But then stopped. "I'll see you soon, Leah."

The sticky thoughts in her head stole her voice. She only nodded back.

Melaina strode up to Ouranos and wrapped him in a hug. "Take care of yourself."

"Always." He hugged her back then pulled away. She warmly gripped Zeke's hand, though his smile for her felt fake and broken.

Then they walked through the portal.

Leaving Leah alone.

Melaina breathed deeply. "I greatly worry for Philip. I… have mostly kept this to myself, but I struggle to imagine that Ackerson has still kept him alive. He would be a lot of trouble for no benefit." She stared at the floor. "A sentiment my father often kept with the young children he captured during the war…"

Leah's heart sunk.

"He's still alive," Ethos said. "I'm sure of it. He's still useful to Ackerson. They all know we're looking for Jaden and we have better tech to find him in Pilot. They'll wait until we make a definitive move toward Jaden then use Philip as a distraction or a bargaining chip to get Jaden's exact location." She shook her head. "He's as good as dead at that point though. Angel will get the location out of us one way or another and take out Philip then. Sacha's right. He's a priority right now. In fact…" Her voice grew dark. "Even if Pilot found Jaden at this moment, I'd keep it a secret until we got Philip." She put her hands on her hips and looked up. "That being said, we need to be ready the *exact* moment we have both Philip and Jaden's location." She pulled out her phone. "I need to see if I can secure transportation. I'm gonna head through the portal a moment, find a Wi-Fi signal, and see what I can do. Leah, can you watch over Pilot in case he discovers anything?"

Leah picked at the bald spot on her tail. She nodded.

Ethos frowned. "Hun… don't let Zeke's words get to you. He's scared. For you and for Andre. He's not trying to hurt you."

Too late for that, Leah thought. She nodded again.

Ethos stepped forward, her hand out like she wanted to hug Leah, but Leah stepped back, squeezing her tail close to her. Ethos pulled her hand back, her ears splayed. "Sorry. I'll give you your space." She nodded to Leah and Melaina. "I'll be right back." She vanished through the portal.

Leaving Leah totally alone now.

Melaina helped Leah find her way back to Pilot. "I will retrieve some food and tea. Will you be okay alone for a moment?"

Alone forever? The Thought Factory translated.

She only nodded.

Melaina smiled and left.

Leah sat on a chair next to Pilot's base and stared forward, drowning in her thoughts while the Thought Monster ate at her brain.

Pilot manifested next to her. "Hey. For what it's worth, you made the right call."

She slowly turned to him, frowning.

"The narrow copy," Pilot explained. "It was *-bzzt-* brilliant."

Leah shrugged.

"We'll find them," Pilot said. "Philip and--" His hologram suddenly froze and flickered. "Aha!" Pilot spewed colorful fire and did several loop-de-loops. "I've got it! I've *-bzzt-* cracked the encryption!"

Leah stood, eyes wide.

"Give me a moment." Code washed over his hologram, then vanished. He grinned. "Got it! He and the others are in a town in *-bzzt-* Canada," Pilot said. He vanished and pulled up a map of Canada in the hologram. A little red dot showed up in the middle of Alberta. "Here." He flickered a bit. "….Or here." A second dot appeared, this time high up in the province. "The first town is Jasper, *-bzzt-* the second is Pine Cove." He flicked his tail. "Sorry I don't have anything more concrete. I think he put two towns deliberately, *-bzzt-* just in case. The math conversions make it hard to know though." His grin faded. "A shame this had to break *now*. Ethos won't even say anything about it until they find Philip. And I get why, but still."

Leah frantically waved her arms, pointing at the Canadian map. *But he's right there! He's there and in danger and we need to get to him! Dang it, work voice!*

Pilot seemed to pick up on her message anyway. "I know. He's *-bzzt-* right there and we can't do anything. I'm… I'm sorry," Pilot said. "But… if it helps, I agree *-bzzt-* with you. We need to find Jaden sooner rather than later. I just don't see how *-bzzt-* you're going to convince Ethos. Hopefully they'll get Philip quickly so we can go after Jaden."

She stared at the A.I. Something bubbled inside her, making the green glow on her fur come back. A fierce determination beat against her chest.

"I don't need to convince Ethos," Leah said, her tinny voice cracking. "I'm going to go after Jaden myself."

CHAPTER 32

FINDING PHILIP

Neil sat back against the wall, pulling yet another long string on his jacket, feeling the fabric vibrate as he tugged until it stopped. He balled the string in his palm and ripped it, freeing it, before putting it in a pile on the floor with the others.

Half a day of string-pulling had made a significant nest.

God, he was exhausted. But every time he tried sleeping, images of Philip flashed in his mind and woke him up immediately. Nothing to do but pull stings and hope he could stay awake.

Zeke and Ouranos had showed up in record time and Andre immediately got Pilot to work. The A.I.'s additional work on Andre's computer soon made the heat dump unbearable in his tiny room, so they pieced together a bunch of extension cables and connectors to get Andre in the main warehouse. Both he and Chad complained loudly about the daisy chain, but Andre eventually gave in after he had soaked through two shirts trying to fight through the heat dump. Andre and Pilot now worked overtime at the computers, though it looked more like a boring day at the office, despite the tension.

With some luck and help from the Fawns, Andre had been able to find limited records of Philip and Theophania (Labeling them as "insurance" and "bait" which set Neil's teeth on edge) but finding out where they were now seemed just out of reach. Pilot's limited software was right on the cusp of getting through the layers of encryption, but some firewall, some bug, some… who knows what, blocked him. Neil didn't know shit about computers, so when Andre went off explaining the technicalities, he tuned out.

Angus was in the corner scrying with his mirror again, though he hadn't said anything in hours. Tension wracked Neil's shoulders, making them ache.

So Neil kept pulling out loose strings.

Sacha eyed him. "You're going to pull the whole jacket apart if you don't stop that."

"Like I give a shit," Neil said. "Any news yet?"

"I'm -*bzzt*- trying," Pilot said, his hologram flickering as he spoke. The image in the tiny hovering holoprojector distorted it to the point where it almost vanished. "Hold your -*bzzt*- cattle."

"Hold your horses," Chadwick corrected.

"Yeah well, -*bzzt*- we don't have -*bzzt*- horses on -*bzzt*- Zyearth," Pilot said. "Doesn't -*bzzt*- work."

Trecheon frowned. "You don't? Not even feral ones?"

"Both feral and -*bzzt*- zyfaunos died in the -*bzzt*- Great Dragon War-*boar-score.*"

Sacha frowned. "Pilot, don't strain yourself."

"I'm -*bzzt*- fine-*mine-chime.*"

Sacha perked her ears. "You're word-vomiting."

"Let me *work*," Pilot said, his avatar vanishing into colorful pixels before reforming again, draining all the humor from his normally cheery personality.

Sacha sighed. "And this is why we don't copy A.I.s. Totally distorts their personalities."

Pilot threw a four-letter swear at her.

Andre growled. "Shit's locked down tight as hell. I have to reengineer a way inside." He tapped away, brow furrowed. "Sure you can't go faster, Pilot?"

Pilot's voice barely registered on the tiny hologram. "Your encryptions and firewalls are *-bzzt-* so *primitive.* It's a *-bzzt-* wonder the intelligent races of this *-bzzt-* planet got anything done."

Andre sat his elbows on the makeshift desk and leaned on his hands. "Not what I asked, butterfly."

"I'm a *fae, -bzzt-* thank you very much," Pilot huffed. A pause. "No, I *-bzzt-* can't go faster." The fae dragon snorted, his tiny hologram spitting rainbow pixels. "If I was a *-bzzt- smart* copy--"

"Then you'd be just as broken as you are now," Sacha said. "And more annoying." She reached for Damianos and worked a little more on his wound. He groaned quietly. "I don't know how you have as much awareness as you do with a narrow copy. You should basically be nothing more than a software program."

"I'm *-bzzt-* built different," Pilot said.

"But you still can't find a way in," Andre said, crossing his arms. "Not that different."

Trecheon swore. It had been the first word he had said since Neil berated him. Neil's tail twitched watching him. Trecheon leaned against the wall near Chadwick, as far away from the Fawns as he could be. Which Neil couldn't blame him for.

Maybe Neil had been too harsh on him. But he was still too angry and too worried to think about apologizing. After they got Philip. *If* they got Philip. His stomach grew queasy again.

"We'll get it," Andre said. "We gotta." He glanced at Zeke. "How'd Leah take you leaving her behind?"

Zeke perked his ears. He paused, crossing his arms. "She doesn't see it like that. She's being useful."

Andre eyed him. "You're dreamin' if you think she doesn't see it that way. She's a soldier being told to sit on the bench."

Zeke looked off. "She's safer there."

"But not happy," Andre said. "Bet my dog tags. Stubborn as a goat, just like you." He eyed the room. "Sorry fuzzballs, meant no disrespect."

Sacha paused her healing and glanced at him. "I thought that was a slur."

"'Fuzzy' is a slur," Trecheon said. "Like furball, hairball, or in the wrong context, furry. Thought that one's changing lately. Fuzzball is a term of endearment."

Sacha shook her head. "Earth is so strange."

"Language is strange," Trecheon said. He sighed. "It's probably better she stays there. I lived the war. I know how terrible it was, and I know the signs of PTSD." He crossed his arms and met Zeke's gaze. "It's also why you're staying here. I promised Matt I'd take care of you, and by Draso, that's what I'm going to do."

Zeke snorted, but didn't contradict him.

Neil kept pacing, stewing in his own trauma, which came back full force with Dami's injury. His breathing quickened, his tail lashed out, his fur puffed up and his whiskers twitched. Bits and pieces of the war flashed through his senses – the hot smell of burning gunpowder, the screams of civilians, of children, of the dying, the bright flashes of explosions and tracer rounds in the air, the taste of dust and blood on his tongue, the grime and sweat building on his fur and skin. He--

"Neil."

Neil paused and looked at Sacha.

She frowned, ears flat. "Sit. Do your grounding exercises."

Neil stared at her a moment. Her words bounced around in her head, but he couldn't seem to get his body to move.

"Neil," Trecheon said. "I'll do them too. Okay? We'll do them together." He sat on one of the cots.

Neil frowned. He took a deep breath, then sat where he was. He looked around and slowly went through his exercises, counting off as he did. *Five things I can see. Four things I can hear. Three things I can touch...* Trecheon did the same, mumbling as he did. By the time he finished, his heartrate had slowed and he breathed easier. Thank God.

"Glad to see you more yourself again, love," Damianos said. Neil turned. Dami sat up now, smiling, though clearly weary.

Neil's heart warmed and stress sloughed off him like a heavy blanket falling to the floor. "Thank *Christ.*" He reached for him.

"Careful," Sacha said. "He's not whole yet. But he's close."

"Better than I was," Dami said. He took Neil's hands, which lifted huge burden off Neil's shoulders. He pressed his forehead to Dami's.

"Oh, thank the Sisters," Natassa said. She leaned forward and took Dami's hand. "We were so worried."

"I got it, I got it!" Pilot said. "I -*bzzt*- found a way in!"

Andre immediately turned his attention to the computer. His face broke in a grin. "*Hell* yeah, that's what I'm talkin' about." He tapped away, eyes darting back and forth as he stared at the screen.

Trecheon stopped immediately.

Neil stood too. "Well?"

Andre clapped his hands. "I got it," he said. "We're in. Give me a mo'."

"Way ahead of you," Pilot said. His tiny hologram glitched slightly and he danced in the air with loop de loops. "Everything's *-bzzt-* here. Philip and Theophania are… Oh…"

Andre's eyes grew wide. *"Shit."*

Neil moved forward and glanced over Andre's shoulder. "What? What is it? Where are they?"

"Here," Andre said. He pointed to a map with a massive ranch property and a clear fence covering at least 20 acres. Somewhere miles out of town.

Trecheon narrowed his gaze. "The hell is that?"

Andre's eyes grew dark. "Ackerson's home."

Ouranos' pendant beeped suddenly and he pulled it up, frowning. "Melaina?"

"Ouranos, we have a serious problem," Melaina said, shifting from foot to foot. "Leah is *missing.*"

CHAPTER 33

PROBLEMS

Neil stared at Melaina, his fur puffed up. "What?"

Melaina rubbed her hands together. "I… I went to go make tea and gather some food, but when I returned to Pilot's base, Leah was not there. I thought perhaps she had gone for a walk to clear her head, but hours passed and she never returned. I searched the palace with our staff, but no one can find her anywhere."

"Lady Melaina?" An Athánatos sentry entered the room. "We cannot find the doe Ethos either. She is not on Sol that we can find, nor is she in the palace."

Neil's heart dropped into his stomach. "Christ on a *crutch*. They *didn't.*"

Logos cursed and gritted her teeth. "Ethos, you *idiot.*"

Zeke's quills stood on end, but he held out his hands. "Calm down. Maybe she's just… hiding?" He shook his head. "Before we all freak out, lemmie contact her." He closed his eyes.

Sacha poked her head near Ouranos. "Did you search for her pendant signal?"

"Oh," Melaina said. "No, I have not." She fiddled with something on the holographic UI. "It lists her pendant in the room where we put up the evidence wall. One moment." The pendant's camera followed her as she rushed through the palace.

"I... I can't feel her."

Neil turned to Zeke.

Zeke's wide eyes betrayed a fear Neil had only felt himself in the war. Zeke stared at his hands, his jaw loose and eyes glassy. "She's not answering. I can't feel anything. I can't *smell* anything. I..." He wrapped his arms around himself. "Is she..."

"She's not dead," Sacha said. "You'd really know it if she was. There's a... dark feeling that comes when a bond is severed through death. It's one of the reasons why we stopped the practice."

"Then she's just blocking me," Zeke said, his voice cracking. "Blocking me so completely it's like we don't have a bond." He pressed his eyes tightly shut. "Damn it, it wasn't supposed to be this way."

"Ouranos." Neil turned back to the pendant's projection. Melaina held up a Defender pendant, black with a green band around the corner. She turned to Ouranos, tears in her eyes. "She left this behind..."

Neil's fur stood on end. "We're in deep shit."

Sacha stepped forward. "Melaina, wake Pilot up."

Pilot appeared next to Melaina. "Already -*bzzt*- awake. What do you want?"

"Why would Leah take off?" Sacha asked. "Did you finally decrypt Jaden's message?"

Pilot crossed his tiny forearms and snorted rainbow smoke. "What do you mean *-bzzt-* 'finally'? This is difficult stuff! Give *-bzzt-* me some credit!"

Sacha held her hands up, twitching her long tail, though she rolled her eyes. "My bad, sorry. Can you answer the question?"

"Can you *-bzzt-* not be so *rude?"*

Neil glared at the A.I., adrenaline pumping. "What makes him do that?"

Sacha sighed. "Age, mostly."

"Watch your *-bzzt-* mouth," Pilot snarled. "I'm *special."*

"You're old," Sacha said. She turned to Neil. "Since Pilot *is* older, we were able to restore a lot of his broken code. Less to fix. But he just doesn't have the computing power that most modern Defender A.I.s have."

Pilot scoffed, turning to the pendant on the wall, glaring as hard as he could with those tiny eyes. "I don't *-bzzt-* need *-bzzt-* more computing power. I'm *-bzzt-* doing just fine-*mine-sign* without it, if you'd *-bzzt--bzzt-* *just leave me be!"*

Sacha stood and moved to the pendant hologram, narrowing her gaze. "Pilot. Something is wrong."

"Nothing's *-bzzt-* wrong," Pilot said.

"Horse spit," Sacha said. "Don't blow me off. You should not be word-vomiting like this no matter how much you're straining your processors. And I have never heard you shout at someone like that. So what the hell is wrong?"

Pilot snorted a flurry of glitchy, holographic fire at the pendant. Andre held his hands up and leaned away. Pilot growled, deep and throaty, though a number of squeaks worked their way through. *"Back. Off."*

Sacha glared back. She crossed her arms. "Fine. We do this the hard way. Pilot, display A.I. properties, Defender override code 75623."

Pilot froze in place and his avatar melted into words, showing the A.I.'s properties. Pilot's voice read them off, deadpan. "This A.I. is a smart copy of Defender A.I. codenamed Pilot, originally commissioned in *-bzzt-* for the Defender Refugee Program during the Great Dragon War--"

Sacha bared her teeth. "Thought so."

Andre drew in a sharp breath. Chadwick's ears perked and his jaw dropped.

Trecheon stood. "Oh *shit.* "

"Pilot must have finished the decryption and gave Leah a location," Sacha said. "Pilot, display transcript of final message before copying."

Pilot's properties melted away again and a paragraph of text appeared instead, displaying his last message to Leah. Neil looked it over. Sure enough, he had finished the decryption and now they had a location. Well… two locations. The map accompanying the message showed two tiny mountain towns, over a hundred miles from each other, buried deep in the mountains of Canada.

Trecheon growled. "Sounds like she got the location and took off with Pilot."

Zeke bared his teeth. "I'm going after Leah." He turned to the door.

"Hold it, Prínkipas," Trecheon said, moving in front of him. "Like hell you are. We've already had this conversation."

"She's going after Jaden, and damn it, I'm not gonna let her go alone!"

Trecheon crossed his arms. "Do you know which town?"

Zeke wrinkled his snout, then dropped his shoulders. "Shit."

"Exactly," Trecheon said.

"But it does not mean we should allow her to go on her own," Ouranos protested. "Someone must go after her."

"I don't think we can," Neil said. "They're already on to us, and they might even know where we are. If we all start charging off toward Canada, they'll follow and we'll lead them right to Leah and Jaden."

Trecheon cursed and crossed his arms, looking away.

"I agree with Neil," Andre said. "Best bet is to go after Philip. Get him out before they figure out what's going on with Jaden and try to use Philip to get his location. Our hands are tied."

"So we go charging Ackerson's McRanch then?" Neil asked.

"Not without intel," Andre said. He typed away at the computer. "Give us a mo' and we'll get all the info we can on the property. This is delicate."

Neil threw his hands up. "Great. More waiting."

"This'll go faster if I have the full Pilot," Andre said. He paused. "Well, the copy. Better than just this infiltration blip."

"Ex*cuse -bzzt-* me." Pilot's tinny voice barely registered.

"I will get him to you," Melaina said. "Please send someone to get me from the beach." She cut off the communication.

Zeke sat on a beat up plastic chair. "Damnit, Leah…"

"I hate to say it, Zeke," Trecheon said. "But Leah is on her own. The best thing we can do for her is to distract the people going after her and hope we get them all. If we're lucky, she'll find Jaden in good shape and we can regroup."

Zeke formed a fist. "Then I'm coming with you to Ackerson's, and don't you dare tell me I can't. I need to protect my partner." Little beads of magic floated around his head.

Trecheon lowered his gaze. "You can't control your magic. You'll give us away."

Then Ouranos started singing. Neil had heard him sing that song before, usually while working on something that needed a lot of concentration.

And Zeke's magic vanished. Ouranos stood straight. "We are working on it. Let him come. I take responsibility for him."

Zeke turned to him, ears flat.

Trecheon wrinkled his snout, but threw up his hands. "Fine. Let's get this info and get Philip ASAP."

"With us," Logos said. "We'll hide nearby with snipers." She crossed her arms. "Like it or not, we're professionals. We won't be found."

"Ackerson may be a disgusting criminal, but he's not stupid," Pathos said. "He knows we're looking for Philip. It's why Philip is in his ranch home. He probably has a bunch of his Angels there too. They're looking for a fight."

"Or a negotiation table," Logos said. "Either way. You need help."

Trecheon stared a moment, then shook his head. "I hate everything about this." He turned to Andre. "Can you get into the security cameras?"

"Already got it," Andre said, grinning. "I can see things, but I need to be closer to actually affect things. I'm limited here."

Zeke eyed him.

Andre narrowed his gaze. "Don't tell me to stay behind, Zeke. This is for you and Leah as much as it is for Philip. You hear me?"

"And if you go, I go," Chadwick said. "I can help."

Zeke folded his arms. "I don't like it."

"None of us do," Trecheon said. "But we work with what we got."

"And hopefully we can save Leah from her own stupid decisions," Neil said. He turned to the team. "Alright, people. Let's move out."

Then Angus opened his eyes.

UNION STATION

"This is fantastic!" Pilot said into Leah's earpiece as she crossed the marble floors of Union Station. *"I've never been on an adventure before! Normally I get left behind. What fun!"*

Leah gritted her teeth as she padded along the cold floor. Big white pillars lined either side of the long hall leading to the ticket booths, and signs pointed them every which way – to the platforms, the baggage area, the ride pickups, tickets, food, bathrooms, you name it. People and zyfaunos wandered the halls with a purpose, often in crisp suits and loud formal shoes, which made her in her black yoga pants, blue T-shirt, bare feet, and tiny blue backpack stand out. The highly-polished, bare-rafter ceiling gave the building a warm glow, but the cold floor shot ice through her paw pads and right up to her brain. She hiked her backpack up and tried to keep her eyes focused. No darting around like she was doing something wrong.

Even though she was.

This was pretty much the most foolish thing she had ever done in her life. The relative calm of the station gave her the first opportunity to think, and the Thought Monster frantically ran through her flight from Athánatos, taking inventory of everything she did wrong.

Taking off without telling anyone.

Stealing Ethos' phone and wallet.

Leaving her pendant behind.

Then taking the portal to Sol, stealing one of the motorboats, landing on Casino Beach and hitching a rideshare from Ethos' phone, on her account, to the train station. Good Draso, if they ever caught up to her… this was such a terrible idea.

But… she had to get to Jaden before Angel did. And she was the only one willing to attempt it while Philip was in danger.

She had no choice.

"Automatic ticket counter on your left," Pilot said. *"Plug me in and I'll get you a ticket. Where'd you wanna go first?"*

"You pick one," Leah whispered.

"You got it," Pilot said. *"Look up Jasper, Alberta. It's closer and sort of on the way to the second location."*

Leah tapped away at the touch screen, looking for the fastest way to Jasper. She frowned. Even at full speed, she'd need to make several transitions and it'd take nearly a week to get there because the town was so remote.

The Thought Monster rumbled deeply in her mind, which she took to be a dark giggle. She shuddered.

It took a good twenty minutes to settle a route to Jasper. Three separate trains, five buses, and she could get… near it. The final drop would leave her twenty-five miles in a nearby town with only dirt roads to get to Jasper.

Much too far to walk on her own. She checked the rideshare app, but nothing in the area lit up.

She'd have to walk it.

"They have outfitters there," Pilot said. *"You can get some warm clothing and walk."*

That'd be her only choice. She punched it through and the price displayed.

$1387. Her jaw dropped.

"I can pay for it," Pilot said. *"In a matter of speaking. Just hook me up."*

"That's a lot of money…" Leah said, an ear flicked back. And a lot of… fraud. Wouldn't that flag the system? What if she got caught? She twitched her whiskers. "Don't I need ID…? How do I do that?"

Pilot took a second to respond. *"I really should have thought of that before we left. And we left the fabricator behind."* Another pause. *"Earth databases suggest that fake IDs happen all the time, but I don't know how to get one. And they might figure out it's a fraud."*

Dang it. A fake ID was a terrible idea. *All* of this was a terrible idea. How in Draso's name was she going to get there? Maybe she should just go home… But then she'd have to face everyone back on Athánatos. And Jaden…

"Having a rough time?"

Leah turned, her heart racing. A golden doe with deep brown eyes raised her eyebrows with a smile. She winked at her.

Then Leah caught a glimpse of the green Wishing Dust in her eyes. "Ethos?"

"The very same," Ethos said. She leaned closer. "But don't call me that out here. Call me Ana."

Leah blinked at her, her ears flushing. "Ana."

"Certainly." She grinned. "You didn't think Ethos was my real name, did you?" She winked. "You weren't exactly subtle, sneaking off like that." She frowned. "I should drag you back, but since you already signaled while using the ride app, we might as well continue." She gently cupped Leah's face. "And you shouldn't go alone."

Leah's ears flushed harder. A wave of Ethos' past injuries flooded her mind, though it faded fast with Ethos' eye batting and seductive look. "Um. Right. How uh… how'd you change your fur color?"

"Makeup is a wonderful thing," Ethos said, removing her hand and cutting off Leah's connection to her. "Especially when created to respond to my enhancement magic. Zeke was right. The pink doe thing caught up to us pretty quickly, so disguises became necessary." She batted her eyes at her. "Pretty convincing, huh?"

Leah turned away, feeling hot. Images of Ari flirting with her back in the small town in Eastern Canada filled her mind. Her eyes burned.

Ethos frowned, flattening her long ears against her head. "Oh… sorry, love. I forgot Ari's death is so much nearer to you than to me. I'll stop the flirting."

"It's… it's fine," Leah said. "It's just… hard. And makes me think of the war." She rubbed her arm. "Sorry."

"Don't be," Ethos said. "That was insensitive of me." She turned to the ticket master. "Trying to get to Jasper?"

Leah shrugged. "It's the closest city Jaden listed. Pilot said he could… 'buy' the tickets for me."

Ethos smirked. "So you did take Pilot."

Leah flushed again and turned away, ears back.

"Don't shy away," Ethos said. "I would have too." She reached into her purse and pulled out a small rectangular card, completely blank. She glanced at Leah. "What do you want your alias to be?"

Leah blinked. "What?"

"Fake name, hun."

"Uh…" She scratched her chin. "Opal? I guess? My mom's name. No one here will know that."

"Got it." Ethos eyed her like a painter observing the scenery. "You look like a 'Grayhair' to me. Opal Grayhair. Real simple, common last name." She turned to the rectangle and stared at it. "Don't move for a moment."

Leah stood real still.

The seconds passed, then Ethos perked up and grinned. "There! All done." She passed the rectangle to Leah.

A fake ID. Name, address, picture, everything needed. She stared. "Dang. Your magic is something else."

"It comes in handy." She turned to the ticket booth and erased what was there. "We're not taking coach. If we do this, we do it in style. We need a sleeper car." She added their IDs to the tickets, paid for them with a credit card, and printed them. Big packets came out with all their various tickets. "There. No apps. Less chance of us being tracked. Shall we get on our way, Opal?"

"How are we going to get to Jaspar after our last stop?"

"Hun, we trekked all the way across the Canadian wilderness," she said. "One little dirt road isn't going to stop us." She held out a hand. "Let's do this."

Leah stared at her hand. There were so many unknowns. Why was Ethos so intent on going with her? Why did she suddenly trust Leah with her real name, after all this time?

…Why did she and her sisters kill Neil's family?

But… like it or not, she needed help. And Ethos was help.

She took the doe's hand. Ethos squeezed it tight.

CHAPTER 35

STAKEOUT

Trecheon stood on the muddy ground right outside their safehouse with the entire team, several hours before dawn. Neil, Damianos, Natassa and Sacha on one team. Trecheon and the Fawns in another. Zeke, Ouranos, and Andre on the final team, there for support only. Evenly distribute the healers. Get there before dawn when their enemy's guards were down. Keep everyone close.

Of course, right before they were going to get started, Angus woke up from his long trance and threw a monkey wrench into the mix. And after all those hours scrying, he only had three things to say.

"Neil cannot touch Theophania or Philip will die."

"Chadwick and Melaina cannot leave this safehouse until Matt and his team return to Earth or they will die."

And the last he said only to Trecheon.

"Your friends will not abandon you. Don't despair."

That should have been comforting. But instead it made Trecheon's belly flip on its side. Because if Angus was telling him that, that meant that in some part of his future, he would *feel* abandoned.

Why?

No amount of pushing and prodding would get Angus to explain what that meant. Even now, Trecheon's chest ached thinking about it. Because it was one more thing out of his control. One more thing to fill him with dread.

Neil, though, wouldn't take Angus' vague comment sitting down, and demanded to know what Angus meant about Philip.

Angus had leaned close to Neil and looked him right in the eye with his dead gaze. "Listen to me. There's a lot of branching paths up ahead. So many that I can't even make a proper map. Every step, every breath, every *piss break* is going to change what happens in the future. I can't predict exact outcomes – it's too unstable. But I saw one constant branching path. If you touch Theophania, even briefly, Philip will die. Every path leading from you touching her led to his death." He waved a finger at Neil. "So stay the hell away."

Neil hadn't taken that well. Especially after everyone else suggested he stay behind. The best they could get him to commit to was sitting in the van while the others handled it.

That was gonna backfire, Trecheon was sure of it.

Angus had nothing to say about how their actions would affect Leah, Ethos, or Jaden and his team. That wasn't comforting. And the Black Cloak had vanished again, so no help there either.

"Why can't you just scry where Jaden is?" Sacha had asked. "See if he's alive at all."

"Gotta have a recent starting point first," Angus said. "I could map out the flight through the docks because the Fawns caught a glimpse of them on Casino Beach in one of their cameras and we had a starting point. Jaden's starting point is *years* ago. It'd take years to map from there, assuming our info was accurate on his location to begin with." He shrugged. "Sorry."

The best Sacha could do was growl at him.

Trecheon couldn't get Angus or the Fawns to tell him why they had cameras at Casino Beach.

At least Andre and Pilot's copy had some info on Ackerson. The map was right – big horse property an hour and a half from the base, buried in the hills of local wine country, surrounded by big flat pieces of land, towering hills and cliff faces, and secured by state-of-the-art defenses.

He had every inch of the property covered by cameras. If they got within fifty feet, the camera would catch them. It made them quite limited in what they could do, but then Ouranos suggested using the summons. They passed as normal birds well enough, they could fly over the camera's line of sight. Pax, Archángeli, and Jústi could swoop in, scare off any of Ackerson's Angels, snatch up Philip, and get out of there.

They'd need at least one Gem user though, to shield Philip from retaliation. Sacha volunteered.

Trecheon immediately volunteered too, and was shot down. "We need a healer on the ground, Trecheon," Sacha said.

"And you need a partner," Trecheon countered.

She crossed her arms. "We need a quick exit. Can't get bogged down with a big team. I'll go alone and you support me from the outside."

Trecheon started to protest, but then remembered what his last selfish act did. He shut his mouth. "Okay. Sure." Though his heart burned with fear.

Your friends will not abandon you. Don't despair.

"They're here," Logos said, nodding to three white, unmarked vans that pulled into the parking lot by the broken-down warehouse. That familiar gray cat with a crisp suit and dark yellow eyes got out of one. She stomped on a stunted cigarette and waved at them. Logos nodded. "Let's go."

It took a good two and a half hours to traverse the heavy city traffic until they finally reached the tiny road that would take them to a village of McMansions, one of which was Ackerson's. The ride was completely silent, leaving Trecheon alone with the city noise, the high-pitched whirr of the hydrogen engine, the stench of tobacco, and his own thoughts.

Closer to the ranch, the vans split up. Trecheon's team took a perch high on one of the cliffs overlooking the property, and Neil's team set up on the ground, near the edge of the camera's view, ready to dive in. Zeke's team pulled up just close enough to get Andre on the cameras.

Pathos pulled the van onto a dirt path hidden by palm trees and killed the engine. "We're about a mile from the property."

Trecheon contacted Neil and Zeke. The hologram warmed and projected against the wall of Trecheon's van. "You guys ready?"

Neil sat in his van, arms crossed, his ears quivering. He wouldn't even look into the hologram. "I don't like this."

"We'll get Philip out safe," Sacha said. "I stake my life on it."

"Don't do that," Trecheon and Neil said together.

Sacha perked her ears, frowning, but didn't respond.

Andre tapped away at the computer, pulling up Theophania's cameras. "Hey uh, just a heads up… things changed."

Trecheon cursed. "Explain."

"Ackerson has visitors over," Andre said. "A *lot* of them, awake and alert in the living room. Most are Angels, but there's one I ain't seen before. Built guy. A puma." He frowned. "Kinda looks like you, Neil."

Trecheon and Neil both perked their ears.

"That's not good," Sacha said. "They might be trying a hide-in-plain-sight tactic."

"One more problem," Andre said. "He's got Philip in the living room with them."

"Christ," Neil said. "There goes our chance with the summons." He punched the side of his van. Damianos and Natassa both lit up with magic. Sacha let out a low rumbling growl.

"We've got to coordinate this right then," Logos said. "They may know we're on to them, but that doesn't mean they know where we are. And they won't hurt Philip randomly. He's a bargaining chip. It'd be a waste of resources to kill him when they aren't in immediate danger."

Trecheon flattened his ears.

Ouranos leaned back. "Do we know who is at Ackerson's? It would be helpful to know what magic they have."

Andre pulled out a folded sheet of paper and laid it out. "Got the rap sheet here. I recognize four. Kitta, a shielder and cloaker. Florina and Luana are there too, those Ei-Ei jewel users from Neil's big fight. And… this guy. Fedir. Big stag, also with Ei-Ei jewels."

"Luana has healing magic," Neil said. "Kind of. She gets hurt when she heals others. And I'm pretty sure it was Florina I saw trading magic with Natassa."

"She has Ei-Ei jewels," Natassa said. "And for some reason they recognize her as royalty. She can command all elements. I can only assume the same of the stag."

"One more," Andre said. "A black and orange bat. He has some goopy thing next to him."

A spike shot through Trecheon's heart. "Ronan. With Judgement."

"That… complicates things," Ouranos said. "Judgement will recognize the Phonar, and her allies will counter their magic."

"Hey," Andre said. "Any of you fuzzballs recognize this device in the living room?" He pulled up a picture from the security cams and showed them the computer. A three-foot-tall box stood in the center of the room, with a colorless Gem in it.

"Lighting and *air*," Sacha said. "Shield enhancer. Probably got the whole building shielded."

Andre stared at it again. "Why's that Gem got no color?"

"Gems with no color or sheen are unbound," Sacha said. She lowered her gaze. "Could be Jordan's missing Gem."

Everyone grew quiet.

Trecheon tapped his chin. "How long would Jústi have before someone could counter his magic?"

Ouranos shrugged. "I am unsure."

"Long enough to take out the shield?"

"Perhaps."

"It won't stay down though," Sacha said, her voice tinny on the communicator. "Shield enhancers can power cycle in just over a minute."

"That gives us a time window though," Trecheon said.

"Maybe we can get the other summons in there once we take down the shield," Neil said. "Get Philip and blow up that shield enhancer."

"Places then," Neil said. "Trecheon, watch from the cliff with the snipers and keep us updated. Zeke, Ouranos, protect Andre and be ready to be a distraction if necessary, and get the summons ready. We'll get as close as we can and Natassa, put your summons on standby. Let's get this done."

"You mean let *us* get this done," Sacha told Neil. "You're staying here."

Neil flicked an ear back.

"You better not get yourself killed, Sacha," Trecheon said, pointing at the camera. "Or I'll… I'll kill you myself."

"You'll have to catch my ghost first," Sacha said with a wink. She met Trecheon's gaze. "Good luck."

“You too.” He cut communications.

Pathos got out of the driver’s seat, opened the back, and started assembling her rifle. “You both ready for this?”

“Not at all,” Trecheon said, his heart pumping. “Let’s do this.”

CHAPTER 36

Open Heart

Leah and Ethos had traveled overnight in relative silence.

The sleeper car cabin was nice. Plush bunk beds, a private shower, great view, tables for working, good soft pillows. And privacy, which allowed them to use familiar names.

Pilot was absolutely ecstatic, staring out the window and spitting facts about whatever area they were in whenever he got the chance, almost like he had forgotten Leah and Ethos were even there.

But Leah still wasn't sure she could trust Ethos. Ana. Whoever she was. On the surface, she acted like the Ethos she knew in war, but there was something hidden, something darker, that Leah couldn't quite name. She was overly flirty, defensive, and clearly hiding… something.

This was a mistake.

But it was a mistake Leah was stuck with. Stops were few and far between, and even if Leah wanted to get off, it's not like she could find another way to Jasper. She just had to endure it.

For the most part, the day consisted of sleep, silence, and meals, most of which were taken in the dining car. Leah had gotten a simple sketch journal from the little gift shop on the far end of the train. It wouldn't be safe to write a journal of what they were actually doing, so Leah started up a simple comic of talking heads. Her main character, Auburn, was a little ginger cat arguing with the creator of the comic. It was a good way to pass the time and try to bring a little humor to this dark errand.

A shame it didn't stay humorous. By evening, Auburn was chasing down summons and fighting a literal Thought Monster with nothing but her own anxiety. Leah had to put the comic away after that, for her own mental health.

By the time dinner came by, she was almost bored. She went to get dinner early, if only to pass the time. But the diner car was full when she got there, so she took her food back to their car.

Ethos was showering in their tiny bathroom, steaming up the windows. Leah sighed. She couldn't even enjoy the view…

You can't trust Ethos, The Thought Monster spat.

Leah growled. "Shut up."

Pilot manifested next to her. "I'm sorry, did I say something to bother you?"

Leah frowned. "No, no. Sorry."

Pilot eyed her a moment, then turned to the window. He droned on about the trees outside, even though he really couldn't see them through the steamed windows.

She killed Neil's parents, the Thought Monster continued. *And she wouldn't even say why.*

Leah stabbed a bit of her salad. *"Shut up."*

Pilot stopped immediately and hunkered down like a dog scared of its owner. "I'm sorry, Leah, I'll--"

She held her hands up. "No, Pilot, not you. Sorry again, I just…"

She'll take you out too, the Thought Monster said. *The moment you're no longer useful.* She imagined it tossing her an evil smile. *She's probably just looking for Jaden to hurt him… You know she's with Ackerson…*

She held her hands over her ears. *"SHUT UP!"*

"Leah?"

Leah looked up. Pilot's hologram vanished.

Ethos stood outside the shower, wrapped in a towel, still dripping water from her ears. The shower had worn off her makeup, removing the golden brown in favor of that shining pink fur.

Leah's ears grew hot.

See, even now she's trying to lower your inhibitions…

Leah gripped her head and growled.

Ethos frowned. She sat on the chair opposite Leah. "Everything okay?"

"No," Leah said. "My stupid brain…" She'd have to apologize to Pilot.

Ethos smirked slightly. "Sorry, did my towel do something to you?"

See?

"Argh!" She pressed her head to the table. *Shut up, shut up, SHUT UP.*

Ethos pressed her hand to Leah's shoulder. Leah expected a wave of her injuries to flood her mind, but she just got… fear. A deep, penetrating fear. She looked up at Ethos.

Ethos frowned. She opened her mouth like she wanted to speak, but remained silent.

Leah flicked her ears back. "You're afraid."

Ethos' long ears lay back against her head. "I am."

"Of me?"

"No," Ethos said. "Well… not of *you* but… of hurting you. Scaring you." She shuddered. "Taking you down with me." The fear doubled, then Ethos removed her hand. "Sorry."

Leah sat up. "What do you mean?"

Ethos looked into her eyes a moment, then shook her head. "Let me get dry and dressed." She pulled pajamas out of her backpack then vanished into the bathroom again.

The Thought Monster chuckled. *She's going to hurt you.*

No, she's not! Leah snarled back. *Shut up!*

She hurt Neil's parents, the Thought Monster said. *Innocents. And you're not even an innocent. You're a liability.*

Leah hands balled into fists.

Ethos walked out now, in tiny pajama shorts and a spaghetti strap shirt. Her ears were still pinned against her head.

Leah chewed her lip. "Did you have to kill Neil's parents?"

Ethos flicked her ears back. "Ah. So that's where this all comes from."

"Answer the question, please."

Ethos licked the tip of her nose, one ear tilting back. She sat in the chair. "We didn't want to, Leah."

"That's not what I asked," Leah said, speaking just a little too fast. "Did you *have* to?"

Ethos placed her hands in her lap, holding herself rigid. "Ackerson has controlled our lives from the moment we returned to El Dorado after the Wall fell."

Leah lifted her chin and narrowed her gaze. "You're still dodging the question."

"Let me finish," Ethos said, lifting a hand. "Ackerson controlling our lives dictated that we had to have control over Trecheon and Neil's lives. But that didn't mean we intended to hurt them. But Ackerson..." She paused, tightening her mouth. "He knows how to… persuade."

"What could he have possibly done to persuade you to do exactly what you told us you *hated?*" Leah said, her voice cold. "Neil and his parents didn't deserve that."

Ethos glared back, both ears flat now. Though her eyes glistened. "Can I sit next to you?"

Every bone in her body screamed at Leah to say no, but she nodded anyway.

Ethos sat on the bed. "I was married, once."

Leah flicked her ears back. That didn't... but she kept her mouth shut.

"Ironically she was also a gray cat," Ethos said. "A Russian blue, if you really want to pick out breeds, though she never put much stock in that. Her name was Mara and she was my world. We met not long after we had recovered from the war and hit it off immediately." She smiled sadly. "I expected her to run the moment she learned of my connection to the mob, but she didn't. Instead she encouraged me to find a way out. It was one of the things that inspired our push to get Matron Fawn out. It'd be a way to cut ties and start fresh. We got married the year before we hatched the plan to leave."

Leah leaned back.

Ethos picked up a napkin and dabbed her eyes. "Ackerson was all for it. The Matron was overstepping boundaries, directing hits through us and Neil and Trecheon that could potentially compromise him. He wanted her gone. *We* wanted her gone. And with her gone, it'd be a chance to work our way out from under Ackerson too, and right the wrongs we committed against Trecheon and Neil." She paused and folded her hands in her lap.

Leah's tail twitched. "That clearly didn't work out."

She shrugged. "We thought it did. Neil killed her, through our subtle directions, giving us several layers of deception. No one would know who did it." She formed fists. "But Ackerson wasn't satisfied with that. Because he wanted Neil and Trecheon crushed too. So he ordered us to kill Neil's parents in retribution for Matron Fawn's death, as an excuse to hurt them."

Leah drew her hands to her snout.

"We fought it," Ethos said. "And Ackerson responded by kidnapping our families, including my wife. For a whole week he tortured them, threatening to kill them. He sent regular videos of their torture at all hours of the day and night." She lowered her head. "Mara, for her part, fought valiantly. She wouldn't give them the satisfaction of screaming during the torture. She begged me not to give in to what Ackerson wanted. Said her life wasn't more valuable than the people Ackerson wanted to hurt. And I knew that was all true… But I wanted her back. I couldn't think straight. I *needed* her."

Leah's ears lay against her head. "…So you killed Neil's parents."

"We did," Ethos said. "We were desperate." She looked off. "Didn't matter though. We did the deed, got Philip stuck in foster care as a bargaining chip and for a few glorious months, we had our families back. Glorious, but agonizing, because of the cost. Mara wouldn't speak to me for two weeks. Not because of the pain she endured, but because we gave in.

"So we tried again to leave Ackerson." Ethos bunched her shorts into her fists. "But the second we did, he swooped in again and took them all. This time there was no negotiation. Just hours and hours of torture and pain and death, all recorded for us. Ackerson told us who held all the power."

Leah's whole body buzzed. "Ana…"

Ethos glanced off. "So yeah. We didn't have to kill them. We didn't want to. But we did, and this is the consequence." She wrung her hand together. "It's been four years since Mara's death. I hope… she knew how much I loved her." She stared at the floor. Slowly, her face changed – ears drooped, black lips tilted in a frown, eyes glassy and dark.

She's manipulating you, the Thought Monster said.

Leah watched her. Tears coursed down her white cheeks.

Leah didn't care if this was manipulation. She wrapped her arms around Ethos and held her tight. Waves of her injuries and illnesses washed over Leah's body, but so did her fear, her guilt, her shame.

Images ran through Leah's mind. Ethos walking through the park with Mara, the pair kissing, being intimate… then Mara sitting in a chair, face bloodied, mouth open in a silent scream, Ethos' despair ripping through Leah's body.

She leaned her head on Leah's shoulder and wailed. Not just quiet, bleating sobs, but sorrow so deep that no comforting gesture can touch it. Leah held her tongue. Nothing could be said for grief like that.

Her healing magic activated at some point, making them both feel warm. Over time, Ethos' wails calmed into sobs and slowed into sniffles. And Leah held on.

It wasn't the same as losing a spouse to torture but… Ari's death visited her again. Her strong spirit, squelched by a knife. Leah unable to save her.

She should have given in to Ari's flirting. Let them enjoy each other before that horrible event. She should have been able to save her.

You should have killed Sharp.

You should have stopped Ronan.

You should be better than this.

She shoved it aside and locked it in a box. This wasn't about her. It was about Ethos. She needed to put Ethos first.

Draso's horns you're selfish, the Thought Monster spat. *Making Trecheon and Neil's injuries and troubles about you. Going off looking for Jaden when no one was ready, putting everyone in danger. Making Ethos' grief about you failing Ari. You're pathetic.*

Leah didn't fight back this time. Because it was true. Everything she was doing was selfish. She let the guilt stew. A reminder, she thought. Make this about Ethos, not her.

Eventually Ethos let out a shuddering breath and pulled back. Tears stained her fur. She picked up a napkin and wiped her eyes and nose. "…Sorry about that."

"Don't ever be sorry about mourning," Leah said. "It's necessary. You're okay."

"Thanks." She leaned back. "Draso's breath. I thought I was over Mara."

"Wounds leave a scar," Leah said. "And sometimes they still hurt."

Ethos stared up at the bunk bed. "Yeah. That makes sense."

They were silent for several minutes.

"What was Ari's real name?"

Ethos sat up. "I'm sorry?"

You selfish, disgusting--

But Leah fought that time. She had to know. "Ari. Was that a code name too?"

Ethos blinked, but then chuckled. "Yeah, it was." She smiled. "Her name was Dawn."

Leah smiled, but then tilted her head. "Wait. Dawn Fawn?"

Ethos laughed. "Yeah, our mother wasn't great with names. Dawn loved it though. She said it suited her. She was a sunrise."

Ari's bright laugh echoed in Leah's ears. "Yeah. She really was."

Ethos leaned on Leah's shoulder. "Guess my mourning made you think of her. Sorry."

"Don't be," Leah said. "I… don't think I'm finished mourning her either."

"Understandable." She scooted closer. "Don't answer if you're not comfortable, but… I know Ari was flirting outrageously with you on our trip through Canada, because *I* was flirting with you outrageously. Did… anything come of that?"

Leah's ears flushed again. "Well, she certainly got physical with me. But I put it off. I wanted to focus on the mission." She sighed. "I regret that now."

"Hmm." Ethos nuzzled her, just a little. "I see. Thanks for sharing."

Leah pulled back. She gave her what she hoped was a flirty smile. "Why do you ask?"

Ethos smiled back, eyes half lidded. "Oh, no reason." Then she frowned and leaned away. "Sorry. I've been flirting with you nonstop even after I said I wouldn't, but now it feels like I'm using my grief as a way to force you into something. Or maybe… maybe looking for a replacement for Mara. That's not right."

Leah flattened one ear. She lay back on the bed. "Honestly, I appreciate you admitting that. And… I kind of feel the same way. Like I'm using you to get what I missed out on with Ari." She sighed. "But it won't bring her back. I shouldn't be looking to 'fix' it. And… I can't be Mara. I'm not interested in romance anyway. The physical stuff is all I need."

Ethos leaned back too, laying an arm over her head. "Curse our consciences."

Leah snuggled close and wrapped an arm across Ethos' stomach. "We could always just cuddle. And I wouldn't mind the company tonight."

Ethos faced her, and gently stroked her cheek. "That I think I could do."

"Let me get into PJs first," Leah said.

Ethos grinned. "Can I watch?"

Leah lifted her brows and smiled. "Sure." She slipped her shirt over her head.

A few minutes later the two of them were cuddled under the blankets on the bottom bunk. Leah lay on her back and Ethos snuggled into her side, nuzzling into her neck. She sighed happily. "I think I like this better."

Leah stared up at the bunk, gently rubbing the fur between Ethos' ears. "Yeah, same." She pulled the covers closer.

Pilot didn't manifest, but he purred curiously. "Should I, uh, leave you two alone?"

Leah chuckled. "Probably." She frowned. "I'm sorry I shouted at you."

"It's fine," Pilot said. "I'm an ancient A.I. I know how difficult it is to shut off your brain sometimes. Goodnight." The light from his datashard faded.

Ethos fell asleep surprisingly fast. Maybe this was what Leah needed. If only as a chance to escape her selfishness.

If only the Thought Monster would shut up.

It took her a good thirty minutes to fall into a restless sleep.

The sun poked beams into Leah's eye way too soon. She blinked sleepily.

Ethos was still cuddled close. One dainty strap had slid down her shoulder. Leah smiled and rubbed her arm. Ethos yawned and opened one eye. She tightened her grip around Leah's stomach.

The gentle whine of Pilot's datashard warming hit her ears. Guess that was the sign to wake up. She turned in the bed.

And froze.

"Ethos…"

Ethos stretched and turned, but then tensed up next to Leah.

Pilot's avatar hung by its neck, his eyes dead and black, and big, bold words hovered over his head, covering the entire wall.

GET OFF THE TRAIN.

CHAPTER 37

TEAM BUILDING

Philip Black sat on the couch in an unfamiliar living room, watching the blue otter Kitta tinker with the shield generator. The early morning dawn barely shone through trees outside the ceiling-high picture windows, painting leafy shadows on the beige carpet. One of the humans, someone called Ackerson, took a sip of his water, wiped his mouth and neatly-trimmed beard, then placed the glass on the clear side table with a loud clunk.

Everyone in the room looked at him. Except Kitta. She kept her gaze on the generator. Her hands shook.

Philip pulled his knees up to his chin.

Ackerson carefully folded his hands in his lap and held his chin high. His team watched a moment longer, then went back to whatever they had been doing prior. Ackerson kept his face neutral.

Philip shivered. The tension in the air sent his heart racing and tears built in his eyes. What was going to happen to him?

Where was Neil?

Millie, a gray rat, tossed the rat-shaped crystal that she shared with her partner, Ralph into the air, over and over. A gray lump that could almost be mistaken for used bar-b-que charcoal like when he cooked at the beach with Neil. It weirdly matched her own scraggly gray fur and thick bare tail. Ralph's black fur was also a mess, like he never cleaned himself. He picked at his ear, then held up his hands. "Hey Mill, toss me a bone."

She grinned, held her hand out, and threw it forward. A blast of white-hot energy flew from her fingertips and smashed into Ralph's outstretched hands in a shower of sparks. Ralph laughed, but Kitta yelped and shielded herself. Luana let out a little gasp, but Florina just sighed.

Philip pulled down his ears, shivering.

"Hey assholes," Theophania said, walking into the room. She brushed her long blond braid across her broad shoulder and scratched the stubble on the side of her head. "Don't waste your magic on games, okay? I know how long it takes for that Blood Crystal to recharge and we need everyone at full strength." She sat on the couch next to Philip, too close for comfort. Philip resisted the urge to scoot away. He wasn't sure what punishment that would land him.

When he had first met Theophania, she had been so nice. She liked taking him for ice cream and reading stories to him and telling dramatic tales of her time in the war. She reminded him a lot of Neil.

But one day Philip woke up to find the house completely stripped of everything. Theophania grabbed him by the arm, shoved a backpack in his hand, and threw him into the back of a van with the windows blocked out. They stopped in an underground garage and then he found himself here. It had been almost a week now. Maybe. He had hardly slept.

The only other person here who seemed to care about him was the blue otter, Kitta. She was kind at least, making sure he got fed and bathed. She even got a couple of books for him.

But only when no one else was watching. He had a feeling she wasn't supposed to help.

He hugged his knees. He was going to die here.

Ralph leaned back in his chair, letting the remaining magic dance between his fingers. "The hell for? The magic comes back fast enough. Just because the old man is paranoid."

Ackerson crossed his arms.

"It's not *paranoia,*" Luana said. She rubbed her brown arms. "Vincent is *dead* and that rat Neil killed Jaska."

Philip perked his ears.

Millie raised an eyebrow.

Luana rolled her eyes. "It's a figure of speech, god."

"Oh, get over it," Millie said. "Jaska was a ticking timebomb anyway. He just wanted to destroy. It was only a matter of time before he turned on us all."

"One could argue we all fit there," Kitta muttered, though no one seemed to hear her.

Luana narrowed her gaze at Millie. "Point is, I didn't think *anyone* could kill Jaska, and that puma did. And he's not even a mage."

"We're certain about that then," Ackerson said. His perfectly controlled voice boomed through the living room and instantly everyone turned their gaze to him, even Kitta. "I ask because I was certain *no one* in Outlander was a mage. I built them that way on purpose. But it turns out nearly *all* of them were."

"You also told Corbin and me that the cat and Prínkipas from Mage were harmless," Fedir said, his thick Eastern European accent rolling off his tongue. He shook his head, fluffing up his fur, his sharpened antlers catching shed fur from the air. He pawed at the Ei-Ei jewels around his eyes. "And yet now we learn they took down Judgement. Ronan told us Judgement could not be defeated."

"She can't," Ronan said, his voice deep and menacing. His wings glitched in an out of view and he glared at Fedir in a dare. Judgement, the strange, gloopy monster next to him, flicked a black mudball into the air and caught it. Like Ronan, she twisted and turned like a computer glitch, though not nearly as much.

Philip recoiled to a corner of the couch. Theophania eyed him, then moved closer too, trapping him. Kitta shot her a glare, but Theophania didn't notice.

Fedir crossed his arms. "Then what do you call the defeat at the Desert Wall?"

Tiny mudballs flew across the room, hitting everyone square in the forehead. Words swelled in Philip's mind, along with a deep, nauseating smell. *A retreat,* Judgement said. She nodded to Ronan. *This one was the one defeated. I am anchored to him, and need him in order to act.* She glanced around the room, flicking more mudballs. *Unless there is a volunteer to replace him as summoner?*

"We all see what you've done to him," the strange puma that looked like Neil said. "I don't think any of us are suited to that… responsibility."

Judgement grinned with a too-wide mouth dripping with black ink. *Your loss.*

"You shouldn't even be here anyway," Florina said. "You're supposed to be looking for Jaden in Canada."

Ronan snorted. "Until Trecheon and his friend actually finds him, we're staying here," he said. "Canada is far too large to try and investigate without any kind of guide."

"So what you actually mean is," Florina said. "You're *useless.*"

Ronan snarled at her, though Judgement stopped him with a gloopy wing against his back, spraying ink everywhere. Several dropps landed on Philip's tail. *Patience, master. You will win. Have faith.*

Ronan stayed silent.

Millie nodded to Fedir. "Aren't you supposed to shed your antlers soon?"

"It is the season, yes," Fedir said. "But they are not yet loose. Do not detract from the question."

"Then why do you bother sharpening them?"

"The better to impale you with, *pizda*," he said, then turned to Ackerson. "Answer the question."

Ackerson lifted his chin. "Maybe you should actually ask one then," he said.

Fedir narrowed his gaze, rumbling. "Why did you tell Corbin and me that the cat and quilar were harmless?"

Ackerson waved a hand. "They were when they worked for me. Can't help it that they found some way to get magic."

"Hrumph," Fedir said. "You have lied before. Outlander is proof of that."

Everyone stopped and stared at Fedir and Ackerson. The silence was deafening, but Ackerson refused to back down.

"Being ignorant is not the same as lying."

"It was your job to vet them," Fedir said. "You know the signs of a mage. Yet you missed all of them."

Ackerson stood. "You are treading on thin ice, Fedir. Mistakes happen. Even for me."

Fedir snorted. "That is evident."

"Them being mages doesn't change anything," Ralph said. "We'll still have no problem taking them out."

"Knowing what *kind* of mages would be helpful though," Fedir said. "One could argue it *necessary.*"

"I don't think they're *all* mages," Florina said. "If Neil was a mage, he wouldn't have had to use a knife to take out Jaska." She juggled fireball marbles in one hand.

"Absence of proof is not proof," Ackerson said.

"Can't see him having any *useful* magic," Millie said. She pulled a tuft out of her own fur and nibbled on the end of it. "If he was smart, he would have used a Wish to keep track of his baby brother." She grinned at Philip, fur tuft between her teeth, then held her hands out, lighting them with magic again.

Philip hunched down, staring at her.

Ackerson narrowed his gaze. "Millie, put that damn thing away and save it, for God's sake."

Millie rolled her eyes, but snuffed the magic. "Paranoid."

"Prepared," Ackerson said.

"There," Kitta said. She patted the big machine, though still wouldn't look Ackerson in the eye. "Good as I can get her. When we're finally off this planet, we can have a proper shield generator, but for now, this colony ship one will do. Though without the infrastructure, I can't get the bubble bigger than the house."

"It'll do," Ackerson said.

Theophania crossed her arms. "Are we still planning on getting off this rock?"

"In time," Ackerson said. "That's why all you stick with me, isn't it?"

Millie grinned. "Well, it sure as hell isn't because of your winning personality."

"Funny," Ackerson said.

"Only as long as you keep your promise to us," Fedir said, his voice dark and dangerous. "I do not like the idea of getting killed waiting for you to finally get us to greener woods."

Ackerson held himself high, chin raised. "I'm not planning on us getting killed." Theophania scoffed and looked off, a strange sadness covering her features. Philip almost felt sad for her. Ackerson continued. "But I do expect patience. The Fawns destroyed their communication equipment when they fled, so we're floating dead in the water until we can get the Zyearth tech we need to catch Sharp's contacts."

"Why didn't we do this sooner?" Florina asked through gritted teeth.

"I had *planned* to do this sooner," Ackerson said. "Then the Zyearthlings showed up. Can't exactly escape the planet illegally while the crown jewel of Galactic InterPol is watching the skies."

Theophania leaned back on the couch. "I was under the impression that the Zyearthlings left Galactic InterPol. That's what Sharp said."

Ackerson's eye twitched. "They still work with them, even if they aren't members. Any suspicious activity is going to set off alarm bells. So while they were here, we could do nothing."

"The Zyearthlings left Earth," Kitta said.

"Astute observation," Ackerson snarled, making her cower. "And Sharp was sending out calls when he could. Then the Fawn's betrayed me and ended all that. But the Zyearthlings have an established connection to Earth now. They left behind everything we need. Defender pendants, an A.I., and I can only imagine the equipment we'll find on Athánatos when we get there. And Outlander's little ragtag team can't best us without their Zyearthling allies. Florina just needs to get the hang of creating rips in their strange Veil. We'll get this. Give it time."

Philip's eyes grew wide again. Athánatos… Neil talked about it all the time. It was the place Damianos and Natassa came from. He kept saying he'd take Philip after he got adopted. It was safe. No one could get there.

But Ackerson could. He'd destroy it. He shook himself.

Then the electricity went out, shutting off the AC and dousing them in darkness. Ackerson sighed. "I thought you said that generator didn't need much power to stay on."

"It doesn't," Kitta said. "Most of its power is from Jordan's old Gem."

"Then what--"

The house shook and everyone's fur and hair stood on end. Ackerson gripped the arms of his chair. "Status, anyone!"

Judgement moved in the dark, her shining inky skin catching a little light. Large mudballs hit everyone around them. Philip hastily wiped it away, but he couldn't help hearing the words.

It is the Phonar.

Kitta gasped. "Are they *serious?*"

"So *shut it down,*" Ackerson spat.

Florina held up a hand, drawing in a bolt of magic from somewhere, sucking the static from the air. Fur and hair settled down. Philip covered his ears.

But the shield generator snapped and sparked. Kitta leapt back with a yelp. Then all the lights on the machine shut off.

Ackerson's heart skipped a beat, but he kept his face neutral. "The hell happened?"

Kitta looked over the generator. "It's *dead.*"

"Get it back online," Ackerson said.

"I'm *trying,*" Kitta said. "It'll need a minute--"

"There's a second summon!" Florina said. "Hold on!" She pressed her hand to the floor.

Everything rumbled. Not an earthquake… earth magic. The windows shattered as panic started to settle in. Philip screamed and Theophania leapt off the couch. Ackerson stood now, covering his head with his arm, though the glass fell harmlessly to the floor.

Then the shaking stopped. Florina growled. "Damn summons…"

Kitta huddled in on herself. "Any more…?"

Fedir stood tall and sent out a flash of fire, then ice, then water, then stone, but nothing happened. "The air is clear. I'm not feeling any of the others."

Theophania narrowed her gaze. "You got all the elements except one. What about Zeke's bird?"

Florina laughed. "What, afraid of a little wind? I'd love to see what they think Zeke's little pet could do, because it ain't much."

Fedir's voice rumbled. "His bird should not be underestimated." He whipped up a small twister.

But while everyone's gaze was on the upper parts of the windows, Philip had his trained on the ground. A black bird, a crow or a raven, hopped around among the broken glass, completely silent. He met Philip's gaze with a piercing purple eye. A single ember flew at him, landing in his fur, and a comforting voice cooled his mind.

When the fire starts, the voice said. *Run to me.*

Philip stared, but he nodded, very slightly.

The raven opened his wings, shooting purple flames in all directions. Fire caught the rafters and hanging lights and crashed down on the group.

Florina screamed and she and Theophania ran for the door, but they crashed into an invisible shield. The shield generator had gone back up. Florina waved a hand, trying to put the fire out with water, but for some reason that only fed the fire. Fedir pushed sand instead, though it did little to stop the smoke.

Several phoenixes flew in now, diving on Angel, their magic filling the room.

Florina shot massive bolts of electricity at the three of them. The owl and kestrel took the hits head-on and crashed to the floor, vanishing in wave of particles, but the golden eagle vanished before it got hit.

Millie and Ralph ran into the kitchen trying to escape the flames. "Turn off the shield, Kitta!" Millie shouted.

"I'm *trying!*" Kitta pounded on the machine, waving her hands, trying to get the smoke and fire to clear. Falling debris bounced off the little shield she had around her, cracking it.

Philip saw his chance. He ran for the raven.

But Theophania saw him and snatched him up, lifting him off the ground. "Don't you *dare,* you little *shit.*"

The raven cawed at her and divebombed her face, but the inky monster blasted him away with a disgusting blast of black mud. The bird fell to the ground and vanished in a thousand tiny purple particles. Philip cried and the monster laughed, gurgling with a sick pleasure.

"Get the brat to the vans!" Ackerson shouted. "We'll wave him in their faces and get them to stop. Luana, get over here!"

Luana stumbled through the smoke. She stared at Ackerson's terribly burned hands. "Are you *insane?*"

"Heal it!" Ackerson demanded.

She held her hands up. "I can't heal that! It'll kill me!"

He pressed a pistol to the side of her head. Philip struggled in Theophania's arms, crying, but she held him tight. Ackerson glared at Luana. "Heal it or you'll die anyway."

She stared, wide eyed. "But--"

"Either you heal it now and take a chance at survival, or you take a bullet to the head and die for certain." He drilled the muzzle into her skull. *"Last chance, Luana."*

She blinked, tears building in her eyes. Then she got to work fixing his burns. Ragged cuts slashed through her skin while she worked, making her wince with every psychic mending.

Luana groaned. "It's enough… You can heal normally now. Just--"

He shook the gun. "Don't stop."

She dropped to her knees, still working the healing. Blood ran down her skin, staining the carpet underneath her. She lay in a puddle of her own blood, convulsing, coughing. She held out a hand to him. *"Help... don't leave me..."*

Then the shielder powered down. Kitta waved a hand, coughing, clutching the colorless Gem. "Everyone out!" Theophania pulled Philip toward the underground garage. Philip watched Ackerson and Luana.

He left her. Bleeding on the floor. Philip caught a glimpse of Fedir bending over her as he left.

Philip coughed, his lungs aching. *Neil, save me... please.*

CHAPTER 38

GUARDIAN

Trecheon leaned against the van, hoping the thick trees surrounding it was enough to keep them hidden. Unlikely, with Pathos and Logos' massive snipers and thick, reflective scopes, but he could still hope. It was a terrible plan, leaving Ouranos and Zeke to tackle Angel without the summons, especially with Zeke's powers not fully under control and Andre with no powers at all. But he trusted Ouranos with his life, so he figured he could trust him with Andre and Zeke's lives as well.

But he didn't trust the Fawns with anything. So he went with them.

Even though he had never worked with them directly during his time as their assassin, the proximity to them while they held those massive sniper rifles unnerved him. They both lay prone on top of the van, hidden behind the live oak foliage, watching everything unfold through the scopes. Trecheon was directly under their barrels, and though he knew they could do nothing to him in this position, his heart still raced.

"You didn't have to come with us, you know," one of the doe said, though Trecheon couldn't tell which one.

He huffed in response.

Pathos stuck her head over the edge of the van. "I know you have no reason to trust us, Trecheon, but I promise you, we are not your enemy."

Trecheon crossed his arms and looked away. "I don't know who my enemies are anymore. I might even be my own enemy."

"From where I'm sitting, yeah," Pathos said.

Trecheon glared up at her. "I didn't ask you."

"You invited discussion."

"Shut up, both of you," Logos said. "The summons are going in."

Trecheon turned his attention back to the mansion. From his vantage point, it was basically a doll house and the summons were hardly more than specks.

He squinted. "You two sure you can hit them this far back?"

Pathos repositioned herself on the van. "I know it's hard, Trecheon, but just trust me. We have our reputation for a reason."

Trecheon growled and focused his attention on the summons.

Jústi dove in and bathed the house in electricity. Sure enough, the shield held tough, but not for long. It burst in a shower of sparks, forcing Jústi back. Trecheon couldn't even see Pax as he dove into the ground and shook the house, but he did see the shimmer of falling glass as all the windows blew out.

Then Excelsis dove in, setting the place ablaze. Trecheon winced. He had to hope he'd get Philip out in time.

The roof caught fire almost immediately, sending dark pillars of smoke into the air. But no one left the building. Maybe they got them all. Wishful thinking.

"Heads up, ladies," Andre said over the comms. *"Damage is done, but the cameras aren't picking up anyone leaving."*

"There!" Pathos said.

"How many?" Trecheon asked.

Pathos paused. "Just one," she said finally. "Shit. Two. Theophania. She has Philip."

"Where?" Andre asked. *"I can't get them on the cameras."*

"Heading around the side of the house," Pathos said. She cursed again. "They have a van. Andre, get Neil. We need our ground team."

"On it." Andre cut the comms.

Trecheon looked at the Fawns. "Can you get her?"

Pathos tensed. "Cover your ears."

Trecheon pulled his ears down.

Pathos fired, making Trecheon's bones rumble.

"Shit," Pathos said.

Trecheon snarled, his ears ringing terribly. "You *missed?"*

"On purpose," Pathos said. "She picked Philip up. Would have killed him instead."

Trecheon snarled. "If you so much as nick him, you're *dead."* His pendant beeped. He fumbled with it and pulled it up. "Ouranos?"

"Zeke," Zeke answered. "We can see Ackerson's team evacuating, but we can't tell which one has Philip. Should we--"

"Zeke, on your right!" Andre shouted.

A loud bang sounded through the communicator. Trecheon glanced over the cliff, but he couldn't see any of his teammates through the trees. "Zeke? Come in!"

"Damn Paper Wasps!" Zeke shouted. "Ouranos, Andre, look out--"

Another bang. This time the explosion lit up one of the trees. Shouting lit up the pendant's communication, but Trecheon couldn't tell who it was.

"Shit!" Trecheon turned to the van. "We gotta get down there, now!"

A gust of wind brushed against Trecheon's neck. *Eyes up, Guardian!*

Trecheon glanced up. Archángeli rushed the van and landed on the edge of the cliff. Trecheon narrowed his gaze. "I'm not a Guardian."

We haven't the time to argue, Archángeli said with a brush of wind. They lifted up and hovered as best they could. *Hold out your arm. Time is of the essence.*

"Go," Pathos said. "We'll see what we can do about Ackerson's stragglers."

Trecheon lowered his gaze. "If you do anything to hurt my team--"

"Then you have our permission to burn us to a crisp," Logos said. "Draso knows we'd deserve it. Just go!" She lay prone and rested the stock against her shoulder.

Trecheon huffed, then held his arm to the bird, and Archángeli grabbed him. The pair sailed toward Zeke and Ouranos.

Your enemy is savage, Archángeli said. *He forced one of his mages to heal him at her own expense then left her to die in the flames while he escaped.*

Trecheon winced. "Did you see Philip?"

Theophania has a death grip on him, they replied. *But Neil and his team are ready for her.*

Hopefully, Trecheon added.

Archángeli swooped over the tops of the trees and soon Trecheon caught a glimpse of the scene.

Zeke lay on the ground, gripping his arm, elemental marbles flying wildly all around him. Ouranos stood between Zeke and a red wolf with a manic look in his eye. He held a tiny machine in his hand.

Andre lay on the ground behind Zeke, unmoving. *Shit.*

Those damn Nanos. That must be Caster.

"Get me in close!" Trecheon said. He shielded himself pulling on all the strength he could. "Let go now!"

Archángeli let go.

Trecheon flew through the air and tackled the red wolf. Caster snarled, gnashing his teeth, but Trecheon got his hand under the wolf's snout and pushed his head hard to the ground. He wrestled the Nano out of the Caster's hand and threw it as far as he could. It exploded several feet away, blasting Trecheon's face with heat, but at least the flames didn't touch him.

The wolf kicked Trecheon in the stomach, sending him flying off. Caster scrambled up as Ouranos ran to Trecheon.

Caster bared all his teeth. "So Ackerson was right. Outlander rides again."

"Outlander is *dead,*" Trecheon spat. "You're looking at a …Defender." Damn it, this was not the time to hesitate!

Caster laughed. "Such conviction." He dug into his pockets and pulled out a half dozen more Nanos. "Let's see what you're worth, *Defender.*" He tossed them all up. The golf ball-sized drones caught the air and flew about.

"Scatter!" Trecheon called, and shielded everyone.

CHAPTER 39

OPERATION RESCUE KIT

Neil sat in the van as they pulled up close to the ranch, trying to calm his beating heart.

He had never known fear like this before. Not even in the war. War at least had expectations. He'd to come to peace with the possibility of his own death dozens of times in war. He had learned how to suppress it.

Sort of.

But this… This wasn't just fear for his own life. This moment could strip him of almost every person who meant something to him. Dami, Natassa, Sacha.

Philip.

Trecheon.

And he could do literally nothing. Couldn't be the leader he needed to be. Hell, couldn't even *help*. He had to rely fully on the family he was afraid to lose. He curled in on himself, hoping he wouldn't explode.

Natassa wrapped her arms around him. "Courage, my Heart. You have a support network."

"Trust us, love," Dami said, gripping Neil's hand. "We'll get Philip out today, safe and sound." He smiled, though his ears twitched. "You told me that we will have peace again. Philip is part of that. Think of this as a step toward peace."

Neil looked into their eyes. He gripped both their hands. "You could both die today…"

They pressed their foreheads against Neil's head.

"No one is going to die today," Sacha said. "Unless it's Ackerson or his cronies. I stake my life--"

"Sacha," Neil said. *"Don't.* I don't want to lose you either. You understand? You're valuable too. Life wouldn't be the same." He flicked his tail. "Trecheon wouldn't be the same."

Sacha flattened her ears.

Andre called on Neil's comm. *"Heads up! The summons attacked the mansion and Theophania is escaping with Philip! They're in a gray van, heading for the east exit."*

"Shit!" Sacha put their van into gear and drove off. "Where's the east exit, Andre?"

"Head down Brockton, left on Foxcove--gah!"

Neil's heart froze. "Andre?"

"Watch out, Andre!" Zeke calling. Then the pendant dropped communication.

"Damn it!" Sacha said. "Hang on, I'll do what I can!" She made a left on Foxcove.

A gray van peeled out of a hidden driveway and tore down the road.

Neil stood, steadying himself as the van rocked, and plopped into the passenger seat, his heart threatening to burst. "Is that them?"

"I can only assume," Sacha said. The van pulled ahead. "Shit, they're fast!" They drove several minutes until they cleared the ranches and entered a small housing tract, with undeveloped desert on the left side.

Neil pulled out a pistol, a Collins .225, that the Fawns had supplied him with. Tiny and useless in most situations.

But if he could hit a tire…

He rolled down the window and leaned out. "Hold us steady!" He squeezed off two shots, puncturing the back tires.

The enemy van hit the brakes and swerved, before turning on its side and crashing, sliding down the asphalt. Before Sacha could get to them, the backdoor flopped open and Theophania rolled out with Philip.

Wait. Two Theophanias. With two Philips.

Neil stared, slack jawed. Her magic. It made him see his worst fears.

Twice.

The two blonde humans stared as Sacha's van skidded to a halt, then they took off in opposite directions, dragging their Philips with them.

Sacha ripped off her seat belt and ran right. "Natassa, with me! Give Dami a blast of lightning, then Dami, you go after the other one!"

But Neil couldn't wait. Collins in hand, he ran after the other Theophania, following her into the bare desert.

"Neil, wait!" Sacha shouted. "Stay here!"

Neil tuned her out.

To hell with predictions. He needed his brother. So he ran.

Damianos appeared at his left, hands lit up with electricity. "Neil, you cannot do this!"

"I can't sit here and do *nothing!*" Neil said. Theophania and Philip weaved around a series of tumbleweeds and Neil followed. "Just don't let me touch her and it'll all work out, but I can't let Philip be alone!"

Dami ran alongside him, but he nodded. He squeezed his magic-laden hands into fists. "What should we do?"

Neil ducked under a low-hanging Joshua tree. "Can you hit her without hurting Philip?"

"Not likely," Damianos said. "Not while she is holding his hand."

"Then can you… Wait."

Philip turned back to Neil, tears running down his fur… then he vanished. And suddenly it wasn't Theophania running from them anymore, it was a grown puma.

Neil snarled. That damn *magic*. Deceptive, rotten *bullshit*. No more playing around. He paused, aimed, and fired the Collins. The puma dashed left, but the bullet still caught his collarbone and he crashed to the ground with a yelp.

Neil dashed over and kicked the puma onto his back. He yowled. Neil aimed the gun at his face. *"Where the hell is my brother?"*

The puma spat blood at Neil and muttered something in some harsh language Neil couldn't recognize. But he didn't need to know the words to understand the meaning.

Go to hell.

Neil gritted his teeth. He roared and unloaded the entire magazine into the puma. All ten remaining shots peppered the puma's chest and head, shooting blood and brains into the air, his body convulsing with each shot until the mag emptied, the slide locked out of place, and the trigger clicked against nothing. Neil only saw red. He couldn't stop firing.

Damianos gently gripped Neil's wrist. Neil shook himself and stared down. Blood everywhere. Clothes, flesh, and fur torn apart by bullets. The desert soaked up the puma's remains. One eye had been shot out, but the other stared up, permanently shocked, spattered with blood, his mouth unnaturally wide. Unmoving.

The carnage burned into Neil's brain. He had seen this before. In war. Vicious, violent, desperate attacks, leaving nothing but broken bodies in the dust. Adrenaline flooded his system and suddenly he was back in battle, fighting for his life, for his team's life, for Trecheon's life, hoping to survive and see Philip once more. Just *once more.*

Then the shakes started. His heart wouldn't slow. His breathing quickened. His vision blurred. All his senses ripped him away from reality and plopped him in a world made entirely of fear.

Damianos wrapped his arms around Neil's shoulders and held him. Neil reached up absently and gripped his arm, only mildly aware of his surroundings. Dami's arm grounded him… but only just.

Good God, what had he just done?

"We need to return," Damianos said. "And find your brother."

"…Y-Yeah." Neil's voice squeaked. He turned slowly away, absentmindedly messing with the pistol's slide before pocketing it. He walked back toward the van way too slow, but he couldn't make his body move. Everything kept him in that world of fear.

Philip needs you.

But Dami just saw the assassin in me.

He stopped. Dami saw that. The assassin. Because no matter how much Neil had tried to put it away, it was never completely gone. It was just hidden.

He was broken. He could never marry Natassa or Dami like this. He couldn't help Athánatos.

He couldn't save Philip.

Dami gripped his shoulders. "Neil?"

"I'm… sorry." Neil said, his voice shaking. "I'm sorry, Dami."

"You are forgiven."

Neil met his gaze. Dami smiled, for whatever that was worth. Still that same love he had always had in his smile, his eyes, his gentle touch. This was Neil's reality. Not war, not assassins. Just… love. "You are forgiven, Neil. As you always have been. But you need to learn to forgive yourself."

And that finally chased the trauma monster back into his cave. A fire lit on Neil's tail, dragging him back to reality. "Philip."

Dami nodded, determined. "Let us hurry."

And they ran.

CASTER

Zeke scrambled to his feet and dashed left, trying to keep his eye on Trecheon.

And Andre. He hadn't moved since that first explosion knocked them all on their tails. *Draso, let him be alive!*

God, his arm felt like it was on fire.

Trecheon leapt to the right and threw a fireball at one of the Nanos, blowing it up. Zeke held up his good hand as the bomb hit him with heat and flame, though Trecheon's shield held, but barely. Trecheon snarled. "Take these things out!"

Zeke pulled on his magic, but all he got was frantic blasts of dust, fire, and stones flying every which-way. He ran for a tree instead. *Damn it, not now! Not when Andre needs me!*

Ouranos dashed to one side and froze several drones, dropping them to the dirt. Trecheon kicked them hard and they flew off, exploding harmlessly.

Zeke bared his teeth, determined to make his magic work. He aimed a fire marble at one of the Nanos, but the marble zigzagged around it before crashing into a bush, setting it ablaze. Zeke cursed.

"Remember the song!" Ouranos called as he put out the flames. He dodged another Nano as the drone chased him.

Zeke bared his teeth, and threw an iceball forward, smashing the drone chasing Ouranos. He ran through the song in his head. *Sisters brave, Sisters free, Meeting under mahogany tree...*

Something heavy fell on his head and crashed to the floor – a large stone. Zeke rubbed his head and found blood. Was that his own magic? He glanced up.

Large pockets of elemental magic floated over his head – water, iceballs, fire, stones, all swirling about in a slow-moving wind.

Then they all fell at once.

Zeke dove out of the way, pulling hard on the magic. *Go after Caster, not me!*

But the magic chased him. He had to get it away from Andre.

"Zeke, ground yourself!" Ouranos shouted.

Zeke snarled. Not the time!

Two more drones headed for Trecheon. The red quilar turned and ran, though the drones followed close by.

Zeke rushed after him. He couldn't control his magic normally but maybe... "Trecheon, shield me!"

Trecheon whipped about and threw his hands forward. A shield shimmered around him. He dove under the drones.

The wild magic crashed into them, exploding them to bits. The elements vanished in the explosion, burning through Trecheon's shield and singeing Zeke's skin under his fur. He crashed hard to the ground and his arm cracked, shooting fire through his bones. He screamed, holding the arm close.

Trecheon turned. "Zeke!"

Zeke stood. He couldn't stop now. Not with those paper wasps. He had people to protect. He fought back the pain and rage, running the song in his head, determined to keep a hold of his magic, then turned to Caster.

But Caster wasn't pulling impossible amounts of drones out of his pockets anymore. Instead, he lay on the ground, convulsing, foaming at the mouth. A colorless, dull rock lay near his hand as if it had just come out of his pocket.

Caster looked up at him, eyes blank, choking on foam, but for a brief second, his gaze focused and he shakingly tapped the dull rock at his side. Then his head jolted to one side and he stopped moving completely.

Trecheon looked him over. "What the hell just happened?"

Zeke glanced down at the rock… no, the crystal. Shaped like a simple wolf. He immediately thought of the pink doe crystal the Fawns had. A Blood Crystal? He picked it up with his good hand.

Caster's body cracked and shook, then slowly crumbled to a fine dust. Trecheon yelped and leapt back. Ouranos winced, hands up.

Zeke turned to the side and threw up. He wiped his mouth.

Andre groaned.

Zeke stood straight up. "Andre!" He ran for him.

But something black and gloopy snatched him and pressed him hard to the ground. His immediate thought was Cast… but it wasn't.

It was Judgement. Zyfaunos-sized, with gloopy black fur, huge inky wings, and blue Cast eyes. She watched him with a wide, drippy grin, glitching left and right like he had seen Ronan do. *Hello, Prínkipas,* she said. *So good to see you… up close.*

"Zeke!" Trecheon and Ouranos ran for him.

My stay is short lived, Judgement said. *But I see... potential in you. In the Azure family line. Such passionate people you are. Exactly what I need.*

Zeke's magic exploded off his body, flying through the air, though none of it affected her. He struggled under her, frantic. She smiled. *There it is, little Prínkipas. The desperation of the Azure. The focus on one goal, one need.* She held out a hand. *It is early, but maybe...*

Wind whipped about her and she shrieked. Though it almost seemed like a laugh.

Archángeli dove on her, claws out, wind magic ripping through them. They slammed into her, tearing her off Zeke. Though how much Archángeli's attack did, Zeke couldn't tell. She gave a muddy, goopy wink to Zeke. *Not yet then. Until we meet again.* She vanished into the desert as Archángeli rushed after her. Trecheon moved like he wanted to chase her down, but Ouranos held him back, thank god.

Zeke brushed the leftover mud and gunk off him, fighting the desire to throw up. He gripped his arm.

Andre was on his knees now, shaking himself and gripping his head. "Good god, the frick happened?"

You got hit by a paper wasp and I couldn't save you. Zeke stood up, shaking off the ick from Judgement. He shoved the experience aside, burying it in the recesses of his mind. Andre was more important. He kneeled beside Andre. "...You okay?"

Andre coughed. "Could be better. Christ, my ribs..."

The Fawn's van rolled up now, crunching tires against the dirt. Logos threw open the door. "If you all are done gawking, Ackerson and Angel are escaping. Get in!"

Zeke pocketed the crystal and he and Ouranos helped Andre into the van.

Andre shook his head several times and pulled up his laptop. "Gimme a sec, I'll get the gate." The door slowly opened and Logos burst through it, heading for the mansion.

Zeke hissed in pain. Trecheon frowned and pressed a hand to the broken arm, though with all that magic expenditure, the heal went slow. Zeke frowned. "Andre--"

"I'm good," Andre said. "I've had worse. Don't worry about me. Get yourself healed up."

But it was all Zeke could focus on.

EXPOSED

Neil ran as fast as he could back toward the crash site. Logic dictated one thing. If the Theophania he had been chasing wasn't real, then the one Sacha and Natassa ran after was.

And Neil wasn't going to let them chase her alone.

As they neared the van, Dami turned to him. "Should you replenish your firearm?"

Images of that dead puma still haunted Neil's brain, warping and morphing into Philip, dead on the ground, forever staring blankly. He shook himself. "No. I don't want to risk hitting Philip and I don't know if shooting Theophania counts as 'touching' her."

"Wait, Neil. Look!" Dami pointed back toward the neighborhood.

Neil's own motorbike stood outside. He hadn't brought it there though. The hell did that come from?

But then he saw the figures.

Theophania stood in one of the driveways, holding Philip by the arm, dragging him along the lawn. She held a long shining object in her hand, but Neil couldn't tell what it was at that distance.

Sacha was nowhere to be found.

Dami took off toward them. Neil followed, pure adrenaline running his every movement. *Don't hurt him, don't kill him, just let me get to him, PLEASE!*

Then Theophania looked up and spotted them. She turned to run, dragging Philip with her.

Philp held a hand out. *"NEIL!"*

Dami snarled and threw his magic forward, crashing lightning into the grass, throwing up dirt and vegetation, making Theophania and Philip's hair and fur stand up. Philip shouted, but they did stop. Theophania pulled Philip close to her, wrapping an arm under his chin and holding the long object near his head. Neil finally saw what it was.

A machete.

"Stay the hell away, Black, or your brother will be pieces on the dirt."

Philip wailed. "Neil, help, *please!*" It stabbed Neil right through the heart.

Neil and Damianos stopped near the edge of the lawn. Neil held his hands up, but couldn't stop the shaking. "Theophania, *don't.* For God's sake, he's just a *child.*"

"I'm not an *idiot,*" Theophania said. "The moment I let him go, I'm dead." She held the machete close to his head. Philip sobbed loudly. Theophania shook him, but he didn't stop. She glared at Neil.

Neil stood there, torn. Was this like before? Was that Theophania's magic? Or was that really Philip? His vision blurred and his eyes burned. *Touch Theophania and Philip will die.* God, what was he supposed to *do?*

She drew the machete closer. Neil's heart threatened to burst out of his chest. She stepped back, shaking. "Effective, isn't it? Far more than a gun. Just imagine… ripping your baby brother's flesh to pieces, bit by bit."

Neil held a hand out. *"Don't--"*

"Should have kept better tabs on him," Theophania said, though her voice trembled. "Maybe paid better attention to who was pulling the strings going after Matron Fawn. Should've known better."

Dami bared his teeth, lightning flying all about him. "You speak too much."

"Give over, Athánatos," Theophania said. "All power but no strength." She glared at Neil. "You're probably wondering whether or not this is real." She lifted her head. "Do you want to risk it?"

Neil took one step forward. He couldn't help himself. "Come on, he's just a *kit*. How heartless are you?"

"Very, as it turns out."

"So what, we're at a standstill?" Neil said, though he took another step. "What do you want from me?"

"Maybe I don't want anything," Theophania said. "Or maybe I want to slowly lob pieces of his body off and watch you wallow in despair." Philip's sobs doubled. Snot ran down his face and he shook.

Nei's stomach dropped.

But Damianos lifted his head and relaxed, just slightly. "She is stalling."

Theophania frowned, brow furrowed. "Well then. Cleverer than you look."

Neil stared a moment, then glanced around. That meant the rest of Angel was on the way.

She held up one of Philip's hands. He tried pulling it back, but she held it rigidly in place. "Should we see how many fingers it takes for my team to come back?"

Neil stepped forward again. *"No!"*

Theophania raised the machete.

Sacha leapt out from the side of the house and slammed into Theophania with a loud roar, separating her from Philip. The pair rolled across the lawn toward Dami and Neil.

Neil leapt out of the way and ran to Philip. The young puma wrapped his arms around Neil's neck. Neil picked him up and held him tight, shutting his eyes to the world, taking in his brother's hug, his sobs of relief, all the snot and tears. He was afraid to open his eyes, afraid to let go. But he had his brother. He had him… Thank God.

Sacha roared again. Neil flashed his eyes open.

Sacha and Theophania wrestled on the grass, rolling around, each trying to pin the other. Theophania didn't have a machete after all, but a simple hammer, masked by her magic. She swung the thing left and right, aiming for Sacha's head, but Sacha kept building up a shield, blocking each attack. The hammer shattered each shield after a couple of blows. It was only a matter of time before Theophania got the right window.

Neil held Philip close. *Gotta rely on the mages.* "Dami, Natassa!"

Damianos shot electricity at Theophania, but it bounced off Sacha's shield and vanished into the air. "I cannot hit her! The shield is protecting them both!"

Neil turned to Natassa.

Natassa held her hands out, but she stood frozen. "I… I fear hurting her with any of my magic. Even the summons--"

Sacha called out. Theophania had her pinned to the grass, hammer above her head.

"Natassa!" Neil shouted. "Summons, *now!*"

Sacha raised her left hand, claws out, roaring so loud Neil's bones shook.

Natassa called Excelsis and Deo. They appeared in a flash of white and purple fire and rushed forward towards Theophania, trailing embers and the strong scent of smoke.

With a panic in her eye, Theophania aimed her hammer blow at Sacha's arm and smashed it into her palm, shattering it.

Shattering it. Not fur and bones, but wires, bolts, and jagged metal burst from the hand and arm, spraying the summons with scraps. Both squawked and flew back, raking their feathers free of fragments with their talons.

Neil's jaw dropped. She had *biomech?*

Theophania stared, breathing hard.

Sacha roared and thrust the jagged metal bone deep into the side of Theophania's neck. The metal punctured all the way through the neck, spraying blood and flesh everywhere. Sacha ripped it out and shoved her enemy aside. Theophania didn't even have a chance to gasp. Blood shot from the wound and exploded out of her mouth as she fell over, eyes wide, grasping for her neck, choking on her own blood, quivering, before she stopped moving all together, staring blankly. Sacha gasped for air, slowly standing.

Philip stared, tears still running down his snout, then he buried his face in Neil's shoulder, gripping him tight. Neil gripped him back, but couldn't take his eyes off Sacha. Blood splattered everywhere, mixing with the blood already on Neil's clothes.

She cradled her broken arm and turned to the group. "Everyone okay?" Her voice sounded hoarse and broken.

Neil took a step forward. "Are you…?"

She glanced quickly at the janky arm, gagged, then ripped off her uniform jacket and wrapped the arm in it. "…I will be."

Sirens echoed across the neighborhood and three police cars rolled up, lights blaring. Several cops poured out of the cars, guns drawn.

Quickly, though reluctantly, Neil put Philip down and raised his hands up. He urged everyone else to follow his example.

One cop dashed over to Neil and wrenched his arms behind his back, slapping cuffs on him. Neil expected that dull, familiar drone of the cop reading his Miranda rights, though the officers cuffed them in total silence. Neil's legs turned to jelly. Not good. *Definitely* not good.

Two more policemen put Dami and Natassa in cuffs, though Sacha and Philip were saved the humiliation. They carefully put them all in various cars. Oddly, Angus was in one of them. He grinned and flashed a thumbs up at Neil, though it did nothing to put him at ease.

Neil watched a policewoman direct Philip to the backseat of her car. Neil called out. "Philip!"

Philip looked up at him.

Neil struggled to find his voice. "It'll be okay, kiddo. I promise. Everything's fine now." It was all he could get out.

Philip smiled at him. Really smiled. And all the heaviness on Neil's heart sloughed off. He relaxed for the first time since Trecheon had first called him about Leah. Philip was alive. *Alive.* Who cared what happened next. His brother was alive…

Philip messily wiped his face, his smile growing into a full grin. "I know."

THE ANGEL ATTACKS

Trecheon gritted his teeth as he pressed his hand to Zeke's wound. The bone knit, but so, so slowly. His whole body ached and his mind raced.

Where was Philip?

Where was the van that took off with him?

He had to hope Neil would get to him in time. And that Ackerson wouldn't just throw him away.

And that everyone would survive. Too much to hope for.

Draso, please take care of them. Keep them safe until we can get there.

The Fawn's van pulled up next to the mansion just as a gray SUV shot out from an underground garage and slid to a halt while the east gate opened. The blue otter, Kitta, leaned against the still open sliding door, fur flying in the wind, blood staining her shoulders, her expression fearful. She mouthed one word.

Help.

Adrenaline shot up Trecheon's spine. "Pathos, she wanted--"

But then a scraggly gray rat shoved Kitta out of sight, lit up her hands and blasted the van with some kind of wild magic. It hit them straight on, destroying the sliding door sending them tumbling through the dirt.

Trecheon scrambled for purchase on anything he could get his hands on, flying about the cabin with the rest of the team, desperately trying not to get thrown from the vehicle. His Gem whined and the air shimmered with chaotic shields, but with everyone bouncing around, nothing stuck. His nose burned and the deeply disturbing smell of burning flesh assailed him.

In a bright flash of light, Trecheon was thrown from the van into the open air, making his world spin, then he crashed hard in the rusty dirt and slid along while his shield shattered to dust. His vision blurred, a sharp pain bit into his side, and his foot felt like it was on fire, but things could be worse. He groaned and tried to stand.

Ouranos was a few feet away from him, moaning, but alive. Andre coughed and sat up, brushing dust off his shirt and gripping his side. Zeke was already on his knees, taking deep breaths. Now the Fawns--

"Logos!" Pathos' voice echoed from the van. The vehicle was on its side, two wheels spinning.

Trecheon coughed, forced himself to his feet, and dashed as fast as his broken body would let him to the van, hopping on one foot. Zeke ran with him. They peered through the door.

Pathos held Logos in her arms. Blood covered Logos' chest and she gasped for air, gurgling and bubbly. Dying.

Dying.

For a terrible, awful, disgusting moment, elation filled Trecheon's chest at the idea that the Fawns were finally getting comeuppance for their crimes. He could let her die and in her own words, she'd deserve it. He'd finally have his control back. His agency.

But the thought sent Trecheon's stomach churning, especially after Ackerson had left his own teammate to die. After all the pain he had caused himself.

Besides… this he could control.

Zeke narrowed his gaze and bared his teeth. *"Trecheon--"*

Trecheon carefully lowered himself into the van. "Hold her still." He pressed his metal hands to the massive wound in Logos' chest.

It was a good five minutes of healing while the flesh knit. He got a alarmingly vivid image of her lungs stitching back together in his mind, while his metal hands grew slick with her blood, but soon Logos was breathing normally again. Blood still stained her pink fur and gray tracksuit, but she was able to sit up. Trecheon held a hand to her shoulder. "Doing okay now?"

She glanced at him, shock still in her eyes. She swallowed. "You could have let me die."

Trecheon pressed his lips together. "Yeah well… Defenders… don't do that."

Zeke's ears splayed.

A tinny ringtone rang from somewhere in the van as Ouranos and Andre carefully walked up. Pathos cleared her throat and picked up the phone off a pile of broken glass.

It read El Dorado Police Department on it.

A shock ripped through Trecheon's heart.

Pathos took a deep breath and answered. "Yes, hello?" A pause. "Angus? Oh, thank Draso. And Theophania… Good. It worked out then. Officer Johnson? Yes, very good." A pause. "Oh hell, is she okay? Oh, good. We'll be there as soon as we can and maybe Red can do something about it. Yeah, had a bit of a snag, but seems we got the main goal. We'll be fine. Hang tight."

Logos relaxed. "Well, at least one thing worked out okay..." She coughed.

"What the hell is going on?" Trecheon said. "Why is Angus calling you from the *police station?*"

"Neil and his team have been arrested," Pathos said.

Trecheon fur stood on end. *"What?"*

"Don't panic," Pathos said. "We planned this. Trust us." She stood shakily. "We... may have another safehouse nearby. Close enough that we can get into something that doesn't scream 'just survived a gang war.' Then we'll head to the police station." She shifted. "Theophania is dead, and Philip is fine. Sacha is injured, but everyone else made it out okay."

Trecheon flattened his ears and furrowed his brow.

"Trust us, Trecheon," Pathos said. "It'll work out. I promise." She softened her expression. "We aren't your enemy."

Trecheon took a deep breath. "Fine." He turned to Zeke. "Let me finish fixing that arm, Zeke. And the head injury."

Zeke sat hard on the dirt. His magic swirled above his head, and his throat burned. "I really screwed that up."

Ouranos squatted beside him. "Zeke--"

"Don't," Zeke said. "I know what happened." He turned to Trecheon. "You're right. I don't belong here. I'm...I'm a danger. I can admit that now."

Andre frowned. He sat next to Zeke and pulled him into a deep hug. Zeke took a shuddering breath and leaned into him.

Trecheon took a deep breath. "Come on. Let's get you back to safety. And get you some help."

CHAPTER 43

EPD

Neil sat in a cheap plastic chair in front of a long gray table in an empty white room with a one-way window. A scenario all too familiar.

The aftermath of their battle and arrest blurred in his mind. He remembered only a few things – Angus' odd, knowing grin, Philip's smile, the rough handcuffs, Sacha rocking back and forth in her seat while they waited in the station, Damianos freezing up completely when spoken to, Natassa pulling Philip away when they called Neil in for questioning. That was probably the right order of things, but Neil couldn't be certain.

But the septic smell, the bright light, and the hard plastic chair brought everything into crisp sharpness.

There was no way he was getting out of this. They'd lock him up for life.

But Philip is alive.

He was alive… and out of Angel's hands. He couldn't ask for more. Well, he *could,* but that was selfish. He just had to hope that Angus was a really damn good lawyer. Maybe he'd shorten his sentence enough that he'd get to spend time with Philip in his twilight years.

Christ, he was screwed.

A police officer with rounded shoulders and a thick broom mustache walked into the room with a clipboard and a folder. All Neil's hair stood on end and he gripped the arms of the chair.

Stay calm. Don't freak out.

Philip is alive.

"Greetings, Mr. Black," the officer said. "I'm Officer Johnson. I'm sure you've probably suspected it, but this interview is being recorded." He sat down opposite Neil. "Sorry we had to meet this way. I imagine that was a harrowing ordeal."

Neil's heart beat against his chest. That wasn't how he expected to be talked to. Not while he was sitting here splattered with blood. Reverse psychology maybe? He kept his guard up. "Yes, sir."

The officer opened the folder and flipped through some papers. "Says here you were a Marine in the War of Eons. Honorably discharged for PTSD."

Neil pressed his lips together. "Yes sir."

"Have you been managing that?"

"Best I can, sir."

The officer smirked. "You can drop all that 'sir' nonsense. This ain't your war troop, son."

That only made Neil tense up more. "Apologies."

Johnson sighed. He pulled up the clipboard and clicked a pen. "Describe what happened, please."

Neil stared at the gray table recounting everything, though he left out the part with the other puma, and thankfully the officer didn't question it.

"The tigress that leapt in after the victim," the officer said. "She was a passerby, yes?"

Neil looked up. That was fishing for something. He met the officer's eyes.

He squinted one eye, just enough that it could almost be a wink. Neil fought the instinct to flip his ears back.

"Yes."

"So you don't know her name." Another subtle wink.

"No, sir." He shook himself. "Sorry. No… I don't."

"The victim," Johnson continued. "Was seen holding a puma kit hostage. Can I assume he's related to you?"

"My brother."

"And the victim?"

"His new foster parent."

The officer raised an eyebrow. "New?"

"Yes," Neil said. "He's only been with her two months."

The officer fiddled through papers from the folder. "The address you were at wasn't her registered address."

Neil perked an ear. "I'm sorry?"

"Her address is listed here," He slid the paper to Neil. "Can you confirm this is the address Philip's social worker provided you?"

Neil glanced it over. It was the same old address she had been at since Philip first moved in with her. The house they had fought Jaska and his ilk in. "Yeah, that's the address."

"Hmm." He tapped his chin. "But that's not the house she was living in."

"No," Neil said. "I tried visiting that address a few days ago and the house was stripped bare."

"Bare?"

"It smelled of fresh paint," Neil said. "Like it was just getting ready for new residents."

"Had it ever been that way in past visits?"

"No."

"And were you aware of the move?"

"No but… his social worker was. She mentioned it a few days ago when I called about why Philip wasn't at the address I was given."

Johnson made a note on the clipboard. "Interesting. We'll check out the registered address."

Neil hoped to God that the Fawns had sterilized the place like they had promised.

"One more question if you don't mind," Johnson said. "What is your connection to Bob Ackerson?"

Neil perked both ears now, his tail puffy. He pulled it under the table, out of the view of cameras. "I, uh, worked for him in the war."

"In what role?"

Neil kept a straight face. "Sorry… that's classified."

"Hmm," Johnson said. "Like so many things his hands touched. Did you have any contact with him after the war?"

"No," Neil said. "I was deemed unfit for service after my terrible PTSD episode and spent over a year in therapy. I avoided all war contacts."

"Except Trecheon Omnir."

Neil's body buzzed. "Only because he was in therapy with me. The man lost both arms in the Battle of DC. Neither of us were fit for anything other than a hospital bed."

"I suppose that's fair." He made a note on his clipboard. "Were you aware of any of Ackerson's connections to Matron Fawn?"

Neil's ear twitched, despite his efforts to stay still. He didn't like where that was going. "No, sir."

"Hmm." The officer held a finger to his ear and tilted his head, clearly listening to something. Then he nodded and stood. "Welp, Mr. Black, you're free to go."

Neil's jaw dropped. "What?"

"Let me escort you outside." He gathered his papers, placed them neatly in the folder, then waved toward the door. Neil reluctantly stood and followed him. They headed for the lobby. "We may contact you for more information, but considering your condition, likely your testimony here will be enough. Wouldn't want to aggravate a war hero's PTSD." He smiled. "Enjoy your freedom, Mr. Black." He walked back into the offices.

Neil blinked. The hell just happened? This had to be a trick. He waited a good two minutes, but no one bothered him, so he walked into the waiting area.

Dami and Natassa were there, with Sacha, and--

"Neil!" Philip leapt out of his chair and ran. Neil wrapped his brother in a hug and held him tight. Finally. *Finally.* He was safe. It didn't feel real, except for Philip's sobs, his warmth, his close hug. Eventually Philip pulled back and grinned, though tears and snot stained his muzzle. Neil couldn't help but laugh.

Natassa walked over and handed a box of tissues to Philip, who took it gratefully and wiped his face. Natassa gently headbutted Neil.

Dami stood. "I am confused. They had every right to arrest us, but now they are letting us go?"

Neil shook his head. "Don't ask why because I haven't got a clue." He sighed. "I'm just glad everyone's okay." He frowned and turned to Sacha. "Well. Alive."

Sacha sat in her chair with her arm in a sling, staring at the floor, rocking slightly. She hadn't even looked up. Neil squeezed Philip's shoulder, then walked to Sacha. She blinked and shook herself like coming out of a trance, then looked up. She stood.

Neil knew that look in her eyes well. Still living in the trauma. He wanted nothing more than to take it all away from her. But the most he could manage was two words.

"Thank you."

She stared a moment longer, then her eyes focused. "Ah… you're welcome."

Carefully, Neil pulled her into a hug, giving her the space to push him away if she needed to. But instead she wrapped her good arm around him and held him tight. Really tight. He tightened his hug in response and let her hold him as long as she needed. He couldn't take the pain from her, but he could be a safe space while she worked through it.

She buried her face in his shoulder and shook with poorly contained sobs. But soon she calmed, taking deep breaths. But she still held him tight. He only let go when someone tapped his shoulder.

Angus smiled up at them, not quite meeting Neil's gaze with his own. "I'm glad we all got through this, but we aren't out of the woods just yet. Let's get going, shall we?" He headed for the door, walking stick clacking on the ground. Sacha nodded to Neil.

Philip walked over and took Neil's hand. Dami took the other, and Natassa gave Neil a squeeze. Neil took a deep breath. Not out of the woods. But ready to get there. He led his family out of the station.

CHAPTER 44

THE LONG VERSION

Trecheon leapt out of the new van as soon as the driver pulled into the station, careful of his sprained ankle. It had been an hour since Angus had called them and Trecheon couldn't calm his churning stomach. The faster he got to Sacha the better.

But Pathos had made a good point about their bloodied clothes, so a stop at the safehouse had been necessary, even if it meant Trecheon was stuck in too-tight jeans and a dull gray shirt. Ouranos, Andre, and Zeke were impossible to find clothes for, so they took a detour to a big and tall store while Pathos, Logos, and Trecheon took one van to the station.

But it didn't matter. As long as Sacha was okay. He dashed for the station doors, fast as his injured foot let him.

Angus walked out first and grinned wide before Trecheon even hit the sidewalk. "We're all fine, thanks for asking." He leaned against the wall.

Trecheon faltered. "But I didn't--"

Then Neil walked out, Philip at his side.

"Oh thank *Draso.*" Trecheon hugged Philip tight.

Philip hugged him too. "I'm fine, Uncle Trecheon." Tears welled up in his eyes. "I was so *scared.*" He gushed about everything that happened – the frantic move, the time in Ackerson's mansion, Theophania with a hammer. "And then Sacha came rushing at Miss Theophania and pulled her away and they wrestled around on the grass and Theophania hit her with a hammer and shattered her arm and--"

Trecheon's heart sank. "Wait, *shattered it?*"

"Yeah!" Philip said. "And then she stabbed Miss Theophania in the neck with her *bone,* and--"

"*What?*"

Neil put a hand on Trecheon's shoulder. "It's not what you think."

"What the hell am I *supposed* to think?"

Then Sacha walked out, blood splattered all over her outfit, arm in a sling. And a metal bone protruding from it. Biomech.

She had biomech. Just like him. And she had never said anything about it. His jaw dropped. "Sacha--"

She bared her teeth. "I don't want to talk about it." She walked off and sat on a bench.

Neil's squeezed Trecheon's shoulder now. "Give her time. 'Traumatic' doesn't even begin to describe it."

Trecheon's quills stood on end. "But is she hurt?"

"Beyond the biomech and her own damn mind, no."

Pathos and Logos walked up now. Angus grinned again. Pathos smirked back, even though he couldn't see her. "Great work, Angus. Make a note to contact Johnson and get this settled on his end soon as, okay?"

Neil's ears twitched. "Of course he's working for you. Should have figured that out."

Pathos winked at him, then turned back to Angus. "How quick can you have the paperwork filled out?"

"We can stop at a print shop," Angus said. He waved a folder. "Got the police report here. Did you get my suit?"

"It's in the van," Pathos said.

Neil flicked his ears back. "What's that all about?"

"We're going to get you Philip," Logos said. "Legally."

"Just leave it all to me," Angus said. "Well, except the driving. You'll have to do that part."

"It's the least we can do after everything we did to hurt you," Pathos said. She rubbed her arm. "I know it doesn't make up for everything. As much as we want to… we can't. But we can right this wrong at least." She frowned. "For whatever it's worth… we're sorry."

Neil pressed his lips together. He lowered his gaze. "You said Ackerson 'negotiated' with you to make you do all you did to me. That was the 'long version.' So what did he say to make you do that?"

Pathos and Logos exchanged glances, ears flat against their heads. Logos hugged herself, but nodded. Pathos took a deep breath and turned to Neil. "It's… not what he said. It's what he did."

Trecheon flattened an ear. "And what did he do?"

"He kidnapped, tortured, and killed all our families," Logos said. "All of them. Spouses. Children. I had a two-month-old at the time. He sent videos of the torture, telling us that if we wanted our families back, we'd do what he asked."

Neil's tail puffed up and Trecheon's stomach grew sour. He swallowed hard. "So you did."

Pathos nodded. "Whatever he wanted, we did. And he still killed them all." She stared up, shaking, tears running down her snout.

Philip gripped Neil's arm. Trecheon's gut turned inside out. He knew Ackerson was heartless, but this…?

"We should have known better," Logos said. "We should have put our hooves down. But when your family's on the line, you don't think straight."

Pathos turned to Neil. "It's why we're such advocates for families. Because we lost ours." She looked off. "So we advocate for families we can't have." She met Neil's gaze, her eyes shining with tears. "Hold on to yours."

Logos wrapped an arm around her sister's shoulders and guided her toward Angus and Sacha.

Trecheon watched them walk off.

That was why Leah went after Jaden. Why Zeke kept insisting on joining the fight. Because Jaden, Embrik, and Alexina were family. Andre was family. And they needed to hold on to that family. Before they lost them to Ackerson too.

A strong desire to pull Sacha into a hug made his arms twitchy. But she needed her space. And Matt was still lightyears away.

He reached for Neil's hand instead and gripped it tight, wishing he could feel it. Neil leaned close to him though, perhaps understanding Trecheon's need.

Damianos cleared his throat. "I should check on Sacha."

"Philip," Natassa said, a gentle smile on her face. "Would you like to see me make a dragon out of fire magic? So you know that not all magic is for ill. It can be a beautiful thing."

Philip watched her a moment, then looked at Neil. Neil took a shaky breath. Philip hugged him again. "Everything will be okay." He turned to Natassa and smiled. "I'd love to." She smiled and the three of them walked toward Sacha, leaving Neil and Trecheon alone.

Trecheon still gripped Neil's hand, watching Angus and the Fawns talk. Philip walked up to Pathos and the two of them spoke, but he couldn't make out what. But for the first time since this started, there was no fear. Pathos and Logos would protect Philip as their own.

Turns out, he didn't know who his enemies were. He was looking for them in all the wrong places. But he was learning.

"I have never felt more fear in my life than when Theophania had that hammer to Philip's head," Neil said. "Not even when I raced through the house trying to find Mom after the Fawns… after Ackerson killed her."

Trecheon turned to him.

"But… Philip is fine. He's alive, unharmed. He had so many people working to free him and protect him."

"But they had no one," Trecheon said, finishing the thought.

"No," Neil said. "They didn't."

They stood in silence for a moment.

"So you believe them then," Trecheon said. "Because you didn't before."

Neil glanced down. "After going through what I did with Philip, yeah, I do." His fur stood on end and he rubbed one arm. "That's not a pain you can fake."

"This doesn't undo all the trauma they foisted on us," Trecheon said.

"No, it doesn't," Neil said. "But they did what they did in a desperate attempt to save their families. Just like we did for Philip. If we can't forgive them for it, how can we forgive ourselves?"

Ouch. Right to the heart. But there was a lot of truth to it. "Yeah."

Neil's tail swished slowly side to side. "If we get out of this, maybe we can all heal together."

Trecheon looked up. "I'd like that." He hugged Neil.

Neil hugged him back. "You know, in all the years we've known each other, I can't think of a single time before now that we've hugged."

Trecheon frowned. "I can't either."

Neil hugged him tighter. "Let's make sure this isn't the only time."

"Yeah, let's not." Trecheon gave him a squeeze. "I love you, brother."

Neil chuckled. "Love you too, asshole." He broke the hug, all grins, finally back to the puma Trecheon knew and loved. "Great to hear you finally call me brother."

Trecheon smiled. "Something I should have done sooner."

A second van pulled up and Ouranos, Zeke, and Andre piled out in plain clothes. Zeke rushed over, magic marbles swirling around his head. He kept his distance though. "Is everyone okay? Tell me everyone's okay."

Neil smiled. "We're fine, thank God."

Ouranos sighed relief. "Sisters be praised." He turned to Trecheon. "What is our next course of action?"

"The Black family will be coming with us to get Philip formally adopted," Angus said walking up. "All we need is a signature from his social worker and we're good to go. I've got a courthouse date this afternoon."

"Already?" Neil said.

Angus grinned again. "We've been planning this a long time."

Trecheon winced. "Good luck getting Piper to sign your brother off."

"We have a plan for that," Logos said. She sniffed and dabbed at her eyes with a tissue. "Trust us."

Trecheon's shoulders relaxed. "For the first time, I believe I can."

She smiled.

"So what do we do now?" Andre asked.

The door to the police station opened and two officers walked out, talking and laughing. Trecheon flicked his ears back. He pointed across the parking lot to a little park. "Let's not talk about this here."

Best Laid Plans

Slowly Trecheon led the group to the park. There wasn't much to it – a few flowering bushes, some bright orange trees, and big dying lawns ready to wait out the winter. A man-made river flowed through it like a big fountain, which thankfully drowned out their voices a little.

Trecheon sat on a rock. "Right then. We got Philip safe and sound."

"Which means the next step is getting to Jaden," Zeke said. "Or… letting Leah and Ethos do that." He crossed his arms. "Don't like that one though."

"So who's going after Jaden then?" Neil asked. "Because I'm ready to kick some ass after that fiasco."

Philip shifted, flicking his ears back. "You need someone to protect Athánatos…" Everyone turned to him. Philip twitched his nose. "I heard the Angels talking about it. They're planning on invading it because there's a bunch of… Zyearth tech? I didn't know what they meant but… they want to get it from Athánatos because they're planning on leaving Earth. Whatever that means."

Trecheon shared a dark look with Ouranos. "That's not good."

"It is not," Ouranos said.

"And they have several members with Athánatos jewels," Neil said, his tail lashing.

Zeke flattened an ear. "Natassa, you said they were 'royalty.' Does that mean they could create rips in the Veil and get on the island?"

"Potentially," Natassa said.

"Ackerson said they were working on that still," Philip said.

Trecheon sat hard on a rock. "Great. So we still have a bunch of trained mages on our asses. And we still don't know who all of them are. Like that rat. I don't know what magic she used, but it packed a hell of a punch."

"Millie," Pathos said, snarling. She pawed at the grass with her hoof. "And her partner Ralph. Guess that confirms Ackerson got his claws in them. They have a Blood Crystal and they use it for its intended purpose – big destructive spells."

Trecheon stood straight. "We need a change of plans. We can't do this on our own."

Natassa furrowed her brow and sat hard on a rock. "We have run out of allies."

"We have allies coming," Trecheon said. "The best thing we can do is gather everyone up, get to Athánatos, and hold our ground until Matt and the others come back. And I mean *everyone*. Jaden and his team included."

"So we go after Jaden," Andre said.

"No," Trecheon said. "*I* go after Jaden. I'll meet up with Leah and Ethos, find Jaden, and head back ASAP. The rest of you go back to Athánatos and protect it. We can wait them out."

"Now hold on a second." Neil stood. "You aren't going to do this alone. Not with all the mages still out there. You go running after Jaden and they'll follow."

"You've got to get Philip legally while you've got the chance," Trecheon said. "You can't come with me." He turned to Ouranos. "And before you say anything, you have the whole Athánatos population to take care of. It's not a matter of 'if' but a matter of 'when' Angel penetrates Athánatos. They need everyone there."

Zeke flicked his ears back. The elemental marbles raced around his head.

Trecheon nodded to him. "Everyone, Zeke."

"You're not going alone."

Trecheon turned. Sacha. She lifted her chin, jaw tense. Just what he needed. "You're injured. You wouldn't let me go with a busted arm, so--"

Sacha ripped off the sling, tugged the broken arm free of its socket, and threw it to the ground. "There. Broken arm gone. I have a spare. I'm going with you."

"Sacha--"

"Don't Sacha me," Sacha said. "I spent two and a half *years* looking for Leah and I'm not going to let her vanish after we just got her back. And damn it, I'm not going to lose you either!" She waved a finger at him. "I'm a senior Defender. I'm not some grunt you can order around and force to stay behind. This isn't a *request.* I'm *coming with you.*"

Trecheon winced. He nodded to her arm. "And where's the spare?"

"Back at Athánatos."

"We don't have time to go back."

"You don't have a choice," Pathos said.

Trecheon flicked his ears back.

"We can arrange a private train to Canada for you," Logos said. "It'll make up for the time lost while Ethos and Leah were traveling. But it's very unlikely we can get one in the next hour. Likely you'll leave tomorrow."

Trecheon sighed. He leaned against a tree. "Fine. We'll go back, get packed up, and get on the road tomorrow. And get your arm fixed." He flicked an ear. "And I guess you're coming with me."

"Damn right, I am." She picked up the broken biomech and headed back to the parking lot and one of the Fawn's vans.

Pathos took a long look at Neil. She faced him fully. "Your brother… forgave us." Her eyes shined with tears. "I-I don't…" Her voice trailed.

Neil flicked an ear back, but his face lightened. Philip buried his face in Neil's side.

Trecheon's heart softened. Leave it to Philip to be so understanding and empathetic. It was time he and Neil took after him.

Neil ruffled Philip's fur, then turned to the Fawns. "I forgive you too. For what it's worth." He breathed deeply. "Ackerson killed my parents and used me all these years. Not you."

Trecheon crossed his arms, but he nodded, unable to find the words.

Logos smiled sadly. "Thank you. It's more than we deserve."

A sleek black sedan pulled into the parking lot and the gray cat who had originally brought them a van got out. She nodded to the Fawns.

Logos nodded back. "We'll get Philip's paperwork all settled and get back as soon as we can," she said. "Expect your train to leave early tomorrow morning."

"Will do," Trecheon said. "And thank you. I mean that."

Logos smiled. A real smile.

The group separated into the vehicles and took off. Trecheon fiddled with his thumbs sitting opposite Sacha in the back of the vehicle.

Just hold on a little longer, Jaden.

DERAILED

Before Leah could even piece together what was going on with Pilot's strange message, Ethos shoved her to the mattress, reached between the bed and the wall and pulled out a pistol. She darted her gaze to each corner of the room, gun ready. "Pilot, what happened? Who did this to you?"

"GET OFF THE TRAIN," Pilot said, deadpan and robotic.

Leah frantically pulled Pilot's datashard and power pack off the floor and poked around at the control. "It's still locked to me."

Ethos turned to her. "What?"

"GET OFF THE TRAIN," Pilot said.

"How?" Leah said. "We don't have another stop for at least six hours!" She looked out the window. They were deep in a dense forest. "Do you expect us to *jump?"*

"GET OFF THE TRAIN," Pilot repeated. "IN SIX HOURS."

Leah flicked her ears back. She turned to Ethos.

Ethos narrowed her gaze at Pilot. "Who are you?"

350

Pilot lifted his head and met Ethos' gaze. "YOU KNOW WHO I AM."

Leah's tail twitched. "Ethos?"

Ethos snorted. "Shit." She reached for her bag. "Pack up. I think we should get off the train."

Back in Canada. Leah stood on the platform with her backpack, Pilot's A.I. crystal, and Ethos' hand in hers. She was back as Ana, a golden doe with sparkling eyes and an unassuming outfit. Leah had cut off Pilot's external speaker, so he could only speak into her earpiece now. He almost made her go deaf with the constant shouting of "get off the train." But the moment they did, the shouting stopped.

Now they were really without direction.

The last time Leah had been in Canada, she had fought Sharp and lost Ari. She squeezed Ethos' hand. She wasn't going to lose her too.

But even though they were in a fairly large border town and the war was long over, her anxiety chewed away at her stomach and made her feel dizzy. Flashes of their trek through the Canadian wilderness fed the Thought Monster.

In a lot of ways, their return was worse than their initial visit. Fewer allies, more danger, worry for Jaden… and she didn't even have Zeke.

She didn't even have *Zeke.* She should have brought him with her. She needed him. Her walking slowed as the Thought Monster bit at her.

You chased him away.

He won't want you anymore.

You betrayed him. He'll hate you.

You've lost everything.

Ethos squeezed her hand, temporarily fighting the Thought Monster back. Leah glanced at her. She smiled and gently wiped away an escaped tear. "Courage, hun. We're not at war anymore. And I won't let anyone hurt you."

Leah stared at her, then sighed. "Thank you." Ethos pressed her forehead to Leah's.

Pilot beeped in her ear. *"FIND A HOTEL."*

Leah tapped the earpiece. "Hotel? I thought we were going to Jasper."

"FIND A HOTEL."

"I really don't like this," Ethos said. "It's one thing to get off the train, which I question the wisdom in that in the first place when Pilot is clearly bugging out, but it's a totally different thing to *stay* here." She squeezed Leah's hand. "We're renting a car and getting out of here."

"FIND A HOTEL!"

"He's still telling me to find a hotel…"

"And he can *shove it,*" Ethos said. She headed into the station.

The line to the rental counter had at least twenty customers, and only one worker, a white wolf who spoke too fast and hid as much as he could behind the big, darkened window. By the time they got to the front, the worker didn't have great news.

"Sorry, ladies, but I've just rented my last car." He flicked his big white ears back.

Ethos frowned. "You really don't have *anything?"*

"Not today," he said. "But I can get you one tomorrow around noon, if you don't mind spending the night."

Ethos narrowed her gaze at him, but he didn't budge. She sighed. "Fine." She got the paperwork together to reserve the car.

They walked down a street full of hotels and stopped at a boutique placed called The Hunter's Lodge. Ethos wouldn't let Leah's hand go. It kept her grounded, though it couldn't fight the Thought Monster back completely. It kept coming back to Zeke.

Zeke really would be angry with her. She shouldn't have done that. *I'm sorry.*

Several minutes passed. A gentle smell of chocolate chip cookies entered her nose, though they were nowhere near the shops yet. She glanced around, searching for the source of the smell.

Then Zeke spoke to her.

I forgive you.

Leah's eyes widened. Her mind raced. She had reestablished the connection. It was vague and hard to recognize, but it was there. A thousand thoughts manifested at once, each one chewed up and spit out by the Thought Monster, ripping them apart before she could settle on anything.

You don't have to say anything, Zeke said. *It's okay. We're fine. I'm not going to leave you.*

YES HE WILL.

I WON'T, Zeke said, a fierce scent of spice hitting her nose. Aimed at her anxiety, not her. *You don't have to believe your anxiety, Leah. I would never leave you. Ever. Okay?*

She chewed her lip. *Okay. Yeah.*

Just... don't leave me either. A pause. *Even though I'm broken.*

Leah frowned. *You're not broken.*

I am.

You're not!

Leah... The chocolate chip smell faded in favor of too-hot oil in a pan. *Promise me you won't leave me.*

Leah flattened an ear. *I won't leave you, Zeke.*

Good... Good.

A deep urge to pull Zeke into a hug made her feel slightly numb. *Zeke... we'll get through together. Okay?*

A long pause.

The Hunter's Lodge was a tiny cabin-like hotel with a massive fireplace, big comfy chairs and a small restaurant. Their room had only two small beds, an antique dresser, and a single tiny table. The window had a window seat, and the bathroom had a tub big enough that both of them could fit in it if they wanted, which clashed with the bare-necessities feel of the rest of the room.

It reminded Leah far too strongly of the hotel she had shared with Ari right before she died.

Ethos seemed to know this so she gave Leah space while they got settled. She was cautiously chatty at dinner, though slightly bitter about their situation. However, she was quiet and distant in the room, spending the evening staring out the window as the sun set.

Leah needed a distraction. She turned on the TV and flipped through the channels.

"Ugh, hotel TV is the worst." Ethos stood. "I'm going to take a bath." She smiled at Leah and ran a finger under her chin. "I don't suppose you care to join me?"

Leah's fur all stood on end and her ears flushed. "I… Um…"

Ethos drew close and touched noses with her. "I promise no sexy times."

"You absolutely cannot keep that promise in a bathtub like that."

"I second that notion," Pilot said.

Ethos shot him a glare. "Now you're going to speak normally. I see."

Pilot appeared and tilted his head. "Pardon?"

Leah frowned. "You've been shooting us strange cryptic messages for hours. It's why we're not on the train anymore."

"Have I?" He vanished into light motes then reappeared. "Well then… you're right. My logs are quite clear."

Leah flicked an ear. "Do your logs say where the messages came from?"

"Nope!" Pilot said. He crossed his little arms and fluttered his wings. "You know, you really shouldn't be listening to random cryptic messages I spew off and can't remember later."

Ethos rolled her eyes. "A lesson learned too late." She turned to Leah, eyes half lidded, and nuzzled noses. "I'll leave it up to you, hun." She walked toward the bathroom, shaking her tail.

Leah licked her lips, but remained rooted to the spot. The Thought Monster threw her brain into thought paralysis, unable to settle on a single idea.

"And in tonight's news, a major passenger train derailment has been reported in Alberta."

Leah and Ethos turned to the TV.

"The CrossTrek Express from El Dorado into Alberta derailed over Lake Eliza when it was caught in a sudden lake storm, officials say," the reporter said. *"Excess water got into the electric system and shocked the passengers, raising questions about train safety. Dozens are confirmed dead and dozens more are missing. Officials say they will continue through the night to search for survivors."*

The three of them sat in uncomfortable silence for a moment.

"Water and electricity," Ethos said quietly.

Leah tightened her jaw. "That wasn't an accident. That was Sharp. That was his summons."

Pilot flickered. "Calculating odds of survival." he said robotically. "0.053%." He hunched down. "I'm… glad you listened to my cryptic messages after all. Maybe keep doing that if I say another one."

Ethos hugged herself.

Leah stood and turned to Ethos. "I think I'll join you." She furrowed her brow. "Life's too fragile."

Ethos jolted slightly, like coming out a trance. She blinked at Leah, but then nodded and held a hand out to her. Leah took it and they entered the bathroom.

They spent that night wrapped in each other's arms. Leah hardly slept. She had to get to Jaden as quick as possible.

COMPLETE FAMILY

Neil parked outside the office of Child Safety Services and put the van in neutral. He stared at the steering wheel.

Angus gripped his shoulder, still staring forward. "It'll work out. I promise."

"Did you scry that," Neil asked. "Or are you guessing?"

Angus touched a finger to the side of his snout and smiled. "Just trust me. And remember what I said."

"Let you do the talking."

"*All* the talking."

"No final retort," Neil said. "Or I ruin it."

"Exactly." He adjusted his suit and tie, then slipped on his dark glasses and extended his walking stick.

Neil breathed deeply. He turned and leaned into the backseat. "Ready, bud?"

Philip shifted in the middle seat, fiddling with his jacket. Natassa and Damianos sat on either side of him, and he gripped their hands tightly. He flattened his ears. "What if they take me from you?"

"Then we will use the pendant to find you," Damianos said. He smiled and patted Philip's shoulder. "And we will bring you to Athánatos."

Philip met his gaze, then stared at the floor. He fidgeted with the pendant Damianos had graciously donated. "And if that happens, we'll be on Athánatos forever. Because Neil will be a criminal."

"It is not ideal," Natassa said. "But it will be home."

Philip leaned against her. She wrapped an arm around him and gave him a squeeze.

The Fawns' sleek black car parked next to them and Pathos and Logos got out.

Neil squeezed his eyes shut a moment. "Let's get this over with." He opened the door and everyone piled out.

Like Angus predicted, no one said a word when the Fawns led the group into the building. Hell, the Fawns didn't say anything either. They didn't need to. No one challenged them. Neil was able to walk freely down the same familiar hallway to Piper's office. He opened her door.

"I don't *care* what happened to her," Piper screamed over the phone. "If you don't find him--" She stopped and stared wide eyed at Neil, then slammed the phone down. "What the *hell!* What did you do to Theophania? Where is Philip? What in Draso's name is *wrong with you?*"

Neil sat in a chair across from her desk and folded his hands in his lap, grateful he had been given the chance to change his bloodied clothes. *Not a word. Or you'll mess this up and lose Philip.*

Piper bared her fangs and flicked her tail. "What do you have to say for--"

"Greetings Miss Piper," Angus said, his voice dark and professional. He walked into the room, his wings scraping the floor. Philip walked in behind him and sheepishly made his way to the chair next to Neil.

Piper stood and reached for Philip. "Oh god, Philip, thank *heavens.*"

He hissed at her, baring fangs and flattening his ears. "Don't touch me."

Piper paused, but she nodded and sat back down, her ears flat against her head.

Neil bit back a smirk.

Angus pulled out a folder and ran fingertips over the papers, reading the braille markers. "I'm here representing Philip and Neil Black for their adoption case."

"Adoption case?" Piper shouted. She wagged a finger at Neil. "This man just murdered a foster parent and kidnapped a child!"

"The police report says otherwise, Miss Piper," Angus said. He pulled a paper packet out, carefully made his way between the chairs, feeling around, and passed the packet to Piper.

She scoffed, though she took it from him. "A blind lawyer? That's original. Let me guess. You can 'see' because of echolocation, since you're a bat, right?"

Neil turned to Angus.

Angus frowned, shaking his wings. "Your ableist and xenophobic *ad hominem* attacks have been noted, Miss Piper."

She made a face, then read in silence. Her eyes widened as she read.

"I'll save you the trouble of reading the entire document right now," Angus said. "This is a police report on your foster parent, Theophania Dubois, stating that she threatened to kill a child in a standoff against that child's brother, who *legally* is allowed to visit him, regardless of what your notes say."

Piper flattened her ears and furrowed her brow.

Philip winced in his chair. Neil tightened his fists, but kept his face as neutral as possible, refusing to speak.

"Theophania held a hammer to Philip's head," Angus said. "Threatening to bash in his skull, while Neil begged her to let him go. And the record is *very* clear. Multiple witnesses confirm it. Neil did nothing."

Piper frowned. "I… What? Then who killed her?"

"An unknown passer-by happened to notice what was going on and tackled Theophania to the ground, in an effort to save Philip," Angus said. "Theophania retaliated, shattering the bystander's biomechanical arm in an attempted murder. The bystander defended herself and incapacitated Theophania."

Philip huddled in his chair and whimpered. Neil gripped his hand and held it tight.

"Police were called," Angus continued. "It should be noted that the home Theophania and Philip were staying at was not the home this office has recorded as her address. The police were very interested in why she wasn't at her proper address."

Piper leaned down.

"Regardless," Angus said. "While investigating the home, they discovered something quite peculiar. The proposed murder weapon of Matron Felicity Fawn."

Piper dropped the papers on her desk. "That is far too much of a coincidence to be true."

"Police were very sure of the original weapon," Angus said. He pulled another report out. "As you can see here."

Piper snorted. "I don't need to see it. I know what it says. The murder weapon was a military-issued rifle." She nodded to Neil. "One that Neil used as a sniper in the war."

"One that most US snipers used," Angus said. "And one that has a very small supply, yet high demand on the black market, especially with known mobs. The US military retired the weapons after the war in favor of new, more efficient snipers, and destroyed most of the old ones for spare parts and metal. Only a few exist now."

"Neil could plant it."

Angus scoffed. "Because self-employed HVAC men make more than enough money to acquire a rare weapon worth tens of thousands of dollars."

"Neil had it in the *war.*"

"And I'm *sure* the Marines let a man with an infamous PTSD case take home a retired military-issued sniper rifle as a souvenir." Angus' large bat ears twitched. "Neil's DNA signature was nowhere on the rifle, in case you were wondering. It'd be a stretch to suggest Neil carried it fully assembled on his motorbike anyway."

So that's why his bike had been parked there. Alibi.

Piper glared. "I don't appreciate--"

Angus flipped a braille-covered page in his folder, ignoring her. "Along with this weapon, they found a slew of others, as well as communication connecting Miss Dubois to the Brown Fox mob." He adjusted the dark glasses on his snout. "As a social worker, I'm sure you're quite familiar with what that implies, Miss Piper."

Neil's heart raced. Just before he and Trecheon and met Matt and the others all those years ago, they had taken out Assistant Mayor Sheldon, who actually had worked with the Starshine sex trafficking ring of Brown Fox. This was a big accusation. The Fawns weren't messing around.

Piper sunk in her chair. "I don't have anything to do with Brown Fox."

"No one is suggesting you do," Angus said. "And as of right now, the investigation is incomplete. Though it does raise the question of how someone so closely connected to a known child trafficking ring managed to slip through the cracks and get into foster care. And why that carefully vetted foster parent was living at the wrong address."

Piper spoke fast now. "I swear to Draso, I don't--"

Angus held up a hand. "We might be willing to overlook such a... *careless* transgression, if you would be willing to sign off on Neil's adoption of his traumatized younger brother." Angus smiled slyly. "After all, the Fawn Family wishes to make this right by the Black Family."

Piper's ears grew pale and she squeaked. "The... Fawn Family?"

"You know as well as I that the EPD openly suspected Neil of killing Matron Fawn," Angus said. "He was never formally accused, but certain... parties kept the rumors alive."

Neil bit his tongue against the wave of rage against Piper and her loud and constant insistence of his guilt. This was on the Fawns... no, not the Fawns. Ackerson. He orchestrated all of this. He had to remember that. Especially after all he had done to Ethos, Pathos, and Logos' families. They were victims too.

But Piper helped. He glared, his only weapon at the moment.

Angus turned a page and continued running fingers over the paper. "But since there is now evidence that a rival and frankly, despicable company had taken out the Matron in cold blood, the Fawns have taken it upon themselves to correct this mistake and help reunite a family once broken." He grinned. "It's why they put their own lawyer on this case." He jerked a thumb behind him. "It's also why they're waiting in the lobby. If you wanted to speak with them."

Piper held up her hands. "I-It's not necessary, I promise."

"Excellent," Angus said. "Then signing off on this adoption will be simple." He pulled out another packet and passed it to her. "I've taken the liberty of filling out the paperwork ahead of time. I've already had a judge look it over. All that's needed is your autograph." He cleared his throat and adjusted his glasses again. "I'd appreciate it if you signed quickly, Miss Piper. We have a court appointment to make this official in less than an hour, and the Fawns are *very* busy people. Wouldn't want them growing impatient."

She gawked. "You already…" She shook her head. "Never mind. I don't want to know." She flipped through the packet, signing in various places, then tossed it at Neil. "There. I hope you're happy."

Neil pressed his lips tight. He looked over all the places Piper was supposed to sign, then passed the packet to Angus, saying nothing. He stood.

Piper shook her head and turned to Philip, her brow furrowed sympathetically. "I am so sorry, Philip."

Philip narrowed his eyes and lifted his chin. "I'm not." He stood too. Neil took his hand.

Angus tucked the paper away. "Wonderful doing business with you, Miss Piper. I'm sure the Fawns will be in touch."

Piper's eyes widened. "Wait, what?"

"Good day." Angus left with Philip and Neil behind him.

The Fawns still sat in the lobby, taking up the chairs and lounges, flipping through magazines as casually as could be. The secretary stood frozen at his desk, staring at them. Natassa and Damianos leaned against one wall, holding hands. They stirred when they saw Neil. Natassa reached out. "Well?"

But Neil just shook his head, not yet trusting his voice. Angus nodded in the vague direction of the doe, who stood as one, and the party left the building.

The moment the door shut, Neil fell to his knees and drew Philip into a big hug.

Philip hugged him tightly back, shaking with sobs. Neil sobbed too, gripping Philip's coat. His family was whole again. There was a light at the end of the tunnel. Both Damianos and Natassa kneeled near them too, placing hands on Neil and Philip's backs.

A whole family. Neil's heart swelled.

Angus gently tapped his shoulder, though he didn't look down. "I don't wish to break up a tender moment," he said. "But we really do need to get to the courthouse before we lose our window. Our judge only has so much spare time to dedicate to the Fawn's business. Then we can celebrate all we want."

"Yeah," Neil said, his voice raw. "Yeah." He broke the hug with Philip and smiled at him through teary vision. "We're free, bud."

Philip grinned bigger than he had ever seen. And he kept grinning all through the trip to the courthouse… and home.

Home.

Neil could only hope Trecheon would have half his luck over getting Philip in his search for Jaden.

SEVERAL MODEST PROPOSALS

Neil slumped into his room after helping Damianos find a temporary guest room for Philip. He promised he'd stay nearby in case Philip needed anything.

Philip had been ecstatic to be on the island. He stared at everything with stars in his eyes, and could hardly stop talking, even through dinner. It was good to know that the days' events hadn't broken him.

Neil would need more time though.

Natassa was already lying on the bed waiting for him. She smiled. "Everything settled then?"

"Yeah." He stripped down to his boxers and flopped on the bed. "God, what a day. Hell, this last week and a half even."

Natassa wrapped an arm across Neil's stomach, laid her head on his shoulder, and nestled close. "Thank the Sisters it is over. At least until we are able to get Jaden."

He rubbed the fur on her shoulder. "I'm sorry."

Natassa glanced at him. "For what?"

"For not relying on you and Dami sooner," he said. "I keep forgetting I have a support network now. For so long it's only been me and kind of Trecheon. I'm so used to having to do this on my own. That was a mistake."

"You will never fight alone again, love." She snuggled near him. "No need to apologize. I understand it is an adjustment."

"I know that now." He rubbed the fur on her cheek. "Thanks for reminding me. And for being there for me."

"Of course, my Heart." She sighed and snuggled into him. "We work best when we work together. And I plan to be together for as long as time will let us."

Neil's mind wandered back to Ouranos' throwaway comment from several weeks back. *I would rather the title of Basileus go to someone more capable.* Being capable was more than just being a leader. It was building a support network and making sure to use it. Something Theron never did. Neil would have be better about that if he were to truly help Athánatos. And also be a good spouse. He played with a tuft of fur at the tip of Natassa's ear. "If you don't mind me asking, what would it mean for me and Athánatos if we got married?"

Natassa giggled. "Well, that certainly took a turn." She gently kissed his neck. "You would have to ask me first."

Neil's ears flushed and he froze. "I-I.. I mean…"

She ran her finger down his bare chest. "I promise you will not be disappointed if you ask."

Neil turned on his side and faced her. God, she was beautiful. Those gorgeous violet eyes, her cream-colored snout, her gentle smile. He traced her cheek where the cream and black fur met.

Yes, he could spend the rest of his life with her.

"Natassa," he said, his heart racing. "Will you marry me?"

Her smile exploded into a grin and she nodded, eyes shining. "Of course." She leaned in for a kiss, which he happily accepted, holding her face in his hands. She pressed her tongue into his mouth, then pushed him on his back and straddled him, running her hands over his chest. He moaned against her lips, running his hands down her sides and holding her hips. She pulled back, tracing kisses along his jawline and neck, then sat up and pulled her shirt over her head. He licked his lips, then ran his hands up her sides, rubbing the fur the wrong way, making her shiver. He cupped her breasts and caressed them. She closed her eyes and tilted her head back, mouth open, moaning softly. Then she lay over him for another kiss while he slipped her skirt and panties off.

Neil lay back on the bed, wiping the sweat off his brow, wishing for the umpteenth time that Athánatos had electricity so he could put a fan on him after that kind of exercise. Something they'd have to work on when he made Athánatos his permanent home. "God, I needed that."

Natassa let out a long breath. "I daresay we both did."

"So," Neil said, pulling the covers over his and Natassa's waists. He took a deep breath, trying to calm his heart. "About that marriage thing."

Natassa giggled. She hitched herself up on her elbow and traced little circles in Neil's chest fur with her finger. "I fully expected our lovemaking to distract you."

"Well, it *did,*" Neil said. "But once the little guy is out of commission, the brain starts working again."

She laughed now. "I suppose that is fair." She ran her finger down his stomach, making him shiver. She smiled, then spoke. "The roles of Basileus and Basilea are equal. So when we marry, you will be considered the Basileus and you will be treated as such. That includes the respect and place of high status, but also the responsibility." She leaned her head on his shoulder. "You have shown yourself quite capable of that already."

"Have I?"

"It is why our people already show the respect and courtesies of a king to you," Natassa said.

Neil flicked his ears back. "Well. Some of them anyway."

"The Archons will come around," Natassa said. "You have demonstrated that you are a leader, capable of compassion and self-sacrifice. And now you have shown that you can turn to your support network instead of battling alone. That puts you higher than the previous Basileus."

Neil frowned. "I don't think I've done great at that support network thing. But I'm trying."

"And you will only improve," Natassa said. "Your attitude alone proves to me that you will. And I daresay that trying is better than ignoring it as Theron did."

He glanced up at the ceiling. "What would happen if I… if I asked Damianos to marry me too? I mean, can I even do that? I know you said Athánatos are a poly culture, but does that apply to the royalty?"

"Of course it does," she said giggling. "Dami will have a choice. He can marry you as a husband and rule alongside us as another Basileus, or he can instead be King's Consort. It grants all the same privileges of marriage without the responsibility of a ruler."

He gently rubbed her arm. "So… which one do you think he'll take?"

Natassa pulled the blanket up to their shoulders, kissed his cheek, and snugged into his neck. "I suppose you will find out tomorrow."

Philip and Dami showed up at Neil's bedroom at 8AM with news that Trecheon and Sacha were planning on leaving in an hour. Natassa gave Dami a telling look, which he returned with a smile, then the group walked to the dining area of the royal wing. Everyone was there already, sitting on various wicker chairs and lounges, munching on pastries and eggs. A smell of coffee and cooked meat filled the room.

Ouranos stood when he saw them, a big grin on his face. "The happy family joins us."

Zeke flicked his ears back. The magic marbles appeared over his head again and he moved to a place in the far corner, away from everyone else. Ouranos watched him with a frown.

Neil pressed his lips together and padded right up to Ouranos before he lost his nerve. *Deep breath.* "I know this isn't exactly tradition, but I don't have anyone else to ask so…" He met Ouranos' gaze. "I'd like to ask your permission to marry Natassa."

Ouranos laughed, deep and hearty. He took Neil's hand into both of his. "My friend, nothing would please me more than to call you brother. It has been a long time coming." He smirked at Natassa. "Though my sister is far too strong-willed to let something like permission stop her from marrying whomever she wishes."

"W-Well, good," Neil said. "Because she already said yes."

"As expected." Ouranos patted Neil's hand. "The title of Basileus will fall to the shoulders where it will be the most useful, and our family will be better with you in it."

Neil smiled. "I hope so."

"I know so," Ouranos said.

Neil breathed deeply. He turned to Dami now and took both of his hands in his while the adrenaline still pumped. "Dami… will you marry me?"

Dami's face lit up like a sun. "Of course, my love." He pulled Neil close and they shared a kiss. His tenderness sent chills up Neil's spine. He stepped back and held Neil's hands tight. "Though I would prefer the title of King's Consort, if you approve."

Neil nodded, the nerves making him move too fast. But he smiled. "Anything."

Dami laughed. He stroked Neil's cheek. "Then I accept, my emerald prince."

"Hooray!" Philip leapt up and danced around the room. "Neil's gonna be a king! Neil's gonna be a king! I knew it!"

Andre grinned. "Now that's a happy ending." He nudged Chadwick. "So, Chad, when are you gonna ask me to marry you, huh?"

"Oh," Chadwick said. "Now, I suppose. Will you marry me?"

Andre jolted and his jaw dropped. Zeke spit out his water. Andre's eyes widened. "You serious?"

"I wouldn't ask if I wasn't serious, hun."

"I… I accept." He smiled, then took Chadwick's hands in his, eyes glassy. "I'd love nothing more." The two shared a kiss.

Zeke wiped his mouth, staring, but he did manage a smile.

Andre grinned back at him. He waved away the elemental marbles, drew him into a sideways hug, and ruffled his quills. "Already got my best man picked out."

"I should hope so," Zeke said.

Trecheon walked up now and patted Neil on the shoulder. "So when you marry Natassa, does that make you Matt's uncle-in-law?"

Neil wrinkled his snout, then laughed. "Oh man, I can't wait to rub that in his face."

Trecheon chuckled. He pointed to Neil. "If I'm not best man, we're gonna have to have a serious talk."

"Naw, I'm gonna make Matt my best man, since I'm apparently going to be his uncle," Neil said, smirking. "You can be best idiot."

Pathos walked into the room holding a bag. "If we're all done celebrating, we need to settle down and finish up with breakfast. Trecheon and Sacha have a train to catch."

CHAPTER 49

APOLOGIES

"You are sure it is wise to go alone?" Ouranos said.

Trecheon and Sacha stood with Ouranos, Zeke, Andre, and Pathos by the portal to Sol Island. Sacha had replaced her arm and carried a small metal case with more spare parts and repair kits, as well as her backpack with a few changes of clothes. Trecheon still wasn't sure how he hadn't noticed the biomech before.

Sacha didn't have a cover anymore though, since she didn't have a spare. The arm was just bare metal below the elbow now. She wouldn't use it or look at it – it hung at her side like it was nothing more than a decoration.

Ouranos frowned, twitching his tail. "Trecheon?"

Trecheon shook his head. "Sorry." His ear flicked. "Honestly it probably isn't, but considering the situation, I think it's the best course of action. And you really do need to protect Athánatos. Especially since we know now that at least two of Ackerson's cronies can likely get past the Veil."

Zeke rubbed his arm, then reached over and took Andre's hand. Andre squeezed it and leaned into him.

Ouranos crossed his arms. "Let it be known that I do not like this plan, though I see your reasoning. Please take care of yourselves, both of you. We have lost enough."

"Yeah," Trecheon said. "Will do."

"Uncle Trecheon!"

Trecheon turned. Philip ran up with Neil behind him. He hugged Trecheon around the waist. Trecheon smiled and ruffled his fur. "Hey, kiddo. Enjoying your time on the island? Did Neil and Dami give you the full tour?"

"Uncle Trecheon, this place is *amazing,*" he said, grinning, and he launched into a long-winded description of all he had seen. "No wonder Neil wants to spend all his time here. Are we gonna live here *forever?*"

Trecheon glanced at Neil with a smirk and a raised eyebrow. Neil smirked back. Trecheon patted Philip's back. "Pretty sure Athánatos kings are required to live on the islands they rule. But I don't know if you'll move in permanently just yet."

"I'm totally gonna convince Neil to move in permanently now," Philip said, determined. "We'll be settled by the time you get back." He paused, leaning on his chin. "You are coming back, right?"

"He better," Neil said. "I'd hate to have to hunt him down like a common hedgehog."

"Funny," Trecheon said. "Don't worry, I'm coming back."

"Be safe, okay?" Philip said. He gave Trecheon another squeeze and ran off with Dami and Natassa, squealing.

Neil gave Trecheon a big hug. Trecheon settled into it. Despite it being so new to them, it felt like home.

"I want more of these," Neil said. "And I want my best man at my wedding. Or weddings." He grinned. "I can't believe I'm getting married. Twice!"

Trecheon smiled. "You deserve it."

Neil squeezed Trecheon. "So you better come back here, okay?"

Trecheon squeezed him back. "I promise."

Neil gave Sacha a hug too. She held him tightly, though she didn't speak.

Pathos handed Trecheon the bag. "Everything you need. IDs, passports, tickets, paperwork, whatever." She lowered her gaze. "I couldn't get you a private *train,* but you do have a private cruiser for high class passengers and an entirely private car, so that'll count for something. No long stops like a common commuter train." Her ear twitched. "You sure you want to head for Pine Cove? Jasper is closer."

"Exactly," Trecheon said. "That's the logic Leah and Ethos will have too. I predict they'll go to Jasper first. If we're lucky, we'll meet up in Pine Cove." He smiled. "Though if we're *extra* lucky, they'll find Jaden in Jasper and head back and we can get home without fuss. But I don't think we'll be that lucky."

"Wishful thinking," Pathos said. "Since this is a private travel train, you'll get there in about three days. Hopefully that'll be fast enough to catch up with Leah and Ethos. Missy's on the shore. She'll get you to the station." She flicked her ears back. "Come back safe, okay?"

"Thank you," Trecheon said. "I mean that."

Then they left.

The trip to the train station was quiet and uneventful, and because they were on a private travel train, the path they took through the station itself kept them mostly out of the public eye as well. Not that Trecheon was too concerned with the beating Angel had taken.

Though Sharp was still out there.

The dark gray cat Missy led them through the station, eyes forward, headed for their platform and train. They found their private car and she flashed their tickets at the conductor.

The conductor looked them over and nodded. "Just a fair warning, we have a slight delay. Big passenger derailment in Alberta."

Sacha and Trecheon exchanged glances.

Missy frowned. "Everything alright?"

"I'm not at liberty to say, ma'am," the conductor said. "But the news is all over it right now."

"Oh Draso…" Trecheon muttered.

"The investigation's likely to take a long time," the conductor said. "So they're rerouting other trains. But the goal is to get us to our destination within six hours of our original arrival time."

"Understood," Missy said, and dragged the pair of them on their train car, settling them in the bedroom.

"Bathroom is there," she said, pointing. "Bedroom here, lounge next door. You can order food through this datapad and it will be delivered to you. This is totally private – no one else has access to this car, except for emergencies. Even the food will come to you through a chute."

Trecheon flicked his ears back. "Okay, thanks."

Her face softened. "Mr. Omnir. I was at Sheldon Manor when you took out the Assistant Mayor."

Trecheon's fur stood on end. That was why she looked so familiar. Exactly the memories he didn't need.

Sacha took a step forward.

Missy continued. "I know you hate your time as an assassin. You have every right to do so. It is a thankless, mentally destructive profession, that strips you of control." She took a deep breath. "But you did a lot of good during that time. Cling to that, okay? Control or not, you changed this world for the better. And you are not a bad person. Quite the opposite."

Trecheon frowned. What do you say to that?

Then Sacha walked up and slipped her hand into his. Her biomechanical hand.

Missy bowed to him. "It was a pleasure working with you. But I'm sure I speak for both of us when I say I hope we never do again."

"Yeah," Trecheon said. "Same."

"Take care, Mr. Omnir." She left.

Sacha and Trecheon stood there in silence for several minutes. Memories rolled over him. Assassinations, the Fawn's control over him, Ackerson pulling the strings, all the way back through the war, boot camp, Granddad's iron grip--

"I'm sorry."

Trecheon turned.

Sacha met his gaze, tears rolling down her cheeks. "I'm sorry. I should have told you about my arm. I shouldn't have made such a stink about going to your apartment. I should have let you have control." She wiped her face and glanced at her biomechanical arm. "I should be able to tell you what *happened,* damn it, but--"

"Hey, hey, hey," Trecheon said, placing a hand on her shoulder. "You have nothing to be sorry for. You have a right to privacy, Sacha. You only tell the people you trust when you're ready to tell them."

"But I do trust you," she said. "It shouldn't be so hard."

Trecheon pressed his lips into a thin line. He wrapped an arm around her and gently pulled her into a hug. She laid her head on his shoulder. "Sach, I know how hard it is. I've lived it myself. You never have to worry that I won't understand why you're not ready."

To his surprise, she buried her face in his neck and squeezed him tight.

He leaned his head on hers and locked his arms across her back.

"Don't let go," she whispered.

He closed his eyes. "I won't."

CHAPTER 50

SHARP

Leah slept in, though Ethos took off early the next morning, hoping to grab the car sooner. But no such luck. The reservation stood firm at noon. She came back with sandwiches, drinks, and a sour mood.

Leah pulled her into bed after lunch and lightened things considerably. Ethos lay naked on the mattress after they finished, breathing hard.

"You sure you're not interested in a relationship?" she asked, huffing.

Leah smiled, tracing circles on Ethos' bare stomach. "Sorry, not into that romantic stuff. Just the physical stuff."

"Damn." She pulled Leah back on top of her.

They were packed and ready to go by noon. Leah threw her bag in the trunk of their blue sedan, got in the passenger's seat, and yawned.

Ethos took the driver's seat, grinning. "I hope I wore you out."

"You did, thanks," Leah said, yawning again.

"You seem… surprisingly confident in the bedroom," Ethos said. "No offense."

Leah's ears grew hot, but she smiled. "None taken. I know my anxiety ruins a lot of my life, but when I feel confident in something, the anxiety goes away. I struggle with relationships sometimes, because of my magic. No one wants to be near me because seeing their medical history is a huge invasion of privacy. But those few who have let me into their lives have made me feel comfortable and welcome. And the very few who I've been intimate with have helped boost my confidence. So that kind of intimacy, I'm very confident in. No anxiety. I hope that makes sense."

"It does." Ethos chuckled. "Lucky me then. Planning on sleeping for the trip? I've got a blanket in the back."

Leah glanced back. It was the comforter from the hotel. "You did not steal the comforter."

"It has sentimental value now," Ethos said grinning. "SatNav says we should be there by nightfall, assuming we don't get much snow. Get some sleep."

"I'll keep Ethos focused," Pilot said cheerily. "We can tell ghost stories!"

"We absolutely cannot," Ethos said.

Leah chuckled, then leaned back in the seat and fell asleep.

It seemed like only minutes had passed when the car suddenly stopped and Leah jolted awake. She sat up, fully alert, glancing around.

They were on a small, single-lane road deep in an evergreen forest covered in snow. Evening light just barely filtered through the tree canopy. A gentle snowfall darkened the area, making it hard to see beyond the headlights. A spike of lightning ran up Leah's spine, and she instinctively tensed, looking for Ackerson's goons.

But this wasn't the war.

And yet.

She frowned. "Why'd we stop?"

"Keep your head down," Ethos hissed. "And stay in the car." She opened the door.

Leah grabbed her arm. "You are *not* going out there alone and unarmed."

Ethos flicked her ears back. "Okay, you're right." She pulled out her pistol, removed the magazine, and gripped it in her palm. It lit up bright white, then faded, leaving a full-moon clip in its place. She squeezed the .22, transforming it into a 357 Magnum, then slid the rounds into the chamber. She met Leah's eyes. "Stay. Here. I'll be back soon." She vanished into the darkness.

Leah slipped her collapsible staff out of pocket and tore off her seatbelt. She would not lose Ethos like she lost Ari.

She's going to die, the Thought Monster spat. *You already lost.*

Anxiety ripped through her body. But before she could get out, the driver's side door opened. Ethos threw herself into the seat and slammed the door shut. "Leah, shield the car. Hold on!" She tore off.

Leah leaned her head down and wrapped the car in a shield. Ethos kept her revolver up and ready, darting her gaze from window to window as they drove as fast as they could in the dark. Leah's magic gave the car a slight sheen like it was trapped in a big soap bubble.

It did little to protect them when the lightning hit.

The woods flashed a split second before the bolt smashed the car, shattering the shield and sending the vehicle careening into the woods. Ethos screamed and Leah built another shield as the car tumbled over and over through the trees. Leah bounced around in her seatbelt, unable to see or slow herself at all. Everything came to a halt when it crashed roof-first into a massive tree trunk, shaking them in their seats.

Leah hung sideways in her seatbelt. She groaned, hit the release button, then collapsed on top of the broken window.

Something sticky dripped on her head. She glanced up.

The low light barely illuminated Ethos' broken body. Blood dripped from her injuries as she hung lifeless in the seatbelt. The Thought Monster's voice echoed in her mind at a thousand miles a minute.

I told you so-I told you so-I told you so--

Leah gasped. "No!" She reached into the front seat, released Ethos from the seatbelt, and pulled her into her arms. She pressed her hand to the big wound on Ethos' neck and started healing it. Ethos groaned and stirred.

"Don't move." The injuries were extensive. Deep lacerations all through her body, bruised bones, organ punctures… She worked as quick as she could, fighting tears. *I am not going to lose you too!*

A deep, throaty roar echoed through the trees, followed by the staccato sound of an eagle cry. Leah froze. The wyvern and the gryfon.

Sharp's summons.

Leah turned the lights off the car. That wouldn't hide them long though.

Ethos coughed blood. "S-Sharp's coming."

"You're injured." Leah patched up the lacerations and started in on the internal bleeding. "If I don't finish this, you'll *die.*"

Ethos gripped Leah's hand. "If he finds us, we're *both* dead…"

Another roar blasted through the woods, shaking the car.

Pilot's hologram drone flittered out of his power pack. "I'll distract them."

Leah stared wide-eyed. "What do you plan on doing? You're a hologram!"

Pilot turned to her, a fierce look on his draconian features. "I'm saving your lives." He flew off, brightening his hologram.

She's dying... The Thought Monster's words echoed across her skull, tearing her away from Pilot. She pulled his power pack close to her and went back to healing Ethos.

"Over here, you dragon wannabe!" Pilot's voice echoed through the trees. A loud roar followed it.

Leah huffed, spent, then ran her hands over Ethos' body. Still had some bruised bones, still had some internal damage, but she'd survive now. Her body buzzed with energy and heat from the magic, but she had to get to Pilot.

Ethos heaved breath after breath into her hands, eyes pressed tightly shut, tears running down her face.

Leah placed a hand on her shoulder. "The pain will subside soon. Stay here." She passed Pilot's datashard pack to her. "Hold on to this. We can't let Sharp get Pilot."

Ethos coughed and took in a shuddering breath. "W-What about his hologram drone?"

"Useless without the power pack," Leah said. "He--"

The power pack lit up briefly and faded. Pilot spoke quietly through it. "It got my drone."

"Stay here," Leah said. "And stay down." She picked up Ethos' revolver and her staff and climbed out of the broken passenger door, all her battle instincts kicking in.

Keep Sharp away from Ethos.

She dashed through the woods back toward the street, feeling every bruise and sprain, revolver in hand. She purposefully crashed through the brush as loud as possible.

Keep the summons away from the car.

Kill the summoner... stop the summons. One shot. One shot against Sharp and it'd all be over.

The attack came from the left.

Leah lifted the revolver in both hands and fired, lighting the area up just enough to see the wild, angry face of the wyvern attacking, claws out, wings flared. The bullet cut through the black scales of its neck. It gripped the wound with the tiny claws on its wing joints and slithered away into the darkness, leaving a trail of bright blue blood dust. Leah gripped her chest and reflexively gasped for air, still feeling the boom of the revolvers recoil. She shook her staff to length.

A white bolt of lightning shocked through the sky.

Leah caught the magic on her staff and it spun around it like a flashing tornado. Her hands burned and buzzed and her vision blurred, but she managed to whip the staff in the direction the lightning came from. The magic shot forward, bouncing through the forest, reflecting off the snow.

The gryfon attacked in a quick flash of pale purple, talons out and beak open.

Leah ducked, rolled to her back, and stabbed her staff into the gryfon's belly as it flew over her. The gryfon squawked and dashed off into the darkness, leaving a trail of electricity and charred trees.

Leah swooped her staff around and caught the magic, using it to light up the area.

A pair of arms wrapped around her chest and neck, making her drop her weapons. *Sharp.*

He pulled her face toward his, "looking" at her with mangled, dead eye sockets. He grinned.

"Boo."

Leah bared her fangs and let out a feral yowl. She reached behind her and dug claws into Sharp's shoulders, then pitched her whole weight forward and pulled him over her head, heaving him several meters away, spraying blood in the air.

Sharp crashed through the underbrush, kicking up snow and pine needles, shouting and grunting with pain. He rolled to his hands and knees. "Get her, you frickin' dragon!"

The wyvern. She picked up her staff, but a torrent of water spun around, dragging up debris from the ground and catching her in a waterspout and spinning her in circles, cutting off her air and chilling her to the bone.

But there were words in the water.

I... am not... dragon... it said. *I... am Kaoru...*

Kaoru. She extended her staff out of the waterspout and it caught on a tree. The force stopped her spin and pulled her from the spout. She fell to the ground, soaked and coughing, but she shook herself and stood. "Kaoru!"

The waterspout collapsed, raining all around her. She darted her gaze left and right until she spotted the soft glowing eyes of the wyvern. He walked to her slowly, using his wings as forelegs instead of putting all his weight on his back feet like most wyvern. He stumbled along like he didn't quite know how to move properly.

Leah stood, holding her hand out, shivering from the cold soaking her clothes and fur. "You are Kaoru... yes?"

"Kill her, you stupid beast!" Sharp shouted.

"You don't have to do what he says," Leah said. "You have a choice."

Kaoru stopped. He raised himself on his back legs. A gentle rain fell on Leah's head. *I... have choice?*

Leah furrowed her brow. Something was terribly wrong. "Of course... you always have a choice."

The wyvern shook his head. *No... no choice... Grand Master... he assigns...* He shook himself, fluffing his black and blue feathers. *He forces...*

Leah's jaw dropped. "Forced?"

"That does it," Sharp shouted. A second later a gunshot echoed through the trees and a bullet whizzed by Leah. She shielded and dove toward Kaoru. "You hear me, you damn summons? Kill her or I'll kill you myself!"

Leah couldn't believe her ears. He was abusing his summons and they still chose to stay with him? She turned to Kaoru.

Kaoru sunk to the snow. More rain fell. *Death... would be welcome...*

Leah's heart ached. "Kaoru. What is the gryfon's name?"

She... is Drifa... Kaoru said. *She... does not speak... Trauma... stole her voice...*

Another gunshot through the air, another near miss.

Leah scooted closer to Kaoru. His pain was evident on his face this close up. She carefully placed a hand on his neck.

A wave of fear, pain, and trauma washed over her. A flash of some faceless beings, bright white lights, then Sharp's ugly mug, but that was all that he associated with whatever it was that bound him to Sharp.

She had never felt trauma or pain from a summon before. Not ever. What in Draso's name had happened to them?

"Kaoru... You and Drifa can leave. You don't have to be his summons."

Can't... leave... Kaoru said. *Binding spell... binds for life...*

Leah's eyes widened. "What?"

We cannot... leave... while he... lives...

A fire lit in Leah's belly. "Then let me help end him."

"There you are, you *coward.*"

Leah turned. Sharp had Drifa cornered against a bunch of trees. She pressed against them, wings flared in fear, clicking her beak at him as if trying to chase him away. He came after her, his gun aimed at her head. She couldn't die as a summon, but that *fear.*

Leah grabbed her staff and rushed him.

But just as she got close, he faced her, gun forward. "Gotcha." He fired.

She slid under him as the bullet raced over her head, the shockwave burning the guard hairs. She swept her staff under his legs, knocking him to the snow. "Drifa, quick, give me some of your lightning and I'll free you from him!"

The gryfon looked up confused, but then water rained down on them. *Drifa... trust her!* Drifa keened and threw a bolt of lightning at Leah. Leah caught it in her staff and dove for Sharp, careful to keep the staff away from her soaked clothing.

But the lightning vanished the moment her staff got near him, blowing her back. He laughed, then kicked her in the stomach, sending her flying. He wiped his mouth.

"You think I'm helpless?" he said. "Think I can't learn? Turns out you don't need *eyes* to make a Wish. So I covered all the bases this time. Full magic immunity – from mage, summon, and borrowed magic." He beat his chest and held his hands out. "You can't touch me." He lifted his pistol.

Leah barely leapt out of the way as he fired. Drifa squawked and took off into the woods. Leah dashed between the trees. "Kaoru! The revolver! Get me the revolver!"

The big wyvern shook himself, shedding feathers and he crawled around in the snow, sniffing.

Sharp shot again, the boom echoing through the night sky. Leah thanked her past self for having the insight to take out his vision, but it meant she couldn't get close to him – his hearing was too sensitive. She needed the gun.

Kill the summoner, save the summons.

Sharp shouted and fired randomly into the woods, over and over. Leah shielded and rolled, though a bullet caught her shield and shattered it.

Gray cat...! Leah paused, searching the woods. Kaoru stood to his full height and lifted one foot.

Her revolver.

He tossed it to her. She leapt through the air and caught it.

BAM. Sharp's weapon tore through her shoulder. She shrieked and crashed to the ground.

Sharp walked toward her, releasing the empty magazine. "I've been waiting too long for this." He fumbled in his pockets for a new one.

She gripped the revolver tight. "You said no mage magic can touch you."

"That's what I said, you--"

"Then I can't change my mind on this and heal you." She fired.

The bullet ripped through Sharp's chest and he fell surprisingly fast to the snow and stopped moving instantly.

It was over so fast, Leah didn't know how to process it. She coughed, dropping the gun and shaking her hand as the pain from the recoil raced through it. She gripped the gaping wound in her shoulder, shivering with cold, her mind a battlefield.

She killed him. *She killed him.* Ari's choking last breath ripped through her memories, then Zeke's parents, shot through the head, then the Battle of DC, all those screams, *all those screams—*

Footsteps crunched in the snow, drawing her into crisp focus.

Drifa walked cautiously to Sharp's body and sniffed it, ears perked. Her long, feathered tail fanned out and she turned to Kaoru, head titled.

Kaoru sniffed him too, then turned to Leah. *He... is gone.*

Leah nodded. "He is."

What... now?

Leah flicked her ears back. "You don't know?"

Kaoru and Drifa exchanged glances. *A summon... has a master... follows all orders... or dies.*

Leah furrowed her brow. "Oh, Kaoru. No, summons don't. Summons are supposed to *choose* their master. They can leave when their master abuses them. And they don't die." she frowned. "Ever."

Both Kaoru and Drifa's ears perked. Drifa shook. Kaoru spread his wings, glancing around in fear. *We... never die?*

Leah shook her head. "Summons are forever."

Drifa's beak opened. She hunched down and held her head in her talons and trembled. No. Sobbed.

Leah sat up as best she could. "What in the name of Draso happened to you two?"

Drifa stood and let out a sorrowful shriek. She spread her wings and leapt through the trees into the air.

Kaoru's eyes widened. *Come back!* He took off after her.

Leah tried standing, but the injuries and cold had caught up with her. She held out a hand. "Wait, don't go!"

"Leah!" Ethos shouted.

Leah turned. Ethos hobbled toward her, phone flashlight on. She got to Leah and peeled her hand back. "Oh heavens."

"Bullet," Leah said. "In my shoulder. Get it out."

Ethos furrowed her brow. She glanced quickly at Sharp's body, still oozing blood, then she ripped a piece of her coat and passed it to Leah. "Might want to bite down on this." She dug into the wound.

Leah screamed into the rag.

"There," Ethos said. "It's done." She dropped the bullet into the snow and took the strip of cloth from Leah. "Take off your jacket."

Leah groaned, but did so. Ethos scooped up a handful of snow and held it in her hands. It transformed, steaming. She pressed the liquid to Leah's wound.

Leah hissed in pain.

"Warm water, to clean it. Can't risk trying to make it an antiseptic though. Too much can go wrong." She held the strip of cloth, transformed it into a roll of cotton bandages, then began wrapping the wound. "I can fix your jacket after I've had a moment to rest. I think I can technically use my magic to make the clothes dry again too."

Leah shivered, the cold setting in with shock. She leaned against Ethos. "How… how far is Jasper?"

"Another forty miles."

Leah's heart sank. "How are we supposed to get there?"

Ethos held her close. "We'll figure it out." She helped Leah to her feet. "Come on."

Leah let Ethos lead her back toward their battered car, glancing around the woods, desperate for something to focus on to distract from her burning shoulder.

But the summons were gone. And she couldn't help them anymore.

You lost them, the Thought Monster said. *They needed help and you let them go. How are you supposed to help Jaden? How can you help ANYONE? You're pathetic.*

Yeah… she was.

JASPER

Leah stood next to Ethos, staring at their broken car, shivering in the cold. Her shoulder burned and ached, making it hard to focus on anything.

Ethos worked quickly, using her magic to transform their clothes into something dry, warm, and clean and the car mats into tarps for a makeshift tent. After a bit of a rest, she was able to use a few fallen branches as leverages and got the car back on its wheels.

Leah crunched the snow between her toes, letting the cold sink into her paw pads and ground her.

Ethos pulled the comforter, Pilot's power pack, and their bags to the big tarp in the snow, then nodded to the car. "I can use my magic to restore it, slowly." She sighed. "Without the Blood Crystal giving me extra power, I predict it'll take half the night to fix it, assuming the engine is still mostly intact. But I'll do it. Then we can take off tomorrow."

Leah snuggled into Ethos' side, trying to ignore the pain in her shoulder. Thankfully Ethos seemed relatively fine, despite the internal injuries. She pressed a little magic into her, healing a couple of wounds, but the shoulder pain and her exhaustion prevented her from recognizing any of Ethos' past history.

Everything ached. Her legs, her arms, her shoulder… her heart.

Poor Kaoru and Drifa, flying off to who knew where, with no knowledge of their states of being, prime for being abused.

Summon abuse. Of all the things she had researched over her five-year thesis, that was one thing she had never come across. She didn't think it could happen. Despite having a "master," in the long run, summons were masters of themselves. Or at least that was the belief.

But… forcing a summon's oath…

Was that even possible? She never would have thought so, but seeing Kaoru and Drifa… maybe it was.

Ethos pulled a thermos out of her bag, scooped some snow into it, and pressed her hands to the mug. Soon a gentle smell of brewing tea filled Leah's nose. She took a sip and passed it to Leah. "Penny for your thoughts?"

Leah sipped tea and stared at the ground, pushing the burning in her shoulder out of her mind as best she could. She picked at a few guard hairs on her tail, but then noticed a bald spot and stopped. Dang it.

"A summon's oath needs to be taken willingly," she said carefully. "And I mean *very* willingly. Someone could say the oath, but unless the magic feels their will to commit with their whole body and soul, it won't stick. Any doubt at all and it will fail. The history of summons aren't always clear about everything, but they are *very* clear about that." Her eyes burned. "But Sharp's summons… I think they were forced somehow. How does someone force someone else to become a summon?"

"Indoctrination," Ethos said. Leah turned to her. Ethos piled up some sticks and transformed them into big logs. She pulled a lighter from her bag and lit it. Embers took to the sky. "Social pressure. Promises. There's more ways than you might believe." She took a deep breath. "When you believe it is your destiny to become something, for whatever reason you're fed, you go with it."

Leah flicked her ears back. "That's what happened to you, isn't it? That's how you got stuck as your sister's assassins."

Ethos nodded.

She leaned against Ethos again. "…I'm sorry."

Pilot's datashard lit up and his hologram appeared from the power pack. He frowned. "Are you two okay?"

"We'll live," Ethos said.

"Pilot," Leah asked. "Is it possible to force someone to take the summoner's oath?"

Pilot rubbed his chin with a thick claw. "Not that I know of. History has never recorded it."

Leah growled. "How much access do you have to the greater intergalactic networks?"

Pilot shrugged his wings. "Decent access. It's why I was able to scrounge through the Summoner's Database."

Leah huffed. "Well, if you can, scan the networks for anything about forced summons. Whoever did that will *pay.*" She pushed her glasses up higher on her nose and leaned back. "And I couldn't even help them…"

"Hun," Ethos said. "You can't blame yourself for that. You can't control them." She furrowed her brow. "Maybe you shouldn't even try. Being controlled is what got them to that state in the first place."

Leah's ears flattened. She hunched down. "…You're right. I just hope they find a master who will treat them with kindness. They need it."

Ethos rubbed Leah's good arm. "I'm sure they'll be fine." She stood and stretched. "Rest. I need to start on this car." She helped Leah lay her head on her bag and cuddle in the blanket.

Despite the pain, Leah fell asleep almost instantly. She woke up several times in the night though. Sometimes Ethos was sleeping next to her, other times she was working on the car. When she woke up the fifth time, Ethos had cuddled close to her under the blanket, snoring, and the dawn was just peaking through the trees. She glanced at the car.

All fixed.

She sighed and went back to sleep.

She had no idea what time it was when Ethos gently shook her awake, but late enough that the sun had penetrated the tree canopy. She blinked awake, shading her eyes against the blinding light on the snow and groaned. Her shoulder was stiff and aching. Moving hurt.

Ethos smiled and passed Leah some more tea and a pastry from her bag. "Morning, hun. Snow tea and smashed pastries. My magic is spent so I can't enhance them. Hopefully Jasper has a good coffeehouse. Gotta get going if we wanna make decent time."

Leah sat up and rubbed her shoulder. Ethos changed her bandage again and they piled into the car. Getting it back on the road was easier than Leah expected and soon they were back on their way. Every bump reminded her of her injuries – bruises, cuts, sprains, that shoulder. It was the most agonizing ride she had ever experienced.

"What are we supposed to do when we (ow) get into town?" Leah asked.

Ethos frowned. "Good question."

"CHAOS DINER JUST LOST A REALLY GOOD COOK."

Leah glanced in the backseat. Pilot had activated again, starting with blank eyes, head tilted unnaturally.

Ethos growled, baring her teeth. "I only have a vague idea of who's doing this, and if I see them, they're getting a punch in the mouth. I *hate* cryptic messages."

Leah frowned. "It's the Cloak isn't it?"

"Likely. He's been sending us cryptic signs ever since he vanished after the war."

Leah shrugged. "At least we have something to go off of."

They got into Jasper just after noon and it was bustling. All the buildings had the feel of an old mountain town – log cabin façades, big well-kept pine trees, crude but highly polished benches and tables made of fallen trees, and gravel trails instead of sidewalks. The air smelled of bacon, coffee, and fireplaces. But regardless of the façade, it was clearly a high-end commercial center, like a theme park dress up, rather than an actual logger town. Every building in sight was a shop with modern signs, bright lights, and inviting fronts. And while many of the people wandering the town were clearly backpackers, laden with supplies for a long hike, there were equally as many families and groups of teens and young people more interested in the shops and food than the woods around them.

The Chaos Diner was off to the left of the main road. It had fenced off several parking spaces with large wood barriers and had put up a bunch of simple tables and chairs which were all full up. The smell of sausage, roasted veggies, and eggs hit Leah all the way from here. She licked her lips.

Ethos patted Leah's good shoulder. "Let's go. I have an idea on how to get some information. We'll see if we can get some proper bandages and painkillers after this. And keep your jacket over your wound. Wouldn't want people asking awkward questions." Leah nodded and they entered the diner.

The inside was just as busy as the outside, with patrons of all species crowding on the rugged tables. A strong smell of bar-b-que filled the room. Old lanterns converted to electric lights hung from the low ceiling, and firewood lined all the walls in big boxes. A big burly human in overalls, a messy apron, and no shirt stood at the counter, chatting with customers and taking orders, though with all the talking, Leah couldn't make out what they said.

Ethos walked confidently to the counter.

The proprietor turned to her. The apron had a tag that said "it/its pronouns, please." It grinned. "Greetings, lovelies. What can I getcha?"

"Two lunch specials, please," Ethos said, passing it some cash. She batted her eyes. "I've heard you just lost an amazing cook. I hope they moved and there wasn't something more serious."

The worker chuckled as it got Ethos' change. "Uh oh. Rosé Café must be spreading rumors about food poisoning again."

"Shut it, Chuck!" someone shouted from the dining room.

"Says the man eating here instead of his own restaurant, *Barry,*" Chuck said, though it laughed. Barry raised his coffee and shouted cheers. Chuck passed Ethos the change. "You're looking for Dyne and his buddy Tymon."

Leah's heart seized. Those names were no accident. And… just two of them. Jaden and Embrik. So where was Alexina?

"They left about a month ago. Something about a rather urgent need to move." Chuck rubbed the thick beard on its chin. "Though I'll admit, it was rather sudden. Said he didn't have time to leave two weeks notice, but he apologized for it." It pointed to the bulletin board. "They left that jumbled riddle on the wall before they left. I have no clue what the hell it means, but if you can figure it out, meal's on us. Been puzzling through it ever since they left." It handed them a number on a stand. "Good luck, lovelies."

Ethos nodded. "Thank you."

It nodded back, then went to the next customer.

Ethos picked a table near the bulletin board and took a picture of the riddle. She squinted at it. "What kind of riddle is this? It's just a mess of words." She passed it to Leah.

Leah glanced it over. That was definitely Jaden's handwriting. And sure enough, it was just a tangled disaster. *Squirrel, dragon, nest, free, flutters...*

Wait. "I know this," Leah said. "Give me a piece of paper and a pen." Ethos passed her a notepad and a pen from her bag, and Leah began rearranging words. It took their entire meal, but she ended up with a familiar poem. The Zyearth nursery rhyme Jaden had recited to them when he was testing Leah and Zeke's mental connection before they went after the British dignitary Rosanna May in Idaho.

Well. Somewhat familiar. Jaden had changed it.

"Here," Leah said. "I think I got this right. Based off an old Zyearth nursery rhyme, but the second and fourth lines end differently." She laid out the paper and wrinkled her snout. "'Grove' and 'cove' could probably be switched, but I'm not sure it matters."

> *Squirrels climb the branches, birds seek the divine*
> *And the winged dragon flutters high over the pine*
> *But when the sky darkens and we leave the cove,*
> *Squirrel, bird, and dragon return to the grove.*

Ethos tapped the paper excitedly. "Look. Pine Cove. That's where he's telling us he moved."

"Makes sense," Leah said. "No one but me or Zeke would know that poem." She sighed. "Draso, what a disappointment… We're back at square one. How do we get to Pine Cove from here?"

"Carefully," Ethos said. She picked up the paper with the solved riddle, held it in her hand, and turned it into a blank sticky note. Then she ripped it up. While no one was looking, she walked over to the bulletin board and did the same thing to Jaden's original note. Then without another word, she dropped a tip on the table and left.

Leah followed. She didn't know what chased Jaden and Embrik away, but the fact that he had been here, recently, filled her with hope.

Hang on, Jaden. We're almost home.

CHAPTER 52

PINE COVE

Trecheon exited the train and stepped down on the platform with Sacha at his side. Snow covered the roofs, though the platform had been cleared of it. Bright morning sun lit everything up, reflecting off the snow, blinding Trecheon as he disembarked. He shaded his eyes and glanced around.

Here we are. Pine Cove.

Now he just had to hope he'd find Jaden. And that Matt's father wouldn't see his red quills and try to murder him like Matt had done all those years ago. He probably should have thought of that before he volunteered for this.

He ran a hand over the Defender pendant around his neck. Hopefully that'd be a deterrent. If that wasn't, then Jaden's faded Golden Guardian pendant might be. Or it might be an aggravator. Who knew.

During the trip, Trecheon had kept a sharp eye on the train derailment news, counting the missing passengers and looking up the ever-growing list of the dead. Thankfully nothing came up about Leah or Ethos, though they were likely using aliases and he'd have no idea what those would be. On top of that, it wasn't a coincidence that both electricity and water were involved in the crash.

That was Sharp and his summons.

Sacha glanced around. She had spent the majority of the trip sleeping or mindlessly scrolling through the TV. Probably as a distraction. At least it kept her from waking up in the middle of the night screaming after the hell she'd been through. He'd probably do the same thing. She flicked her long golden tail. "So now what?"

"If I were on the lam," Trecheon said. "I'd be hiding in plain sight. Take an unassuming job, pay my bills, never stand out. Maybe work somewhere as a line cook or a barback or hell, a hotel cleaner where I could work mostly alone and see fewer people. Less likely someone remembers your face."

"So we should start with the diners then," Sacha said. "Got it." She grabbed his arm and pulled him through the station.

They split up and spent the better part of the day visiting diners, hotels, bars, and even a few shops here and there, asking about white, or red, or black quilar. Every inquiry was met with a no. Sacha also asked about Leah and Ethos, but that also led nowhere. It was a dead end.

By evening, Trecheon was hungry, tired, and defeated. Jaden wasn't here, or if he was, no one knew. Or they were hiding it. It's not like Jaden or his friends would be expecting an Omnir and a tiger to be looking for them.

Sacha suggested a break after their measly dinner of sandwiches and chips and found a park overlooking the cove for which the town got its name. It was early enough in the season that the cove hadn't frozen yet, but snow covered most of the trees and grass. Trecheon found a clean bench and sat, staring out over the water. Sacha sat next to him. Both remained silent.

He longed for control he worried he'd never get back.

Trecheon's pendant beeped. He glanced quickly at Sacha, then fumbled the pendant and pulled it up, expecting Ouranos calling with bad news.

But it wasn't Ouranos. It was Matt.

Sacha chewed her lip. "I'll give you some privacy." She walked off.

Trecheon's heart raced. All this time and he had nothing more to report. He took a deep breath and answered the call, not bothering to hide his disappointment. "Hey, Matt."

Matt flicked his ears back. "Your expression tells me you don't have good news."

"Afraid not," Trecheon said, and launched into an explanation of everything they knew and what had happened – breaking Jaden's encryption, Philip's predicament and rescue, Leah's disappearance, and Trecheon's frantic attempts to chase her and Jaden down. All ending with the unfortunate news that at least one of Jaden's locations seemed like a dead end.

Matt's expression grew darker with every word. "I'm glad Philip is okay. That's a victory. But… damn, I should be there. You all are going through hell."

"I won't disagree," Trecheon said. "But considering how things could have gone, we're holding our own pretty well. It definitely could be worse. Angel is subdued for now and most of us are packed away and safe."

Matt nodded. "True. I suppose you've got that chaos under control somewhat at least." He smirked. "I always did love a zyfaunos who could take charge in bad weather."

Trecheon's heart fluttered. He smiled and raised his eyebrows. "That makes two of us then. Maybe that's what attracts me to you so much."

"Attracts?" Matt said laughing. "From subtle to overt in two seconds flat."

Trecheon's ears grew hot. "Don't read too much into it."

"Too late," Matt said. "Maybe I'll take up that invitation to share your bed after all. Let you prove to me how good you are at taking charge."

Heat built in Trecheon's belly and between his legs. *"Now* who's being overt?"

"You started it."

"Don't tempt me with a good time," Trecheon said, trying to keep calm.

Matt chuckled. "I'm glad I'm coming back whether you find my dad or not." He paused, his grin fading slightly. "I hope you find him though."

"I hope so too." Trecheon's chest ached. "Just… get here soon." He chewed his lip. "I need you."

Matt's eyes grew wide a moment, but he smiled. "Yeah." He stretched. "That's actually why I called to be honest. We messed with some settings on the engine and gave it some more power. We're going to be there early. Just a couple of days."

Oh, thank Draso. "We're in Canada still, just so you know," Trecheon said. "Not sure how to direct you."

"I'll follow your pendant signal," Matt said. "We'll get there. Just hang on, okay?"

"We will," Trecheon said. "See you soon."

"Not soon enough." Matt waved and ended the call.

Trecheon dropped the pendant, letting it hang around his neck. He ran his hand down his face. Good Draso…

"You really love him, don't you," Sacha said.

Trecheon turned. Sacha stood behind him next to one of the snow-covered pine trees. He flicked his ears back. "I thought you were giving me space."

"Sorry," Sacha said. "I wanted to make sure you were okay. You sounded… desperate."

Trecheon leaned back on the bench. "Shit. Did I?"

Sacha sat next to him. "So why haven't you said anything?"

Trecheon flattened his ears. "I clearly *have.*"

"You know what I mean," Sacha said. "How come you haven't outright told him? Are you afraid he'll reject you?"

Trecheon chuckled darkly. "After that comment about my bed, no."

"Then what's holding you back?"

Trecheon pressed his lips tight.

Sacha's whiskers twitched. "You don't have to answer if you don't want."

Trecheon covered his face with his hands. "My whole life has been run by someone else. Theron ran my life when he took my father and forced me on Granddad. Granddad ran my life right up to putting me in the Marines. Ackerson ran my life all through the war, and the war ran my life after that. I don't have to explain how the Fawns have run my life too, even if it was really Ackerson pulling the strings." He shook his head. "And now my own heart betrays me and starts doing its own thing without my permission. I need control."

Sacha furrowed her brow and pinned her ears back. "Trecheon, your heart and you are the same thing. If your heart needs it, *you* need it."

Trecheon scoffed. "It's not a *need.*"

"Clearly it is if your heart won't let it go," Sacha said.

"I need *control,* damnit," Trecheon said, forming fists. "It doesn't matter if they're needs or wants or whatever, I need to *control them.*"

"Why?"

Trecheon frowned.

Sacha leaned next to him and looked him in the eye. "Hun. All those other things you've mentioned. The family, the war, the enemies. All of them controlled your life for the worse."

Trecheon leaned back. "Obviously."

"But your heart isn't trying to hurt you," Sacha said. "It's trying to bring you joy. It's not the same kind of control." She took his hands. "It's trying to balance all the pain you've faced. Why are you fighting it?"

Trecheon looked down, his heart aching.

"I understand your need for control," Sacha continued. "I've been watching you struggle with it ever since this started. But often times when we have that need, we're afraid of something. So what are you afraid of?"

Trecheon winced, biting his tongue. That's where the core was. Fear. Damn it all. "I'm… afraid of opening up. I've been so closed off for so long, I…" He stared up at the darkening sky. "I'm afraid of letting someone in. Of getting hurt." He turned to Sacha. "…Of losing you. And Matt." He pressed his lips tightly together. "I can't… I can't close up again. I can't be alone anymore. I can't be without you."

Sacha squeezed his hands. "We would never hurt you, Trecheon."

"Not on *purpose.*"

"Not ever," Sacha said. "Not if we can help it." She leaned closer to him. "Both Matt and I have seen you fight to control your life. It's why we've been giving you as much control as we can. And it's why we've waited on *you* to come to *us*. On your own terms."

Trecheon stared out over the cove. The fading light painted the sky a dark purple. Draso's breath. His cheeks flushed. "So you know."

"I've known for a long time, hun." Sacha laid a hand on his knee. A shiver ran up his spine. "But I wanted you to take control of your life again.

I wanted… I wanted you to recognize your own fear before you faced it head on.”

Draso's breath. Was that really the problem?

Was he afraid to love again?

Images of Rebekka flashed in his mind. Ironically, their one romantic escapade had happened in the woods of Canada.

But that was war. That was… desperation. Maybe it was love… but it wasn't what he felt for Sacha or Matt. This was *real* love.

And he was running from it.

But the distance, his brain said. *They're so far away. Soon they'll be back on Zyearth and you'll be alone again.*

But not right now, his heart said. *Matt's coming for you. Sacha's right there. She's waiting.*

Sacha smiled. A soft, gentle smile, chasing away his fears. Putting aside her own. Waiting. “You can kiss me if you want,” she said quietly. “But your choice. You're in control.” She rubbed his knee.

He furrowed his brow. Neil's grinning face flashed in his mind, of all things. Him gleefully hugging Natassa. Sharing kisses with Damianos. Asking both of them to marry him. The family he had built for himself, despite his terrible past and awful mistakes. Trecheon wanted that.

Maybe… maybe he could actually have it.

He caressed Sacha's cheek, and, heart beating fast, he pressed his lips to hers. She returned the kiss, leaning into him, right hand running up and down his chest, left hand holding his head. He couldn't convince himself to move fast or do more than a simple kiss… so he let her lead. Have control. Let the feelings of her caresses run through his body.

It ended all too soon, his body begging for more, though his mind struggled with the fact that she was the first person he had kissed since the war. That's how broken he was.

But his heart wasn't trying to hurt him. He had to cling to that.

She smiled, her eyes shining. She pressed her forehead to his and closed her eyes. He closed his too, trying to slow his heartbeat.

"Thank you." She pulled back, smiling lightly. "I hope there's more where that came from."

Trecheon's ears grew hot. "Yeah… I hope so too."

She giggled and kissed his forehead, then gave him a sly glance. "Now don't think that gets you out of telling Matt your feelings."

Trecheon narrowed his gaze. Well, shit. "No way. A bird in the hand is worth two in the bush."

She raised a finger and smirked. "Ah, but a Gem left untouched is a Gem left unbroken."

Trecheon blinked. "What?"

She laughed. "Sorry. Not sure if there's a comparable Earth idiom. Basically it means if you don't take risks, you'll never earn rewards."

Trecheon rolled his eyes. "I have my reward right here."

"You have one," Sacha said. She kissed his nose. "But I know you want both. And before you ask, I'm happy to share. As long as Matt is." She winked. "Hell, I'll share him too, if he's interested."

He frowned at her.

Her smile softened. "If you want. In your own time." She tapped his knee. "Listen to your heart, hun."

"It doesn't want to hurt me," Trecheon said. "I get it." He sighed. "Maybe sometime. After we find his father."

"Good enough for me," Sacha said. She stood and held out a hand. "Let's find a hotel for the night and see what the morning brings us."

He eyed her warily.

"When I said in your own time," she said. "I meant in your own time. Whatever happens tonight in that room is up to you. You're in control."

He glanced at her hand, then took it, and the pair of them walked back to town, fingers laced together. He couldn't feel her hand in his, but it didn't seem to matter. The warmth was there anyway.

He hoped the morning wouldn't come too soon.

CHAPTER 53

INVASION

"Concentrate," Ouranos said. "Let your senses ground you."

Zeke and Ouranos were in the palace gardens, in the ArchDragon Park, surrounded by elaborate dragon statuary and big trees. Many of them had their fall leaves, a few were already bare, and a handful were evergreens, making everything feel colorful and cozy. The pine smell wafted through the air, and Zeke and Ouranos had crunched through a lot of fallen leaves on the way to the clover lawn. They had found a space in the shade and sat cross-legged.

Zeke was still broken. He knew that. And it was something he had to fix before he lost everything. Andre, Leah…

His new family. If he could accept them in the first place. His parents' claws dug into his shoulders, begging him to stay with them.

He scrunched his snout. If he was going to fix himself, he had to fix his magic.

Ouranos held his hands in his lap and his eyes closed. "Let your mind rest. Tell me what you see."

Zeke twitched his snout and focused on the scene around him. "I see… a fountain." The moment he said it, little globs of water floated around his head. He glared at them.

"Describe it," Ouranos said.

"It's… calming," Zeke said. "Shooting streams into the air, letting sunlight catch it. When the water hits the trees, the leaves shine like jewels."

"Good," Ouranos said. "Now, what do you feel?"

"I feel… cold." A wind blew now, catching the water globs and spreading them out in a ring around his head. He growled, his eye twitching. "It's… crisp. Gives me goosebumps under the fur." He paused. "It cuts under my shirt. I can feel it build behind my glasses, making the metal cold." Then a fireball appeared and whirled around the water hoop. Zeke gritted his teeth. *"Damnit."*

Ouranos started singing, slowly and quietly.

Tension left Zeke's body and the magic faded. He tried the next sense. *I hear… water. Trickling down little streams.* His nose twitched, and he pressed his eyes closed. Again. *I hear… singing. Songs of the past, in the Athánatos language. My heritage. My uncle…*

A pebble smacked him in the head. He opened his eyes. Little globs of magic floated around him again in their ever-moving solar systems. He focused on Ouranos singing again and it faded, though it didn't vanish completely. He sighed and held his head in his hands. "This isn't working. It's not a solution if I can only hold on to my magic while you're singing."

Ouranos frowned. "I am sorry, Zeke. The meditation seems to do you good, but you may need more intervention."

Zeke scoffed. "Like, what, a therapist? Can't exactly get that here."

"Unfortunately, no," Ouranos said. "Hopefully we can on the mainland though, once we are in a better place." He stood. "I wish I could do more for you."

Zeke slumped down. Then panic rose in his spine. His moms. They had faded. He tensed up, willing them back to him, desperate to hold on to them. They slunk over him like ghosts, hands on his shoulders, grasping his shirt. But he couldn't relax. "Yeah. I wish that too."

Ouranos smiled sadly and gripped Zeke's shoulder. "I sense you would like some time alone, so I will leave you to it. But if you need anything at all, remember you have family here."

Mom and Mama tightened their grips.

"Feel free to wander the gardens," Ouranos said. "Mona's Garden is to the east. I recommend it. I find it very calming."

Zeke folded his arms and stared at the clover.

Ouranos flicked an ear. He patted Zeke's shoulder. "Find me if you need anything." He left.

Zeke watched him walk off. He looked so dejected. Zeke growled. He should be *better* about this. Ouranos wasn't doing anything wrong. He was trying to *help*, damnit.

But he couldn't bring himself to let Ouranos in. Not with his moms clinging so tightly to him.

He took Ouranos' hint and wandered into Mona's Garden. He found a patch of clover and sat cross-legged again. Keeping his eyes on the statue of Mona, he focused on the flowing golden silks around her arms waving in the wind, trying to remember all Ouranos had taught him about meditation. The sight (golden silk), the smell (fall flowers), the sounds (wind rustling through the garden trees), the feel (late November, chilling his skin), and the taste.

Bitterness.

Fear.

Marbles of magic floated around his head.

Shit, he lost it again. He shook himself, resumed his relaxed position and attempted it again. But his concentration had broken too far, and worry crept in its place, making the marbles spin faster. His moms' sharp phantom claws dug their way into his shoulders again, coaxing him into the imaginary world where they still lived. Zeke fought it, but only just.

He shook his head. *No.* Now was the time to focus on the present. No matter how bleak it was. He had to let his parents go. Even he didn't want to.

Focus on something else.

Leah immediately came to mind. He held his head in his hands. Draso, he needed her… She shouldn't be out there alone.

But he also shouldn't be with her while he was such a danger. Screw all of this.

Zeke stood up from his meditation position in front of Mona and sat down on a marble bench. Battles were supposed to be the worst part of war. No one had told him that the waiting was just as bad. Slowly the magic floating around him faded, though not by his own will.

"Hey, Zeke," Neil said. "Sup? You trying that meditation thing again?"

Zeke opened his eyes. Neil walked up, all smiles. He was entirely different than the puma Zeke had met back on Casino Beach a week and a half ago. Happy, joking all the time, grins with every greeting, a lover of food, and someone who treated everyone as his equal. Even the palace dwellers, who would be his subjects after his marriage with Natassa.

He fell into his new family like it was nothing. And Zeke hurt watching him.

Neil frowned and waved a hand. "Yo, Zeke, you there bud?"

Zeke frowned. "Can I ask a difficult question?"

Neil's face turned more serious and his whiskers twitched. He sat on the bench next to Zeke. "Sure. What's on your mind?"

"You lost your family very similarly to how I did," Zeke said. He wrung his hands. "Hell, it was practically by the same person."

"It was by the same person," Neil said. "My parents' blood is on Ackerson's hands, not the Fawns. They were just desperate to get their families back." He smiled sadly. "That's what I'm trying to believe anyway. It's hard, but I think it's the right mindset."

"Right." Zeke flicked his ears. "And now you have a new family here on Athánatos."

"I do, yeah."

"How do you do it?" Zeke asked.

Neil raised an eyebrow. "Find a new family?"

"More like… accept a new family."

Neil shrugged. "It's not like there's some special formula I followed. I just fell in love and there it was. I accepted it without question."

Zeke stared at his hands. His mom's phantom claws dug deeper, to the point where his shoulders ached. "Great. Just what I needed to hear as an ace/aro person."

"I didn't mean you *needed* to fall in love to accept a new family," Neil said. "Like I said, there's no formula for it. It's just what *I* did."

Zeke leaned back. "But… what about your old family? How did you get them to let you go?"

"I didn't," Neil said. "I had to let them go myself."

Zeke turned to him, a stab of pain running through his heart.

Neil rubbed his hands together. "They didn't want to let go. They clawed at me, whispering in my ears, telling me I messed up, and their deaths were my fault, and letting them go was just as bad as killing them a second time." He formed fists. "I fought that for years."

Zeke pressed his lips into a thin line. The phantom claws dug deeper, drawing invisible blood.

Neil lowered his gaze. "I couldn't go through the stages of grief. I kept getting stuck at denial. Tracing all the steps back to see where I messed up. What could I have done to prevent their deaths? I fully embraced the thought that their deaths were my fault. I killed them." He shook his head. "Honestly, I probably would still think that if Pathos hadn't told me that Ackerson was orchestrating the whole thing. There wasn't anything I could do."

"But… you said they let you go."

"I said *I* let *them* go," Neil said. "Big difference. I had to recognize that they didn't control me in death. At that point, everything was on me. *I* needed to let go. I had to. Because I was living in the past and I needed to live in the future. I had someone to fight for."

Zeke furrowed his brow. "Philip."

"Exactly." Neil glanced at Mona. "Philip gave me a goal to work toward. An urgent, terrible goal, but one nonetheless. Singularly focused. Couldn't sit there wallowing in guilt over dead parents when I had a living brother." He shook his head. "I admit, I wasn't in a good place mentally. But Trecheon kept me afloat. Then Matt and his team showed up and gave me a new reason to fight." He smiled. "Then Dami and Natassa gave me a new reason to hope. I could see a future that wasn't all pain." He turned to Zeke. "I could let my dead folks go."

Zeke flattened both ears now.

Neil pressed his lips together. "Honestly. They'd want me to let them go."

"They'd want to be *alive,*" Zeke said.

"Of course," Neil said. "But they aren't. And they wouldn't want me clinging to them. That's not representing them fairly. They would never hold me down." He sighed. "Much as I struggled to get along with my folks after the war, they still loved me. Wanted the best for me. They'd never hurt me." He turned. "Neither would your parents. Love is supposed to strengthen you, not disable you."

Zeke's heart snapped. His parents clung tighter to his shoulders now, growling in his ear, hissing at Neil.

But… that couldn't be his parents. Neil was right. They'd never drag him down. They even said so at the end of their lives. These were just phantoms.

Right?

"Remember you have a family to fight for too, Zeke," Neil said. "You have Andre and Leah."

Zeke's took in a sharp breath.

"And Jaden, and Embrik, and Alexina," Neil said. "A goal to work toward. Family. You accepted *them,* right?"

"I mean… yeah."

"And you deserve to have them." He gripped Zeke's shoulder. "Your moms deserve rest. You're not being disloyal letting them go. You're honoring them." Then he stood and headed back for the palace.

Neil's warm hand on his shoulder had loosened his moms' phantom claws. Though they still kept their arms around him.

Don't let go, Mom said.

We need you, Mama said.

Zeke bit his lip. He couldn't let them go. If he let them go, it'd be like they died all over again. Neil had only faced that once. Zeke had lost them twice already. He couldn't do it again.

You can, Zeke. Zeke jolted. Leah's voice. A warm, comforting smell of baked apples filled his nostrils. *It's okay to let the past go.*

Zeke shut his eyes. *I can't.*

You don't want to, Leah said. *...Honestly, I don't want to either. But... we can. Together. And build a new family. Your parents would want that for you.* He could almost feel her hug him. *Starting with us.*

"Zeke?"

Zeke shook his head and glanced up. Ouranos, holding a tray with tea and snacks. He wore a frown. "I am sorry, I did not mean to bother you but I thought you would like some tea."

He stared at Ouranos. All he had tried to do since Zeke had shown up was make him feel welcome, with warm smiles, comforting touches, advice when he needed it, distractions otherwise. All he had ever craved with Leah, with Andre... with his moms.

And he had still pushed him away. He shouldn't. He mentally shrugged off his mom's hugs. *I can't accept him while I'm still clinging to your phantoms.*

They still pulled on him. But he pushed them back. He was done giving in. This wasn't his moms. They would never hurt him. And he... he had a family here.

Then his moms vanished.

Ouranos put the tea tray down on the bench. "My apologies. I will leave this here and let you relax." He turned to leave.

Zeke stood. "Wait, Ouranos!"

Ouranos turned back.

Zeke flattened his ear. "Uncle... Thanks."

Ouranos' eyes widened. He grinned, full faced. "You are welcome, nephew."

Zeke smiled back.

Then Andre ran into the garden. "Zeke, Ouranos!"

Zeke frowned. "Andre?"

Andre skidded to a halt and leaned on his knees, breathing hard. "Some… Some Archons showed up. Said they were from the far end of the island."

Zeke tensed.

Ouranos furrowed his brow. "What happened?"

"We're compromised," Andre said. "Ackerson's goons have invaded the island."

TOGETHER AGAIN

Leah and Ethos pulled into a parking space at Pine Cove's train station. Despite having little of it left after the accident, Ethos' magical makeup was able to hide her well. No one seemed to notice the two of them.

Leah had used the long trip to memorize Jaden's modified poem, reciting it over and over again. It might not mean anything, but better to have it and not need it than to need it and not have it.

Pilot offered to analyze it too, looking for patterns and ciphers, but he didn't find anything. "I don't like that this is so simple," he had said. "Feels... unfinished."

"And very unlike Jaden," Leah agreed.

Ethos had decided to spend the night at a hotel in Jasper and start the journey the next day, to give them another day of rest. Leah's shoulder still ached and stung, but at least the wound didn't look infected.

If Jaden and Embrik had seen fit to work at a diner in Jasper, they were probably doing the same thing in Pine Cove.

"And I bet he'd pick one close to the station," Ethos said. "A place where it'd be mostly travelers passing through – less time for people to get used to his face."

Leah nodded. "Good point."

They walked to the town's main street. It looked hardly different than Jasper – no more than a commercialized, theme park façade of a mining town, albeit much bigger than Jasper, with paved sidewalks and busy streets.

Leah pointed. "There." A big diner called Amalia's. The signage didn't even try to hide the commercialism like most of the rest of it, using big fancy light-up letters to attract guests. It was bustling with customers, and a line went out the door, despite the fact that lunch had come and gone.

Ethos nodded. "Might as well start there." They headed for the building and got in line.

"Well, well."

Leah turned and winced, ears splayed.

Trecheon and Sacha.

Trecheon crossed his arms and tilted his head. "Fancy meeting you here."

Leah's system immediately went into overdrive. Her ears grew hot, her belly roiled, and an overwhelming need to hide wracked her body. *He came looking for you! You're in deathly trouble now!* the Thought Monster screamed into her mind.

She swallowed hard and forced herself to stand straight. "Trecheon, I am *so sorry--*"

Trecheon held up a hand, brow furrowed. "Don't apologize, Leah. I know why you ran off."

She wiped at her eyes. The Thought Monster clawed at her, but Trecheon's gentle expression chased it back. "Y-You do?"

Trecheon nodded. "You're worried about your family, and Jaden is family. I mean, hell, Neil and I did the same thing for Philip." He rubbed an arm. "I shouldn't have held you back. That was stripping you of control. I should have offered to go with you instead." He turned to Ethos. "So thank you for covering my ass with that."

Ethos' ears drooped, but she nodded.

Leah flicked her tail and glanced at the floor. "Still, I shouldn't have taken off like that. And I stole a phone, money, *Pilot--*"

"It's okay, Leah," Trecheon said. "Really. If anything, it lit a fire under our tails and we actually took some initiative. It's probably what we needed."

Leah's hair stood on end. "What do you mean, took initiative?"

Sacha glanced around at the big crowds. Several people stared at them. One person whispered to his partner while pointing. "Let's find some place more private." She led them to a park overlooking what Leah expected was the actual cove the city was named after, and they sat down on a bench. Thankfully the park was pretty quiet and the bench far off the main path. Trecheon explained everything that had happened with Philip, Ackerson, and Angel.

"The worst part is, we think they might be able to get into Athánatos," Trecheon said. "That's why everyone else stayed behind. Fawns included. And speaking of…" He turned to Ethos. "Ethos. Pathos and Logos told Neil and I what Ackerson did to your families."

Ethos grimaced. Leah gripped her hand, and glared at Trecheon, daring him to call her a liar, or belittle her pain. Ethos' fear rushed through her own body, almost overwhelming her, but she stood firm.

But she didn't have to worry.

Trecheon drooped his ears and he frowned deeply. "For what its worth," he said. "I'm so very sorry. And I forgive you."

Ethos' eyes widened.

Trecheon looked down and fiddled with his hands. "I know it doesn't bring back your family, and it doesn't undo all the damage from the aftermath." He met her gaze. "But hopefully it eases your heart a little."

Ethos stared at him. Tears built in her eyes. "I… Thank you…" She shook herself. "I… I don't…"

Trecheon held out a hand to her. "We've all got a lot of healing to do. Neil was hoping we could all do it together. If you're willing." He smiled.

Ethos looked at his hand. She reached out and squeezed it, tears running down her snout. "I could use some healing, yeah…" Leah squeezed her other hand. The fear lessened.

"I'm glad this all worked out," Sacha said, crossing her arms. She eyed Leah. "But please never do that again, okay? Next time we work together."

Leah nodded, but then her eyes widened. "Captain, your *arm*. What happened to the covering?"

Trecheon lifted a brow, turning to Sacha, but then he rolled his eyes. "Of course you'd know. I should have figured that."

"She's one of the few," Sacha said. "And let's just say Theophania was a deft hand with a hammer."

Ethos tilted her head. "Was."

Sacha rubbed her biomechanical hand. "Was."

"Leah," Ethos said. "You have two healers in front of you. You need to take care of *your* arm."

Sacha's ears colored. "What happened?"

Leah carefully pulled back her jacket and shirt, revealing the big bandage. They hadn't been able to change the dressing for hours and it had started bleeding through.

Sacha immediately went to work on it. "What was it?"

"Bullet wound," Leah said. "I fought Sharp in the woods." She narrowed her gaze. "He's dead now, by the way. And I doubt they'll find his rotting body in the wilds of Canada." She frowned. "His summons got away though…"

"You're an absolute mess," Sacha said, moving to other wounds. "You've been picking your tail again. It's bald."

"…I know."

"Let me take care of you, Ethos," Trecheon said. Ethos flicked her ears back, but nodded. Trecheon got to work healing her up. "I assume you haven't found Jaden since you're all alone. Did you come from Jasper?"

"We did," Leah said. "Jaden wasn't there, but he left us a clue that he came here."

Sacha flicked her ears. She finished up with Leah. "Well, he's not here either, that we can see. We've been here two days now."

Leah slumped. "So what now?"

Pilot's datashard warmed at Leah's side and his hologram appeared. He did some loop de loops and posed. "Greetings, Trecheon. Sacha." He winked. "I think I might have an idea. There a church around here?"

Leah twitched her whiskers. "A church?"

"Look back at the poem," Pilot said. *"Squirrels climb the branches, birds seek the divine.* He was dropping a hint. If he couldn't hide in a diner… maybe he could hide in a church."

Ethos pulled up her phone and did a search. She frowned. "There's seventeen different churches here."

"Then we better start looking," Trecheon said.

Churches were significantly harder to search without looking suspicious, Leah realized. Especially when every church here was a different denomination or religion or deity. Each church leader seemed excited to see a fresh face, but got quite standoffish when Leah asked about someone staying there. It made *all* of them suspicious. They'd never find out for certain if any of them actually had Jaden and Embrik if they all clammed up the moment they asked about it.

Leah was about to enter the final church in her section, the Pious Church of Draso, when she heard Zeke's voice in her head, mixed with panic.

I can't let them go, he said. *If I let them go now, it'd be killing them again, and I can't do that a third time.*

Leah frowned. He was talking about his parents. He still felt their pull.

She knew that feeling. Exactly what she faced with Ari.

That one was your fault, the Thought Monster spat.

But… Zeke's wasn't. He needed to let them go.

You can, Zeke. She didn't know if it'd make it through the distance, but she tried imagining a scent for him. Baking apples. Warm and cozy. *It's okay to let the past go.*

The smell of burning eggs hit her own nose. Panic. *I can't.*

You don't want to, Leah said. *…Honestly, I don't want to either. But… we can. Together. And build a new family. Your parents would want that for you.* She hugged herself, hoping he could feel it. *Starting with us.*

She waited. He didn't speak again, but the burning eggs smell drifted away in favor of… tea. Which she immediately associated with family. She tried reaching out again, but couldn't quite get there. But he was safe. She could feel it. She took a deep breath and walked inside the church.

The moment she walked in the door, she knew she was in the right place.

A white wolf with piercing blue eyes stood near the front of the church wearing the robes of a High Cleric of Draso, nose buried in a book. He

looked up when Leah walked in and smiled. "Ah, welcome in! Can I help-
-"

"You were at Suzy's Diner back in El Dorado," Leah said. She covered her mouth, but the accusation had already escaped.

The wolf lifted a brow, tilting his head. "I promise you, I don't know what you're talking about."

She stared at him and narrowed her gaze. She wasn't wrong. "Yes, you do. And actually… you were the bus driver too, on Casino Beach when Zeke and I came back from the war. And the car rental worker." Her eyes widened. "And the medic in Neil's tent in DC!" She pressed her hands to her mouth. "Fire and *ice,* you're--"

The wolf splayed his ears. "Don't say it."

Leah's tail lashed, but she bit back her words. "You know where Jaden is."

The wolf pressed his lips together, then sighed. Without another word, he walked down from the pulpit, and walked up to her. "I suppose it was inevitable with you, Leah. But… keep it to yourself, please." He passed her a piece of paper then narrowed his gaze. "Hurry."

She took the paper and ran out.

The Black Cloak was waiting at the bottom of the stairs for her. Leah's heart pumped and her jaw dropped.

He had green eyes.

She turned back to the church. Empty. The wolf was gone.

"Well?" the Cloak said. "What's it say?"

Leah flicked her ears back. "You don't know?"

"If I knew, I wouldn't be *asking,* " the Cloak said.

She twitched her tail. "You and your counterpart have terrible coordination."

He glanced into the empty church and sighed. "More than you know."

Leah bit her lip and opened the paper, expecting another riddle. But it was just a series of seemingly random numbers on one line, and 2-4, 3-10 on the next.

Leah met the Cloak's gaze, then ran for a nearby clump of trees away from the main road. The Cloak followed her. She pulled Pilot out of his bag. "Pilot, display Jaden's poem from Jasper."

Pilot nodded and the hologram showed it off.

Squirrels climb the branches, birds seek the divine
And the winged dragon flutters high over the pine
But when the sky darkens and we leave the cove,
Squirrel, bird, and dragon return to the grove.

Leah nodded. She held up the note. "Display letters based on the first row of numbers."

Pilot tilted his head, but nodded. The letters popped up quick. V-A-N-C-O-

"Vancouver!" the Cloak said. "He's in Vancouver!" He looked over the remaining numbers, then squinted at the poem. "Line two, word four, line three, word ten writes out--"

"Dragon Cove," Leah said.

"Pilot, do a blanket search in Vancouver for anything with the name Dragon Cove," the Cloak said.

"Nothing," Pilot said.

"Switch the words," Leah said. "Search Dragon Grove instead."

A second passed, but it felt like a year. "One result," Pilot said, his image flickering. "Small bar buried in downtown, dressed up to look like an American speakeasy--"

"Address!" the Cloak shouted.

Pilot's hologram jolted left, displaying the full address.

The Cloak pulled out a phone and took a picture. He held out his hand and Rashard appeared in a flash of snow and ice. The Cloak leapt on his back. "Get your people and meet me there." He took off to the sky.

Leah ran back for town, wishing she hadn't left her pendant back on Athánatos.

Vancouver was fourteen hours away, much to Leah's dismay, but at least they had three drivers now, so aside from a six-hour stop to allow them all to sleep, they made good time and got to the city limits around 9:30 the next morning. According to the website, Dragon Grove didn't open until noon, but Leah was anxious to find it and they headed into the city anyway, fighting rush hour traffic, and finally getting there around 11AM. Sacha and Trecheon napped in the parking lot while they waited, but Leah couldn't calm herself enough to follow them. She held tight to Ethos' hand instead.

The moment noon hit, the group was in the door. Not surprisingly, it was completely empty, full of nothing but chairs, tables with white linens, low lights, and soft music.

A silver fox stood at the bar at the far end of the restaurant. She flicked one ear back.

Trecheon immediately froze, and Leah couldn't blame him. This fox looked remarkably like one of their proposed hits – Rebekka.

It didn't help that she immediately pulled out a pistol and aimed it at the bunch.

Leah threw up her hands and shielded the group, as did Sacha and Trecheon.

"Put the gun down, Rebekka!" Trecheon shouted.

"I'm *not* Rebekka," the fox said. "But you have one of the Fawn assassins with you, so I assume you're *Ackerson's.*"

"We're not!" Leah said.

"We just ripped him and his cronies new assholes," Trecheon said, teeth gritted.

"Then explain the Fawn."

"We've broken ties with him," Ethos said coolly. "At great expense. He screwed with us too much." She narrowed her gaze. "But how do you know him?"

The fox lifted her snout. "Say the poem."

Trecheon raised an eyebrow, but Leah stepped forward and recited it. "He modified it from a Zyearth poem and left it in Jasper, then used it to drop hints in Pine Cove to get us here." She furrowed her brow. "Please, we have to know where he is. His son is on his way here and we promised we'd get Jaden to him safely."

The fox pressed her lips together. "His son... Zeke?"

"His son Matt," Leah said. "But Zeke is looking for him too. He's my bonded partner."

The fox slammed her fist on the bar. "Shit! I gave it to the wrong person..."

Sacha frowned. "Gave what to the wrong person?"

"Jaden left here two days ago with his buddy Embrik," the fox said. Leah's heart dropped. The fox crossed her arms and spoke through gritted teeth. "Ackerson was on his tail. He left a piece of paper with information about where he was going with strict instructions saying not to share it with anyone who couldn't say that poem."

Leah's ears grew cold. "Who did you give it to? When?"

"A bat named Ronan," the fox said. "Last night. He knew the poem, knew Zeke…"

"Oh, *hell.*"

Leah turned. The Black Cloak stood in the door, green eyes wide with fear.

Trecheon glared at him. "Where the hell is Jaden?"

"I don't know," the Cloak said. "Because I was supposed to find out with that message."

CHAPTER 55

REFUGEE

Zeke and Ouranos ran back with Andre to the palace. Zeke's heart pounded with every step and he struggled to keep his magic under control.

Neil was already talking with the Archons when they got there, looking deathly serious. Melaina and Natassa stood off to the side with several dozen Athánatos in streaks of silver and green. They had a hunted look in their eyes, a gaze Zeke knew all too well from war. Damianos was off to the side with Philip. The young puma clutched his hand, fear in his eyes.

Neil looked up when they walked in and met Ouranos' gaze. "We're waiting this out."

Zeke's eyes widened. "What?"

Ouranos lifted a brow. "Explain, please."

"Ackerson's team came in between the borders of Windrik and Frostrik," Neil said, indicating the two Archons, one streaked in silver, the other in green. "The Archons had the sense to release their mule deer and get their people to safety through the rips, then seal everything."

"I will admit, the portals to the palace were helpful," Windrik said. "I apologize for doubting you." They bowed.

Neil nodded to them, then turned back to Ouranos. "There's nothing in the Archon boarders for Ackerson. I don't know what they're looking for besides us, but regardless, they'll be headed here. And it's a long damn walk." He nodded to Melaina and Natassa. "In the meantime, we're taking care of our own. The Phonar have already been disbursed to the other Archons, so more should be coming in soon." He lifted his chin. "This is the Athánatos stronghold. This is where we fight."

Ouranos smiled. "Well, then. Seems you have everything under control. Acting as our Basileus already. I could not be prouder."

Frostrik lifted a brow. "So are the rumors true? Our Prinkípissa is marrying the feline warrior who helped bring down Theron?"

Neil's ears colored. "We were trying to keep that *quiet.*"

Windrik laughed. "It is better as an open secret. We need something to celebrate." They grinned. "Can I assume that includes our own Damianos?"

Neil rubbed the back of his head. "I mean… yeah. I wouldn't have it any other way."

"Good." They turned to Dami, a sly smile on their face. "You know your fathers have had a celebration ready to go at the first sign of an engagement for a good while now."

Damianos flicked his tail. "Papa knows."

Frostrik grinned. "He does." He nodded. "A good match, all three of you." Philip relaxed and gave Damianos a big hug. Dami smiled and hugged him back. Frostrik waved a hand. "Proof laid bare."

"Basileus," Windrik said, their voice growing serious. "I know you do not carry that title yet, but know that the Archons stand fully by you."

"Even the ones who doubted you in our last meeting," Frostrik said. "Your actions with the rips and with fighting for Philip have softened their worries."

Windrik bowed. "It will be an honor to have you serve alongside Lady Natassa and Lord Damianos."

Natassa nodded, smiling.

Neil smiled too and gave a short bow. "Thanks. That means a lot." He clapped his hands together. "Alright, let's get to work."

The preparation began. Other Archons and their citizens joined soon after, having also sealed their portals. Neil called on everyone for help. "As I should have done a long time ago," he said. "I have a support network now." Natassa gripped his hand and agreed.

Andre and Chadwick carried bedrolls and pillows, the Fawns helped pass out blankets, clothes, and supplies, and even Angus kept the children entertained, juggling various objects with help from his telekinetic magic. Philip ran around helping him find new and strange things to juggle.

Pathos asked Angus if he had seen anything about Ackerson's approach. He could only say that the time paths branched out too much to be useful. But to have hope.

He looked directly in Zeke's direction when he said that. His blank stare burned through Zeke's heart.

Neil was right in the thick of it, consulting with the Archons, comforting refugees, and directing efforts to find everyone food and places to stay. No one questioned his authority, and in fact many of the Athánatos bowed to him, thanked him, and several even called him Basileus. There was an air of joy and relief around the word, despite their desperate situation.

Neil took everything with grace, smiling the whole time.

Zeke watched most of it from afar. Neil took to this so easily. As much as Zeke was now willing to admit this was his home, he still didn't know how to navigate it. He fought jealousy. Neil could handle it, but why couldn't he? He had finally let his moms go. Finally accepted his family. Why did everything feel so distant?

The stares and whispers didn't help. All of them recognized him as a royal Athánatos, but of course, no one knew who he was. It seemed like every time he tried to help with something, the resulting stares and subtle gossip halted everything and backed everyone up. He finally had to step aside to keep everything running smooth.

He sighed and sat on a marble bench in the Great Hall, watching Athánatos pour in.

Andre sat next to him. He took a cloth napkin, wiped the sweat off his skin and turned to Zeke. "Feeling overwhelmed?"

"That's an understatement," Zeke said. He cautiously leaned his head on Andre's shoulder.

Andre smiled and wrapped an arm around him. "It's fine, dude. Everythin's changing too fast for you. Ain't gonna be easy."

"I guess not."

They sat there for what felt like a long time. Andre rubbed Zeke's shoulder. Neither spoke. Zeke took a deep breath.

"Andre…" he said quietly. "Where do I belong?"

Andre wrapped his other arm around Zeke and held him tight. He laid his head on Zeke's. "Right here, man. In the present, with your family. With me, with Leah. And Jaden, Embrik and Alexina too. All on this wild, unbelievable island full of amazing people." He squeezed him. "It's where your heart is."

Zeke squeezed him back. A wave of fear for his friend shot through his body. Andre was out here in the open without any magic at all, when

Ackerson's full mage team was headed right for them. And Zeke couldn't even keep his magic under control to protect them. Proof of that lay in their last encounter with Ackerson. Little marbles of fire, ice, and water floated around them both.

Andre squeezed his shoulder. "You got this, dude." He stood. "Magic and all." He waved his hand through the water marble, making it slosh around. "I'm gonna go help Chadwick." He walked off.

They continued on for a good eighteen hours. Zeke busied himself by running food from the kitchens to the staging area. Something that drew less attention from the incoming refugees, keeping things running smoother. Simple pastries, pasta, a variety of fruit and veggies, water, and temporary beds had been laid out for the refugees and workers, and the night blurred into periods of rest, food, and labor. Zeke managed to get a few hours of fitful sleep.

It was just after dawn when Ouranos stood in the middle of the room and called for attention. "My people. The invaders have been spotted ten miles out, sneaking through our forests. The Phonar have found them, but were met with heavy resistance and could not fight. Our enemies know we are aware of them."

Fearful murmurs washed over the Athánatos.

Ouranos stood tall. "I will be heading out to face them head on. Those who stay behind will protect you should I fail to stop them. Fear not. You will be defended."

"I swear on it," Neil said. Melaina, Natassa, and Damianos stood by his side. Andre and Chadwick stood nearby too, swords in their hands, and the Fawns and Angus also raised their fists in solidarity.

Ouranos nodded. "I will hold you to that, Basileus." He turned to leave.

"I'm coming with you," Zeke said.

As one, everyone in the room turned to Zeke. Several gasped, and others whispered to each other. A child gripped his mom's hand. "It's a Prínkipas!"

Zeke dropped a plate of cheese at the buffet, pushed aside the discomfort, and held his ground.

Ouranos turned to him, brow furrowed. He opened his mouth to speak, but someone cut him off.

"Who are you?" a voice demanded from somewhere in the crowd.

Zeke pushed his glasses up higher on his snout and stood tall. "Zeke Brightclaw." He faltered slightly, the words sticking to his throat. The magic marbles returned full-force, floating around his head and even his tail. But he kept going. "I am the son of Prinkípissa Alexina and Jaden Azure." The crowd let out a collective gasp and fell to murmurs. Zeke met Ouranos' gaze. "And I have lost too much family, Uncle. I'm not going to lose any more. Besides," he glanced at Andre, "I have people to protect." He breathed deep and formed fists. "I'm coming with you. It's not a question." *Even if I'm broken.*

Leah's voice echoed in his head. *You're not broken.*

Ouranos nodded, smiling slightly. "It would be an honor to have you, nephew."

The magic around his tail vanished.

Andre hugged Zeke from behind. "You better come back, asshole."

Zeke took a deep breath, trying to calm the frantic beating of his heart. "I plan to."

Ouranos and Zeke entered the stable as they had before, though as they walked down the long hall, Ouranos opened all the stall doors. The mule deer responded in kind, snorting and pawing the ground. Zeke stayed close to him.

Finally they came to Caj and Kia's stalls. Caj raised his head high and snorted, though he met Ouranos' gaze. Ouranos ran a hand down his neck. "You know what I am here for, old friend. Today we go to war."

Caj leaned his head forward and bellowed, a weird mix of deep-throated roars and a haunted, high-pitched whine that sounded like a wailing ghost. The others joined him, filling the stable with their cries, so loud that Zeke had to cover his ears. The deer emptied their stalls and trotted out into the open, then stood in wait for their sire.

Caj left his stall and leaned down for Ouranos to climb on. The pair walked out.

Zeke watched him, his heart pounding. Kia pressed her snout against Zeke's cheek, then kneeled, letting him get on. He patted her neck, and she nodded in response. He gripped the reins and they pulled up next to Ouranos.

Ouranos frowned. He reached up and plucked a ball of ice floating around Zeke's head. "Unfortunately, Zeke, this is not a time for songs of peace. It is a time for war." He met Zeke's gaze with such an intensity that it sent shivers up Zeke's spine. "Channel all you have learned. From peace and meditation, but also from war. We need it now."

Zeke nodded.

Ouranos held out his hands and called Jústi and Pax. "What do you know about the invaders?"

Jústi alighted on a branch and waved a wing. Tiny electric bolts hit their shoulders. *There are at least five, and Ackerson is among them. They have firearms as well as magic.*

"Do you know which ones?" Ouranos asked.

Jústi clicked her beak. *At least two have Ei-Ei jewels, but that was all we could ascertain before we were chased off.*

Ouranos nodded. "Take us to them." The birds took to the sky, trailing lightning and dust, and dove between the trees.

Zeke called Archángeli, but rather than fly off after the others, they landed on Zeke's shoulder. Their claws clasped gently – a welcome, grounding feeling against his skin, unlike his moms' phantom claws. They headbutted Zeke.

Prínkipas, Archángeli said. *No matter what happens here, know it has been my pleasure to be your guardian.*

Zeke stroked Archángeli's chest feathers. "Thanks… I mean that."

Always, Zeke.

Ouranos gently tugged the reins, turned toward the forest, and broke into a full gallop. Kia called after her father and followed, with the rest of the pack on their tail.

Zeke held on tight, determined. Ackerson was going down.

CHAPTER 56

THE BATTLE OF ATHÁNATOS

Zeke held tight to Kia's bridle as they paced quietly through the forest for the next hour.

Ouranos and Caj had scattered the pack throughout the woods while he and Zeke followed the Phonar to Ackerson's last known location. Archángeli stayed on Zeke's shoulder, darting their gaze left and right, ever alert. Pax flew from branch to branch, pausing to listen.

Silence. No feral animal sounds. Not even any wind.

Zeke shivered. He guided Kia closer to Caj. "Is it possible we passed them?"

Ouranos lifted his head. "I do not--"

A wailing shriek from one of the mule deer echoed through the forest, followed by the panicked cries of the others of its pack. A loud bellow followed.

Caj stood to his hind legs and bellowed back, nearly bucking Ouranos off. Kia backed up, baring fangs and hissing.

Zeke's heart raced. "I don't suppose your wild mule deer would willingly attack your tame ones?"

Ouranos narrowed his gaze. "I think… only one."

Dust blew against their ears. *Prínkipas warriors, duck your heads!*

Zeke ducked. A dozen magic marbles manifested around his head.

Pax swooped in front of them, forming a wall of earth, tearing up trees and forcing the deer back. The violent staccato of rifle fire stung Zeke's ears as puffs of dirt peppered the wall, though nothing penetrated.

Ouranos held out his hand. "Jústi!" The lightning bird dove behind the wall, filling the air with electricity, but another round of fire silenced her and her magic with a squawk.

Zeke held out his hand and threw bolts of lighting behind the wall. Someone shrieked. Archángeli left Zeke's shoulder and whipped around the wall of earth, but a flash of fire chased them back.

Ouranos swore. "Pax--"

The massive stag Fedir rushed between the trees and crashed antlers-first into Caj and Ouranos, throwing them into the wall of earth, forcing Kia and Zeke back. The wall collapsed and the group fell in a pile of dust and stones.

Fedir recovered first, and with elements lighting his fur, he charged Ouranos, stomping heavy hooves, maw open, spitting saliva everywhere. Ouranos blasted sharp ice spikes at him while scrambling out of the way. One grazed Fedir's shoulder, though he didn't slow down. He called hot flames to his hands and brought them down on Ouranos.

Caj got to his feet and charged Fedir, smashing his sharp antlers into the stag's face, piercing one eye and ripping two big wounds in his snout, making him flinch and roar in pain. He flailed about and caught part of Caj's flank with his flaming hands. Caj reared up, blood spilling from the wound while his fur and flesh burned, but a wave of ice and snow knocked him off his feet and he collapsed.

Zeke lit the air around him on fire and Kia charged Fedir. The stag countered with a wave of water, which threw the pair of them to the ground. Kia moaned, but wouldn't get back up. Zeke shook himself, water flying everywhere.

Fedir charged.

Ouranos shouted and blasted the area with hurricane winds. Fedir countered with his own wind magic then charged him. He dashed right, grabbed Ouranos' arm, and threw him bodily into a tree. Ouranos called out, blood staining the ground.

Zeke snarled. "Not my family!" He held his hand out and gathered the first element that came to mind.

Ice.

Like Jaden's magic.

A massive swirl of ice and snow whipped around them like a blizzard, blocking their vision. He called on his wind magic next and spun a tornado of diamond dust around Fedir. The stag roared, batting at the magic as it cut through his fur down to the skin, spilling blood everywhere.

A vicious dust tornado appeared from the left and crashed into Zeke, throwing him into a tree. He groaned. His blizzard spun wildly out of control and threw Fedir somewhere into the woods.

Ouranos leaned against the tree and spat blood on the ground. More blood ran down his damaged arm. Zeke stood and rushed toward him.

A flash of blue stood out against the dark green bushes next to Ouranos' tree. Kitta. The cloaker.

Way too close to Ouranos. He stumbled toward his uncle. "Kitta," Zeke said.

Kitta's big eyes met his, fearful and wide.

Zeke's ears splayed. "You asked for help at the mansion. Let me help you. Ackerson doesn't have to control you." Against his better judgement, he held out a hand toward her.

She bit her lip, her pupils tiny with fear, then reached for him, hand shaking.

A heavy gray rat crashed on top of Kitta and stuck a thick knife through the back of her neck. She stared up, pawing at the blade, choking and gasping before she finally stopped moving. Zeke scrambled back, pulling Ouranos away. Ouranos stared, gasping.

Millie grinned at him, bare tail flailing. "Nasty traitors, both of you." She held out a glowing hand.

Zeke pulled Ouranos left, his heart pounding.

The rat threw a ball of energy forward, lighting the woods, crashing through the trees, barely missing Zeke and Ouranos. The trees around them splintered and cracked, throwing bark, sticks, and leaves into the air. Zeke created a wind pocket around them, trying to throw it all off, wishing Leah was here to help shield them.

Archángeli dove in and grabbed Zeke's shoulders, attempting to lift him out of the way, but he struggled in their grip. "Not me, Ouranos!" He pulled at Archángeli's claws until they let him go.

Ouranos hobbled off, though Millie had him in her sights. She raised another ball of energy.

No time. Zeke dashed in and tackled her, throwing her off balance, just as she released the energy. Archángeli snatched up Ouranos and pulled him to safety though he lost some fur on his tail to the massive attack.

Zeke rolled on the ground with Millie, his magic flailing out of control, though he couldn't pin her down. She kicked him hard in the stomach, sending him flying. He rolled off, gripping his middle.

Millie snarled, hand raised, but no energy formed on her fingers. She frowned and glanced around. "Ralph!"

"Busy!" Ralph ran by with a half-dozen mule deer on his tail.

Zeke saw his chance and rushed her again, but a wall of stone shot up between them and he crashed into it. He glanced around, rubbing his snout.

Florina stood there, a blank look on her face, hands out. "I'll handle this, Millie."

Zeke glared. The woman with "royal" Ei-Ei jewels. Stealing magic.

She lifted a hand, catching it ablaze, then threw a barrage of massive fireballs at Zeke.

Zeke raised a wall of ice to block the fireballs. They blasted through the ice, shooting steam into his eyes, burning them. He cried out and shut his eyes tight. *Damn it!*

Ouranos' voice echoed in his head. *Tell me what you hear.*

He flicked his ears up, listening.

A twig snap on the left.

He threw his hands in the direction of the noise, kicking up a dust storm, and was rewarded with the sound of Florina crying out and coughing.

Tell me what you taste.

The sharp, tingling sensation of electricity bit the tip of his tongue. He threw his hands out, surrounding himself with walls of stone. The lighting crashed against it in loud thundering bursts that shook his very bones, but it didn't hit him.

Tell me what you smell.

Fire, strong, tearing through the woods. He snarled, pulling down the stone slabs and expelling waves of water through the trees.

Tell me what you feel.

The warmth of steam, the sting of smoke, the tingle of vanishing magic rippled through his fur. He had shut down the fire.

Tell me what you see.

He flashed his burning eyes open, blinking tears out, trying to focus through the steam and smoke.

Florina attacked from the right, her hands ablaze with fire magic.

Zeke threw out a hand, shooting sharp ice spikes at her center of mass. The spikes ripped through her flesh, extinguishing the magic and throwing her to the ground. She stared up, pawing at the wounds and shaking, unable to make any sound above a gurgling squeak.

Zeke leaned down and pressed a hand to her forehead. "I'll make this quick."

He shut his eyes and froze her brain.

Her body shook, then she stopped moving entirely, staring up at the sky with wide, bloody eyes. He sighed, trembling. Draso, how the hell did Jaden do that?

A gust of wind blew through his quills. *Zeke!* Zeke turned. Archángeli rushed past him. *Follow me, quickly!*

Zeke rushed after them. "Ouranos?"

Safe, for now, Archángeli said. *He has Kia and Caj protecting him. But the others are attempting escape. Fedir is ripping through the Veil and it must be sealed immediately!*

Zeke's heart stopped. "Ouranos said that ripping through it takes ages! How'd they do it so quickly?"

I do not know, but it needs sealing!

"I can't do that! I failed last time!"

Ouranos is out of commission and cannot do it, Archángeli said. *If you cannot, our enemies will escape and we leave ourselves vulnerable!*

"Damnit!" Marbles of magic appeared over his head, but he waved them away. "Take me to them." Archángeli tore off into the woods.

Zeke felt the rip before he saw it as he crested over a small hill. Sure enough, Fedir had his fingerhooves in the Veil, with Millie standing next to him, bouncing on her feet. The stag ripped a finger down through the air, drawing a thin red line. Dozens of tendrils floated out of the line, wiggling like seaweed in the waves. He tugged at a thin line.

A flash of white light split the red line. Millie leapt up and clapped.

"Millie, *help!*" Ralph shouted. Zeke turned. The mule deer nipped at his tail, bellowing.

Millie threw her hands forward and Ralph's hands started glowing. He turned the energy on the deer.

Zeke gritted his teeth. "Oh, hell no." He called on his ice and wind powers and shot a blizzard down the hill into Ralph. Ralph shouted and tumbled over and over in the snow, his energy lost.

Fedir frantically pulled at the red strings in the Veil, forcing more light through the rip.

Zeke directed the snow toward him.

Fedir roared, turned away from his work, and blasted the ice with fire, steaming up the area. Zeke coughed, but whipped up a twister, blowing the steam away.

Fedir charged him, magic trailing him.

Archángeli dove down on him, digging talons into his eyes and pulling him away from Zeke. Zeke stumbled back, barely avoiding the attack. He turned back to the rip.

Millie tugged at the strings now, and the white light transformed into a portal, a back alley somewhere. She called. "Ralph, hurry!"

Ralph stumbled for the portal, drenched.

Zeke rushed for the portal. "Don't you dare!"

Millie gasped, then vanished into the rip. Ralph tumbled in after her.

"Damnit!" Zeke slid up to the portal, ready to dive in.

A rush of wind hit his ears. *Prínkipas, seal it!*

"But they're getting away!"

Let them! Archángeli said. *They cannot return without an Ei-Ei jewel user. Seal it!*

"I don't know how!"

Remember what Ouranos taught you!

He snarled and tried to remember Ouranos' instructions. *Pick a familiar element. Weave the magic through the rip.*

He held his hands out, calling on any element and what appeared was… ice. Jaden's magic, once again. He formed a thin needle-like ice shard and wove the magic "through" the edges of the rip.

Slowly the rip sealed up.

Yes! He kept at it, slow and steady, magic draining out of him, until finally he got to the top of the rip and dissipated the magic. The rip sealed. No more shimmers, no more bad feelings, no more portal. Zeke sighed, and fell to one knee, his magic spent. He took several deep breaths.

But he had done it.

Prínkipas watch out!

Zeke turned just as Fedir dove full force at him, roaring at him. He held up his hands, but he couldn't get his magic to activate. *No!*

Andre appeared at his left, holding a sword. He rushed between the stag and Zeke and thrust the sword into Fedir's chest, spraying blood everywhere. Fedir's roar cut short, his body going limp before crashing on Andre, burying him under his weight.

Zeke leapt to his feet. *"Andre!"*

The body stirred, then slid to the side. Andre stood, spitting and coughing. He shook dust off, but it clung to the blood on his shirt.

"Oh *god,*" Zeke said.

"It's not mine," Andre said. "Damn stag's."

Zeke waved a hand in the air. "What the hell were you *thinking?"*

Andre grinned at Zeke. "Sorry man, you were taking too long."

"Don't ever do that again," Zeke said. He hugged Andre, despite the blood and dust. "But… thanks."

Andre grinned. "Guess I can handle myself after all, magic or not." He patted Zeke's back. "Can't lose my best man." He shook himself again and stuck out his tongue in disgust. "God, I need a shower."

"Everyone alright?"

Zeke turned. Neil walked up with Damianos. Ouranos leaned on Dami but his arm was bandaged and overall he seemed okay, considering. He smiled at Zeke.

"Well done, nephew."

For the first time since this whole endeavor, Zeke smiled with pride.

Our celebration is hollow, Pax said, flying in and landing on Dami's shoulder. *Despite our success, we have seen nothing of Ackerson.*

Zeke's tail lashed about. "Shit."

Neil's pendant started beeping. Neil frowned and glanced at it. Trecheon.

He answered the call. "Trecheon?"

"We have a problem," Trecheon said. "And we need Angus."

PREPARE FOR WAR

Trecheon impatiently tapped his foot on the hardwood floor. "Come on, Neil…"

The group sat in a sparse back room in the Dragon Grove restaurant while they waited to hear from Neil about Angus. The proprietor of the place, the silver fox that looked far too much like Rebekka, had brought them food and drinks while they waited to see what to do next.

Leah and Sacha sat at a table, silently sipping water and sharing a plate of poutine while Ethos typed frantically away on Trecheon's phone doing who knew what. The Cloak paced back and forth, muttering under his breath in a different language like had all those years ago on Sol before they tackled the Cast on the shipping docks. Speaking with the "entity" in the cloak itself. Or whatever.

He had green eyes rather than the striking blue eyes Trecheon had always associated with him. Leah told him her Cloak had green eyes. Which suggested there was more than one Cloak. He racked his brain, trying to recall his Cloak's voice. Was it different than the Cloak here? He couldn't remember. Just another layer of mystery around this not-quite-an-ally, not-quite-an-enemy.

Worse, he was just as clueless as the rest of them, which terrified Trecheon more than anything else they had encountered so far. If the time traveler didn't even know what was going on, they were truly boned.

"Here." The fox placed a thick glass on the table next to Trecheon full of a deep amber liquid. "To calm your nerves a bit."

Trecheon eyed her. It was the first time he had noticed a bright streak of pink through the fluff on her head. He snorted. "You'll forgive me if I don't entirely trust a drink made by a complete stranger who, but an hour ago, aimed a *pistol at my head.*"

The fox rolled her eyes. "Name's Safiya. Now I'm not a stranger. And that's some of our finest bourbon, so maybe don't look a gift horse in the mouth."

Trecheon pushed it aside. "No, thank you. I gave up alcohol after the war."

Safiya flattened one ear. She picked up the glass and put a cup of water and a plate of fries down instead. "At least hydrate yourself and eat a little something." She nodded to the Black Cloak. "If your strange cryptid's habit of speaking in tongues is any indication, you're in for a hell of a ride to get Jaden."

Trecheon winced. Just the reminder he didn't need. He had to get Jaden.

He *had* to.

Safiya tilted her head. "Just *try* the fries at least. I promise I didn't poison them."

He pinched a fry between his fingers until the hot innards exploded steam into the air, then slowly brought it to his mouth.

Safiya sighed. "Thank you." She furrowed her brow. "Hold out hope. Jaden and Embrik are too tough to let these assholes take them down."

"And yet, they seem to have taken Alexina down," Leah muttered quietly. "There was supposed to be three of them."

Safiya splayed her ears, her fluffy tail swishing side to side. She nodded. "Just have faith." She left.

Trecheon's fast heartbeat pounded in his ears. *Where are they?*

The pendant beeped. Everyone looked up and the Cloak froze in place.

Trecheon fumbled it and pulled up the hologram. "Neil?"

"Hey Trech," Neil said. He was in an open room with Pathos and Angus. "Sorry that took a while. Had a bit of an issue with Ouranos and Zeke."

Leah gasped. "Are they okay?"

"They'll be fine, but Ackerson's goons took a lot out of them. They could use healers soon as."

Trecheon flicked his ears. "And we have all the healers here. Damn it."

"We're taking care of them," Neil said. "In the meantime, we've got Angus on the case. He says your info was good. He found a solid starting point for Jaden."

"And?"

"See for yourself." He passed the pendant and Angus came into the picture. The black and green bat still sat cross-legged with a mirror on the floor in front of him. He stared into Trecheon's gaze with blank eyes.

"I hate to say this, but this is going to be… complicated," Angus said.

Leah moved in close to Trecheon, trembling. "I-Is Jaden alive?"

"For now," Angus said. "And I have an unusually clear path for his future movements. Where he is, who's going after him, when they'll attack, down to the minute. But that's not a good thing. It means the timeline is fixed – no room for error."

"So then tell us where the hell he is so we can save him!" Trecheon said.

"You can't go after him yet," Angus said. "For Jaden to survive, you need to wait two days. And Neil, Zeke, and Ouranos need to fight alongside you."

"What?" Trecheon said. "Why?"

"Ackerson has more on his team than we anticipated," Angus said. "A bunch of stays, all mages. You'll need the help."

Neil crossed his arms. "How the hell are we supposed to get there in *two days?* Ackerson will have all of us blacklisted at every airport from here to Albuquerque!" He turned to Pathos. "Got any way to get us there in two days?"

Pathos flicked her ears back. "Not likely. Trains are one thing, but it was impossible to hold on to any planes or airport connections when we escaped Ackerson."

"There's a derailed train anyway," Sacha said. "Slowing everything down."

"Blame that one on Sharp," Ethos snapped.

Trecheon slammed the table. *"Shit."*

Sacha leaned over. "I don't suppose your scrying map has a way for them to get here?"

"Give me a moment." Angus settled again and closed his eyes, but then immediately flinched and gripped his head, hissing.

Neil's ears perked in surprise. "Angus? What happened?"

Angus' eyes grew wide. He picked up the mirror, wiped it, and tried again, but opened his eyes a moment longer. "Oh *crosswinds* and *mistrals.*"

Ethos frowned. "Angus?"

"The map is gone!" Angus said. "My entire prediction map, completely trashed! Someone's interfering with it."

Trecheon lifted his head and glared at the Cloak.

The Cloak held his hands up. "It's not me, I swear to Draso."

"There's *two of you,*" Trecheon snapped. "Where the hell is the other one?"

The Cloak glared. "If I knew, I wouldn't have had to race here to find out where Jaden is. But I promise you, he's not interfering. That goes against our code."

"Look," Angus said. "I have Jaden's coordinates and the exact day and time he'll get attacked. I'll pass them to you. Let Pilot get you there."

Leah's ears flushed and she slunk away.

Neil's tail lashed. "But how the hell are *we* supposed to get there?"

"I can help with that," Chadwick said, coming into the room. "Time to call in a favor with Commander Reddy."

Neil stood near the portal leading to Sol with Ouranos and Zeke the following morning, a bag hoisted on his shoulder. Anxiety ran through every vein.

Commander Reddy came through – they had promised they could get a troop transport and the clearance to fly it by the next morning. It'd be cutting it close, but with luck, they'd get there just in time to get to Jaden. The only problem was, he couldn't promise them a pilot.

That was Zeke's job.

Zeke didn't seem too happy with the idea considering his malfunctioning magic, but Neil had faith in him and made sure to tell him so. They'd get through this.

"After all," Neil had told him. "Jaden is depending on us." And it was time they learned to depend on each other. A hard lesson learned.

That seemed to calm him a bit.

Andre stood near Zeke, a deep frown on his face. Zeke drew Andre into a deep hug, burying his face in Andre's shoulder.

"You better be alive when I get back."

"Trust me, I plan on it." Andre squeezed him tight. "Same to you. Love you, brother."

Zeke took a deep breath. "Yeah. Love you, too."

Natassa and Damianos moved close to Neil. He pulled them close to him, taking in the memory. He had to have faith – he'd be back for them, no matter how dangerous this whole thing was. But just in case, he had to make this memorable. "I love you two more than I could ever say. Thanks for being there for me in all this. Stay safe. We'll be back soon as we can be."

"We will," Natassa said.

Neil smiled. "I know."

"Take care," Dami said. "And come back to us."

"Of course." He kissed both their cheeks.

Ouranos hugged Natassa. "You are sure you will be okay without us?"

"We will be just fine," Natassa said.

Neil nodded. "I've got faith in them. About time I put my trust in my family."

Zeke raised his head and met Ouranos' gaze. Ouranos smiled at him. Zeke smiled back.

Ouranos patted Natassa's shoulder. "Keep us informed if you find Ackerson. It is quite disturbing that it has been so long and we have seen nothing of him."

"Of course."

Pathos and Logos walked up to Neil. "Philip is in good hands," Pathos said.

Neil smiled. "I know. Thank you." He pointed to them. "But you better not get yourselves killed. We all have a lot of healing to do."

Pathos winked at him. "We'll be here for it."

"I'll get you all to the beach," Chadwick said. "Let's go."

Zeke stood on Casino Beach with Neil and Ouranos, trying to calm his nerves as the Humvee pulled into the parking lot. He gripped Jaden's faded Defender pendant in his hand. Commander Reddy got out and walked toward them. Zeke instinctively saluted, though he was surprised to see Neil did too.

Commander Reddy laughed. "At ease, gentlemen," they said. "War's long over. Though I suppose us soldiers never really rest."

"Who's that with you?" Neil asked.

Another human eased out of the car. Their long, wild black hair fluffed about and they smirked. "Ah. Good to see at least one of the heroes of the war. Thought you all died after storming the Desert Wall, but I'm glad to see that's not true."

Zeke squinted. "You look strangely familiar."

The human laughed. "Yeah, I was the little shit giving Goodwin a hard time about counting on the deck of the *Invictus.*" They poked their breasts. "I've changed a bit since then, so I'm not surprised you don't recognize me. She/her pronouns, please."

"Oh," Zeke said. "Um… congratulations."

The woman grinned. "Thanks, big guy." She gripped her breasts and bounced them up and down. "The girls thank you too."

Zeke's ears grew hot. "I... uh..."

Reddy turned to her, frowning. "Hilde..."

"Sorry," Hilde said, gripping Reddy's arm. "Can't help myself. Feels too good to be *me,* you know?" She held a hand out to Zeke. "Brunhilde Mendoza. Nice to meet you properly this time."

Zeke gingerly took her hand. "That's quite a name."

"Yeah, didn't want to go for traditional Latino names when I transitioned," Hilde said. She flexed, muscles bulging. "I want to be a German warrior woman."

Neil flicked his ears back. "You said... Mendoza." His tail stopped its slow swish.

"I did," Hilde said. "And before you ask, yes, I'm Christian's sister." She frowned. "That's... that's kind of why I convinced Reddy to bring me along."

Neil's whiskers drooped. "Hilde... Christian... I am so sorry..."

Hilde held up a hand. "Don't apologize. My brother was a stubborn ass and we both know it. Got himself into all kinds of shit he shouldn't have been in. And if my understanding of what really happened on the shipping docks three years ago is correct, then I assume he was in far over his head. Christian wouldn't want you blaming yourself for what happened. It's not your fault."

Neil breathed deeply. "Sure as hell feels like it is sometimes. We couldn't even tell you all what happened."

Hilde smiled gently. "Well. I'm here now. I'd love to know the story."

Neil smirked. "Well. He got to punch a mage king in the face."

Hilde laughed. "Sounds like him."

"Something to discuss on the way to the base," Reddy said. "From what I understand, you're on a tight schedule. Everyone in."

The drive was tense, though quick, and soon Zeke faced the pilot seat of a familiar transport – a Raven troop carrier, like the one he had flown into the Battle of DC. Anxiety rippled through him, making him shake. Magic marbles formed over his head.

Ouranos pressed a hand to his shoulder, steadying him. "Courage, nephew. Remember your mediations. They saved us both against Angel."

Zeke met his uncle's gaze. And the magic faded. He nodded, slipped into the seat, and took the controls.

Jaden, here we come.

Leah shifted from foot to foot, trying to keep her anxiety under control. The afternoon sun had nearly touched the tops of the trees near their designated landing zone.

They were running out of time.

She and the others were gathered in a tight clump of trees near a big clearing by the water's edge, not far from an old mining operation that had been left to rot. The very place Jaden and Embrik were hiding, according to Angus. She itched to go find them. Prediction or not, Jaden needed her. But after everything Angus had already predicted as truth, she forced herself to wait.

Zeke, Neil, and Ouranos would be there any moment.

But Jaden was right *there*. She stood and paced, hugging her arms, trying to calm down. She had trusted Angus up to this point. She'd just have to trust him now.

The Thought Monster chewed through her brain. *Assuming Jaden isn't already dead.*

Her ears burned.

Sacha adjusted something on her biomechanical arm, though Leah suspected it was more from boredom or anxiety than from necessity. Trecheon moved from rock to rock, trying to find some place comfortable and failing. Ethos had taken her revolver and transformed it once more – this time into a sniper rifle. She fiddled with various parts of it.

The Black Cloak just stood on the beach, staring out over the water. Waiting.

The apprehension was palpable.

Trecheon stood suddenly and pointed. "There."

A small but familiar troop transport headed their way through the sky, silent as could be. Trecheon waved everyone into the trees.

The transport landed and Zeke, Ouranos, and Neil got out. Zeke glanced around before laying eyes on Leah.

She froze in place, unsure. Zeke stood still, his expression blank. She didn't even get any smells from their bond.

See? The Thought Monster said. *He hates you.*

But then Zeke moved toward her with a purpose, taking big strides. He drew her into a tight hug.

She wrapped her arms around his middle and hugged him tight, nuzzling into his chest. An overpowering smell of comfort food filled her nose – fresh cookies, baked apples, the perfect cup of coffee. The tension left her body.

"I'm sorry," he said. "I chased you away. I got after you for your magic when you can't even help it. I didn't listen. This is my fault."

"Don't say that," Leah said, squeezing tighter. "I'm the one who made the stupid choices. I just don't want to fight anymore. I'm sorry."

He lay his head on hers and stroked her fur. "We're here now. That's all that matters."

She pulled back and smiled up at him, wiping away tears. "Always."

Zeke smiled. He held up Leah's Defender pendant and slipped it over her head. The Thought Monster retreated… just a little.

"Zeke, Ouranos, come here and let us heal you," Sacha said. She and Trecheon fixed up their injuries.

Neil walked up, sword in hand. "I'm glad for this touching reunion," he said. "But we have some family to save."

Leah nodded.

And they ran.

CHAPTER 58

END OF THE LINE

Jaden ran as fast as his injured leg would let him. Embrik ran on his left, pulling him along, his eyes wide with fear. The same fear churned in Jaden's stomach, making him nauseous.

Everything had gone so very, very wrong.

"Come out, Guardian!" a singsong voice said. The rabbit Jaden had met at the Battle of DC just before he had run a sword through Caster's gut. But now a full-on mage with Continuum Stones. *Continuum Stones.* They had tried so hard to bust that smuggling ring and they had failed. Now they were paying the price.

His leg gave out completely and he tripped through the underbrush to the ground. Embrik caught up, but they couldn't help the noise.

"I heeear youuu," Corbin said, like this whole thing was a game.

Embrik pulled Jaden into a dense thicket and glanced at the injury. Blood pooled on the ground, the bone exposed. He winced. "Jaden…"

"I know." He tried activating his magic, but he got only acid biting the tips of his fingers. He wasted it fighting back the rest of Angel.

Embrik held out a hand. A few sparks floated on his palm, but nothing more.

They were done.

Jaden leaned against a tree trunk, then gripped Embrik's hand. Tears of pain gathered in the corners of his eyes. He couldn't run anymore. "Embrik… thanks for staying with me all these years."

Embrik narrowed his gaze, his red quills shining in the moonlight. "You are not allowed to give up. You still have not seen your children. Your Guardian son."

Jaden shut his eyes tight. Either of his sons. Either of his *wives*. Hell, *any* of his family. He had lost them all. Over and over and over again. Destined to create new families and lose them immediately.

Time to accept defeat. He was tired of running. Tired of losing everything. They hadn't found him in time. Assuming they wanted to find him at all.

"Come out, little Guardian!" Corbin called. He stomped his foot and the heavy grating of rock on stone hit Jaden's ears. He glanced through the thicket. A bunch of stones surrounded him, ready to be used as weapons.

This was the end. He shut his eyes tight and squeezed Embrik's hand. Embrik, to his credit, leaned up against Jaden in the thicket. He just hoped that--

"Jaden."

The pain in his leg vanished and a warm, comforting energy rippled through his body. *Healing.* He opened his eyes.

Leah kneeled next to him, working her magic through his leg.

Leah.

He stared, dumbfounded as she worked. She finished healing his leg, flawlessly, then smiled at him, her eyes glistening. She threw her arms around his neck.

He froze a moment before hugging her back. This was real. It was *real*.

"Hey," another voice whispered. Jaden turned. Zeke. He smiled too, touching a finger to his snout. "Sorry we took so long."

Embrik released a long breath. "Thank the Sisters." He gripped Zeke's hand. "You have no idea how good it is to see you."

Relief ran through Jaden like he had never felt before. Finally, light at the end of the tunnel. Assuming they survived. He gave Leah another squeeze, then sat up and rubbed his healed leg. "Tell me you didn't come alone. Corbin has Continuum Stones and--"

"Hey Corbin!" a voice called. Jaden peeked through the thicket.

A red and black quilar stood to the left of their hiding place. A puma holding a sword stood next to him.

Jaden's heart raced. *That's him. That's the Omnir.* He swallowed hard. *That's my son's best friend. Trecheon.*

Trecheon stood firm, facing down Corbin. He crossed his arms and raised an eyebrow. "Ackerson has you chasing down old men now? Pathetic."

Corbin glared, flattening his long ears. "Finally Outlander resurfaces. I thought you all died in the war."

Trecheon dropped his fists and narrowed his gaze. "We did. Outlander is gone. You're looking at Defenders."

The puma tugged on a necklace and grinned. He leaned on Trecheon's shoulder. "We even have the pendants to match."

Jaden squinted, then his eyes widened.

Defender pendants.

They had *Defender pendants.*

Corbin spat. He raised his hands and a dozen fist sized rocks floated into the air. He dug his massive bare feet into the ground. "Can you defend against this?"

Trecheon lifted his chin. He threw a hand in the air, and a Gem glowed and whined at his side. Fire sprang up in a vicious tornado, wrapping around him. He glared.

The puma sparked something on his sword – an *Athánatos sword* – and lightning traced the outline of the blade.

Trecheon glared at Corbin, his eyes glowing, reflecting the fire magic. *"Try me."*

Corbin raised the rocks.

A sharp *boom* shot through the trees, echoing against the mining buildings in a crescendo of reverberation, as if a giant cymbal had been struck. A human in the trees to their right crashed to the ground, blood flying. An Angel trying to sneak up on them.

Jaden frantically searched the tree line and caught a flash of pink. One of the Fawns.

"Ethos," Leah whispered.

Trecheon caught his fist on fire and charged Corbin, trailing flames.

Corbin gasped and leapt back. He threw rock after rock at Trecheon. Trecheon countered with fireballs, exploding each rock in turn, filling the air with dust. Corbin's fur puffed up. "Damnit!" He threw a dozen at once, then turned and ran.

The puma rushed in and smashed his way through the boulders while Trecheon threw waves of fire at them. They rushed after the rabbit.

But then they stopped. Trecheon glanced around, panic in his eyes.

The puma's tail lashed. "Philip? Philip!"

Trecheon held out a hand, trying to calm him. "It's not real, Neil. It's one of those fear mongering mages."

"Not for long it isn't." A golden tigress rushed out from the trees on Trecheon's left and dove behind a bush. Someone shouted and the tigress rolled out into view, wrestling with a human Jaden didn't recognize.

The tigress roared and shoved the woman to the ground, then pulled out an expanding staff. She pressed it against her enemy's eye socket and activated it. The staff punched through her eye. She screamed, then stopped moving.

The tigress fell to her knees. "…And stay down." But then she perked her ears and looked up. "Trecheon, at your nine!" Trecheon turned.

A moose slid out from behind a tree, glowing jewels nestled around his eyes, his antlers glistening and bloody.

Trecheon stopped. "Break!" He, the tigress, and Neil ran in opposite directions. The stag bellowed and threw fire, ice, and electricity into the air.

Zeke stood. "That's my cue." He rushed out into the open. "Ouranos!"

Embrik perked his ears and glanced around. *"Ouranos?"*

Jaden turned too. A black figure ran out, hands alight with ice and fire. Jaden's jaw dropped.

Embrik gripped Jaden's hand. "The prince lives."

Ouranos raised his hands and shot twin beams of magic at the moose. The stag stomped a foot to the ground and raised a massive wall of stone, blocking Ouranos' power.

Leah tapped her pendant. "Ethos!"

"Gun's jammed, and it's not responding to my magic!" Ethos shouted over the comm.

Zeke gritted his teeth. He closed a fist and pounded it to the ground. Massive ice spikes shot up and raced toward the stone wall, crashing through it and collapsing it on top of the moose. Zeke and Ouranos waited a moment, but the buck didn't move again. All they could see among the stones were his bloodied antlers. Zeke sighed.

Trecheon and the puma walked out. Trecheon glanced around, fire engulfing his hands. "Is that it? Did we get them all?"

Ouranos pressed a hand to his chest and released a breath. "It appears we did." He smiled at Zeke. "Excellent work, nephew."

Embrik stepped out into the open. "My prince…" Ouranos turned. Embrik's eyes shined. "To see you alive… here… whole." He bowed.

Ouranos smiled wide. "Embrik, my dear friend. Surely our relationship demands more." He drew him into a hug. Embrik hugged him tightly back. Ouranos broke away and grinned now. "Melaina will be thrilled."

Embrik perked his ears. "Leah was correct then. She is restored."

"All of Athánatos is," Ouranos said.

Embrik covered his snout with his hands. "Thank the Four Sisters…"

Jaden walked out now, Leah at his side. "Zeke."

Zeke smiled and wrapped his arms around Jaden. "Thank Draso. We had a hell of a time finding you." Leah grinned and hugged them both.

Jaden gave them a squeeze, his heart considerably lighter. He broke the hug and gripped Leah and Zeke's hands. "And I'll be eternally grateful that you kept at it."

Leah grinned and held up a pendant. "Here." She slipped it over his head. His Guardian pendant. "Now it's official."

He smiled. "Thank you."

Zeke flicked his ears. "Jaden… Where's Alexina?"

Ouranos turned to him, ears splayed.

Jaden exchanged a glance with Embrik, his heart breaking. "…Let's get somewhere safe before we explain."

Trecheon walked up with Ethos, Neil, and the golden tigress. She wore a full Defender healer's uniform.

Ethos hugged Jaden tight. "Thank Draso… We thought we lost you."

He hugged her back. "Trust me, I thought we were lost too."

The tigress gave a Defender salute. "Guardian Azure. It's good to see you alive." She smiled. "I can see where Matt gets his devilish good looks."

Trecheon flattened his ears. "Really, Sacha?"

"I second that," Neil said. "Can't wait to tease the shit out of him for it." He winked at Jaden. "Name's Neil by the way."

"Introductions later," Trecheon said. "I don't think we're clear just yet. We need to get out of here. We've got a transport."

But Jaden kept his gaze on Trecheon. "You… you're…"

Trecheon furrowed his brow. "An Omnir. I know. Matt does too, before you freak out on me."

"No," Jaden said. He pointed to the pendant. "You're a Defender."

Trecheon frowned. He ran a hand over the pendant. "Honorary."

"You threw yourself out there to protect Embrik and me," Jaden said. "A core tenant of the Defender Oath. You're a Defender." He smiled. "I'm… glad to see it. Really glad."

Trecheon smiled back. "We can talk about it more later. Let's--"

The Black Cloak ran out from the trees, waving a hand, his green eyes wide. *"Shields up, now!"*

Jaden glanced up. Four massive boulders flew through the air toward them. Jaden threw his hands up and tried to shield, but got only a cloud of Lexi acid instead. But the Cloak, Trecheon, Sacha, and Leah followed his example and wrapped them in shields. Ouranos, Zeke, and Embrik blasted the boulders with various elements, smashing them to bits, raining gravel over the shields, sticking them with sharp rocks. All but one cracked and vanished. Jaden turned.

Ronan stood in the clearing, eyes wide with rage. The black and orange bat raised his wings, lifting more boulders into the air. His body glitched violently, out of sync with time.

Zeke threw up a stone wall, blocking Ronan's attack, but he had panic in his eye. "How'd he find us?"

Jaden pulled out his sword hilt, though he knew it'd be useless. "It doesn't matter, we just have to take him out now, before he summons--"

The boulders smashed Zeke's wall to bits, throwing sharp stones everywhere.

"Scatter!" Jaden shouted. He shielded again, this time managing a weak one, but several stones broke through, crashing into them as they fled, knocking them to the ground. One sliced through Zeke's arm, another wounded Trecheon's side, and another landed square on Leah's tail. Several pounded Jaden down, pinning his legs. The attack left them all on the ground nursing injuries. The Cloak stood between them and Ronan, arms out, shielding them, though the shield was a weak purple.

Ronan huffed at them, his eyes wild with anger. *"How are you still alive?"* he snapped.

Jaden spat blood on the ground. He shook himself. "Ronan--"

"Don't," Ronan shouted. *"You're ruining* everything. *"* He fluffed up the fur on his chest and arms. "Now I don't have a choice." He lifted his hands again. The sickly smell of death and decay filled the air.

Zeke coughed and gripped his injured arm. *"No!"*

A tall figure formed behind Ronan.

Ouranos stood, favoring his left leg. He stared, wide-eyed. "Judgement."

Judgement appeared through the darkness, towering over the group, foot claws digging into the ground, wearing a grotesque facsimile of the traditional Athánatos garb.

She smiled, her mouth nothing more than a black void. Drops of ink landed on their heads. *Ah. The little rats return. And you have brought me a second Azure. How fitting.* She glared at them with deep yellow eyes and spread inky black wings, dripping with viscous black liquid. The drops crashed to the ground and sprouted tiny, glowing blue eyes.

Trecheon's eyes widened. *"Cast?"*

"They aren't real!" Leah said. "Hit them hard enough and they'll vanish!"

Jaden threw his hands forward and coated the growing number of Cast with a thin layer of ice. They popped like balloons one after the other, but for every one he eliminated, another three took its place.

Trecheon wasn't having any better luck with his fire. He threw fireball after fireball, but couldn't keep up with the growing mass. He hobbled to his feet, gripping his side and waved a hand. "Hurry, back to the transport!" Everyone stood and ran for the shore.

Judgement laughed, a loud, echoing sound that hurt Jaden's ears. *Oh, I don't think so.* A wave of Cast cut off their path, looming over them like a tsunami from hell.

Jaden blasted the wave with more ice, but every hole he created filled immediately. He stepped back, Lexi acid building on his hands. Fire and *ice,* they couldn't escape!

Zeke, Ouranos, Embrik, and Trecheon pounded the wave with elemental magic of all sorts, but the wave continued growing, rising up through the tree line. Leah held out her staff, her brow furrowed, her eyes wide open, panting with fear. Trecheon and Neil stood in front of Ethos and Sacha, hands outstretched, staring at the wall of Cast. Embrik and Ouranos continued blasting magic, but nothing changed.

Jaden stood in front of Zeke and Leah. He wasn't going to lose another family. *Not again.*

Then everyone's pendants beeped at once and the dragons' eyes lit up electric blue, making them all pause.

The Cast wall wavered, rippling like water. Panicked shrieks peppered the air and holes formed in the wall. A stiff breeze cut under Jaden's fur.

Wind. *Wind magic.*

Strong gusts ripped through the Cast, pulling them apart and throwing them back toward Judgement. The wall fought to stay together.

A flaming battle hammer sailed through the air, crashing into the Cast with a loud boom, shooting sparks all through their bodies, burning them up into nothing. The wall vanished.

Jaden turned.

A white, blue-tipped quilar and a golden quilar stood between them and Judgement, in full Defender uniforms. Fists formed, standing firm.

Matt and Izzy.

Jaden's heart raced as his mind flashed back to the last time he saw them – scared children facing down an Omnir in the inner Sanctum, tears running down their faces, begging Jaden for help.

Those were not the zyfaunos who stood there now.

And they weren't alone. Two stags and a fox stood at their sides, and… and a white wolf, a maroon badger, and a gray rabbit. Lance. Larissa. Viri. His coworkers, fellow soldiers… friends. They had all come for him.

Matt took a step forward. He pointed at Ronan, a thick inky sludge on his fingers. "I don't know who you are. But you have gone after our brothers. Our sisters." He breathed deep. "My *father.*"

The Defenders around him lit up their elements – Lance's ice, Larissa's stone magic, Viri's patented element-wielding sword. Matt and Izzy's allies called on their magic too, filling the air with fire and earth, making the whole area buzz with power. Trecheon and Ouranos stood behind Matt, calling magic to their hands. Matt swirled a twister around him, picking up the other elements in a slow-moving tornado of power. He lifted his chin and bared his teeth, glaring at Ronan.

"That is not a safe place to stand."

CHAPTER 59

JUDGEMENT'S WAY

Jaden's heart pulled in a thousand different directions as everything seemed to happen at once.

Judgement raised her wings higher and sent a mess of Cast at the group. Everyone split up and tackled them, vanishing in a storm of magic, monsters, and darkness. Lightning, fire, water, and wind mixed with the inky Cast, fighting for dominance. A dozen voices rose up to fight.

And every warrior here meant something to Jaden. Magic tingled on the tips of his fingers.

Who was he supposed to protect?

Someone gripped his shoulder. He turned.

The Black Cloak. His Cloak, with green eyes. He met Jaden's gaze. "Your Master Guardian needs you first." He pointed.

Lance faced a pocket of Cast, ice crystals flying about his head, his white wolf tail puffed up and frosted. He pulled his lips back in a snarl, growling loudly, shooting ice spikes into the fray. But a pair of Cast snuck up behind him, rising up for an attack.

Jaden ran forward. *"Lance!"* Lance turned, eyes wide. Jaden built an ice blade on his sword hilt, and sliced through the Cast, tearing them apart and freezing whatever remained. The Cast fell in tiny frozen pellets. He paused, his heart racing, meeting Lance's gaze. Both of them froze, like they had seen a ghost, unable to react.

"Ice-wielders!" Larissa called. They turned. The silver and maroon badger lifted her chin. "Stage one!" She threw several large stones over their heads.

Instinct took over and Jaden shot ice at the stones, breaking them apart and frosting them with sharp crystals, turning them into spearheads. The spikes rained down on an advancing wall of Cast, ripping them to bits. Those that escaped fell to Lance's blanket of frost.

"Jaden!" Viri called now. Jaden followed her voice. Cast surrounded the gray rabbit, and while she fought off several with her long sword, she was overwhelmed. Jaden threw a hand forward and iced the sword. She swung the sword in a wide circle, shooting Jaden's magic in all directions, eliminating the threat. She faced him, her eyes wide.

Lance gripped Jaden's shoulder. He turned and they stared at each other. Lance's mouth hung open slightly, like he was trying to find words. He licked his black lips. "Jaden... You..."

"Reunion talk later, Guardians!" Larissa called. She brought down several heavy stones on a storm of Cast. "Let's do this!"

Jaden placed his hand on Lance's. He nodded at him.

Lance pressed his lips together and nodded back.

Embrik appeared on Jaden's left, fire surrounding him in a bright tornado. "Show us the Guardian, Jaden."

They ran into the fray.

Zeke washed a mess of Cast away with a blast of water toward Ouranos. Ouranos threw his hands up and brought lightning down. Electricity rushed through the water, ripping the Cast to shreds.

But more appeared. And more, and more, and more, and marbles of magic swirled around Zeke's head, blocking his vision, robbing him of power, keeping him from--

"Nephew!" Ouranos called. "Remember your meditations!"

Zeke ground his teeth together. *Tell me what you see.* Cast on his right, rushing for Ouranos. He slapped his hands together and pulled on an element. Wind. He swirled the Cast about into a tornado. *Tell me what you hear.* Cast wailed in the tornado, a mix of high-pitched squealing and deep gurgles. Zeke glared. He'd give them something to wail about.

Tell me what you feel.

Leah's warmth, her power, her strength building inside him. Ouranos' unwavering encouragement. Jaden, alive and well, defending as a Guardian should.

Hope. Community. Support.

Family. All around him. Drawing him fully into the present.

The magic spheres vanished.

Pulling on all his power, he reached for his ice magic and ran it through the twister of Cast, freezing each of them. He spun the twister wide, shooting frozen Cast into the dark mess of monsters, blasting holes through the walls of ink. He leaned down, breathing hard.

He did it. He finally kept control of his magic. He glanced around for Ouranos to thank him.

But Ouranos had already run off. His uncle fought valiantly alongside Trecheon and… Matt.

His brother.

His family.

A bright smell of hot peppers hit his nose. Speaking of family. He turned.

Leah had picked up some residual magic on her staff and now crashed through several piles of Cast, though she struggled.

Zeke ran for her.

Leah leapt over a mess of Cast and tucked into a roll. She spun her staff around, catching several Cast, then slammed them to the ground with a satisfying, inky splat.

But it wasn't enough. More kept coming.

This wasn't like the Desert Wall. They could handle that. Go after Ronan and Judgement. Fight back the Cast. Use their magic effectively.

But here, despite having more allies, they also had more problems.

Kill the summoner, stop the summon.

The summoner was nowhere to be found. And the summon was relentless. The Cast kept coming. No end in sight.

They were *dead.*

Ethos had transformed her jammed rifle into a sword, and kept the Cast at bay, but like with Leah, she couldn't stop the onslaught.

Leah tried to get to her. "Ethos, run for the transport!"

"I'm not leaving you to get killed by Cast!" Ethos shouted. "Not after I lost you once in the war!"

"But--"

A mess of Cast engulfed Ethos. She screamed, muffled by the Cast bodies.

Leah rushed for her. "No!" She dug her staff into the inky blackness and pulled Cast away, their wails stinging her ears. But she couldn't get them all off. *"Ana!"*

"Leah!" Zeke ran for her. "Here!" He threw a fireball her way.

Leah caught it on her staff and ran the fire over the monsters. They wailed and burned away. Leah caught a glimpse of pink among the black. "More, Zeke!"

He threw another fireball at her. She caught it and smashed it on top of the Cast. They wailed, flying off in a flurry of embers, leaving Ethos on the ground. Leah reached for her and pulled her into her arms.

Ethos stared up at her, shaking. "Oh god…"

"You're okay," Leah said, running her hands over Ethos' body, checking for injuries. Her healing powers worked overtime, working through the crush damage from the attack. "You're okay, you're--"

Ethos gasped. "Leah, *watch out!*"

Leah stood, swinging her staff into a storm of approaching Cast. "Zeke, ice!" Zeke threw a beam of ice her way, which she caught and spread through the monsters. They froze in place. "Wind!" Zeke powered her staff and she slammed it to the ground. The gusts ripped through the frozen monsters, leaving behind only tiny black ice shards.

Zeke rushed in, fire surrounding him. Leah pulled fire from him and swirled it through the survivors, burning them to bits.

Lightning! Leah called in her mind. He threw a bolt at her staff then doused the Cast in water. Leah stabbed a puddle, spreading electricity through their enemies.

A strong smell of coffee and cake hit Leah's nose. Perfect harmony.

The Thought Monster ate at her brain. *You're not good enough-you're not good enough.*

But harmony like that fought it back. Not completely, but… better.

When the Cast finally slowed, Leah rested her hands on her knees, panting. Zeke rubbed her back.

Ethos could only stare. "That was amazing."

Leah frowned at her. "Are you okay?"

"I am now." She walked up to Leah, cupped her face, and kissed her. She pulled back, smiling. "You're in good hands. I'll head to the transport."

Leah stared, ears flushed. "Um. Yes. Okay."

Ethos smirked. She pointed at Zeke. "You take care of her, you understand?" She ran through the trees.

Zeke stared at Leah, eyebrow raised. "What was *that?*"

"A story for another time," Leah said. She brandished her staff, heaving every breath. The Thought Monster fought her. *You still aren't good enough. You still can't win.*

"Leah," Zeke said. She met his gaze. He stared back. "Remember what Jaden said. You are Guardian material."

Leah perked her ears.

You hear that, Thought Monster? Zeke said in her head. *No one can deny that. Back off.*

The Thought Monster sunk its claws into Leah's mind, but Zeke's presence pried them off and chased it away. It shrank back. She took a deep breath. "Thanks. I think I needed that."

Zeke smiled and nodded back. "Time for the Guardian to shine." He patted her shoulder, then they rushed another storm of Cast.

Trecheon smashed another Cast with a fireball, adrenaline pumping.

He should have felt elated. Matt was here with all their allies, fighting hard. Roscoe threw waves of earth, burying the Cast. He bellowed, shaking his antlers. Sami and Darvin worked together brilliantly. Darvin collapsed into his Cast form and traded the antlers and hooves for the inky black body. He scooped up Sami's fire magic, and slithered through the mess, catching them all on fire, setting off a chain reaction. Sami's white fox fur reflected her fire magic like a beacon. Izzy ran about catching stray magic with her hammer and blasting Cast to oblivion. Black Bound elixir had snaked up her golden-brown fingertips as she grabbed Cast full-fisted, blowing them apart with the destructive side of her healing magic. They kept the monsters at bay.

But Ronan was still out there. Judgement still loomed over them.

And Matt, with his massive tornados, commanding voice, and bright white fur and quills, was a massive target. He fought off more Cast than any of them, swirling tornados, catching bits of magic from the others, blasting their enemies left and right. Black Bound elixir chased up his fingers, his palms, his wrists, his--

"Trecheon, focus!" Sacha shouted. She held up her staff. "Fire!"

He snarled and threw a fireball her way. She snagged it and punched through a Cast pocket, setting it ablaze. She turned to Trecheon, but then her gaze landed on Matt. "He's burning through the elixir…"

Trecheon's heart raced. That was how he lost Ryota.

"Trecheon," Sacha said. "He needs you. Give me some fire and go after him."

Trecheon frowned. "But you--"

"I can handle myself." She reached forward and quickly kissed him. His face flushed. She met his gaze, brow furrowed. "He needs *you.*" She stepped back and held out her staff. "Fire!"

Trecheon shook himself and lit both ends of her staff ablaze. "You protect yourself, you hear me?"

She nodded and dove into a pocket of Cast flicking fire everywhere.

Trecheon ran for Matt, his heart cleaved in two.

Matt ripped up two twisters, chasing a bunch of Cast away. But Trecheon's gaze was on his arms. The elixir had hit his elbows now.

Panic tore through him. "Matt!"

Matt turned, his eyes wide. He frowned.

Trecheon gripped his arm. "Matt, the elixir."

Matt glanced down. He furrowed his brow. "I didn't...I hadn't even noticed..."

"Don't do this to yourself," Trecheon said. "You have a team. Let us help you."

Matt pressed his lips together.

Ouranos walked up now, forming fists, elements rippling through his fur. "My magic is at your command, brother."

Trecheon stepped back and set his hands ablaze. He nodded.

Matt nodded back. He turned to the ever-growing wall of Cast. "Alright then. Ouranos, ice." He held his hands up. "Trecheon, Ouranos, stage dragon!"

Trecheon drew on all his power, remembering the complex motions for Matt's command. He blasted twin beams of fire into Matt's tornados. Ouranos followed with ice.

Together the three of them wove their magic into massive dragons – wings outstretched, tail lashing, claws sharp and burning.

Ouranos' ice dragon tucked its wings and dove into a havoc of Cast, blasting ice everywhere, leaving heaping waves of frozen black puddles.

Trecheon's fire dragon tugged at him, body and mind, as he and Matt worked to hold its shape. They threw their hands forward and the fire dragon spread its wings and crashed through an onslaught of Cast, burning them into black smoke.

Draso's horns, it was great to have Matt back.

Ouranos jogged up to the two of them. "The Cast are not our enemy. Judgement is."

"Ronan is," Trecheon said. "Stop the summoner, stop the summon."

Matt wrinkled his snout. "That black and orange bat? I haven't seen him since the Cast attacked."

"Then we need a distraction," Ouranos said. "Distract Judgement and her Cast so we may find her summoner." Then Ouranos winced, and in a rush of dust and lightning, his Phonar appeared. They rushed off, elements biting everyone's noses.

The Basileus needs our help!

Matt's eyes grew wide. *"Basileus?"*

"Not who you think." Trecheon pointed.

Neil stood in front of Judgement, sword in hand and several other Phonar surrounding him. Archángeli, Excelsis, Deo, Lumen, Sémini. Jústi and Pax joined them. The only one missing was Kyrie.

Ouranos flattened his ears.

Matt's quills stood straight up. *"Neil?* What the hell?"

"Another time," Trecheon said. "Let's take advantage of that while we can. Find Ronan."

Someone shouted. Trecheon turned. Zeke and Leah were nearly engulfed in Cast.

Matt bared his teeth. "I'll help them. Get Roscoe, Sami, and Darvin and find that bastard." He ran for Zeke.

Trecheon watched him run off. "Keep that elixir under control!" Matt waved a hand and continued.

Izzy ran up with Sacha. "What the hell is Neil *doing?*"

"His duty as Basileus," Ouranos said.

Izzy raised both eyebrows. "Oh. He and Natassa are getting married."

Despite everything, Ouranos chuckled. "They are indeed."

"About time," Izzy said.

"Neil is risking everything for us," Sacha said. "We need to get that asshole summoner. He was this way last I saw him."

"I will get our allies," Ouranos said and ran for the stag brothers and Sami.

Trecheon nodded to Izzy and Sacha and they went hunting.

Neil stood firm in front of Judgement, though his heart pounded against his chest like it was trying to escape. She hadn't yet noticed him. Or she just chose to ignore him.

But he had the Phonar. All of them, save one. And not in their normal bird forms, but their full zyfaunos forms, surrounding him, elements wrapping around them like dust clinging to sunlight, stars in the darkness.

Excelsis and Deo stood on his left and right, their white and purple embers wafting around Neil. They turned to him.

Basileus, they spoke as one. *You have the strength of the Phonar at your side. Consider this an acknowledgement of your status.*

Neil flicked his ears back, his stomach churning.

Justi and Pax spoke, wrapping him in dust and lightning. *Your duty is to Athánatos. But it is also to resist and eliminate Judgement.*

Lumen and Sémini reached for him, tapping his shoulders with pebbles and rain. *But you do not do this alone. You have us.*

You have your allies, Archángeli said in gusts against Neil's ears. *And your family.*

Use them, the Phonar said together, swirling elements around him.

Neil formed fists, glaring at Judgement. "Alright then." He turned to the Phonar. "You've all fought her before. Tell me what I need to do."

The birds started and exchanged glances with each other. Excelsis narrowed his gaze and clicked his long raven beak in what Neil took to be a smirk. *Well then. Someone finally asks our expertise.*

Deo stepped forward, stretching her long neck. *You need all the Phonar to end her anchor in this world.*

Archángeli nodded, shaking his brown tail feathers. *As well as the right conditions.*

Neil flicked his tail. "Neither of which I have."

You do not, Jústi said, eyeing him with one big kestrel eye. *Not with Ronan as her anchor.*

"So we take out Ronan."

We take out his focus jewels, Deo said. *Killing him will free her from his anchor, but make it much easier for her to anchor herself to anyone else with a focus jewel. That includes any of Ronan's allies... or possibly even your own.*

Sémini spoke, waving long fight feathers. *However, if we separate Ronan from his Continuum Stones, it will temporarily break her anchor and make it much harder to anchor another. She will need years to recover.*

"But she could be back," Neil said.

Yes, Excelsis said. *But it is a start.*

Neil tightened his grip on the sword. "Archángeli."

The golden eagle landed in front of him and bowed. *My Basileus.*

"Go find Trecheon and tell him to destroy that son of a bitch's focus jewels," Neil said.

Archángeli bowed again and transformed into their feral form. They took to the sky.

Neil watched them fly off, then turned to Judgement. "Let's give them a chance to find him." He lifted the weapon. "Give me some magic!"

Each of the Phonar raised their feral voices to the sky and wrapped the sword in every element possible. Water and ice swirled around, laying a path for the lightning. Fire swirled in the opposite direction in a double helix, drawing in sharp pebbles and thick sand.

But Judgement still ignored him. She kept her gaze on the others on the ground, flailing her wings and shooting Cast in all directions. Neil growled. "Excelsis."

My Lord.

"Let's make this distraction count." He held up his hand. "Take me up!"

Excelsis cawed, surrounded himself with flames, and emerged in his raven form. He flew over Neil, and Neil grabbed his feet. The other Phonar followed in their bird forms. When Neil was at Judgement's shoulder height, he swung the sword, ripping through her arm with the elemental magic. Fire, ice, and lighting clung to her phantom fur, and black dust spilled out of the wound, dropping to the ground in steamy hisses.

That got her attention. She wailed, gripping her arm, turning to Neil and swatting at him like she was waving away a mosquito.

Neil let go. "Deo!" Deo flew overhead and he grabbed her legs. She flew to Judgement's other arm and he sliced at that one, too.

Judgement roared, her hateful eyes darting all around and her wings shaking with anger. *Why do these flies persist?*

"Well, we've got her," Neil said. "Let's keep her!"

She swung at him again. He let go, this time picking up Pax.

Judgement bared her inky black teeth. *You little rat!*

"A fly *and* a rat?" Neil said. "Jumping species a bit there. So which is it?"

Judgement spread her arms wide, glaring. *You outsiders think you can best me? I am Judgement! I am eternal!*

Neil hovered with Pax in front of Judgement's face, glaring, sword lifted. "Outsider? No. I'm the future Basileus."

Judgement's face fell and her eyes widened. Then she glared. *Traitors.*

"I think they're all just sick of your crap."

You will die! She swung again.

Neil let go and picked up a ride with Jústi, then stabbed her wrist with his sword. She wailed.

Hang on! Jústi flew off and left Neil on Deo's back. They circled around and Neil stabbed at Judgement's neck.

Judgement reached for them. Neil leapt onto Excelsis as Judgement snatched Deo and squeezed. She squawked and vanished in a puff of white fire and feathers.

Neil held tight to Excelsis. "Oh *god.*"

She will return, Excelsis said. *Hold tight!* He dove, gliding along Judgement's side. Neil stabbed her side and carved a long wound, bleeding with black dust.

Judgement roared and slapped her side and caught Excelsis' wing, pitching Neil off. Lumen caught him and dove low.

Judgement peeled Excelsis off and crushed him between her hands.

"Damnit!" This wasn't going to work if he lost all the Phonar. "Keep out of her reach and get her with your magic!"

Lumen nodded and waved a wing at her, pelting her with sharp stones. She shouted, but couldn't move fast enough to catch him.

Neil grinned. "Got 'er." He pointed to the other Phonar and they did the same. He kept her busy, hitching rides between birds, directing attacks, taking a stab at the summon, and flying off.

But it didn't stop the Cast creation. The ground was still slick with them. Judgement was relentless. *Come on, Trecheon, get Ronan!*

Then Judgement fixed her gaze on something. Neil followed her, his heart racing. A flash of white stood out against the sea of black.

Matt.

He whipped up dozens of Cast in twisters, tossing them aside, and worked his magic with Zeke's. The Black Bound elixir ran up his hands past his wrists as he fought.

Judgement grinned, a cavernous, dripping thing. *Ah... Theron's precious potion.* She turned to Matt. *It shall be mine!*

Neil's fur puffed up. "No!" He stabbed her shoulder, but she completely ignored him, fixed on her target. She swatted behind her, knocking Neil and Sémini into the woods, forcing him to lose his grip on the sword. They crashed through the trees, though Sémini padded their fall and Neil landed on the ground with little more than a few scratches and a twisted ankle.

The remaining Phonar swarmed him, pelting him with their elements, panic in their voices. *Basileus--*

"Help me find Ronan," Neil said, speaking too fast. *"Now."*

Zeke stabbed at a Cast with a thick ice spike. But his energy waned. How much longer could they keep this up?

Leah leaned on her knees, panting. "I'm ready to pass out."

"Me too," Zeke said. "I don't--"

Leah's eyes grew wide. "Zeke, look out!"

Zeke turned. A wave of Cast towered over him.

Leah slid in front of him and projected a shield, though it fizzled away. She gripped his middle and he held her tight, a deep burning smell stinging his nose.

Wind whipped around them and caught the Cast wave in a twister, spinning them out of view. Matt stood on the other side, his fingertips dripping black.

Leah perked her ears. "Guardian Azure."

Zeke swallowed hard. His brother.

He nodded to her, then met Zeke's eyes. "Zeke."

Zeke lifted his chin. "Matt."

"You any good with your magic?" Matt asked.

Zeke shrugged. "Ouranos has been training me, but I'm at my limit."

"That's why we rely on each other," Matt said. "I only need a little of what you can offer. If Ouranos trusts you, so do I. Can you trust me?"

Zeke stood tall. "I trust you."

The Cast wailed, echoing through the trees.

Matt breathed deeply, then shook his hands, spraying black liquid everywhere. "Okay then. Follow my lead." The Cast came into view, spreading out like a flood. Matt held out his hands. "Fire on my left, ice on my right!"

Zeke tossed a bit of fire and ice magic, each one barely bigger than a golf ball.

True to Matt's word, he took the magic and ran with it, making massive spinning tornados of ice and fire, then throwing them into the sea of Cast. They ripped through the monsters, tearing them to tiny droplets.

More took their place.

"Again!" Matt called.

Zeke managed bigger orbs of magic that time, and Matt doubled their strength, tearing paths through the creatures. The black liquid on Matt's fingertips ran up his wrists.

"Once again, Zeke!"

"Here!" Leah pressed her power into Zeke's own, and he formed full beams of ice and flames. Matt's tornados grew ever bigger as Zeke fed them, blasting through the Cast like a hurricane blasting through houses. Chunks of frozen and flaming Cast flew out of view, leaving big gaps in the onslaught. Matt guided the magic through them until the Cast wall finally retreated. For a moment, the woods were empty.

Matt grinned, breathing hard. "About time." He turned to Zeke. "You're quite the mage."

Zeke shrugged, though his chest swelled. "I suppose."

Tiny droplets of black rain dirtied his quills. And with it… whispers. He glanced up. Matt did too.

Judgement hovered over them, her void of a grin bearing down on them.

Jaden chased after Lance and Larissa, with Embrik and Viri at his side. His team, his Defenders. Together they could do anything.

Despite everything, he felt at home.

Until a scream made him stop in his tracks. *Leah.* He turned.

One of the bird summons, a burrowing owl, pulled her away from a growing wall of Cast, kicking and screaming. "Let me go, *let me go,* Zeke and Matt are in there!"

Jaden's heart seized. He turned to the wall and caught flashes of Zeke's burnt orange snout and Matt's white quills in the gaps, elements flying all about them, though doing little to the wall of Cast. They stared up. Jaden followed their gaze.

Judgement, hovering over them, blended into the darkness, hands outstretched.

"No!" He ran for them. *"Not my sons!"*

"Jaden!" Lance and the others ran after him.

But not fast enough.

Jaden blasted a hole in the Cast wall with a beam of ice and snow and stood in front of Zeke and Matt, glaring up at Judgement. Pulling on everything he had, he formed a thick wall of ice around them, cutting off the Cast, and threw up a shield between them and Judgement. It shimmered brightly.

Judgement brought a hand down over them, cracking the shield and ice. She pushed hard, shattering the edges of his magic.

"No!" Jaden held his hands out, pushing his powers even further. "You can't have them! Do you hear me? I've lost enough! *I've lost enough, damnit, and you can't have anyone else! You can't have my family!"*

A hand gripped his shoulder. He turned. Zeke. Zeke squeezed him, then held out his hand next to Jaden's and strengthened the ice wall.

Another hand gripped his other shoulder.

Matt.

Matt stared at him, a moment frozen in time, and for a brief second, Jaden saw the little kit he had lost so many years ago. A kit who was now a full Guardian. Matt's golden pendant shone in the light from Jaden's shield.

Matt blinked rapidly, furrowed his brow, and also thrust his hand forward, adding strength to Jaden's shield.

And, together, they pushed.

Trecheon followed Sacha through the woods, Izzy at his left, searching for Ronan.

No Cast in sight. Not a good sign.

A gust blew past Trecheon's ear. Archángeli. *Guardian.*

Trecheon turned to his right. The golden eagle flew at eye level. Trecheon glared. "For the love of Draso, stop calling me that."

Ronan's Continuum Stones are Judgement's anchor, Archángeli said, ignoring Trecheon's protests. *Don't kill him. You will open a door for her to jump summoners. Destroy his Continuum Stones instead.*

Trecheon flicked his ears back, careful to pay attention to where he stepped in the darkness. "How the hell do I do that? Gems aren't easy to break."

Continuum Stones are more fragile than Lexi Gems, Archángeli said. *Ronan wears his on the inside of his ears near the tip. Remove them and destroy them. Otherwise the Prínkipas and your Guardian will fall to Judgement's attack. I am going to help them. Hurry!* They flew off.

"There!" Sacha pointed. A flash of orange in the black.

Shit. "Izzy, Sacha, come here." They turned to him. He explained what Archángeli told him. "Anyone got any ideas?"

"If you can get the stones, my arm can crush them," Sacha said.

"I can get the stones," Izzy said. "But I'll need a distraction."

"Then I'm the distraction," Trecheon said. "Split up. Let's get this done." Trecheon waited until Sacha and Izzy were buried deep in the woods, then lit his hands on fire and called out. "Ronan!"

Ronan actually appeared from behind a tree, dragging his wingtips through the underbrush. His body still glitched like something straight out of a bugged video game, jolting this way and that, vanishing and reappearing in an instant, lagging. It made Trecheon sick, but he held it back.

Ronan lifted his chin. "Trecheon." His voice glitched as badly as his body, making him sound robotic.

Trecheon lifted a brow. "Wow. Didn't actually expect you to answer me."

Ronan rolled his eyes. The green and purple teardrop Continuum Stones caught the little moonlight at the tips of his massive ears. He flicked his head, brushing aside the red, orange, and yellow fur tuft on his forehead, though his hand glitched strangely. "A little fire never worried me and you've got two pathetic healers with you. I like my chances." He lowered his gaze. "You could have been great, you know. Ackerson could have made you so."

"Oh, come off it," Trecheon said. "You don't really think I'll fall for that bullshit, do you? Ackerson's a skunk. Never cared about anyone but himself. Even you know that."

"I never said Ackerson did so out of the goodness of his heart," Ronan said. "He did it to benefit himself, yes, but it still gave me power. Why do you think Judgement chose me?"

"To use you," Trecheon said. "Just like Ackerson is. You're delusional, Ronan. Just like Ryota was when Theron was using him." He furrowed his brow. "Open your *eyes.*"

"You just don't know what power looks like," Ronan said. He held out a hand and lifted two massive rocks out of the ground.

Izzy snuck up behind him, Black Bound elixir on her fingertips.

Trecheon swirled fire around himself. "And you don't understand teamwork."

Izzy leapt on him, gripped the tips of his ears, and pulled, ripping the stones and his ear tips right off with her magic. Ronan screamed and fell, his floating rocks falling with him, blood flying from the wounds.

Izzy rolled off and tossed the stones to Sacha. Sacha held them in her biomechanical hand and squeezed. In a puff of colorful smoke and blood, the stones shattered.

Then Judgement wailed. Trecheon turned.

The massive summon held her hands out as her body crumbled to sparkly black dust. The surrounding Cast popped like soap bubbles, vanishing. Everything collapsed into a muddy puddle before disappearing completely. Gone.

Ronan scrambled off, glitching faster than ever, hugging his body. "No. *No!*" His body glowed, and he opened his mouth in a silent scream before dematerializing with a pop. Just like that… he was gone, like a void. Trecheon's stomach churned.

Sacha held her hands to her snout and Izzy shuddered.

"Everyone alright?" Trecheon asked, frantic.

Sacha nodded. "Yeah… yeah, we're good."

"Good." Trecheon turned and ran for Matt.

But Izzy ran faster.

CHAPTER 60

The Guardian is Home

Jaden fell to one knee, panting. The Cast were gone. Judgement was gone. Draso's breath… it was finally over. If only everything would stop hurting.

"…Dad?"

Jaden stood. Matt stared at him, stunned, ears flat, unmoving.

Jaden's vision blurred and his eyes burned with tears as his heart swelled. He stood, pushing through the pain, and forced himself to speak. His voice cracked. "Hi… son. Sorry… sorry I've been gone so long, I…"

Matt took two steps forward and wrapped his arms around Jaden. He was so strong. Not a child anymore. An adult. A survivor. Jaden hugged him back. *It was real.* Matt was alive, he was here, he was safe, a warrior, a Guardian, healthy, happy...

"Jaden!" Jaden glanced up just as Izzy threw herself on both of them, hugging them tight. Jaden laughed and sobbed at the same time, which came out as a strange, choked sound as he hugged her back. His little piece of Dyne, his best friend's daughter, *alive*...

"Daddy!" Charlotte came running now. Lance and Larissa stepped aside to let her dash past and wrap herself around Jaden. She sobbed. "Oh, thank *Draso*..."

Jaden drank it all in, heaving every breath, every other care thrown aside. His family. He was *home*. Pain meant nothing anymore. Not after this.

Lance cleared his throat.

Reluctantly, Jaden pulled away from his children and turned to meet his Master Guardian. He wrinkled his snout and saluted. "Guardian Tox..."

"Oh, shut up." Lance hugged him too. "Draso, Jaden, we all thought we had lost you. I am so sorry we didn't search harder. We should have kept *trying*."

"Don't," Jaden said. "What's done is done. Don't beat yourself up over it. It's fine now." He pulled back and smiled. "Besides, I wouldn't have Zeke if you had found me. It worked out in the end, even if it was a hard road."

"I should have known you survived, you old goat," Larissa said, and she hugged him tight. Viri squealed and hugged him too, squeezing him. Larissa patted his shoulder. "No worse for the wear."

Jaden beamed. "Missed you both too."

Ouranos and Trecheon jogged up now, with the two stags, the white fox, Sacha, Neil, and Leah. Ouranos smiled. "A happy ending at last." He patted Matt's shoulder. Trecheon hugged Matt then squeezed his hand and his features relaxed. Matt smiled at them both.

Jaden glanced between the three of them. "So Leah was right then. You've made some… surprising friends."

Matt smirked. "Surprising in a good way, I hope." The smirk evolved into a grin. "We have a lot to catch up on." He eyed Zeke, who rubbed his arm. "Especially considering Char and I apparently have a brother and Ouranos is technically our uncle…?"

"So am I, or at least I will be," Neil said grinning. He tapped his chin. "That means your dad will be my brother-in-law too. What fun!"

Matt winced, his eye twitching. "Now that's an image I'll have trouble shifting."

Zeke blinked hard and rubbed his temple. "Good Draso. I need some pictures and string to keep this all straight."

Embrik raised an eyebrow. "I am confused."

"Talk on the way," Ethos said, walking up to the group. "We need to get back to Athánatos before Ackerson gets his way."

"She makes a good point," Ouranos said. "We must make haste." He shifted. "And perhaps you can tell us more about what happened to Alexina."

Jaden flicked his ears back. "Ouranos, I am so sorry…"

"On the plane," Ethos said, gently shoving Zeke and Leah.

"Good thing we've got an X-Zero then," the black stag with silver antlers said, grinning. "Let's get the hell out of here."

Ackerson rushed through the bowels of the Athánatos royal palace, his heart racing.

He had finally lost control. In the worst possible place.

He had tried so hard to get here. He just needed to find the right technology and he'd get off this god-forsaken rock. Or at the very least, get a set of those Ei-Ei jewels…

But he had gotten lost – and a pair of sentries had found him. They bit at his heels as he zigzagged his way through the halls and behind pillars. He had no more ammunition, no allies, no way of fighting back beyond his own fists, which would do little against swords. And if the royal family caught wind…

He was dead.

A dark void caught in his peripheral vision. A black hall, far to his left, roped off, warning away visitors. His savior. For now, anyway. He slid through the ropes, careful not to disturb them, and hid in the darkness, waiting for his pursuers to run by.

But there was more than just a hall. It was stairs, leading deeper into the palace.

Someone shouted in the Athánatos native language. Desperation pulled him down the stairwell. The darkness encroached on him so deeply that soon he couldn't see anything, but the shouting at the top of the stairs kept him going.

And then, a pin prick of light. He followed it like it was an oasis in the Mojave.

The light trickled into a small, severely damaged room – pillars had fallen over, gravel lay all over the floor, shattered glass and some strange black liquid littered everywhere, and everything had a fine layer of dust on it.

But there was one thing. A small, jeweled box on a busted table, the only thing in the room not broken or covered in dust. He picked it up and opened it.

Inside lay a three sets of perfectly shaped gray Ei-Ei jewels.

He frowned. Why on earth would this be here?

A sound of flapping fabric hit his ears, and he whipped about, holding his empty gun in his hand. "Who's there?"

But all he saw was a flash of black fabric vanish into the darkness. Gone.

But there was a small shimmer of light in the center of the room. A visual glitch against the world.

A rip in the Veil. And his escape.

He glanced back at the jewels, pocketed the box, and left through the shimmer, planning on contacting Sharp as soon as he was able to. He smirked, in spite of everything.

I live another day.

Jaden sat on a seat in the X-Zero, nervously tapping his foot, as the plane glided smoothly toward the Vanishing Island. Charlotte sat at his left, holding his hand, but despite everything, it was hard to focus on the good.

Athánatos was in danger.

The rest of their friends and allies had climbed on the plane too, leaving the US plane behind. Commander Reddy assured them that they'd send someone to retrieve it ASAP. Obviously getting to Athánatos was more important and the X-Zero far out sped anything an Earth military could produce.

The only one not on the plane was the Black Cloak. He had vanished after directing Jaden when the battle first began. Jaden longed to have him there, for once. He'd be the only one with news about Alexina. But that kind of luck eluded them.

Neil, the puma and Trecheon's close friend, wouldn't sit. He stood in the middle of the aisle of seats, arms crossed, tail lashing about, his features hard.

Ouranos walked up and gripped Neil's shoulder. "Courage, brother. Athánatos is in good hands."

Neil sighed. "I know, I know, but the fact that we can't even *talk* to them…"

"The Veil has interfered with the pendants in the past," Matt said from the front of the plane. He and Izzy piloted it with skill. Jaden's heart swelled with pride. Matt smiled. "I'm sure it's just a minor issue."

"You all fixed that though," Trecheon said. He sat in a seat behind Matt, fiddling with his thumbs. He hadn't moved from Matt's side the moment the two had connected. Sacha sat next to him, rubbing his back. She, Trecheon, and Leah had healed everyone up, though it didn't do much to lighten the mood. Though it did shock Jaden to see someone with double Gem powers. He hadn't seen that since Dyne's father Vyse had died.

"It's possible they just aren't wearing the pendants," the black stag Darvin said. "If you're hunting someone, you wouldn't want your communicators beeping at you and alerting your prey."

Neil groaned. "God, that's even *worse*. If they got hurt--"

"We're almost there, *Basileus*," Matt said. He smirked. "Congrats on the engagement, by the way. I hope that includes Damianos too."

Neil smiled, despite everything. "Thanks. And yeah, it does. I wouldn't have it any other way."

Zeke glanced over a notebook full of names and colored lines connecting them all. "So according to this, Neil, you're gonna be my uncle by marriage, Ouranos is my uncle by blood, but Damianos is… something…" He cursed, furiously scribbling on the page. Leah and Ethos giggled, holding each other's hands tightly.

"Approaching Athánatos now," Caesum said in that robotic drone of his, though he spoke far too fast. His dragon hologram appeared in the holobulbs. He stared at Jaden for the umpteenth time since they had taken off, though he had yet to speak to him directly.

Jaden smiled. "Hey Caesum. Ready to talk to me now?"

Caesum's scales flared in color, and he hunched in on himself. "Guardian Azure… it is so good to see you. We… we all missed you."

"As I've gathered," Jaden said. Charlotte smiled and pulled Jaden into a hug.

Caesum lowered his gaze, his scales turning a soft blue. "Do… do you have Solas with you?"

Jaden frowned. Solas. Caesum's companion A.I. It had been a long time since he had heard her name. "I… no. The last place I had her was on the hidden X-Zero on Sol."

Matt whipped his head about. "There's a hidden X-Zero on Sol?"

"There was," Jaden said. "We could check, but… I don't know if Solas' datashard would still have power after all these years." He frowned. Hopefully he hadn't inadvertently killed her. He should have thought to grab her all those years ago, but Theron prevented him from visiting Sol again after he had buried his first wife.

"Pilot's did," Ouranos said. "There may be hope yet."

"Maybe," Izzy said, crossing twitching her ear. "We've been all over that island in the last two years and I haven't even seen evidence of Zyearth tech, let alone a plane."

Jaden perked his ears. "What could have happened to it? It couldn't fly. Not on a single Gem anyway, and the Gem shards were scrap. Otherwise I would have taken that home."

Lance shrugged. "Who knows. If we don't find it though, I'll see if Galactic InterPol can help us locate a rogue plane."

Caesum fiddled with his claws. "Sir… Guardian Azure… will you be returning to the Guardianship?"

Jaden's ears perked and his quills stood on end.

Matt turned, frowning. They met each other's gaze.

"I think that's a discussion for a time when we aren't worried about our allies," Lance said, his voice booming in the cabin. He crossed his arms. "Let the Guardian rest, Caesum."

Caesum's scales flared red and he snorted rainbow smoke. "Well, I'm just thinking Matt and Izzy could learn a lot from such an *experienced* Guardian with a long and rich history--"

"Sycophant," Pilot muttered from Leah's power pack.

"Hush, Pilot," Leah and Ouranos said together.

"There." Izzy pointed. "Sol."

Jaden stood now. He leaned over Izzy's seat and stared at the island through the front window. One could hardly tell anyone had ever lived there, it was so overgrown. The morning light forced dark shadows over everything, hiding any evidence of civilization. Jaden flicked his ears back. The first time seeing it since the Sol Genocide.

Matt rested his hand on Jaden's wrist. Jaden met his gaze. Matt furrowed his brow. "I had a hard time seeing too, after all these years. But you aren't alone. And the demons who took this from us are gone." He turned to Trecheon who smiled. "We have allies now."

Jaden stared at Trecheon. A lifetime ago, the red fur would have set him immediately on edge. But today, seeing Trecheon so close to Matt, so willing to put his life on the line for strangers just like any other Defender, he couldn't bring himself to be angry. Hell, even Trecheon's fur pattern was a comfort. The black tipped quills and ears, the sharp black lines in the fur on his head all reminded Jaden strongly of the fur patterns of Sol. His sister-in-law Solana had similar patterns, though hers were white, black, and gold.

It was like having a piece of Sol back – a harmony between loss and gain. Trecheon and Matt's friendship was a fitting end to the terror of the Genocide.

Though it was clear that there was a potential for more than just friendship. He could see it in the way they looked at each other. That… that was good too. Great, even.

"Landing procedures starting," Caesum droned. "Everyone please take a seat and buckle up."

Jaden settled into his seat next to Charlotte. Embrik took up a seat next to him and gripped his hand. "Courage, Guardian. You return here victorious. The genocide did not rob from you as much as you initially thought. It no longer has power over you."

Jaden managed a smile. "Thanks, Embrik."

Jaden followed Ouranos through the rip in the Veil to the center of the Athánatos palace. Getting through the Sanctum would have been much harder had he not had his family.

But they were here. Yet everything was silent.

Ouranos activated his magic and called Jústi and Pax to his side. "This silence does not bode well."

Neil burst through now and the Phonar followed him. "Natassa! Dami!"

"Oh, you have returned." A young Athánatos sentry with all black fur emerged from behind a pillar. He bowed to Neil. "Welcome home, Basileus. Was your quest successful?"

"It was, Baltazar," Neil said. "But where is everyone?"

Baltazar smiled. "In the Great Hall. Fear not. The Halls are cleared of the agents of Angel. We discovered Ackerson likely escaped through an unseen rip in the Veil deep in the palace. Lady Natassa attempted repair, though it is quite unstable. She has sentries posted there until you are able to repair it, Lord Ouranos."

Embrik pushed through the group. "Baltazar. Tell me Lady Melaina is restored."

Baltazar stiffened. "Lord Embrik!" He nodded. "She is. She--"

"Embrik!"

Jaden and Embrik turned.

Melaina came rushing through the palace at full speed and she threw her arms around Embrik's neck. "Oh, thank the Sisters, you live..."

Embrik pulled her close. He said nothing, just peppered kisses on Melaina's fur, squeezing her.

"Sisters be praised," a feminine voice said.

Jaden turned and met the violet eyes of an Athánatos royal standing next to what looked to be an offspring of Electrik. Jaden perked his ears. "Lady Natassa I presume." He bowed.

Natassa giggled. "I assume you are Jaden. Thank the Sisters you were found." She smiled. "No need for titles and bowing, you are family. And being Matt's father, I could not be happier to call you as such."

Neil pushed past them now and hugged Natassa and Electrik's son. "Thank God. Everything okay? Baltazar said Ackerson escaped."

"We believe so, yes," the other Athánatos said. His face grew dark. "It is not the best of endings, but it does mean that we are clear to go home. Assuming there are no more agents of his afoot."

Jaden's hair stood on end and ice frosted his fingertips.

Matt walked forward now, trailing wind behind him. "We're here to help if anyone else shows up."

"At least now the bastard is off our island," Neil said. "And he's lost all the allies that can get him back on. We're safe."

"Once we seal that rip," Ouranos said. "Nephew, would you accompany me?"

Zeke smiled. "It'd be an honor."

"Before you go." Natassa turned to Jaden, her ears flat against her head. "Where is Alexina?"

Jaden took a deep breath, his heart aching. "Rip first. Then Embrik and I have a lot to tell you."

CHAPTER 61

BEST KEPT SECRET

Trecheon sat hard on a wicker couch in one of the private rooms in the Royal Wing, fiddling with his hands, fighting the itch to grab onto Matt, pull him close, and never let go.

But today wasn't about him. It was about Jaden. And Matt had the right to choose who he'd sit with. Besides, he already had Sacha on his right. He gripped her hand – her biomechanical one – and she gripped it back, leaning her head on his shoulder. He nuzzled her fur.

To his surprise, Matt sat on his left, close enough that their hips touched. He side-glanced at Matt and carefully gripped his hand. Matt faced him, eyes wide for a moment, but then he smiled and laced their fingers together. Trecheon's ears grew hot.

The Athánatos royals, as well as the rest of Jaden's family found seats around the room. Jaden took a seat on a big couch, Embrik sat on his left with Melaina, Matt's sister Charlotte on his right. Charlotte met Trecheon's gaze and smiled shyly.

Ouranos stood behind Matt, resting a hand on his shoulder. "In your own time, Jaden."

Jaden took a deep breath, ringing his hands together. "I'm so sorry, Ouranos, but… I don't know where Alexina is. She's missing and it's all my fault."

"Jaden, you are not allowed to blame yourself for what happened," Embrik said. "I have told you that for *years.*"

"Oh, Sisters," Natassa said. "What happened?"

Jaden shook his head. "Angel chased us down. Alexina was heavily pregnant at the time."

"With Zeke," Ouranos said. Zeke flicked his ears back.

Jaden nodded. "I can only assume, since I… anyway. We had found a tiny cabin to hide in just outside Jasper and hoped to stay there while Alexina gave birth and recovered, but they found us. Embrik and I led Angel away. When we came back, Alexina was gone. There was… there was nothing but blood."

"Sisters *alive*," Melaina said. Embrik rubbed Jaden's back.

"I should have stayed with her," Jaden said. "I should have brought her with us, I should have done *something.*"

"Jaden," Zeke said. Jaden met his gaze. "You did all you could. And clearly I got out safely at least."

Jaden scoffed. "I was ready to throttle the Cloak for taking you from us when I first learned about it, but maybe he knew what he was doing." He stared up at the ceiling. "Draso, I wish he was here right now so I could ask what happened to Alexina…"

"Same, honestly," Zeke said.

"I believe my sister lives," Ouranos said. "We have still not seen her other summon, Kyrie. Alexina still has her. She is still alive and whole somewhere. And we will find her. Mark my words."

Jaden sighed. "Thanks, for what that's worth. I wish I had more for you."

"You're here and alive," Izzy said. "That's what matters. Okay? You're more than enough." She grinned.

Charlotte wrapped her arms around him. "We're whole again, Daddy."

Jaden smiled. "Thanks. All of you."

"This calls for a celebration," Ouranos said. "And we have a lot to celebrate right now."

"And we have a lot to catch up on!" Matt said, grinning. He puffed out his chest. "If Alexina is alive, we'll find her. You've got a lot more help looking now."

"Let us eat and rest first. We will be better if we have done both." Ouranos patted Matt's shoulder. "Come, let us talk with the kitchens and get a feast going." Matt smiled up at him and stood.

Jaden stood too. He smiled at Trecheon. "I know I have a lot to catch up with my own kids, but… when we have time, I feel like we also have a lot to talk about. The war, the Omnirs… and the Defenders. If you don't mind."

Trecheon relaxed. That felt right. "Wouldn't miss it for anything."

The next month was a blur of highs and lows. Several teams from both the Defenders and the personnel that Commander Reddy could spare had gone searching for Alexina without any luck. The old cabin had rotted in place, leaving only ancient blood stains and dust. No other traces, which was disheartening. It was like losing Leah all over again. If only the Cloak would show up and say *something* since he had obviously been involved. But no such luck.

"I… trust him," Jaden said. "I should have trusted him sooner. But he clearly knew what he was doing with Zeke. So for now, I trust he knows what he's doing with Alexina."

Trecheon couldn't say the same.

They also couldn't find Jaden's X-Zero, though Jaden was able to get them to the exact place he left it. All they could find was a dead, discarded Gem shard and some flimsy pieces of scrap.

Jaden stared at the spot, ears flat against his head. "Someone took it. You can see the marks on the ground and trees where it took off."

Matt twitched an ear. "But who? No one could fly it without the shards. You'd have to have tremendous power to get it in the air without them."

Trecheon crossed his arms. "Like someone Black Bound?"

Everyone turned to him.

Jaden pressed his lips together. "But that's so *rare.* Who else do you know to be Black Bound besides Izzy and Matt?"

Trecheon exchanged a glance with Matt and Izzy, his heart aching.

Ryota.

Matt rubbed Trecheon's back. "That's a heartache for another time. For now, let's see if we can find it somewhere else."

But no luck. They searched through Sol, Omnir Island, and even Athánatos Island in case Theron had taken parts from it, but there was no sign.

Trecheon stayed out of it. He should never have made that connection to Ryota.

But the time they spent investigating the plane and Alexina's whereabouts gave Jaden a chance to heal among family and friends. Silver linings and all that.

Leah and Zeke stuck close to him and Embrik while the four of them settled into a normal life. Finding Jaden helped Leah find her center again. Zeke slowly adjusted to his ever-expanding family, though he still struggled with his status as prince. For now, he was just Zeke, and the Athánatos people respected that. His relationship with Ouranos continued growing though, and through him, he also bonded with Matt. Of all the family Zeke was suddenly stuck with, Matt and Ouranos seemed to be the ones he connected to the easiest.

And both Leah and Zeke finally got the therapy they so desperately needed. Matt kept true to his word and brought along several Defender therapists trained and ready to help.

Despite knowing he needed it, Trecheon consistently declined therapy. He wasn't ready to open that can of worms yet.

Neil was though, as were the Fawns. While Trecheon had no way of knowing the details of what they discussed, he could see the therapy considerably lightened the mental loads everyone carried. That alone helped him heal his own heart. The Fawns' individual personalities began showing through more than they ever had before. Especially Ethos.

"I'm Ana now," she had told Trecheon. "Ethos died in the woods of Canada. And it's time I shed the assassin."

Trecheon was happy to agree.

Angus, like Trecheon, consistently declined therapy. "Seeing the girls being themselves again is therapy enough, at least for now," he said. "Besides, Pilot is a great listener."

Leah frowned. "He's not a therapist though."

"Sometimes the best therapy is just a person to vent to," Angus said. "For now, that's all I need."

Neil told Trecheon directly that if he was going to help Natassa and Damianos rule Athanatos, he couldn't be carrying the same baggage Theron had been. He needed proper therapy. "Theron let his poor mental health destroy his family and his people. I can't let that happen. Not if I'm going to help fix what he broke."

Trecheon agreed, though it was tough watching Neil come out of every session in tears. Hopefully that wouldn't be forever. It helped that he had Natassa and Damianos to see him through it, especially since they'd be working with him to fix Athánatos, as he put it.

Philip benefited from it too, which helped him work through the trauma of his imprisonment with Theophania. He adjusted to life on Athánatos easily, and Trecheon and Neil got to enjoy the company of the bright, happy child Philip had been before the assassination. He wasn't exactly the same, but he was getting better by the day. Neil was so grateful to have him.

Just as Trecheon was to have Sacha. Adjusting to the fact that they were in a *real relationship* instead of this unrequited flirty limbo took quite a lot of time and quite a bit of light-hearted teasing from his friends until it sunk in. Luckily, Sacha was incredibly patient. In turn, Trecheon remained patient about the secrets her biomechanical arm held. Maybe he'd learn eventually, if she was willing to share.

Jaden reminded Trecheon strongly of his own Granddad. Loving, but gruff, still fighting the demons of his past, but trying to do better for the future. The big difference being Granddad left and Jaden did everything he could to find his way home.

Unfortunately though, it wasn't long before Jaden learned about Trecheon's secret past.

Matt and the others were set to go back to Zyearth again in less than a week, and Sacha had been gently nudging Trecheon to talk to Matt about his feelings for him.

"You're running out of time, hun," she said, as the pair of them wandered through one of the palace gardens. "I know it's still weighing on you."

Trecheon sat hard on a marble bench. "I know, I know, but..." He leaned on his knees, shutting his eyes tight. "I still haven't told him I'm an assassin. I still *can't* tell him. I can't risk chasing him away." He growled. "I can't risk losing him."

"Ah," Jaden said. Trecheon's heart dropped to his stomach and he whipped around. The old Guardian stood off to the side, arms crossed, frowning. "This explains a lot, actually."

Trecheon sat straight up. "Oh god, Jaden, I didn't--"

But Sacha held her biomechanical arm in front of him. "Jaden, if you say *anything--*"

Jaden held up his hands. "You don't have to apologize or explain. I was Ackerson's too. I was also an assassin. War does terrible things to people." He smiled. "But it's over now. Surely Matt would understand that."

Trecheon pressed his eyes shut a moment, then met Jaden's gaze, brow furrowed, frowning.

Jaden's smile faded. "You didn't... you weren't just an assassin in the war, were you."

Damn it, damn it, *damn it,* this was crumbling all around him. "You have to understand, Jaden, I only ever took out the worst people possible and there was a *reason--*"

Jaden's jaw dropped. "Fire and *ice.* You're the *White Assassin.*"

Trecheon pressed his lips together, his ears ringing. He figured that out fast. His brain stalled but his lips kept moving. "...I was, yes. I'm not proud of it. And with all the shit that Ackerson and the Fawn Family put me through, I could have a million excuses for it, but--"

"Did you kill Matron Fawn?"

Trecheon blinked, freezing. "What?"

"I killed Matron Fawn," Neil said. He walked up behind Jaden and crossed his arms, tail lashing. "Her blood's on my hands."

"I helped," Trecheon said, his heart racing.

Neil bared a fang. "You directed, but I pulled the trigger." He turned to Jaden. "If for some god-awful reason you have a problem with that, take it up with me, not Trecheon."

Jaden and Neil stared each other down for what felt like ages. Trecheon couldn't read Jaden's expression, which made his heart stop. But eventually Jaden's face softened slightly. "You… you did what I couldn't then. So for what it's worth… thank you."

Neil winced. "Yeah well, not sure the cost was worth it."

"…I can understand that," Jaden said. "But thank you just the same."

Neil looked away. "Sure."

Jaden turned back to Trecheon. "So… is that why you haven't told Matt you're in love with him?"

Trecheon stood straight up, eyes wide. "I-I didn't--"

"You didn't have to," Jaden said. "I figured it out. You have a terrible poker face, Trecheon."

Trecheon buried his face in his hands. "I know. It's a miracle he hasn't figured it out already."

"My guess is, he probably has," Jaden said. "But he's given control over the situation to you. Because he loves you."

God. Was that it? That almost made things worse. Matt just *waiting* for him, while Trecheon floundered about, being too chickenshit to talk to him like a freakin' adult. He *knew* Jaden and Sacha and everyone else were right. Matt wouldn't leave him for that. They were too close for that. But every time he had the opportunity…

"Trecheon."

Trecheon pulled his hands down and met Jaden's gaze.

Jaden furrowed his brow. "Take some advice from an old zyfaunos who also has a sketchy past. Don't wait to tell him." He wrinkled his snout. "I lost two families and didn't enjoy them while I had them. It was pure luck that I got most of them back, but I'll never regain what I lost. Don't be like me."

Trecheon's fur stood on end. "Um. Yeah. Sure."

Jaden took a deep breath. "I've been a soldier for a long time, and I've had to do some really shady things to get the job done." He breathed slowly. "I know how hard this life can be. So if you ever need someone to talk to about it without judgement… I'm here to listen. Okay? I mean that."

Trecheon pressed his lips together. "Thanks. Really."

Jaden nodded. "I'm supposed to go meet Lance for something, but I'll be around. Take care of yourself, okay? You mean as much to Matt as he means to you."

"Yeah. Sure."

Jaden took a slight bow and walked off.

A few days later, Trecheon took Jaden up on his offer. The two of them sat in one of the gardens while Trecheon poured his heart out about his second assassination against Dr. Lasky. He had intended to give only bare details and see if he could get Jaden talking about his experiences so they could commiserate and maybe build a relationship. Show some trust. But he ended up spending a good three hours spilling everything about it, crying as he spoke. Something he had never done before.

Maybe he did need therapy. But he still wasn't quite ready.

Jaden kept his promise though. He listened without judgement. Talked about his own experiences. Ensured Trecheon that he wasn't a monster.

Jaden quickly filled the gap Granddad had left behind.

Jaden filled a gap for Matt and Izzy, too, Trecheon could tell. The three of them connected almost instantly, though Matt was definitely the one paving the way. To Jaden, Matt and Izzy were still the scared children in the Sanctum all those years ago – Trecheon could see it in the way he hovered over them, like they were going to vanish in a puff of magic. But a few flashy spars with Ouranos and Trecheon and even the Master Guardian, and Jaden slowly accepted Matt and Izzy for who they were - grown adults, fully-fledged Defenders, and Golden Guardians.

Still. Something was missing. And they both knew what it was. Matt's childhood. So whenever he could, Matt told stories about growing up, learning to use his magic, becoming a Guardian… and befriending Trecheon and Ouranos.

Jaden smiled at that. "Befriending your enemies. A good habit to have." He winked at Trecheon. Trecheon smiled back.

Matt wrapped arms around Ouranos and Trecheon and grinned. "I like to think so."

Jaden still encouraged Trecheon to tell Matt about his feelings for him, gently, but Trecheon just couldn't do it. He focused on his budding relationship with Sacha instead. One step at a time.

Despite keeping an ear open, they learned nothing about what had happened to Ackerson and the remaining Angels. His home was abandoned, his contacts lost, and he was officially listed as AWOL by the US Military, according to Commander Reddy. Likely he was still out there, but with the Defenders there, with Galactic InterPol now on high alert for unregistered vehicles leaving Earth, and without Judgement behind him, he had lost his bite.

No more than he deserved.

One thing that still disturbed Trecheon though, was the two Angels who died by crumbling to black dust. He brought it up with Sacha.

"The only thing I know for sure is that both of them had Blood Crystals," Trecheon said. "Is that how they die when a Blood Crystal fades?"

Sacha frowned. "Not that I know of, but I admit, I don't know much about them."

Reluctantly, Trecheon asked Ethos - no, Ana - about it.

She frowned deeply. "That's… not good."

Trecheon raised an eyebrow. "So you do know what's going on."

"I have a feeling," Ana said. "Blood Crystals… they can technically be used to raise the dead."

Trecheon's eyes grew wide. *"What?"*

"It's… a very temporary life," Ana said. "Most only get about a year of life, and you need to have the head of the person intact to attempt it, so you can only do it once." She hugged herself.

Trecheon's quills stood on end. "And you use a Blood Crystal to do that."

"That's one component," Ana said. "It also requires a sacrifice… The Bleeder in the partnership needs to die in order to revive someone else."

Trecheon shivered.

"Ackerson wouldn't care though," Ana said. "Since we only saw two of them though instead of the entire team, I assume Ackerson wasn't the one reviving people." She glanced away. "But let's stay vigilant."

Trecheon gently gripped her shoulder. "We will."

The month moved far too quickly and soon the Defenders were preparing to go home, likely more permanently this time, though Trecheon longed for another excuse to keep them here, especially with the Blood Crystal thing.

And his heart already ached thinking about Matt leaving again. And this time, Sacha would go with him.

Trecheon still hadn't told Matt how he felt. The urgency of it clawed at his chest as he stood next to Matt by the door of the X-Zero while everyone gathered supplies in preparation to leave.

"I better not get home and find out you've also somehow discovered my grandfather is also alive and missing," Matt told Trecheon. "We can't keep meeting like this."

Trecheon lifted a brow and smirked. "I dunno, it's kind of nice to have you on a quick tether."

"Leave tethers out of this," Matt said, laughing. "Seriously though, I'll be back soon enough. Gotta be back for Neil's wedding."

"Wed*dings*," Neil said. "With an S." He rubbed his chin. "I think. I dunno, I'll play it by ear. But give me a couple of years, okay?" He patted Matt's shoulder. "Don't be a stranger. I miss you already, nephew."

Matt flicked his ears back. "That has got to stop."

"Draso himself couldn't stop me," Neil said grinning and he left to go talk to Darvin.

Jaden walked up now, his ears flat. Charlotte stood at his side, ears pinned back, eyes red. Jaden met Matt's gaze. "Matt."

Matt frowned. "Dad? Something wrong?"

Jaden took a deep breath. "I'm sorry to say this son, but… I'm staying here. At least for now."

Trecheon stared, wide-eyed.

Lance poked his head out from the X-Zero, his yellow eyes wide with shock. "You are?"

"I am." Jaden glanced off. "I have to find Alexina. I know she's still alive, and I already lost my first wife. I can't lose her too." He turned to Lance. "You understand."

Lance frowned, crossing his arms. "More than anyone should have to." He nodded. "You stay as long as you need to, Jaden. You'll always have a home on Zyearth."

"And Earth," Jaden said. "I accept that now."

Charlotte hugged him tight. "D-Don't be here long, okay? We miss you."

"I know," Jaden said, hugging her back. "It won't be forever. And we'll talk whenever we can." He gave her a squeeze. "Nothing could keep me from you for long. Not anymore."

"Guardian Azure?" Leah said in a small voice. Both Jaden and Matt turned to her. Her ears colored, but she smiled. "Um… I'm going to be staying here too, for a while, with permission, Guardian Tox." Lance smiled. Zeke walked up behind Leah and wrapped an arm around her, smiling. "Zeke and I need each other."

"And I need to learn more about Athánatos," Zeke said. "It's my home. It's time I accepted that too."

Matt smiled. "I can understand that. But remember you have a home with us too, okay brother?"

Zeke smiled widely.

"Home is where we choose to make it," Ouranos said, walking up now. He wrapped Matt in a bear hug, which Matt returned. "My brother, it was good to have you here if only for a little while. You also have a home on Earth. Never forget that."

"I never could." Matt grinned. He gently headbutted Ouranos. "Take care of yourself, okay? I'll be back sooner than you know it."

"Guardian Tox," Chadwick said, walking up now. He held his black tail rigid and performed a flawless salute.

Lance smiled. "At ease, soldier. Did you think about my proposal?"

"I have, and for now, I must decline," Chadwick said. "I'll also be staying on Earth. Home is where the heart is after all, and my heart is here." Andre walked up behind him and wrapped his arms around him, grinning.

"I'm with Chad on that one," Sacha said, walking up. "I'll also be staying here for the time being."

Trecheon's heart swelled. "You are?"

"I am." She winked at him.

Lance raised an eyebrow and crossed his arms. "Really now. You're not even going to ask permission like the others."

"No, and I dare you to try and take me by force," Sacha said. "You have a deputy head healer, you don't need me. And I need to explore this new life with my new heart. If you can let Jaden do it all those years ago, you can let me do this."

Lance sighed. "Yeah, I understand. Permission granted, not that I'm in charge here."

Sacha wrapped her arms around Trecheon's neck and kissed him. Trecheon drank it in as he always did, fighting back the demons. *You deserve this. You have control. Your heart isn't trying to hurt you.*

And now he had her here for several more years. More time to convince his brain he actually deserved it.

If only he could tell Matt how he felt and make this perfect.

Sacha kissed Trecheon's forehead, then turned to the others. "There's a few more supplies that need sorting. Let's let Matt talk with Trecheon and get those take care of." She shooed everyone away, leaving only Matt, Trecheon, and Ouranos.

Matt smiled that goddamned gorgeous smile of his, making Trecheon's heart flutter. Matt chuckled. "Sometimes I feel like my heart is in a thousand places. But for now I can name at least three." He winked. "You two included."

"I am honored and humbled," Ouranos said. He gave Matt one more hug. "If you will excuse me, I will join the others in helping with supplies." He left.

Leaving Trecheon and Matt alone.

Before Trecheon could say anything, Matt pulled him into his arms and held him tight. "Thanks for finding Dad for me."

"Anytime," Trecheon said. *Anything for you.*

They held each other for what seemed like hours while Trecheon searched for the words he needed. But nothing came out. His brain stalled. He sighed and buried his face in Matt's neck instead, holding him tight.

Matt gave him a gentle squeeze. "Something on your mind? You know you can tell me anything."

Trecheon's heart stopped and his body buzzed. This was it. His opportunity. *Work, brain!*

"I mean that," Matt said. "I'm happy to listen. I'm here for you. Okay?"

Just say it, damn it! Trecheon shouted into his mind. *You're all alone and he's left it open for you, just freakin' tell him you're in love with him!*

But his brain immediately went to one irrefutable fact.

Matt still didn't know Trecheon was an assassin. And how could he try starting a relationship with him when he hadn't even told Matt that? How could he start with a *lie?*

He squeezed his eyes tight and held Matt closer. *Damn it all.*

Matt paused a moment, then lay his head on Trecheon's and rubbed his back. "When you're ready."

Trecheon's whole body seized up and his eyes flew open.

Oh, shit. Jaden was right.

He knows.

But he gave the power to Trecheon. The control. *When you're ready.*

"O-Okay," Trecheon said. "When… when I'm ready."

Matt gave him another deep squeeze, then let go, smiling at him. "I'm gonna help with supplies. But I want one more hug before we leave. Okay?"

"Yeah," Trecheon said, somewhat dumbstruck. "Okay."

Matt patted his back, then walked off.

Sacha made her way to Trecheon, carrying a bag. She frowned. "Couldn't tell him, huh?"

"No," Trecheon said. "But… Jaden was right, Sach. He knows. Said I could tell him when I was ready."

Sacha smirked. "Well, of course he *knows,*" she said. "But good on him for giving you that control. I wouldn't expect anything less." She nuzzled against Trecheon's quills. "You have time. And in the meantime, I have you all to myself."

He turned to her. His wonderful Sacha. He carefully cupped her fluffy face in his hands and kissed her. Sacha wrapped her arms around him and leaned into it.

Nothing felt more right.

She broke the kiss after a moment and smiled. "I hope that's a sign of good things to come."

"Yeah, I hope so too," Trecheon said.

She booped his nose and walked inside the plane holding a bag.

Trecheon glanced out over the group, taking everything in. Draso's horns, what an ordeal. But the future held a lot of hope. Hope he thought he'd never have. He watched Jaden talk with Zeke and Leah, laughing. Damage finally healing. His mind wandered.

But it grasped onto one final thought.

Jaden's Gem had exploded. But it hadn't killed him like Matt thought it had. Instead, it teleported him away and healed itself. Jaden had survived.

So if Jaden had survived a Gem break... could Ryota have survived too?

Ronan floated in the space Judgement had brought him so many times before – a place of no light, no darkness, no *anything*.

And this time, he didn't even have his Continuum Stones to protect him.

You LOST, Judgement spat, hovering over him. *YOU LOST! What is wrong with you?*

"I'm sorry, I'm sorry!" Ronan said. "They overpowered me, and--"

Because you lack the power to hold me to this world, Judgement said. She grasped him with her thick, inky hand. *So now you have a task. Find power. A lot of it. And maybe I can find a proper anchor in you.*

Ronan pulled at her hand. "How do you want me to do that?"

That is for you to discover, Judgement said. *So go discover it!* She lifted him up and threw him through the nothing-world. He screamed, though it made no sound.

Then the world snapped into sharp focus and he was back in reality. A dungeon, to be precise, dark, wet and cold, with his hands chained to a stone wall.

His cell had one companion. A quilar in a black trench coat.

His quills and fur all in red.

THE END

514

About the Author

R. A. Meenan was born in London during the golden age of science fiction, but somehow time traveled to the Modern Era (some say a mad man with a blue box was involved). She was dropped on the doorstep of a house owned by anthropomorphic cats and though they were disappointed she didn't have furry ears and a tail, they took her in to teach her the ways of elemental magic. After setting fire to her furry cat friends' tails one too many times (final score – fire: 2612, cat's tails: 0) they called an exterminator and sent her out on her way.

Others would call this "going to college" and "getting a job" but she disagrees.

Now an adult (physically, not mentally), she ride-hops intergalactic military spacecraft, combing the outer reaches of space and time, writing science fiction and urban fantasy stories based on her experiences. She's also hoping to find the perfect cup of coffee and a better way to grow dinosaurs. Humans kind of look at her funny, but she's managed to make herself an honorary ambassador for furry and anthropomorphic aliens and space dragons.

She carefully feeds and brushes her wonderful husband Joe and the pair have four furry children (which are really cats, but don't tell them that) and a human child named after a video game character. She also spends her spare time teaching essay-writing haters, molding them into people resembling Actual Students and Lovers of English.

She may not win the hearts of stiff military men or students who want good grades for no effort, but she certainly captures the spirit and imagination of time travelers, magic users, nerds, Students-In-Training, and fantasy lovers. Welcome to her nonsensical world. We hope you like it here.

You can email R. A. Meenan at r.a.meenan@zyearth.com. Check out more of her works at www.zyearth.com. You can also follow her on Facebook at https://www.facebook.com/zyearthchronicles or on BlueSky at @zyearth.com as SammieAuburn or on Instagram @zyearthdefender, where she posts snippets and artwork from the Zyearth chronicles.

If you enjoyed this book, consider reviewing it at the retailer where you purchased it!

Enter the World of Zyearth

Liked this book? FREE deleted scenes and extra chapters when you sign up for the newsletter at Zyearth.com! Here's some sneak peeks:

PHILIP leapt into the bed and pulled the blankets up to his face. "I don't know if I'll sleep tonight."

Neil sat on the edge of the bed and tucked the covers around him. "Thinking about today…?"

Philip shrugged. "Maybe." He looked up at Neil, eyes half lidded. "Tell me a story?"

Neil frowned. "I can try, but I'm not really good at stories."

"I can tell one," Dami said, sitting next to Neil. "Once upon a time, there was an Emerald Prince. But he did not know he was a prince. He thought himself a pauper. He sought to prove his worth through combat. He fought a war, chased down villains, and sacrificed himself for the ones he loved. This hurt him tremendously, body and mind. And yet, he still did not see himself worthy…"

IZZY frowned. "You alright?"

"I think Trecheon is hiding something from me."

The adrenaline doubled. Because Trecheon was. Matt still didn't know Trecheon had once been an assassin. She closed the digital book and steadied her hands in her lap. She searched for the words, but nothing came up. A jingle of far-off bells sounded in her ears.

Matt glanced up. "You *knew?*"

Get more information by signing up for the newsletter at Zyearth.com!

Glossary

Learn more about the World of Zyearth at Zyearth.com!

Zyfaunos: Zyfaunos are anthropomorphic animal-like bipeds. All zyfaunos have similar characteristics -- plantigrade or near plantigrade legs, human stance structure in the spine, humanlike eyes and sometimes lips, generally short snouts, and have humanlike, five fingered hands, usually with tiny, somewhat sharp retractable claws instead of fingernails. Zyfaunos tend to have the same height range as humans, with a few extreme examples of very short or very tall species. All zyfaunos can interbreed regardless of the individual's species. Unlike most faunos, zyfaunos are not always "traditionally" colored, and often have unnatural colors in their fur, such as red, blue, green, purple, and others. Though relationships are rare, humans and zyfaunos can produce children. Zyfaunos are named as such because the DNA strain originated from the planet Zyearth and Zyearth has the purest forms of this species.

Quilar: Quilar are perhaps the most unusual of all zyfaunos, as it is unclear what animal they evolved from. They have several key characteristics -- catlike ears and snout, slightly humanlike lips, though usually black or dark pink, humanlike feet and hands, tails, and quills of various lengths on their head in place of hair. Quilar quills are hard, though not usually sharp like a porcupine or hedgehog. Instead of fingernails, quilar have tiny retractable claws on each hand. These claws are not very sharp and are mainly used for scratching. Quilar can be divided by color and physical characteristics into three different categories.

Zyearth Quilar: Zyearth quilar have very short, very soft fur and generally longer, thicker quills on their heads. Their snouts are short and flat and many even have human-like lips. They tend to have catlike ears and human-like eyes. Quilar are the most human-like of all faunos. Human-faunos relationships usually involve a quilar. Zyearth quilar tend to have browns, whites, blacks, and grays for their colors. Jason, pictured on the previous page, is wearing the Defender Elemental uniform colors, indicating his status as an elemental user.

Jason is modeling a Zyearth quilar. Jason's fur is soft golden brown.

Earth Quilar: Earth quilar are physically very similar to Zyearth quilar, though their colors tend to be more vibrant. They also generally have streaks of color in their fur and quills while Zyearth quilars tend to be one solid color.

Trecheon is, reluctantly, modeling an Earth quilar.

Athánatos Quilar: Athánatos quilar are typically taller than their Zyearth and Earth kin. They have ears that bend backwards and more animal-like tails and feet. Their snouts are short and flat and like other quilar, they can have human-like lips.

Ouranos is modeling an Athánatos quilar here.

Focus Jewels: Focus jewels are found on many different planets throughout the universe. The term refers to any jewel that can be bound to a user's skin, soul, or lifeforce that grants supernatural powers. Sometimes focus jewel power only grants simple powers, such as long life, but others exhibit more extravagant powers.

Lexi Gems: Lexi Gems are focus jewels bound to the user's soul and grants users several powers. Average Gem users are granted long life, up to four hundred Zyearth years, and slow aging. Advanced users develop "Gem

Specialties" through the Gem "breaking" usually after a stressful, dramatic, or difficult event in the user's life. Military personnel are the most likely to have broken Gems and most Gems break in training.

There are a variety of specialties that users can develop. The most common specialty is healing, followed by elemental fabricators and manipulators, and a select few specialize in cloaking and shielding. Users are usually granted only one specialty, though a rare few have two. In the case of a duel specialist, both specialties are significantly weaker than those in a single specialist.

Lexi Gems are usually about the size of a user's fist. Gems often take on the colors of their users in one of several forms, but they lose their color if the user doesn't touch their Gem for extended periods of time or if the user dies, which also results in the Gem's bond breaking with their user. Gems can be used again by another user after a previous user has died.

Ei-Ei Jewels: Ei-Ei Jewels, like Lexi Gems, are focus jewels and are the source of magic and power for a member of the Athánatos tribe. Ei-Ei jewels are small and they are fused to the skin of the user just around the edge of their eyes. Ei-Ei jewels also come in pairs. Each eye has one set of the pairs. There are three jewels, but all of them work together to properly function.

The first jewel, the Mind Jewel, is yellow, representing the sophia flower, a symbol of wisdom. This jewel set keeps the user's mind fresh and free of deterioration. They even protect against mind aging issues like Alzheimer's and dementia.

The second set, the Body Jewel, is red, representing the purity of blood and flesh. This jewel set keeps the body from deterioration. Athánatos tribe members are immortal because of this jewel, but they are not invincible.

The final set, the Soul Jewel, is the color of the users eyes, representing the user's soul. This jewel set keeps the soul pinned to the body. Together the three sets make the user immortal.

Wishing Dust: Wishing Dust is created from ground up focus jewels and is used by applying the dust to the eye while making a "wish." Wishes are very specific, detailed spells that do one thing really well, but with a cost. Wishing Dust users are called Wish Dusters.

Wishing Dust is very volatile and a majority of attempted users wish too large for the wish to compensate. If the wish cannot properly compensate, the user will go insane and physically rip themselves apart trying to remove the dust. If a wish goes wrong, the user will

always die. There is no saving them. Because the dust is so powerful and so deadly, most major civilizations in the universe have banned it. As a result, Wishing Dust is mostly found in black markets and smuggler's groups.

Wishing Dust comes in a variety of colors and will add a light, very subtle dusting of that color to the user's eye. It's difficult to identify a Wish Duster until they've used their magic. Common wishes include magic tracking, object manifestation or enhancement, body morphing, and various magical defenses.

Continuum Stones: Continuum Stones are a pair of magical stones that manipulate time and space. They're almost exclusively used by the zyfaunos bat species of Vanguard from the Tribus continent. Users wear the stones attached to the skin in the inner parts of their ears.

Most Continuum Stone users live beyond their biological lifespans, but how long that is depends on their time powers. Powers are granted randomly as the user grows.

Time powers include healing, which reverses time on the user's body, scrying, and very temporary time freezes, with limited range. Each one has their own down sides. Too much healing can put a user outside of time, which takes time and effort to fix. Scrying is very imprecise as a whole. Time freezing robs the user of time off their lifespan – one hour for every second of frozen time.

Space powers include telekinesis, or the ability to lift things with the mind. Telekinesis users can only lift objects that they would otherwise be able to lift with their own strength. Teleportation, or space jumping, which allows users to jump 50 or 60 feet from where they stand. This is very energy intensive and needs a long recovery time between jumps. Finally, gravity manipulation, which allows a user to increase or decrease gravity on an object or in a small radius for a very short period of time. This is also energy intensive and cannot completely negate natural gravity, which means a user cannot eliminate gravity completely and send someone into space.

Jewel Shards: Jewel Shards are a relatively new focus jewel discovered on the Paleofaunos-inhabited planet Erdoglyan. Jewel Shards are pointed cone-shaped jewels and bound physical to a user, usually grafted onto bone or teeth and held in place with ornate metal holders. As they are a permanent fixture, they're often on the face or snout and positioned to face forward like a unicorn horn.

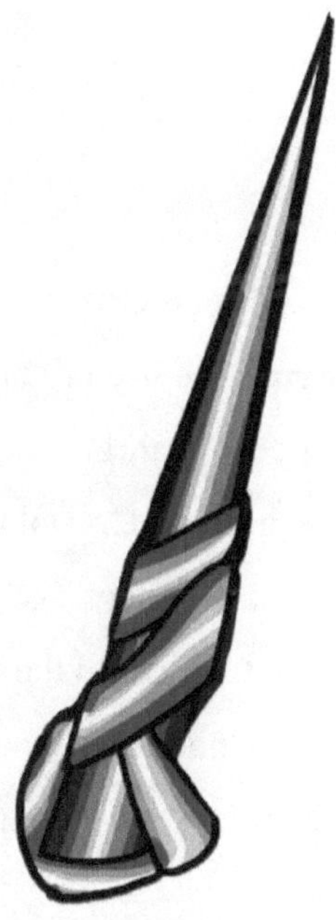

Jewel Shards manifest a single elemental magic, one of the main seven elements. The inhabitants who own jewels call themselves the

Forged and name themselves off the element they have. For example, "Fireforged" or "Lightningforged." The element it manifests will also determine its user's remaining lifespan. Some shorten the lifespan, such as lightning, which only grants 30 to 50 years of life after binding. Others lengthen it, such as stone, which can grant up to 350 years of additional life after binding. Some claim the element manifested is a reflection of the user's personality, though this has yet to be proven.

Jewel Shards are powered by UV rays. If they are left uncharged for too long, it causes psychosis in the user.

Blood Crystals: Unlike other jewels, Blood Crystals are shaped to look like things, typically something that their users find solace in. Blood Crystals are unique in the sense that they need two or more users to work properly. When bound, users will borrow magic or energy from their partner (called the Bleeder) and use it to create massive, destructive spells. Blood Partners can kill each other if they're not careful with how they pull magic.

Blood Crystals are highly regulated by Galactic InterPol because they were once used to bring people back to life, though very temporarily. The process is all but forgotten now, except for the knowledge that in order to use a Blood Crystal to revive someone, someone else had to be sacrificed.

Defender: The Defenders are a military group run by a small country called Zedric on the continent of Yelar on the plant Zyearth.

Guardian: Guardians are an essential part of the Defender military. Guardians are high ranking, highly trained individuals that perform tasks that average Defenders aren't trained for. There are two important types of Guardians.

Master Guardian: The role of Master Guardian is usually held by two people at the same time, often a former Golden Guardian pair. Master Guardians have a duel task – they are both the head of the Defender army and the leaders of the country of Zedric. Master Guardians must be smart, strong, courageous, and influential. Master Guardians are usually in office for life, though there are checks and balances that can remove a Master Guardian if the governing Assembly or the people of Zedric feels like they are not properly performing duties, and some Master Guardians choose to retire. Master Guardians are generally considered by most Defenders to be the most powerful zyfaunos of their time.

Golden Guardian: Golden Guardians are a team of two Defenders specially trained to handle delicate situations and complete covert and difficult missions that need small strike teams. Golden Guardians are selected by the Master Guardian of their era, and are given an extra five years of special training beyond typical Defender training. Usually the team has one healer and one elemental user.

Defender Pendant: Defender pendants are worn by all Defenders, regardless of their position in the army or Academy. They carry holographic identification cards and are the most common means of communication among Defenders. The pendant also carries several symbols. On Zyearth, a legless dragon is a sign of peace, so the Defenders made the legless dragon the center of their pendant. The dragon's  neck is tucked under, a classic move that prevents strangulation in battle. This represents defense. The outstretched wings are a sign of openness and welcome. Finally, the Gem at the dragon's side represents the world of Zyearth, since nearly all native Zyearthlings are bound to Gems.